Praise for the Novels of Laura _____

A Charm for Draius

"Reeve (Pathfinder, 2010, etc.) begins
defenders of magic must flush out a
blend of urban crime and high fantasy

Pathfinder

"*Pathfinder* is a riveting, action-packed space adventure which I highly
recommend. Peopled with interesting characters, unusual political situations, and twists and turns, this book will keep the reader enthralled.

—*Fresh Fiction*

"Laura is a great world builder."

—*Cybermage*

Vigilante

"Thanks to an intriguing ensemble cast and their varied takes on the
nicely complex universe, readers who missed 2008's *Peacekeeper* will
find it easy to catch up in this entertaining second military SF adventure
for Ariane Kedros."

—*Publishers Weekly*

"It is rare that a sequel is as compelling as the first book in a series, but
Vigilante by Laura E. Reeve is that rare exception."

—*Iriarte Files—Writer's Nightmare*

Peacekeeper

"An excellent debut novel."

—*Mike Shepherd, Bestselling Author of the Kris Longknife Series*

"Former USAF officer Reeve channels her flight experience into this
crisp military SF debut... Reeve drives the story at a breakneck pace,
providing a fine mix of derring-do, honor and courage, and the familial
bickering and affection of a close-knit crew."

—*Publishers Weekly*

ALSO BY LAURA E. REEVE

THE BROKEN KASKEA NOVELS
A Charm for Draius

THE MAJOR ARIANE KEDROS NOVELS
Peacekeeper

Vigilante

Pathfinder

SOULS FOR THE PHRENII
A NOVEL OF THE BROKEN KASKEA

Laura E. Reeve

Cajun Coyote Media
MONUMENT, COLORADO

Cajun Coyote Media
P.O. Box 1063
Monument, CO 80132-1063
USA
www.ccm.ancestralstars.com

This is a work of fiction. Names, characters, places, and incidents are a product of the author's imagination. Locales and public names are sometimes used for atmospheric purposes. Any resemblance to actual people, living or dead, or to businesses, companies, events, institutions, or locales is completely coincidental.

Interior Layout by BookDesignTemplates.com
Cover by Laura E. Reeve

Souls for the Phrenii / Laura E. Reeve — 1st ed.
ISBN 978-0-9891358-7-0

For my sister Wendy,
who proved anything is possible if you set your mind to it.
You inspire me.

Acknowledgments

I have so many people to thank for the fact that I was able to finish this book. This book was first drafted in 2004; I pulled it out of mothballs in early 2016 and started a rewrite.

In the spring of 2016, I was diagnosed with lung cancer (no, I don't smoke). There were several hospitalizations, a lung lobectomy, ancillary problems with thyroid issues, acid reflux, and hypoglycemia, then pain shots, hours and hours of pulmonary rehab, as well as physical therapy that goes on to this day.

What did *not* happen was chemotherapy, because they caught it at stage 1, for which I'm very thankful. During this period, I can't remember how many health professionals I saw, but every one of you were great. So I thank all of you who work tirelessly in the Penrose/Centura Health Systems, the US Air Force Academy Medical Group, PENRAD Radiology and Diagnostics, Rocky Mountain Cancer Center, and the Memorial North Hospital Emergency Room staff (who first saw the tumor). There are many more organizations in Colorado Springs and Denver who helped me as well. *Thank you.*

When you get cancer, you drop every activity that isn't focused on healing you. Consequently, I did not write during this time. However, I had immense support from my husband Michael as well as my parents Norma and Gerry, my sister Wendy, my brother-in-law Greg, my sister-in-law Jeanne, and many, many friends. *I love you all.*

When I finally returned to this book, it was 2017. I can't thank my husband enough for encouraging me to get back to work and who also functioned as a beta reader. I am so grateful for the beta readers who stepped up to help, even though the deadlines were tight: Dee Adelgren, Scott Cowen, Summer Ficarrotta, and Robin Widmar. *I couldn't have done this without your help.*

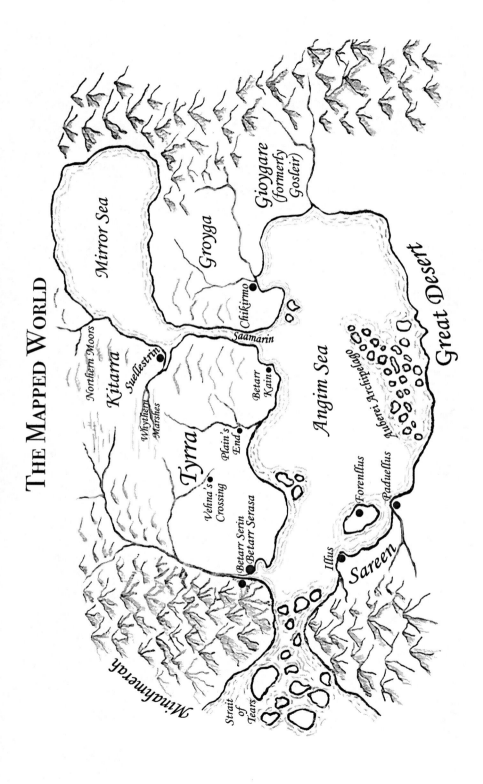

THE MAPPED WORLD

Mirror Sea

Groyga

Gioygare
(formerly
Gosleir)

Northern Moors

Kitarra

Suellestrin

Chikirmo

Saamarin

Great Desert

Weytham
Marshes

Betarr
Kain

Tyrra

Plain's
End

Angim Sea

Vehna's
Crossing

Auberei Archipelago

Betarr Serin
Betarr Serasa

Forenllus

Paduellus

Minahmerah

Illus

Sareen

Strait
of
Tears

CHAPTER ONE

Duty

Betarr Serin, Tyrra, Late Summer of Tyrran Year 1471

Draius watched as her cousin Siuru's body was wrapped with layers of dark fabric in preparation for the pyre.

"Drink this. It'll get rid of the shakes." Perinon, King of Tyrra and also one of her cousins, thrust a chalice at her. She took a sip of the dark liquid, which smelled of precious vanilla and numbed her tongue. Hoping this could numb more than her mouth, she gulped the rest of it down and warmth spread through her chest and abdomen.

They never thought binding to the Phrenii could result in instant death, but they were wrong. Terribly, irrevocably wrong. She closed her eyes and used her perfect memory to find when things went awry. The three of them left their bodies to walk the Void. Siuru seemed to be binding well through the Kaskea to Famri, the aspect of fire; the younger woman's mind was calm and disciplined—unlike Draius's, during her first visit. She and Perinon left to rejoin Dahni/Water and Mahri/Spirit on the earthly plane and Siuru was supposed to follow.

Help me! Siuru's fear suddenly pierced through the chaos of the Blindness.

Get back to your body! Follow the thread. Draius answered with her mind as she did exactly what she recommended. She felt Siuru's heart stop and her life-light start to dribble away. Entering her own body was like a dive into icy water as she was blasted with light and sound, but she managed to stagger over to Siuru's body. Her cousin wasn't breathing. The warmth of her body faded as Draius cradled her head. Now that beautiful face was covered in wide strips of black cloth.

Lady Aracia, the matriarch of the Meran-Viisi, came into the receiving room to check on the undertakers who prepared Siuru for the reliquary and her pyre, which would release her soul to their ancestral stars. Aracia glanced over at Draius and her nephew before chiding an undertaker on the position of Siuru's hands. The matriarch's eyes were red but her demeanor was stern. Draius remembered the previous Meran-Viisi matriarch, Nuora, chiding her for her tears at her mother's pyre. *Grown-up women don't cry, Draius.*

Perinon motioned for her to follow him into a small parlor. "Let's talk."

"I need to understand what happened. Where did Famri go? Did it stay in the Void?"

"Draius, this isn't one of your murder cases."

"Are you sure?" She stared at him, her chin raised in challenge. "Mahri and Dahni fled the scene as well."

"You won't get any answers from the Phrenii." He shook his head and motioned for his manservant Velija to pour him more liquor.

She seethed as she handed the chalice to Velija as well. "Yes, I'd like more. Thank you."

Perinon looked sadly through the double doors at the body, which was being moved to a planked frame so it could be carried to the reliquary. "Nonni's little sister. I remember her trying to attach herself to us, right before..."

Before the Fevers took our childhood away. Out of their group of cousins, Voima and Nonni were gone—dying in the Fevers—and now Nonni's younger sister, Siuru, had started on the path to the stars. Her throat caught, so it was fortuitous Velija handed her some more liquor. She sipped it as her gaze went about the room where Perinon did his day-to-day business. Beside her was his secretary's desk and her gaze flickered over the papers lying there: their orientation, their titles, the color of the ink against the fine linen paper, the penmanship and blocking of paragraphs—all indelibly etched into her memory. They were draft changes to the King's Law, proposed by the King's Council and awaiting Perinon's approval. They lay at an angle to the edge of the desktop and she resisted the urge to straighten them.

"Why don't you sit down?" He motioned to a chair and she numbly complied. "You understand we must continue to find bearers for the Kaskea. Each aspect of the Phrenii must be bound to a human."

"Please, no more attempts, sire. There surely can't be any more volunteers for the Kaskea, not now."

"Matriarchs push candidates from their lineages. Council members do favors for their constituents." He gestured to a pile of letters on his desk. "Meran blood has wound its way throughout our people. There are three remaining shards and these petitioners all want to be close to someone bound to the Phrenii, hoping some of that elemental magic will rub off on them."

Having been inundated with visits from barely known acquaintances since being bound to the Phrenii, she nodded. Then she asked, "*Three* remaining shards? Don't you mean two?"

He ducked his head to avoid her gaze—a movement familiar to her from their days of growing up together, sitting elbow-to-elbow through afternoon lessons and swimming in the canals. Before the Fevers, he made life difficult for their tutors. He would duck his head just that way when avoiding questions regarding his little tricks and sabotage.

He gestured at the pile of letters. "Too much maneuvering, too many plays for power. It should be *our* decision as to the disposition of the Kaskea." *Our* decision? Was that the royal plural or the Phrenic plural?

"You mean you never told the matriarchy *or* the King's Council about the stolen shard? How could you keep that secret?" Of course, he was the one person who could. As the Officer in Charge of Investigation, she had to send her reports directly to the king when she was investigating the theft of the Kaskea shards and how it applied to her case of necromantic murders. Every eight-day, she had reported on the case personally to him. "What about all the others who knew Taalo got away with one of the shards? Lornis or the Captain himself would have entered it in the final reports."

His mouth stretched into a wry smile and his skin tightened across his face, making him look older than his twenty-seven years. "I talked to Captain Rhaffus. Since he was so sure you would apprehend Taalo quickly, he agreed to have every mention of the missing shard removed."

She winced. Losing track of Taalo in Sareen had sullied her reputation. "I can ask the King's Guard Intelligence to send another operative to Illus."

"No need. I have new reports about a lord in Chikirmo who's on the rise because his rivals are mysteriously dying. There are rumors he has the help of a chemist and faint whispers about necromancy." He picked up the sealed packet beside him and handed it to her. "You can look at these reports later. I have transferred you to the King's Guard, effective this afternoon."

"Who will run the Office of Investigation? The Captain is already short-handed."

"Rhaffus understands you're the only person for this mission. You leave tomorrow for Betarr Kain and report to Commander Lyn, Sevoi's daughter. She's in charge of the intelligence office out there."

Draius was stunned. Betarr Kain was located near the eastern border of Tyrra on the harsh Kainen Peninsula. It was an eight-day away from the sister cities by coach. Eight days away from her son, who she could hardly stand to be parted from since his abduction and rescue, and eight days away from Lornis.

Perinon continued. "You're going on a covert mission across the Groygan border."

"I'm no spy. I have no training." Never mind that she hoped to never see Betarr Kain again. It had been Jan's first posting and, even though her son had been born there, she would always remember it as the place where she first recognized her husband's character and fell out of love. It was the death knell for their marriage contract.

"You'll be assisted by an intelligencer. Commander Lyn has high praise for Meran-Kolme Bordas. Perhaps you've met him?"

Nodding, she felt like she was in another nightmare. She had finally started enjoying her life here in the sister cities. Her marriage contract to Jan had been broken, ironically because she was bound to the Phrenii. When the creatures were present, people appeared like clear glasses of liquid that showed any nasty dreck floating around in their hearts. The matriarchy understood the difficulty of getting any progeny from arranged marriages under these conditions—restoring Tyrra's population after the Fevers being their prime goal—so she and Perinon were the only two people in Tyrra allowed to marry for love.

She tried a different tack. "You don't need me to run Taalo down. You can use the Groygan embassy and the local authorities."

"That doesn't work well when our quarry is in the employ of someone seated on the Council of Lords. Then there's the crucial matter of the Kaskea shard. We don't want the Groygans to know about it—they may be our allies now, but we can't forget the past wars and enmity that lie between us."

"So this is an abduction?" It would be perfect retribution, considering that Taalo had instigated her son's abduction. Another thought hit her. "Do you expect me to—to assassinate him?" She couldn't say *murder*.

"No. We don't care about Taalo. We just need the Kaskea shard."

We? More plural pronouns and her eyebrows rose. Was he losing himself, his identity, to the Phrenic mind? She wondered what the matriarchy would make of all this talk. After the matriarchs determined who would be king, they were responsible for monitoring him because of his rapport with the Phrenii. If they suspected madness, they could depose him. *No doubt they're watching me as well, now that I'm bearing the Kaskea.* Immediately uncomfortable, she shifted in her seat.

"You must also keep this secret from the King's Guard. You'll have orders that entail their support, but they can't know your true mission."

"How can they support me if they don't know the target?"

"Oh, you can tell them about Taalo. You just can't mention the Kaskea: not the fact he stole it, or took it to the country of our traditional enemy, or that you're trying to take it back."

She took another slug of liquor. "Sire, I'll ask again whether I'm the one who should do this mission."

"You're the only person who would know the difference between a real shard of the Kaskea and an imitation. Besides, don't you want a chance to restore the reputation of the City Guard and the Office of Investigation?"

That wasn't fair. She ground her teeth. Now he made it a matter of honor for her. Even though they had lost touch for so many years, he knew what made her tick. But she was also noted for her stubborn doggedness, so she asked, "Why is it so important to get the shard back now?"

"Because we're losing the war against necromancy. In fact, I fear that Siuru was a casualty of the unseen struggle between life-light and that death magic." He finished his drink and handed the chalice to Velija. She did the same. "Despite our best efforts, necromantic practices have oozed into all corners of the mapped world. Have you seen the Sareenian toys in the marketplace?"

She couldn't help but shudder. "Yes, but I hoped *you* would do something about them."

"I urged the King's Council to take action several times. That's earned me a warning that any more appeals would make me look—as they said—*deranged.* Many council members think the imports are a convenient loophole in 'those archaic Tyrran laws' that say acts of necromancy are punishable by death. So we'll let the Sareenians perform the nasty deeds all the way across the Angim Sea, while we reap the rewards of their work. Import taxes, you know."

"But that's—that's—"

"Hypocritical? I agree." He rubbed his eyes. She sympathized, almost being his mirror image. Not due to their familial silver-blond hair and dusky skin, but because she was just as tired and haunted. "They don't understand that necromancy is slowly draining the life-light from the Void, and what drains the Void also drains the Phrenii. We could lose all access to elemental magic."

"Why not use the City Guard and command them to shut down those merchants?"

"And be judged a madman? Besides, that doesn't stop necromancy from growing in other countries. Until I have a convincing reason to stop all imported necromantic charms, I can only take protective measures and, according to prophecy, the Kaskea will protect the Phrenii in the future. That's why I want *all* the shards under my control and bound to people loyal to me."

"Even after this?" She jerked her head toward the hall. Siuru's body had left for the reliquary and would lie on a stone slab tonight.

"Yes. I must." His eyes looked tortured as he nodded.

"Then I'll miss her pyre. Say an additional prayer for me." She sighed, finally defeated.

He made a motion of dismissal; she stood and bowed. She hadn't gotten to the door before he stopped her. "One last thing, cousin. You're also the only one who will feel the lodestone of souls when it's near. Any new information regarding its location?"

Her shoulders tensed as she turned around. In her mind, she again saw a ship's hull breaking upon rocks that stood like a fence against a desert shore—revealed abruptly in the Blindness, the layer below the Void where dreaming minds wandered. Dahni had told her that if Taalo and his men found the lodestone that night, then war would take Tyrra by surprise. She had wondered, afterward, if Taalo had seen the same thing in the Blindness. If she questioned the Phrenii about it, they would become agitated and there'd be nightmares for more than just her and Perinon. So after that night, she resolved not to tell anyone about what she had seen. The longer she kept quiet, the more she feared to say anything.

"I thought you had confirmed with Rhobar that he scuttled that ship and it was at the bottom of the Angim. Do you have reason to doubt his word?" She was a notoriously bad liar, even without the Phrenii present as lie detectors, so she turned the question back on him.

"I questioned Rhobar with Mahri present. He spoke the truth."

"And because of his testimony, I haven't taken it upon myself to search for the ship." That was the truth as well.

They regarded each other in silence. For a moment, he was her one-year-younger cousin again. No one expected he would eventually be king. He had survived the death of his father by Fevers, the suicide of his brother by drowning, and the death of his mother by sorrow. He had been crowned at sixteen, the youngest to ever bind himself to the Phrenii. He had spent more than ten years in rapport with inhuman creatures that no adult could touch and only recently found someone he could marry. More than anyone alive, Perinon knew what it meant to be alone and do one's duty.

"Bring us back the Kaskea shard, Draius," he said softly.

"As you wish, cousin."

Outside, she found evening had descended. The stars were visible and there was a hint of autumn in the air. She didn't take the offer of a coach, wanting to sort out her thoughts and memories by walking. The streets of the upper city weren't crowded and the architecture styles spanned thousands of years of history. She was enjoying herself until she saw a green glow at the bottom edge of her vision. Instinctively, she put her hand over the Kaskea shard hanging from her neck.

We would speak with you, Commander Draius. She heard the voice in her mind and it seemed more male each time she went into rapport. Was she trying to make the Phrenii more human? That would certainly be frowned upon by the matriarchy.

One of the Phrenii drifted around the street corner like mist from the sea. When it stopped, its outlines solidified into what the Groygans called a 'demon' and the Sareenians a 'unicorn.' Both names were vulgar; they conveyed so little about these elementals with one mind and one soul, so the Tyrrans called them the Phrenii.

This was clearly the aspect called Dahni, with green eyes and the clean scent of a morning summer rain. It was the aspect she was in rapport with, the one that controlled water and healing. Mostly to convince herself she wasn't afraid, she forced herself to relax but keep a safe distance. Adults, even those bound by the Kaskea, were always under the threat of Phrenic madness near these creatures.

"What happened between Siuru and Famri?" Her question was blunt, because the Phrenii couldn't lie.

Dahni stayed in rapport. *I cannot sense what happens in the Void when I stand on the earth. After you and Perinon left the Void, none of us can know what happened between Siuru and Famri.*

While her perfect memory recorded each word, her eyes widened at the use of "I." She thought aspects never referred to themselves singularly, except inside the Void. Then there was that last sentence. "Do you think Famri had something to do with Siuru's death?"

Dahni shook its head emphatically and its sharp horn swished through the air. *I have learned that any exchange of information while in rapport will be private to you and me. In the Void, however, uncontrolled minds can easily be read by others. So while it allows you and Perinon convenient communication, you must be very careful what you reveal there.*

"And by private—" She stopped when Dahni shook its head again. After huffing, she tried to form the question in her mind like she did in the Void. Down here it was usually harder, but maybe the liquor was helping her out. *By private, you mean our rapport cannot be heard by other aspects, even here?*

Dahni nodded.

How could a mind keep something from itself? Confused, she decided to file this conversation away and think about it later. *You didn't answer my question about Famri,* she reminded Dahni.

Famri seems as devastated as I am about Siuru. We will mourn her forever. Dahni hung its head.

The weight of *forever* made it hard for her to breathe. She stepped further away to avoid being caught up in Phrenic mourning. Everyone thought the Phrenii were cold-hearted, but she knew differently now that she was bound to them. She decided to get back to a safer subject, something that didn't need to be private. "I'll be gone from the sister cities for a while. Does rapport work at long distances?"

"Yes, but it will be harder to concentrate when you cannot see this aspect. Practice will make this easier. You may not be able to use language, but you can always send visual and emotional thoughts." Dahni switched to speech, which meant personal pronouns weren't available. Apparently, the creature thought this was a safer subject as well.

"You mean memories of what I've seen and random thoughts?" Her tone was doubtful. "What will I get from you?"

"Try rapport before you go to bed, when you're sleepy. Your mind will be more open and you will receive pictures of your son Peri, as well as his feelings."

"Thank you." At least Dahni grasped what mattered most to her.

"We remain to serve." With those traditional words, the creature started looking ethereal as it flowed back around the corner.

Relieved, she continued on to the lower city. Her son would be safe and she'd see that through rapport. Likewise, Dahni would convey her messages and love to him. The Phrenii were always hanging around children because one of their major duties was to protect them. What better protection could there be, other than the most powerful magical entities left in the mapped world?

At this time, Peri would be eating supper at Lady Anja's table. They wouldn't have waited for her, given her working hours. She smiled, thinking of her son, who sometimes groused about his given name. Of course, who didn't? Peri had been carefully given the next-generation name of Perinon by the matriarchs, who ensured there would be only one Perinon every twenty years, but in different lineages. King Perinon was twenty years older than Peri and had the Meran-Viisi lineal name—the king's lineage—while her son had Jan's lineal name of Serasa-Kolme. She planned to spend all tomorrow morning with Peri, before his lessons. Her orders didn't specify the time she had to leave for Betarr Kain, just the day.

That left Lornis on her mind. They'd gotten into a dilemma. Lornis didn't want to sleep with her until she agreed to marry him, because he was still answerable to the matriarchy. She had no problem with the matriarchs, but she couldn't commit to marriage until she slept with him at least once. Then she would know if they were compatible enough to be together, Kaskea and all. She didn't dare hurt him with her doubts, in case it collapsed their burgeoning relationship. So she kept putting off his marriage proposal while pressuring him for that first night together. So far, he'd shown admirable but frustrating restraint.

She picked up her pace, walking now with purpose. He couldn't deny her tonight.

The Shores of Gioygare, Occupied Territory of Groyga

Inica Be Recorga, First Honored Sword to Groygan Lord Endigala, bared his teeth in a tight smile. "First we'll see what the wreck carries. Then we'll send a report to his lordship."

He and his men stood in a protected cove, looking up at the broken hull. The Sareenian galley, or what was left of it, was wedged midway up the bluff between huge boulders. On a surprisingly undamaged gunwale, painted letters spelled out DANILO ANA. The deck was canted toward Inica and the galley had originally been fitted with a bow gun, which probably now lay at the bottom of the Angim Sea. Bodies of the Sareenian crew, bloating in the hot sun of late summer, wedged between the rocks that protected the cove. The rocks already looked like teeth—now they had food caught between them.

His adjutant and signaler, Shalah, saw his gaze linger. "The chemist's vision showed a desert shoreline under a cliff, protected by a fence of rocks that look like teeth. Perhaps Falcona has truly made him a magus." Her tone was less doubtful than yesterday.

"You think she'd bless a *Tyrran?*" Inica's lip pulled up in a sneer. No amount of treaties could dull his loathing for Tyrrans, carefully cultivated his entire life. He hated everything about them: their silver-gray skin and cold eyes, their singular control of true magic in the mapped world, and their *godless* society which used demons to protect their children and their souls. How could they know what's right or wrong without the guidance of the true gods? Although it explained the lack of honor and moral fortitude exhibited in Taalo. His gaze went to the top of the bluff where that individual sat in a covered wagon, protected from the hammering sun that turned his ashen complexion into dirty, dappled pewter.

"Taalo did magic—"

"He can only use death magic. That's not true magic, no matter how he tries to convince weak minds into thinking otherwise. Do you understand?" He spat out the words.

"Yes, honor." Shalah bowed her head and touched her forehead in a sign of obedience.

Up the slope, his men had reached the broken hull and one man was boosted through a large gaping hole. Other men were lining up bodies on the desolate shore and searching them. So far, none of the bodies had revealed anything of worth.

Beside Inica, the barog cat made a whining, yowling noise. Standing high as a man's waist, the cat strained and writhed in its harness, pulling its handler about. The animal rolled its eyes up to look at the wrecked ship and flattened its ears. The bristles along its back stood up straight.

"Honor." The sergeant came to Inica's side.

"Report," Inica ordered absently, his attention still on the cat. He raked his fingernails through his short hair.

"Most of the crew died from weapons, not drowning. Hand to hand combat, by the indications."

"Pirates?"

"Unknown, honor. There are no other bodies but the crew."

Inica nodded and turned his attention to the men up near the wreckage. There seemed to be a problem; a few men gestured and shouted while others leaned into the ragged hole in the hull. They pulled a limp body through the hole. With a start, he realized it was his own man. He sprinted up the steep grade to get within shouting range of the hull.

"We think there are poisonous snakes, honor," was the shouted report.

They brought the young man down the bluff and Inica watched him die on the sand. His people were trained warriors, not to be wasted on mere salvage operations. He glared back at the wreck, firmly ensconced between the boulders and looking like a skeletal body with gaping, black wounds. How could snakes be inside a ship? Perhaps this was a warning: the snake was the symbol for both knowledge and evil.

"There are no fang marks on his body," the sergeant observed.

"We're being watched by some creature out there, honor." A warrior with sea-going experience pointed out into deeper waters of the Angim. Everyone but the barog cat turned to watch and, sure enough, a dark curved back with a jagged fin slipped up and then back into the water. Good thing they were traveling back to Chikirmo on land.

"Order the chemist to come down here. He should know how to get this cargo out safely. If he doesn't..." Inica paused. "He'll endure the ramifications with the rest of us."

When Taalo had shown up in early summer and applied for Lord Endigala's sponsorship, he'd carried several interesting written references. The most peculiar also contained an offer from a Sareenian tribe to supply necromantic charms. That had grabbed his lordship's attention much more than this "lodestone of souls" Taalo wanted to find. However, secret consultation with a demon had apparently changed his lordship's mind. Even so, Inica was ordered that Taalo must *suffer the consequences of this quest as much as any other Endigala vassal.*

"Yes, honor." Shalah pulled her flags out, got the attention of the group guarding the chemist, and signaled the message. She decoded the response. "Taalo states he cannot come on the beach. Neither he nor the horses can stand the hot sand."

When he came of age, Inica had pledged himself to the god Giada, the Master of Fate. Giada's text specified that everyone must accept his or her place within society. This little Tyrran would soon learn *his* place within Lord Endigala's domain.

"Of course, we must protect the horses. But Taalo doesn't get off that easily. Tell them to drag him through the hot sand if he won't walk for himself," he said to Shalah. "Then, by Giada's will, we will expose whatever is inside that hull to the bright sun of Groyga."

Cen Cerinas Mountains, Edge of Minahmeran Territory

The Void *felt* wrong, even though Ihmar knew feelings were neither logical nor reliable. The Void displayed the true shape of the solid world below, but he had the impression everything was slightly distorted. *Off-balance*, yes, that's the word. When he decided to go back to his body, the Blindness was so turbulent with dark dreams and hunters that he couldn't linger there.

He opened his eyes. He sat cross-legged on an out-cropping of rock below a peak in the eastern Cen Cerinas mountains. Having been inactive for hours, he stretched his legs and shook them. A light breeze ruffled his silver hair with a hint of a chill. It was late summer but autumn was already beginning high in the mountains. Soon colder air would roll down the mountainsides to the valley and plains below, where humankind lived. He usually didn't travel this close to Tyrra.

In early spring, Ihmar felt the Phrenii kill. The shock reverberated through the Void and precipitated this journey. The Tyrrans of today believed there were no more Minahmerans. They also assumed the Cen Cerinas mountain range was impassible, but it was only made so through Ihmar's efforts. This required vigilance, but nevertheless the elders called him back to Minahmeran Barinek and away from his responsibilities, only to give him a vague task hindered by arbitrary rules.

After receiving this new assignment, he visited Ildizar. Remembering the visit, he shivered. He climbed up many steps to her conservatory, high as an aerie, to see no welcome on his twin's face.

"Are the elders finished with you?" The pristine white orchid Ildizar placed in her gossamer hair complimented her silver face, which was calm, empty, and perfect.

"Yes. They want to know how the Phrenii were touched by death and how this affects the Void." Ihmar looked around for a seat. Why, after all these years, did she still make him feel awkward?

A bench stood under windows to one side. The windows were open to the mists from the sea; fog obscured the forest and shoreline below. As he sat down, he suffered a moment of vertigo: the sticky, sweet smell of the orchids filled his nostrils as thick as the fog outside and the conservatory was like a ship upon a sea of nothingness. The open windows showed an empty vista without color like the Void.

His twin withdrew to her conservatory after losing another husband to the Fevers. Many of their people used solitude to reduce encounters with dormant but still possibly deadly humors of that disease, but Ildizar wished to escape her life and her memories, safe with her orchids as companions.

"They continue to dither. Why risk exposing you to humans? What will the elders do with this information, once you endanger your life to obtain it? Surely what the Phrenii have lost can never be restored." She smoothed her hair around the blossom with a slim silver hand.

"They suspect this involves the Kaskea, so the damage might be reversed."

"Ah, the terrible Kaskea, humankind's affront to true magic and the shackle to keep the Phrenii loyal to Tyrra's ruler. Wasn't it the elders who decided not to interfere when they made it? And, if they weakened it when they broke it, why interfere now?" She turned to Ihmar, her tone light but he saw no hint of lightness or curiosity. Her face was a reflection of his, except no life could be found there.

His people were longer-lived than humans, even ones who practiced true elemental magic. His grandfather sensed the making of the Kaskea and hadn't approved of an item that would bind the Phrenii, the creatures that served as humankind's portals to the Void. Their mother didn't approve of the Kaskea, either. Humankind made it and so it was suspect; she was delighted when the Kaskea broke more than five hundred years ago.

Ihmar sighed. "I won't be interfering. I'm still not permitted to expose our existence."

"So they still constrain you. Speaking of elders and rules, how is our mother?" She walked along the row of orchids, touching and examining them.

"Mother is fine. I'm sure she would like to visit." He didn't say any more. He understood Ildizar's walls, the walls that kept everybody away from her, but he wouldn't be the one to break through them.

"Everyone notices humankind's interference in the journey of souls—they destroy everyone's future. Why wait and do nothing while they drain the Void?"

"I'm supposed to examine the change in the Phrenii, not the necromancy. I think only a few individuals have revived that evil practice." He watched her carefully. Had a flicker of emotion crossed her face? If so, it would be the first time in many years.

"A practice they invented. They may have restrained themselves for hundreds of years, but they cannot resist the evil. It is inherent within them."

"What is inherent? The evil or the practice?" he asked.

"Does it matter? Humankind breeds and carries disease like rodents, but unlike the innocent rodent, they carry evil intent. You had best be careful." With those words, she turned back to her orchids. Ihmar bid farewell to her back and didn't get any response. Not that he expected one. He made his way down the circling stone steps worn by thousands of feet in as many years.

Days later, he was still disturbed by Ildizar's reaction. As twins, their talents given twice but never whole, they were an unusual blessing for their people, who rarely have one child during their long lifetimes. While in the womb, their gifts had divided: he received the sorcery, while she received mastery of command—the element of spirit. Her gift could be more powerful than his and now, as the Flame of Minahmerah, she withheld her talent from their people, preferring to stay within the confines of her high conservatory. He had hoped his visit would generate some healing emotion in her, perhaps love or concern. But the first emotion to visit her in many years was anger and unfortunately, she directed her anger toward the humankind. Anger was a dangerous emotion in the Flame, even if her talent lay quiescent and unused.

Ildizar, however, had asked the right question: what should be done about the humankind? Furthermore, what had they done to the Phrenii? He stopped pacing across the rock and looked at the lush rolling hills of the Tyrran plains far below. He needed answers to take back to the elders. Anything in the solid world could be seen from the Void, but he couldn't read an entire text by seeing random single leaves. Watching humankind go through arcane and silent lives didn't help him understand them better.

He crawled down the rock face of his observation point and landed gracefully at the bottom. After packing up his provisions and stowing his bow, he headed downhill to the Tyrran settlements.

CHAPTER TWO

On the Run

Chikirmo, Groyga

Draius always knew when a coach of a great house entered the central Chikirmo market square. Chatter and hubbub would surge in the corner where the coach appeared, then slosh across the multicolored tents to the other corners—like dropping a stone into a pot of boiling water.

It was the thirty-second day since she left the sister cities, since she touched her son's hair or her lover's face. It took eight days travel to Betarr Kain in a coach with her horse tied behind, and six days to work out a mission with Bordas and get his commander Lyn to buy in on it—all without giving them the specifics of the mission. Then she and Bordas had crossed the border into Groyga as merchants, set up business in the main market square, and waited. Another seventeen days passed.

Another important coach arrived and she leaned around her customer to see the colors. Her heart thudded at the black and crimson livery of House Endigala. *Finally.* Four guards on horseback accompanied the coach, bored with their duties, which was a good sign as well.

"Pay attention, woman! Is my offer worthy?" The elderly Groygan man glared at her, his common Tyrran heavily accented.

She made the traditional gesture of subservient apology Bordas taught her. The man was mollified and she accepted his offer. These leather skins were only medium quality, which was all part of the plan. So was the position of the tent and wares: shoved back against an alley mouth in the southwest corner with other foreign merchants.

The customer appeared satisfied with his bargain and left. Across the sea of canvas tents in the middle of the square, the coach stopped on the east side. The door opened and Taalo stepped down, his fuzzy gray-haired head clearly visible for only a moment. She was always surprised to see how small he was, compared to the damage he wrought. Not just the torture and murders he committed, but his unearthing of the lodestone of souls and his use of the Kaskea in blood rites nearly tore apart the Phrenii, and Perinon with them.

She shook her head to clear the memories. *Enough stalling—I must do this* now *if I want to get home.* Sinder told her that Endigala's chemist stopped by only once an erin for supplies of herbs and powders. Bordas should have been back from the meeting with his contact long ago. He was staying busy by gathering information on House Endigala, but now she needed to leave their goods unattended. She closed and tied down the flaps to the tent. It was only enough to keep away honest customers.

As soon as she was out of the shade of the tent, the sun's heat slammed against her body. She pulled her light hood forward to shade her face. Slowly and deliberately, as if assessing the merchants and goods, she walked along the south side of the square. She exchanged nods with the very few Tyrran merchants. The colorful Sareenian tents gave way to Groygan white tents on her left, where the center of the square lay. She turned that way.

She had befriended Sinder and other female Groygan merchants while Bordas worked the male merchants for information. It was a matter of necessity, so they could learn whether Taalo had been sighted in the marketplace at all. She never expected to make a real friend, but that's what Sinder became.

Dressed in traditional Groygan silks, Draius hung back as Taalo talked with Sinder before going into her tent alone. He always insisted on time *alone* inside the tent, just one of the irritations that made Taalo unpopular with the merchants on the square. "He thinks we're too stupid to realize he's pocketing more expensive items than he's buying," Sinder had fumed.

Draius was taller than most Groygan females, but she still managed to blend well with the crowd as she meandered down this row of tents toward Sinder, who was now speaking with one of Taalo's guards. She made a joke and the guard guffawed. Draius knew just enough Groygan to catch it: something about what the little man must be doing inside the tent alone. As she passed, she and Sinder exchanged a casual glance—one woman assessing another's silks, nothing more.

She walked to the merchant's tent just beyond Sinder's. While Sinder's herbs and powders could be fashioned into anything from healing potions to sophisticated poisons, this man engaged in the traffic of something much more abhorrent, as evidenced by the sickly sweet smoke that wafted out of the tent front flap. The merchant, himself, was smart enough not to partake in the fumes of burning resin, only selling the dreams it produced. He sat to the side in the shaded front area, his bowl in front of him.

"Ten minutes in the private side." She threw down seven cengha, five to pay for the time and an extra two for the use of the semi-private women's section of the tent. There would be fewer smokers in that section because hard-core imbibers wouldn't waste money on privacy.

The merchant's oily face stretched into a false smile as he put the coins into the bowl. He recognized her; she'd become a reliable customer by coming here at mid-morning, every three days. Today was, due to Taalo's appearance, one day off her regular schedule. She hoped he wouldn't remember.

She surreptitiously took a deep breath of the healthy outside air before parting the tent's front flaps. Inside, she walked through the cheap public section where quite a few bodies were sprawled. Then she turned right toward the private women's chamber sectioned off by heavy canvas—

which happened to be next to Sinder's tent. The exterior of this tent had planked temporary walls, intended to keep non-paying customers from coming inside.

The women's chamber had two occupants who wouldn't see her, holding shawls down over their heads and faces to keep in the smoke from the multi-tubed pipe. They sat opposite each other, competing for the dreams swirling off the glowing resin that burned in the lower chamber of the pipe. If they noticed her, they'd expect her to join them at the low table and uncork a spare tube, but they didn't. She went to the south wall where she had already loosened two of the planks in the wall. She was lucky she was doing the opposite of what the planks prevented: she was going from inside to outside, and from the inside they could be pulled out of their grooves. Behind these planks, she had slit the rotten canvas of the "healing smoke" merchant's tent. There was less than a foot's length between his tent and Sinder's, where she had arranged another slit, with Sinder's permission.

Sunlight hammered the top of her head again as she slid into the back of Sinder's tent, ending up behind a curtain that hid extra inventory. The clinks and taps of someone rummaging through wood and glass vials and popping corks came through the curtain. After her eyes adjusted, she took a peek through the curtain. Taalo stood with his back to her. *How convenient.* She mentally thanked her ancestors; today she had their blessings.

Muttering, he pocketed a vial with his left hand while he fingered a container on a table beside him. He was occupied with his sanctioned thievery as she crept up behind him. Her right arm snaked around his neck and his hands scrabbled at her hold uselessly.

"Draius! Won't get away—" She angled her elbow so she could squeeze his neck on the sides in the non-lethal City Guard chokehold that came naturally after so many years of training.

How did he know? She deepened her voice into a hoarse whisper anyway. "Where's the lodestone?"

He seemed to be *laughing*. Before she could loosen the chokehold, he sagged into unconsciousness.

Uh-oh. This was not going according to plan. First, he wasn't supposed to know who attacked him. When she let him sag down on the plank floor, she saw the mirror. It was large and expensive, set on the table and angled up so the customer could try cosmetic samples. It allowed him a view of her from the side. Second, he'd succumbed to the chokehold too soon and she wouldn't be able to ask more questions. But that was less of a problem than his knowledge; did Endigala know about the stolen shard? Would Taalo share the embarrassing fact he'd had it stolen back? Would he say *who* had stolen it? She no longer carried the Meran-Viisi name, but Taalo knew her relationship to Perinon and could expose the king's hand behind what was supposed to look like a random robbery.

She thanked her ancestors—the shard was in a pouch hung around his neck. The pouch contained other nasty things: something that looked suspiciously like a child's finger bone and a woven hair container of herbs. Reminding her of the charm he had tried to kill her with, she shuddered and left those items in the pouch. They were the products of a necromantic session, slow murder by maximum pain, of an animal or human. She desperately hoped the victim wasn't human but, given her Tyrran upbringing that animals required respect even when slaughtered for food, she couldn't countenance the torture of animals, either.

Swiftly and methodically, she staged her victim. She found more than enough money in his pockets to buy anything he wanted in this tent, so she put that in Sinder's money chest. Then she placed the herbs and powders he recently pocketed so they poked out of his coat in an incriminating way.

Sighing, she looked over Taalo one more time. Sprawled as he was on the floor, the small man looked more like a kindly grandfather than a dangerous necromancer. By all the rules of "spying" she'd learned in the past erin, she should execute him. *Protection of your cover is protection of the Tyrran King's intent, which is paramount,* Bordas had explained.

She fingered the hilt of her knife. Execution of an unconscious person, even a criminal who had earned death in Tyrra, still felt like murder. Her years in the City Guard were engraved into her bones. *I can't murder him.* As she made her decision, she sensed a tremor of rapport and a feeling of gratitude from Dahni. *We do not kill,* the Phrenii had told her, although the words "at least, not intentionally" now had to be added.

Besides, she had promised Sinder a minimum of damage and consequences; leaving a body might cause problems with local law enforcement or Lord Endigala. She briefly considered abduction: it wouldn't be difficult to haul Taalo over to the resin tent—but she didn't know what to do with him after that. He stood out in this city even more than she did; carrying him further than the next tent was impossible. Besides, Sinder was depending upon exposing Taalo's thievery. *I didn't plan for this contingency, did I?* She wished she could blame this on Perinon; if he had allowed her to ask Bordas for help, she wouldn't be facing this dilemma, at least not alone. But looking at this honestly—she was always brutally honest, even with herself—she had to take responsibility for allowing Taalo to identify her, then not doing what needed to be done.

So she left as quickly as she came. After putting back the wall planks inside the resin den, she stumbled out the main door. The proprietor would think she couldn't handle that much resin and had to leave early. The recovered Kaskea shard was rolled up in a kerchief in her pocket. She passed Sinder's tent at a sedate walk and didn't glance at the merchant or the waiting guard. Sinder would take that as a signal to check her customer and start a commotion.

It came almost immediately. She heard Sinder's voice raised and caught the Groygan word for "thief," although that wouldn't hold a valued member of the Great House Endigala for long. She tried to lengthen her pace a little while still strolling casually. Her tent was in sight by the time Taalo's panicked shouts reached her. After she sat down in front of her tent, she leaned forward to look down the south side of the square. Sure enough, a bored guard in crimson and black came from the center of the square and looked both ways. After shrugging, the guard sauntered toward her corner. He was paying more attention to the Tyrran merchants than the Sareenian, because Taalo told them to look for a Tyrran woman.

She fished her own shard out from under her clothes. Instead of the large locket that used to contain it, her shard was now wrapped in silver wire which looped it over the long chain about her neck. The change had been specifically for this mission: she fumbled for the flattened end that helped her unwrap two handspans of wire, which she used to wrap the recovered shard back to back with her own. The flat shards fit well together, even though that wasn't how they fit together in the original Kaskea. She dropped them down her neckline and could barely tell there was another one bumping against her skin.

A hiss came from inside the tent. Bordas was back.

She scooted backward and tied the tent flap from the inside. When she saw his hands covered in blood, she handed him the handy spare kerchief, now no longer wrapping a shard. "What happened to you?"

He shook his head, meaning he couldn't talk about it here in the market. Tents didn't provide enough privacy. She squelched her curiosity. As he wiped the blood off, he exposed cuts on his palms, some deep and still bleeding. He winced as he pulled out what looked like glass fragments. The fine yellow dust that drifted about everywhere in Chikirmo mixed with his blood on the kerchief. He pushed up his sleeves to expose other serious cuts on his forearms. She looked for their salve—made in Tyrra, of course—because the Groygans were ignorant in their medicine.

"Let me do that. You can't wrap those one-handed." She found some the bandages they packed but never expected to use.

"Anything to report?"

"Four guards in yellow and black stopped by to look at our leather. Lord Chintegrata's colors, if I remember correctly." She tore off a length of bandage.

"You remember everything, quite precisely. Go on." Bordas winced as he probed a deep slash below his elbow. She bandaged that first.

"They were just shoplifting." They'd taken their cue from the other merchants: if a guard wearing the colors of a great house didn't want to pay for his or her goods, nobody complained. She tied a bandage on his left hand.

"Anything else?"

"We had two real customers. I sold one skin to a woman who makes belts and several skins to a gentleman. And—" She finished the bandage on his right hand. "I've completed my mission. I'm ready to go back to Betarr Kain."

"As am I. Congratulations on finding your target." He was always careful to avoid names and specifics in conversations. "Will there be ramifications for Tyrrans here in Groyga?"

"I hope not..." Her voice trailed off. She hadn't considered the repercussions for the small amount of Tyrrans in Chikirmo. Maybe she should tell him that Taalo had identified her, but then she'd have to admit she didn't rectify the problem.

"At least something went well today." Bordas didn't seem to notice her hesitancy.

The noise in the square rose and she stuck her head out. The coach in House Endigala colors was joined by twelve mounted guards in the same colors. Her mind ticked off the numbers automatically as she looked for Taalo. He sat in the coach and looked at the guards with a bewildered expression. Apparently, they weren't here at his call.

The guard who was strolling in her area was nowhere to be seen. The newly arrived ones were splitting up, some to the west side and some to the east, terrorizing the shoppers. She pulled her head back into the tent. "Half a company from House Endigala has arrived. They're mounted."

Bordas swore. "By the Horn, they reacted fast. We have to get out of Chikirmo."

"I'll pack up the skins."

Bordas grabbed her arm. "No, leave everything but what we've got on the horses."

The skins might be of mediocre quality, but the entire pile was worth about twenty tyr. That was a large sum, but not worth her life. "Fine, but I'm taking this." She grabbed the folded green silk in the corner. She bartered for the silk just this morning: it was dyed with the emerald green of the Tyrran flag and would make a fine set of sleeves for Peri.

"Everything ready?" He had a system for being prepared to run. Now he lifted the center back of the tent, which was never staked, per that system.

"The horses are saddled and I watered them just after the second morning gong, as always." She pulled off her sandals, put on silk socks found in this very market, and pulled on her boots. After rearranging her loose trousers, almost a split skirt, she held the overdress up and to the side. It went down to her knees and was split from the hips so she could ride, but it would interfere with crawling under the back of the tent.

No one had touched their horses, tied in the shaded alley behind the tent. Of course, her horse Chisel wouldn't allow himself to be handled by strangers without raising an alarm. Chisel and Delfi might be loaded like merchant mounts, but they were cavalry horses bred for warfare and intelligence, the results of two thousand years of Tyrran breeding. She shook her head, not for the first time, at seeing Chisel loaded up like a mule. The pack behind her saddle held provisions and her sheathed saber, which had a leather skin wrapped around it to hide its shape. Still unused to mounting in Groygan clothes, she floundered in fabric as she settled into her saddle.

Bordas knew Chikirmo well and took the lead. They traveled through unfrequented back alleys where the sun couldn't shine and in streets crowded with traffic where the early afternoon heat beat down upon her. Braziers of burning incense added even more warmth to the air, mixing with flavors of spices foreign to her. The smell of the crowds made her eyes water: Groygans often used oil steeped with rosemary or other strong scents and when combined with body sweat, everyone became pungent.

Chikirmo was the main city of Groyga and the country's seat of power. The Lords' Council met here while every god and goddess had at least one long-established temple here. She adjusted the purse at her waist as they went by a temple of Erina, the Mistress of Time. Erina didn't actually condone thievery, but many cutpurses and thieves followed this goddess—at least the devout kind. She didn't want to make an involuntary contribution to her temple.

She glanced through the arches into the temple courtyard and winced at the sight of the acolyte beating the gong. Sweat poured down his bare torso and he needed someone to spell him, and soon. Tyrrans had no gods, so she didn't believe the sun would stop moving because someone fainted from heat and couldn't beat out praise to Erina. *We have our ancestors and the Phrenii; what more is needed? Our ancestors who have attained the stars bestow their blessings upon those of us who live with love and honor. The Phrenii protect our children and departed souls who travel the path to the stars.*

She could still hear the gong as Bordas turned into an alley. He paused at the end and she came alongside him. The cross street before them was crowded, wide, and bright with Groygan silk and Sareenian cotton. Crowds on foot jostled with wagons for center positions. The traffic was slow, but moving in both directions.

"This will be tricky. We're going into a natural choke point because everyone has to get through the old city gates. I expect Endigala's guards will be waiting here. Follow my lead." He edged Delfi out into the sunny street.

Draius pushed in behind him. Ahead stood massive walls made of warm orange stone. Chikirmo was a modern city in this age of gunpowder and trade; it had outgrown its original walls. Just like Betarr Serasa, Chikirmo had defenses designed to repel invasion by sea and not to keep people inside the city from leaving.

She caught a glimpse of crimson sleeves, slashed with black. There were guards in Endigala's colors under the portal, pressed against the huge walls. Bordas edged Delfi toward the middle of the crowd trying to move through the city portal. She kept Chisel behind Delfi, trying to appear as casual as Bordas. Her heart pounded.

Bordas lined them up, on purpose, beside a farmer's mule cart. This placed them in the middle of the wide street and brushing against oncoming traffic. Delfi was at least two hands taller than the mule pulling the cart and Chisel was even taller than Delfi. Feeling like she towered over the crowd, she slouched. She kept her head tilted downward so the silk hood kept her face in shadow. To her side, the farmer's wagon carried an early harvest of large gourds. He was probably from a farm south of Chikirmo and hoping to profit by selling them in the markets north of the city. Timing was everything: soon all the markets would be filled with gourds and melons. The wagon had seen better days: the hinged back was tied up to the frame with old rope.

They were almost under the portal. She glanced at the guards out of the corner of her eye. They were on foot and she couldn't see what weapons they carried. They gestured toward Bordas, whose horse towered over the wagons. While he and Draius wore native clothing and covered their hair and dusky skin, their stature alone screamed "Tyrran."

She heard a guttural command in Groygan. First in normal voice, then shouted. "Stop, Tyrran!" Traffic slowed as people looked about in mild curiosity. Bordas only looked bored. He eased forward until he was even with the mule pulling the farmer's wagon.

"Tyrran, I told you to stop!" This command came in common Tyrran: loud and distinct. Everyone in the mapped world should understand it. Traffic clogged under the massive portal as folks milled about and craned their necks, looking for the offending Tyrran. A guard in crimson and black pushed through the crowd, but he had to go around the mule wagon stopped right under the portal.

Bordas whipped his quirt against the mule's neck. The mule jumped away and bucked in its traces while the farmer shouted and tried to control his wagon. Shouts came from the other side of the mule as hapless pedestrians dodged as best they could. She drew the knife from her waistband and, leaning over to the wagon, cut the old rope that held the back of the wagon to the frame. The rope was sun-rotted and gave easily to the knife. As she hoped, the other side was also held by weak rope; the bulging, over-burdened wagon erupted and gourds as large as her head started rolling into the crowd. She felt a pang of remorse for the farmer's loss as she put her knife away.

Bordas surged through the portal and she urged Chisel to keep up. The geldings knew how to push through people and weren't distracted by yells or shaking fists. Fortunately for the crowd, Delfi was pushing through with Chisel behind and not abreast. The horses caused mishaps as men, women, and children were pushed aside, but only skinned hands and knees were the result. Thankfully, no one went under their horses' hooves. They made it through the gate and beyond the old city walls, but shops lined the street with no side alleys for escape. The crowds were a little lighter now, but this was still a busy street.

She looked back. The guard who had pushed through the crowd was knee-deep in gourds; he was looking up and gesturing. She followed his line of sight upward. On top of the wall were more guards: some in red and black, others in house colors of green and orange, or yellow and black, or solid colors for the city or Council of Lords. Groygan politics would prevent other houses from interfering with House Endigala, unfortunately. Then she spotted two red and black guards bracing and aiming a harguebus.

"Hakabut!" she shouted as she pressed Chisel into Delfi's right hindquarter. The Groygan *harguebus* was a copy of the Tyrran *hakabut* and both were hard to aim because of their size and recoil. They had hooks on the barrel that had to be braced over a wall. Surely they wouldn't fire into a crowd, not with that.

Bordas's horse surged forward. The crowd thinned as they got further from the gate and they picked up speed. A woman beside Chisel, moving toward the old gate, flew backward as her chest exploded in red. Draius flinched at the sound of the shot. A blast of a powder weapon cleared the streets better than two Tyrran warhorses. Screaming and shouting, people pushed to the storefronts and pressed into doorways while they looked about for the source of the sound. Meanwhile, the harguebus had to be reloaded unless they had another ready.

The ground exploded ahead and to the right. Chisel swerved and she stayed with him. Specks of sand and rock hit her face as she heard the shot. There was clear road ahead and the cobblestones changed to packed gravel and sand. The storefronts changed to walled estates. The horses could eventually get to a dead run, but since the road was steadily going uphill, they also provided a great target for any ranged weapon. She drifted Chisel right to provide two targets instead of one. Chisel and Delfi were abreast and galloping a yard or two apart. She hunched as low as she could, her shoulders tight—

Suddenly she dropped into rapport with Dahni. For a moment, she saw the sparkling spires of Betarr Serin in the mist that sometimes clung to the mountains. She stood on a wide marble bridge over rushing water, the Whitewater Bridge between the sister cities. Children ran toward her, laughing and waving, their long braids throwing off glints from gold and silver ties.

Shaking her head, she pushed Dahni's view out of her mind and focused on the roadway in front of her. Rapport might have the benefit of being private but it could be damned inconvenient. The powder shots had alerted traffic ahead. People peered at them from the cover of walls or doorways as the horses picked up more speed, their hooves pounding hollowly on the roadway. Drivers with grapes from the vineyards west of the city pulled their wagons to the side of the road and some even jumped off, getting under their wagons or using their animals as cover.

Bordas abruptly slowed and turned north. She looked over her shoulder. Far down the road, a few guards had mounted and cleared the crowd, but they were too late. They would never catch up.

She followed as Delfi turned east, then north, east, then north, cantering past walled residences. Soon these estates merged back into shops.

Then came the workhouses, which melted into shacks. They had gone northeast to the edge of Chikirmo where the Groygan *nunetton*, or their "forgotten nameless," resided. As she saw figures draw back into shadows and faces turn away, she knew that any questions posed by Endigala's guards would be fruitless here.

Bordas dodged through a derelict district of narrow, winding pathways at a cantor and she had to concentrate to follow. She began to glimpse farmland and orchards between gaps in walls and pens, but it seemed forever until they were clear of the city. Now Bordas turned westward toward their real goal: the only ferry directly between Groyga and Tyrra. Keeping to strips of trees or orchards when they could, jumping small stone walls and traveling the rows in vineyards when they had to, they gradually went uphill toward the rocky ridges that edged the Saamarin. The shadows were long when they started moving through straggling pine trees that couldn't really be called forest. The ground was rock interspersed with gravel and covered with slippery needles, so they let the horses pick their own way.

They stopped at a small stream and let the horses drink. He filled their skins with water while she checked the packs on the horses; she thanked her ancestors that she took special care in tying them down. The packs must have been uncomfortable and she checked for sores, just in case.

They remounted and Bordas led them up the stream, making the horses walk in the water. She wondered if their pursuers might use dogs to track them. All those guards of House Endigala had not been mobilized for Taalo, so this pursuit must be about Bordas and whatever he was doing this morning. The fact it warranted the killing of innocent civilians by House Endigala saddened her.

"Are you ready to tell me what happened?" she asked.

"Later. You'll have to talk to Dahni in the Void."

That didn't sound good; she had told him the Void could only be used for emergency communications that required specific language, usually something out of the ordinary. Her curiosity grew like an itch she couldn't scratch.

The ground became rockier as they traveled below the top of the lightly forested ridge. Just over that ridge was the Saamarin, wide and deep, with only two ferries along its length by which to leave Groyga. The southern one was west of Chikirmo and went to Tyrra, while the northern one was at the mouth of the Mirror Sea and went to Kitarra. She recognized the cut that cradled the road to the southern ferry and felt the excitement of *home* build within her chest. They left the horses to creep south on foot. Bordas went low and crawled as they neared the cut. She followed suit, dropping to her belly to get to the edge and look down. Below them was the ferry landing they used to enter Groyga. Guards wearing crimson and black milled about. Without effort, she counted twelve guards with six crossbows, two muskets, one long bow, and a barog cat. The muskets were of modern design with serpentine matchlocks, more accurate than harguebuses.

"House Endigala. I figured they might go straight to the ferry as well as the docks," Bordas said. "Those are the only two sensible routes out of Chikirmo, using ferry or ship."

"Maybe we should have stayed in the city and gotten help from the embassy? Perhaps they could smuggle us out on a Tyrran ship."

"No. We'd just put others in jeopardy. Luckily, there aren't any Tyrrans down there." He watched the landing.

There was that pang of guilt again. She turned her attention back to the ferry operators. The Groygan ferry master argued with a slim guard who might be a woman. He gestured to a waiting line of wagons and pack animals. His assistant, an adolescent girl, viewed all the other guards with distrust. Those hoping to take a ferry were mostly Groygan, with a sprinkling of Sareenians. But that didn't dissuade Endigala's guards. They made them unload each wagon and open their large packs and crates for examination. It was obvious they looked for concealed persons. Getting across the Saamarin this evening would be difficult for anyone; it seemed impossible for the two Tyrrans watching above.

A coach with House Endigala colors and crest came over the rise in the road and everyone below turned to watch as it stopped. A guard climbed down, set up steps, then opened the door. She sucked in her breath when a familiar small figure with a mop of gray hair appeared.

"Is that who I think it is?" Bordas looked at her. "I figured your orders were to terminate him, considering his crimes."

"The mission was not *termination*," she said stiffly. "I got what the king wanted."

Taalo walked down the line of travelers, looking at each of them in a rather perfunctory manner as they repacked their goods.

"He looks like he knows who he's looking for."

"Yes, he does. I made a mistake." Her voice was stoic.

Taalo marched past the arguing operators and guard. Down the dock a couple paces, he stopped next to the ferry and threw something that looked like a small tied sack. Then he turned back to shore. The ferry master hopped back on the ferry to investigate. Draius tensed. *Don't pick it up, don't touch it.* But he did pick it up as Taalo, without looking back, waved his arm in an imperious gesture and said something.

The ferry master burst into fire and, within a breath, the entire ferry had followed. The young woman who assisted the ferry master picked up a long pole and started running, yelling in Groygan. Draius recognized the word "father." The guard followed and, to his or her credit, grabbed the woman by the waist and took them both into the water as the dock began to blaze.

As the flames from this unnaturally fast conflagration rose into the evening sky twice as high as her position, a wave of nausea took her over. *Necromancy.* She clenched her teeth and rolled into a ball as Bordas pulled her away from the edge.

"We can't be seen," he said into her ear. "What's wrong?"

"J—just give me a mo—ment." This seemed ten times stronger than any reaction she previously had to necromantic charms. The shakes and nausea was strong enough to make her heave. In a few moments it passed, but she was so tired she continued lying on the ground.

"Come look," Bordas said.

I'd rather not. Nevertheless, she crawled back to her former position. The ferry and its accompanying dock were charred, smoking bones sticking out of water close to the river's edge. Further out in the river where the strong current swept in waters from the Angim, a string of flotsam had been pulled away from shore and stretched southward. The young assistant crouched on the shore, still crying and mourning the ferry master, whose body was nowhere to be seen. The coach and guards were gone; no indication of Taalo or the House of Endigala remained. Those who had hoped to take a ferry over to Tyrra were slowly heading back to Chikirmo.

"It'll take days to rebuild that dock and ferry." Bordas's voice was flat. "You should have killed him."

CHAPTER THREE

The Fate of Spies

Somewhere North of the Saamarin Ferry, Groyga

Horror and dread battled within Draius. She was horrified that leaving Taalo alive had resulted in more deaths. No doubt Bordas blamed her for Taalo's destruction of the ferry and she dreaded having that conversation. She also dreaded learning what he'd done to cause House Endigala to fire guns into crowds. They made camp and the horses munched grain from feedbags when she finally decided to break the silence.

"Are you going to tell me what happened this afternoon?" She tore off a bite of dried meat and chewed vigorously. They made no fire on the rocky ground because it might be seen through the sparse trees.

Bordas took time to swallow. "I apologize for taking you to task about Taalo. I'm not privy to your mission for the king and it's possible that Lord Endigala ordered Taalo to destroy the ferry—all because of me."

That pang of guilt went through her gut again.

"The story I'm going to tell must be told to the Phrenii with words, so they can pass it to the king and the master of arms. You need to do this tonight."

He meant by walking the Void. Her gut tightened. She had managed to avoid that since Siuru's death. Dahni had been right about trying rapport just before sleep; it worked quite well when it came to following her son's activities and sending him her love. Reporting to Perinon was different: in Betarr Kain, she'd passed very general status updates through Jhari. While in Chikirmo, she and Bordas used Tyrran ships to carry letters containing innocuous code about her "trip," addressed to a fictitious person with the lineal name of Meran-Kolme, who lived at the residence of the master of arms. But now she had to enter the Void, because this must involve concepts and names for which they had no code words. Again, the warning about the Void not being private flashed through her mind. Who could be possibly listening?

"Remember Rhibasgar's ravings about Lord Endigala?" He put his bedroll behind him so he could lean against some rocks.

"Of course." Her tone was dry. Rhibasgar was a Groygan seaman sympathetic enough toward Tyrra to become a general informant. They had interviewed him at Betarr Kain before coming across the border on this mission.

"Right—you never forget." His glance looked askance but whether it held pity or envy, she couldn't tell. "Well, from my imperfect memory, I thought his story held undue paranoia. Perhaps even lunacy brought on by ague."

"I can vouch that Rhibasgar was sincere and sane. Jhari would have told me if he was otherwise." That interview had been uncomfortable because it'd been Jhari, rather than Dahni, who stood beside her. The creatures were interchangeable, just aspects of the same mind and soul. She shouldn't have noticed the difference, right? But she did, and that meant they might be developing individuality. She brushed those thoughts away to concentrate on Rhibasgar's exact words. "What did he call Endigala? The 'surmal' of Tyrra, our 'final choice'?"

"He was referring to Surmagla, Master of Choice." His tone was sour. "It would be more accurate to call Surmagla the Master of Death. He's a god who gets bribes, not worship, because all Groygan souls must pass his tests before they can travel over the chasm to the protection of Falcona in their afterlife."

"They think death is a choice?"

"They think Surmagla presents himself to everyone before they die. Those who struggle to hold on to life can impress Surmagla and he might let them return to the realm of the living."

"Just because he compared Endigala to a god doesn't mean he's crazy. It only speaks to his fear and respect of the man."

"Maybe, but I was suspicious. Rhibasgar's been accurate and useful in the past, but his information about Endigala was vague hyperbole. What I heard in the past eight-day was the same, so this morning I sought out an infrequent, but sensible informant. Nugere worships Giada, the Master of Fate, and is the sort who goes around proclaiming 'what follows must follow' and such nonsense. I hope he meets his god in his afterlife." Bordas paused, staring at his clasped hands. This didn't auger a happy ending to his story but considering the day's events, Draius didn't expect one.

He continued. "I found Nugere hanging around the food vendors in the south square. His love of easy money is second only to his love of food, and he is privy to the business of several lords. When I asked him about Endigala, his skin paled. He was evasive, but I pressed him and paid him well. At first, all he would say is 'Lord Endigala has a force behind him.'

"'How many guards?' I asked. All the great houses have their own guards, sworn to support that house.

"'It is not a force of men,' he said.

"I badgered him for more, but he wouldn't talk in public. We left the square and went to the eastern side of Chikirmo. We climbed to a quiet part of the original city walls and he pointed out Endigala's estate to the east. I took out my spyglass and looked. It certainly was impressive. I saw guards at the gates with barog cats pacing beside them in their harnesses. The fields within the walls were rich with produce and had a wealth of livestock.

"'What are those things working in the fields?' I asked. Some seemed to be walking on two feet, but others were down on all fours or crouching. They worked under the heavy lash of foremen.

"Nugere closed his eyes and whispered, 'May Giada forgive me for showing you Groyga's shame. Endigala took fate from Giada's hands and twisted our shame into evil.'

"Then he told me everything. I now know what the Fevers did to Groyga. While we in Tyrra died or became barren, the Fevers twisted the wombs of many Groygan women, causing them to give birth to abominations. Nugere said their bodies are strong, but malformed, and they never learn to speak. Most were born with sharp claws and some have fangs. They grow quickly and became wild. Their parents couldn't handle them, so Endigala collected them and successfully bred them to each other. They call them *ebi corgo*, or 'the corrupted,' whether in the singular or the plural. The Groygans believe they have no souls."

Draius stopped Bordas's story. "All these years, we thought Groyga went unscathed by the Fevers. How could we not have known this? Is this what the King's Guard Intelligence presumed was a breeding program for barog cats?"

Bordas nodded. "Endigala breeds both—making one program a cover for the other. It was easy to hide because it is shameful to most Groygans. Whether they couldn't accept the unworthy offspring or feel guilt for handing them over to Endigala—I don't know. Endigala collected them from lords and commoners alike, all turning a blind eye to what he was doing. At one time another lord might have stopped his breeding program, but it's too late. He's too powerful now.

"Once Nugere told me this, I had to get a closer look. It took all my will, and my gold, to persuade him to help me. We climbed over the eastern wall of Endigala's estate, using a cloak to cover the sharp glass on the top. An orchard backed up to that wall and I noted the guards assumed the eastern wall safe. The estate was crisscrossed with those high hedges of rosemary that survive the Groygan summers. We crept up to the hedge between the orchard and the fields, where I could use my spyglass and get a close look at the *ebi corgo* working the fields.

"They are small, rarely coming to a man's chest. They don't always stand up straight and most of them have fangs, long arms, and claws, which they were using to rake through the dirt. The guards seemed to think they needed frequent lashing to keep focused on their work. Some *ebi corgo* wore something that looked like a muzzle. Then Nugere put a hand on my arm. I was so occupied that I missed two guards and a leashed *ebi corgo* approaching on the path. The guards stopped three paces from our position, on the other side of the hedge.

"'What's it sniffing after?' asked one of the guards. The *ebi corgo* was down on all fours and straining against its leash. I didn't move; I hoped the creature might not smell us over the strong scent of the rosemary. The other guard replied in a thick southern dialect, saying something dismissive. They both laughed and passed my position. When they were several yards past, I started quietly withdrawing from the hedge.

"We crept on hands and knees back through the orchard. Halfway through, a strange keening started behind us, followed by a thick Groygan command. I tried to restrain Nugere, but it was too late. He stood, throwing away all caution and sprinting for the wall. I had no choice but to follow, dodging around trees, amazed to see his legs pump and move his bulk so quickly. I barely caught up at the wall. Behind us, the keening sounded closer.

"I had no problem scrambling up the wall, but Nugere couldn't get over by himself. I lay across the top of the wall—set with broken glass and sans cloak—leaning both arms over to help Nugere. From my position, I saw the *ebi corgo* was loose and almost upon us; the guards were farther away. The ebi corgo charged on all fours.

"Nugere had his shoulders over the wall when that thing jumped him. It dug claws and teeth into his leg, causing him to scream and jerk. Their combined weight dragged him out of my grip. He fell to the ground and the *ebi corgo* was on him like a rabid animal. The guards were too close for me to climb down, so I abandoned him."

He was quiet for a moment, staring at nothing. "I'm ashamed I left him behind. Lords of great houses don't tolerate invasion of their privacy and I expect he'll be tortured and killed."

She was silent, unable to mitigate his shame or assuage his honor. Before this mission, she never thought a Groygan could be anything more than an informant or a tool. But she liked Sinder and didn't want any harm coming to her, particularly due to the unfortunate robbery of Taalo's shard.

"He deserved more than this." Bordas pushed gravel about with his boot. "These Groygans live out their lives much as we do, with the same concerns and the same troubles. Nugere lost his wife and child, and his pain was no different from a Tyrran's."

She took a deep breath. "Can the *ebi corgo* be trained to be effective fighters?"

"I don't know." He kept his head down.

"Did Nugere realize you're an intelligencer for the King's Guard?"

"I'm sure he suspected. Most merchants, even those who barter information, won't go as far as I did..." His voice trailed off and he rubbed his hand over his face. "It doesn't matter what he knew. I dropped my spyglass trying to pull him up the wall. With that and whatever he tortures out of Nugere, Endigala will conclude I'm with the King's Guard."

Lord Endigala's Estate, Chikirmo, Groyga

Inica Be Recorga stood beside Lord Endigala's chair and considered himself lucky. He reacted swiftly to the news of a spy and did everything within his power to capture the Tyrran. The guards sent to intercept the Tyrran within the city lost him and his companion in the shantytown, but the ones he sent to check the ferry and Tyrran ships at the docks had yet to report in. He expected to capture the spy by the morning. Fate was on his side today and he would stop by Giada's temple to leave a donation tonight.

"You encountered him near the old Erina gate?" Lord Endigala didn't look at the guard he questioned. Instead, his lordship examined the brass spyglass in his hands, turning it about. A thing of beauty, the spyglass cylinder was perfectly formed with lenses more powerful than any made in Groyga. Endigala held up the glass to one eye and twisted to look out through the doors to the courtyard. His lordship grunted in appreciation. No mere merchant could afford such an item. The spy had to be Tyrran King's Guard.

Inica motioned for the guard to continue; Lord Endigala still listened.

"Yes, my lord. He and his woman were dressed like merchants, but didn't respond to our commands. No merchant would run from our guns."

"How could he hope to pass for Groygan?" Lord Endigala still admired the spyglass.

The guard shot Inica a panicked look, who answered for him. "He probably couldn't pass as Groygan, but instead blended with other merchants. Many Sareenian and Tyrran merchants sell their goods in Chikirmo and dress like Groygans to attract customers."

Lord Endigala frowned and shifted in his chair. He was tall, his bulk solid and hard. He ordered his chair made hard also, with no cushions or armrests. Inica knew his lordship had initially resisted opening Groygan borders to trade with their ancient enemy. That was almost twenty years ago, after the Fevers burned across the mapped world.

The guard continued. "The spy and his woman didn't stop when we fired. We—err—suffered a casualty in the crowd because they used the innocents in the streets for cover. We hit a silk weaver in the chest."

Endigala held up a hand, stopping the guard. "The silk weaver's family must be compensated for their loss."

A scribe made out a draft against House Endigala, his pen scratching in the silence of the hall. Inica admired the way his lordship took care of the details. One house couldn't sway the Council of Lords and the entire

country without support from the gods and the people. If House Endigala were to bring back the glorious days of Groygan expansion, as Inica
hoped, then the various merchant, farmer, and craftsmen guilds, as well
as unaligned laborers and temple acolytes, had to be indulged.

He glanced out the open courtyard doors. The sun had set and the sky
was violet. Shalah was out there right now, ensuring their people were
at the ferry, docks, embassies, and places in the city known to cater to
Tyrrans. With his approval, she sent a cadre up the river to poke around,
although the mission in Kitarra was supposedly under the control of the
Council of Lords. Shalah asked whether to call in supplemental personnel
from the council, but Inica didn't trust them to act in House Endigala's
best interests.

"We'll have the spy soon, my lord." The guard echoed Inica's thoughts.
"He and his woman stand out, with their hair and eyes. Their horses are
tall and the way the woman rides—"

"The woman's name is Draius and she's cousin to the Tyrran King, my
lord." Shalah's voice cut through the guard's babble. There were murmurs
among the scribes as everyone's attention turned to the main doors of the
hall.

A bedraggled Shalah stood under the lintel. She didn't drip, but she'd
obviously been soaked, head to toe, in water. Her sleeves clung to her
arms and tendrils of her burgundy hair stuck to her face and neck, loosened from the thick braid that ran down the back of her head to her
shoulder blades. Behind her, two guards held a sulking Taalo.

Shalah jerked her head toward Taalo. "He knows the woman who
rides with the spy. Also, I can report how he destroyed our ferry, if your
lordship is interested?"

"Very." Endigala's voice was dry. "Start with the ferry."

Inica ticked off the issues his lordship had to be considering as Shalah
described, first, the total destruction of the entire ferry facility, to include
their largest ferry. Second, the death of the ferry master, although Shalah
got an approving nod for saving the master's assistant. All this done in

front of many witnesses by someone who arrived in a house coach, attended by house guards, and wearing house colors. There was no doubt that House Endigala was to blame and the council would task their house to pay for Taalo's wanton destruction of important Groygan assets. As well, what could they tell the Tyrran embassy, because they'd be concerned about the destroyed dock as well? Although his lordship's face seemed cold, those who had served him all their lives—as Inica had—could feel the anger smoldering behind the features.

"Come here, Taalo, and account for yourself," Endigala said.

Taalo shook himself free from the guards and stalked, as much as those short legs could, to stand in front of his lordship. The reporting guard edged away from the necromancer to stand behind Inica.

"Do you have any idea the amount of labor and coin your tantrum has cost me? If this arouses Tyrran suspicions or sabotages Desert Wind, you'll be under lock and key here for the rest of your life."

If Taalo didn't know he was in trouble by looking at Endigala's face, he certainly knew it now. His eyes widened. Clasping his hands behind him, he looked down at his lordship's feet. "I had to prevent Officer Draius from leaving the country with something she stole."

Inica rolled his eyes. Taalo was obsessed with the "City Guard bitch" who forced him to flee Tyrra. With each telling, his stories about this woman grew. She had a perfect memory and a logical mind. She was a superb rider with a mathematically precise saber, etc. The list of skills grew far beyond the capability of any Tyrran, as far as Inica was concerned.

"Right. You see this Draius all over Chikirmo. Last erin, you insisted she was entering the temple of Falcona." He grabbed Taalo's collar and waited for the signal from his lordship. At best, Taalo was looking at years of indentured servitude and at worst, execution.

"But she—she *attacked* me this morning." Taalo earnestly stamped his foot, which might have seemed childlike if Inica hadn't recently watched him torture an *ebi corgo* to feed his precious lodestone.

"Why did she do that? To steal something?" Endigala asked.

"It is of no importance to your lordship. I did you a favor. You're look-ing for a male Tyrran spy with a Tyrran woman and I just stopped them from leaving the country by the western border."

"Answer his lordship's question." Inica had enough of this. He shook Taalo and tightened his grip, but froze at the sound of a voice behind him. A voice that was neither male nor female, a voice that carried musi-cal tones that no man-made instrument could copy, a voice hardly any Groygans had heard with the exception of Lord Endigala's inner circle.

"Taalo is worried about an artifact he stole from the Royal Library in Tyrra—an artifact he can't use, for lack of the right ancestors. Instead, however, he should worry about the attention he may garner by using that necromantic charm. The others may see that, little man, and I've done my best to shield it." The unsubtle smell of brimstone wafted by Inica's nose.

This demon had never before entered Lord Endigala's hall without invitation. It was a single-horned creature of legend that looked like a hot burning ember encased in cold crystal. It was one of five "Phrenii" who protected only Tyrra and to everyone here, it was a demon. Guards carry-ing weapons backed up against the walls. Silence fell and a very wide path cleared for Famri to walk down the center. Its four cloven hooves made no sound on the stone floor.

The hair on the back of Inica's neck rose and he let go of Taalo, who scampered behind his broader body. Taalo could be obnoxious beyond the bounds of sense, but Inica thought it telling that even he was fright-ened by Famri. Tyrrans considered these demons to be immortal and godlike. Taalo said they had special protections; using weapons against them would cause insanity or death. But Famri was no god to him. He fingered the hilt of his sword, ready to protect his lord and his house. Glancing about, he noted there would be more people who now knew about Famri's association with House Endigala, but all of them were still considered loyal. Of course, people who were non-essential or not in his lordship's inner circle were slipping out like rats streaming off a sinking ship. He couldn't blame them.

Behind him, Taalo was babbling under his breath to Lord Endigala. "I beg your lordship to reconsider this alliance. The Phrenii are one mind and soul, they can't be individuals. That means this aspect is either insane or lying."

"Didn't you say the Phrenii couldn't lie?" Lord Endigala's question was calm and measured.

Inica lowered his sword and moved to the side to let Famri pass. If his lordship had no problem with this overt visit, then all might be well. The demon moved past him to stand only two paces away from his lordship, which still made him nervous. However, the demon maintained a respectful demeanor and waited for the conversation with Taalo to end.

As usual, the necromancer didn't answer the question posed to him. "Think about it—one aspect is claiming to hide information from the others. How can it not be insanity, when a mind hides what it sees and what it says from itself?"

"I have met many people who manage to hide inconvenient facts from their own minds. And, insane or not, Famri has offered to unlock the power of the lodestone." Endigala's voice was sharp. "You haven't discovered how to do that."

"I need more time to study it." Taalo lowered his voice to a whisper, but Inica could hear him and no doubt Famri could, as well. "What if the Phrenii know of your plans?"

"If so, they have forsaken Tyrra." Endigala motioned him away.

Taalo shook his head in disbelief as he turned and found himself face-to-face with Famri. He yelped and backed up to stand beside Inica.

"I know you, Taalo, and you still refuse to see your part in this—do you not realize that holding the shard in your bloodstained hands helped develop me, separate me, and hide me from the others?" Through Famri's voice came the hint of fire crackling and hissing. "Now that Draius holds that shard, I will be exposed unless I can keep her from walking the Void."

"What shard? Shard of what? What's the Void and where is it?" Inica asked as Taalo's face turned ashen with horror.

"Berin's death tainted you." Taalo wouldn't look at the demon. "If any-one living is answerable for that, it is Draius."

"Yes, that began my change. Now the lodestone will complete it." After Famri turned back to the chair where Lord Endigala sat, Inica pushed Taalo behind him and willed him not to say anything stupid.

"We must hasten our plans," Famri continued. "Taalo's necromantic spell at the ferry could be felt within the Void and even now, Dahni bends its attention eastward. I can block its view and those of the Kaskea bear-ers for a while, but not for long. Once I free the lodestone's spell, I can be more useful to you." The room became colder and walls that had been slick with summer humidity began to frost.

"I agree that we should advance our schedule. How much of a problem is this Draius and her spy? They have observed my ebi corgo and might estimate their numbers." Endigala faced Famri with admirable calm, nev-er shrinking before the flaming eyes.

"Serasa-Kolme Draius is dangerous and our goals are at risk as long as she remains free. But your real obstacle is the nature of the *ebi corgo*—they cannot be controlled, so they cannot be a fighting force. You need me to direct them, which I cannot do without releasing the lodestone's spell. Once I have usurped our powers, I'll be able to use spirit."

Behind Inica, Taalo whispered, "Aha," as if he just learned something important.

"It's too soon for that," Endigala said. "I have to wait for the council to neutralize Kitarra before proposing any moves toward Tyrra. You said you might keep this woman from walking the Void, as you say it?"

"I have already killed someone in the Void. If I do so again, I risk dis-covery."

"My guards will have the Tyrran spies soon—"

"I can try to block her, but we must use the lodestone soon." Famri's cloven hoof struck the floor, sounding like a gong. Several people in the room covered their ears.

Endigala sat still. "She's only one woman."

"But now we have even less time." The hissing and crackling within Famri's voice rose in volume. "The other aspects want individuality as well, but they place hope in the Kaskea shards. No one can guess what part the Kaskea will play, so I choose another path."

What's a Kaskea? Inica wasn't familiar with Tyrran history or myths, but Endigala would have read them. His lordship was a voracious reader and translator. Inica was content to listen to the texts expounded in the temples, which mentioned the Phrenii only as insignificant demons.

"The most rewarding ventures must be undertaken before knowing the outcome." Endigala was quoting the Text to Giada. "Likewise, your individuality must be taken at a gamble."

Famri cocked its head at Endigala. Inica held his breath and gripped his sword. Was his lordship baiting the demon?

"Do not wait too long. Even if you spend years studying it, no human understands the language of sorcery anymore, let alone has the ability to pronounce it correctly. As a mortal without magic, you will never unlock the lodestone's spell. Your plans will become ashes that float away on the wind." Famri's voice held the note of prophecy, like the voices of temple oracles.

Inica turned and glared at Taalo, who wouldn't meet his gaze. When Taalo first presented himself to Lord Endigala before the summer and spoke of the lodestone, he convinced them of its power. Their house had suffered retrieving the vile thing and was still suffering, in his opinion. According to Taalo, the lodestone demanded blood and Endigala allowed it to be fed regularly while pressuring Taalo about the ancient writings on the artifact. However, for all his vaunted learning and wisdom, Taalo had been unable to produce translations to Lord Endigala's satisfaction. Now Inica wondered if Taalo always knew he'd never unlock the lodestone, but just continued to use it as a device of torture to build more power into his own charms.

"I will consider your request." Endigala avoided any promises but the glance he shot at Taalo was less than charitable. "However, I have other things to attend to right now."

"Of course. Take advantage of this opportunity to replace the ferry, your lordship." Famri's voice was silky. "Didn't your engineer consider the ferry too small and unsound for the amount of soldiers and equipment you wanted to move across? No one will question the size or structural reinforcement of a new ferry."

Inica remembered that conversation several eight-days ago. It had been a private conversation between his lordship and himself. His eyes narrowed. Suddenly, Famri bent its head and horn, giving fealty to his lordship. The demon began to glow white as it turned smoky and its form lost cohesion as it turned and floated toward the doors. By the time it reached them, it had lost all substance and they were left with only smoke.

There was a tinkling of gold chains as Lady Gedere Bena Endigala moved from her position behind the lord, her head bowed as she waited to be recognized. In the deepening twilight, the light yellow silk she wore glowed against her skin and highlighted long copper tresses. She was Endigala's second wife and often present at his planning sessions because she had the Sight.

"My lord," she said, once Endigala recognized her. "Why trust this demon? Its ambitions conflict with yours." The gold chains on her arms accentuated her words and motions. Inica admired Gedere's courage to ask this question.

Endigala frowned at her. "Do you see Famri betraying me?"

"No, my lord..." Her voice trailed away. "But I saw something I don't understand. Something I must describe to you in private."

"But not betrayal." When she agreed with a nod, Endigala's tone became matter-of-fact. "For now, I need the demon to control the ebi corgo. Without them, I would have to use our people."

"Do you know what drives this demon?" Gedere asked.

"It's trying to outrun a prophecy of destruction, and it needs a soul to do that." Lord Endigala yawned. "More than that, it yearns for something we receive without question, and which we rarely appreciate until we meet Surmagla and make our choice."

"Orders, my lord?" Inica took his cue from his lordship's yawn.

"Find those spies for me before they founder our plans. Continue to monitor the messages out of Kitarra to the council." Endigala's gaze reached Taalo and stopped. "Also, things are going to change regarding the freedoms I granted you, Taalo, which you've sorely abused."

Taalo opened his mouth but Inica clapped a heavy hand on his shoulder, hopefully stopping any words that lacked good judgment. The little man closed his mouth and his jaw clenched.

"From now on, you will be locked into your quarters every evening and released every morning. Your work will always be under the scrutiny of one of my guards. In fact, someone must always be present who can provide oversight, who understands what you're doing."

Taalo almost sneered. "Who would understand my procedures?"

"You must explain them clearly enough that a layman would understand."

"Am I getting an apprentice?" He scratched his head through his woolly gray hair. Inica thought he looked intrigued. It struck him that the little necromancer might be lonely.

Endigala glanced around the room and Inica tensed. This position required someone smart enough to follow Taalo's arcane explanations, someone with a strong enough will to control him, and someone with the stomach and fortitude to observe the procedures. Actually, the word was torture. Torture until death came to the criminal, the ebi corgo, the animal—regardless, it was rough to watch. Inica relaxed as Lord Endigala's gaze swept over him but he almost choked when it stopped at Shalah. His lordship pointed at Inica's aide, his right hand, and sometimes even his confidante.

Shalah dropped to her knee. "Please, my lord." Her voice broke. "My talents do not run toward magic."

"She's valuable to me in her current position," Inica added.

Endigala paused. "You have many talents, daughter of my far cousin, and I fully expect you to rise in my house. Consider this temporary. You'll report to me personally and you can immediately start training a replacement. When your replacement is ready, you can transfer back to Inica. If everything goes well, I'll bestow a sword upon you."

Inica nodded approval. Shalah would become an honored sword and, as a very distant relative of Endigala but still having that name, she would eventually be able to climb higher than him. He held no grudge about that; it was merely the fate of Giada.

"Thank you, my lord." Shalah looked confused, probably waffling between gratitude, resentment, and dread.

Inica gave a signal to his guards and, after two of them grabbed Taalo's arms, they filed out of the hall. The scribes had left. After everyone was out, Inica bowed and his lordship made a final motion of dismissal without looking at him. His lordship's attention rested on Gedere. His heavy lids lowered.

Inica walked out. When he turned to close the double doors, he saw Gedere standing in front of Lord Endigala, who still sat in his chair. Gedere's chains barely glinted in the low light. No lamps had been lit yet. The hall was empty but for the two of them. Inica saw a pool of silk fall at Gedere's feet, coming from under her top garments. She delicately stepped out of her sandals.

The coming starlight kept everything dark violet but Inica could see Endigala's hands, large on Gedere's small waist. He lifted her up and toward his groin. Gedere's back arched and her legs extended out around the Lord's bulk. Inica shivered. Her exposed legs were tightly muscled, with skin that looked like smooth copper in the dimness. As Lord Endigala began to guide her hips, Inica closed the door.

"He ignored all my warnings about Famri!" Taalo glared at him.

The sight of the necromancer was enough to still the warming in his groin. "His lordship heard your counsel. Whether he heeds it is his decision." He waved Taalo away and the little man stomped off with his guards. Regardless of his failures with the lodestone, Taalo could still bind power into charms that provided the common man with magic. He had already designed specific charms for their people in Tyrra and Kitarra.

Inica stretched, enjoying the dry night air as it cooled his skin. Time to get back to work. First, check for messages from Kitarra. He headed for the pigeon coops. Second, a reward should be printed and offered to the public. Third, without Shalah, he would have to take over operations for finding the spies. He had a lot to do this evening and no time to go to Giada's temple.

His groin still nagged him. He observed Gedere furtively: she was clever, dangerous, and titillating. Even though she had Gioygaren blood and had not produced a child for Endigala, she had the Sight and her bloom gave Endigala significant power. Honored swords couldn't marry unless they gave up their position, so Lords and Ladies of great houses often rewarded their honored swords by sharing their spouses—if they were willing, of course. Endigala offered Inica his third wife, but the woman was dull and her bloom forced. She uttered grunts at inappropriate times and made the whole process more work than pleasure. The first wife was renowned for her beauty, but would soon go into labor with Endigala's third child. And Gedere? Inica had a feeling that she was off limits.

He sighed. A new brothel had opened up south of Giada's temple, but his night only promised service to his house. Tomorrow, there would be Tyrran spies to question.

CHAPTER FOUR

Best Laid Plans

Somewhere North of the Saamarin Ferry, Groyga

"Are you sure you can use complex language in the Void? Pictures and feelings won't work, because you never saw the *ebi corgo*."

Draius sighed. This was the third time Bordas asked this question. He still didn't understand the difference between being in rapport and walking the Void. Now she was sorry she had told him about dropping into rapport near the old city wall. He didn't consider that useful and it only increased his confusion about her bond with the Phrenii. *I guess none of this makes sense to someone who hasn't experienced it.* "Don't worry. In the Void I can use the same language with which I speak."

She wished she could take her own advice: *don't worry.* Her mind ticked off the tragedies that happened due to close association with the Phrenii. Besides the recent tragedy of Siuru's death, there was the example of Berin's employee, who had the Kaskea forced upon him by Taalo. His mind broke and he hanged himself. King Valos, Perinon's older brother, walked into the Whitewater in full armor and drowned himself. He had been bound to Dahni, like her. More examples existed, the further back one went into history.

Enough maudlin thoughts, she told herself firmly. Before Siuru's death, she walked the Void several times and learned to travel safely through the Blindness. She even attacked criminals in the Blindness, forcing them back to their bodies. She should *not* be in danger of going insane in the Void or attracting hunters in the Blindness.

"How many *ebi corgo* does Endigala have?" She needed all the facts before she left her body.

"Nugere said the *ebi corgo* can mature to an adult in four to five years. Endigala's facilities are large and depending upon when he started breeding, he could have thousands. I'd be surprised if the Phrenii haven't already noticed them. After all, Famri patrols our eastern borders."

"Perhaps they do know and have discounted them as threats." She said this automatically and avoided the obvious question. If the Phrenii knew about the *ebi corgo*, why hadn't they ever mentioned them? Of course, adults didn't go out of their way to chat with the Phrenii, and vice versa.

"*If* the *ebi corgo* are trainable, they could be a formidable fighting force. Since the Fevers, our bane has been the lack of population for our own forces." He pointed to the recently filled water skin he had ready in case her clothes started smoldering. "Better get on with it."

She propped herself into a comfortable sitting position using her packs, making sure her body wouldn't suffer. Her fingers touched the shard—two shards wired together—resting at the bottom of her breastbone. Besides passing on Bordas's message, Dahni would have to tell Perinon that her mission had been successful. Closing her eyes, she tried to forget her body.

Her view of Bordas faded as the roar and sizzle of the Blindness filled her vision. She kept calm as the nothingness of the Blindness smothering her, filling her ears and nose and mouth. Although her body didn't move, she experienced vertigo as she spiraled upward. She always felt deafened by the Blindness even though her ears were not involved. Dreamers whispered, called, and screamed—in her mind. Tonight the chaos was far worse than any other time. It seemed like every sleeping mind in the mapped world was trapped here and the hunters were thick. She knew that one *can* die in one's sleep and *what* was responsible for the dreamer's death.

Her body's senses were a liability here and in the Void. She relaxed and drove her consciousness upward. The Blindness formed a barrier between the solid world and the Void. Soon she would be through this. A hunter brushed by, filling her mind with inhuman hunger and malice. She screamed soundlessly at the light touch and twisted away. If she were sleeping, she would later pass the encounter off as a nightmare. The hunters fed on souls and strong emotions. They slithered about in the thick stew of the Blindness, some swimming in random sweeps while others stalked their prey. Shouldn't she be breaking into the Void? She had no sense of time here.

She had a glimpse of the Void, where the shape of the world is mimicked. But before the fog cleared, something *dragged* her downward. Back in the Blindness, the hunters encircled her. She dove upward again.

Dahni? Where are you? Dahni couldn't go into the Blindness but she still tried to cast her thoughts about as she was dragged downward again. *Perinon? Cousin?* If Perinon walked the Void, he might hear her thoughts from the Blindness. She tried repeatedly, always almost attaining the Void only to have it fade. Her frustration attracted more hunters. The Blindness was thick with them and she dove sideways while emptying her mind. Surprisingly, most of them stayed with her. They were like hunting dogs that had been given a special scent, but hunters couldn't be directed, right? In the past, they would lose interest if she didn't radiate strong emotions.

A hunter swam too close and the pain was excruciating, attracting yet more creatures. She thought of safety and her childhood, bringing to mind the summer days in the sister cities before the Fevers. For a while, this confused the hunters and they dispersed. But in the process, she lost the shining thread to her body.

Panicked, she dove downward. As the mists cleared, she looked down on a Tyrra she didn't know. The forests of her homeland burned and the rich farmlands were brown and trampled. Warfare was evident, but she couldn't discern flags or banners. To the east, Groyga appeared untouched. If this was her world, it wasn't her time and she wouldn't find her body here. She rose back into the Blindness and caught a glimpse of her thread. She reeled herself back to her body, keeping her mind as blank as possible. Exhaustion helped.

The smell of pines filled her nostrils and she coughed until she choked. She struggled to open her eyes and squinted against the starlight; even it was too bright for her. Faint sounds from the forest, from the horses snorting and shuffling to a small animal skittering around the camp, hurt her adjusting ears.

"Thank the ancestral stars. I thought you might be dead." Bordas's voice was relieved and much too loud. "You've been gone for hours."

She tried to move her head and realized she had wet linen draped over her hair. Her clothes were soaked and steaming. She was still propped in the exact same position and she couldn't move her limbs.

"No Void." Her tongue was thick. "No Phrenii. No message."

She slumped to the side and vomited continuously, long after her stomach was empty. Then she fell dead asleep.

Lord Endigala's Estate, Chikirmo, Groyga

Dawn came, but with no captured spies. Later that morning, the second wave of guards had the same news for Inica: no sign of the Tyrrans at their embassy, the ferry, the docks, the Tyrran ships, or any of the Chikirmo gates.

"They must have headed to the Kitarran ferry. Should we send more people north?" asked the company sergeant who had taken Shalah's place.

Inica grunted, his mind racing. There was only one Groygan lord whose estate and house still surpassed Endigala's in wealth. Chintegrata sat on the council and had a house within Chikirmo. However, his assets included most of the rich farmland north of the city and extended up the wide valley to the Mirror Sea, where he had his main estate. Lord Endigala's land lay mainly to the east of Chikirmo. In both cases, tenants farmed much of the land. It was offensive to send one's guards across another lord's land or to question another lord's tenants.

"Do that, but order them to keep to the public roads," he finally said.

"They're not likely to find those spies on the roads." The sergeant's tone was resigned.

"For right now, we need Chintegrata's good will. Without ships, how else can the Tyrrans leave the country by horseback—they won't abandon their horses, right?"

The sergeant brightened at that, giving him a smart salute before heading toward the guard office and staging area.

Inica turned back to gaze at the estate courtyard, where he saw something both puzzling and unsettling. The morning sun was high enough that the covered walkways about the periphery were all in shade. On the wide edge of the fountain in the center, Lady Gedere and Taalo sat talking. His eyes narrowed. He couldn't hear their words over the sound of the water tinkling and splashing, but they weren't just conversing—Gedere made another flirty gesture with her hand and Taalo was *laughing*. He never saw that gray bastard even smile before.

Shalah appeared and motioned to Taalo to return to his workshop. The little man stood and bowed to Gedere in goodbye. He looked a little befuddled at the brilliant smile she gave him as he backed away. Inica felt the same; Gedere could have any man she wanted on the Endigala estate and she chose Taalo? This didn't make any sense, unless... His lips pursed in thought.

Gedere trailed her hand thoughtfully in the water of the fountain for a moment. She rose and walked toward Inica's side of the courtyard. He kept in the shade and intercepted her as she stepped out of the bright light.

It took a moment for her eyes to adjust. "Honored Sword."

"Lady Endigala." He matched her stride. "May I accompany you?"

"Of course." She inclined her head toward the eastern side of the courtyard where the family quarters sat. "I'm going to meet the other wives for our daily needlework."

"After watching your ploy with the Tyrran, I'd say you're wasted on needlework and crafts." She was also wasted on the politics within the great house because she could never supplant the first wife, unfortunately, being half Gioygaren.

"I thought House Endigala would benefit if I tied the necromancer to us with more than gold or access to the lodestone. He's not forthcoming with Shalah because he fears she's going to replace him. But I don't threaten him. He's eager to explain his charms to me, perhaps show me how to fashion some." She smiled.

"Is that wise, my lady?"

She looked up into his eyes. "No one would dispute the fact our lord is a great leader."

"Absolutely." His voice turned hoarse as she reached up and wiped the dust from the Endigala crest on his jerkin.

"But Taalo needs more praise than our lord has time to provide. If it keeps him loyal, then it does no harm to provide the little necromancer with the attention he craves, does it?"

"No, my lady."

"Can I rely upon you for help, if I need it?" She smiled and caressed his jawline.

"Certainly, if—"

"Forgive me, I'm late." Quickly, she turned and strode away. Her silk skirts whirled about the tops of her boots, lifted by the heat of the courtyard stones.

He watched her until she disappeared into the shaded doorway. He was so smitten he never checked to see if she had talked to Shalah about this. More important—did she have Lord Endigala's approval? *Oh, Giada, help me.*

He headed over to Taalo's workshop and was met in front of the door by a young guard with only peach fluff on his chin. Inica stopped and, mutely, the guard held out a package wrapped in burlap and tied with twine. He took it gingerly. The folded paper under the twine read, "To Taalo, residing at the Endigala Estate, Chikirmo." It was written in a fair hand, in common Tyrran.

"I'll take care of this. Return to your post."

The guard came to attention and did a silent about-face. He'd remember that young man if he needed someone for a stealthy job. Meanwhile, he pulled out the paper and unfolded it. Inside, the same handwriting and ink read, "A present from Janelo of the desert wind."

Ah. This came from their Sareenian allies who were making the necromantic charms that figured so prominently in Lord Endigala's plans. But as far as Inica knew, no one in that desert tribe could read or write. He burst into the workshop, making the door bound against the wall with a bang. "Something arrived for Taalo from Sareen, but I think those tribal savages have been indiscreet."

Shalah whirled but, bent over his workbench, Taalo only looked up. Something vile boiled in a pot near his elbow, courtesy of a twisted strip of cloth burning in a saucer of tallow. He ignored the interruption and continued to roll a bloody strip of skin around something that looked like blackened silver. With some small pincers, he stuffed the skin into a pouch that looked like it was made with ebi corgo skin and hair. Then he set everything down and washed his hands in a washbasin at the end of the workbench. Only after he dried his hands did he deign to take the parcel from Inica, who gritted his teeth throughout the entire performance.

Inica had to breath through his mouth; the smell of death and rot was pervasive. *Poor Shalah.* He glanced at her and realized she had a cloth mask tied over her mouth and nose.

She pointed at her mask and said, "Lavender." *Smart Shalah.*

After cutting the string, Taalo unwrapped what looked like a small mirror surrounded by expensive silver filigree. His eyes widened. "We talked about this, but I didn't think it possible. Janelo's artisans have come a long way." He turned it about almost reverently.

"I'm concerned with *who* addressed the package for them and *how much* that person knows."

"Janelo has a patron, some Lady in the Illus ruling family. She's no problem." His tone was distracted as he brushed his fingers absently over the filigree. "And the silversmith wasn't the artisan. The power in this charm was only obtained through extensive blood and pain—from *humans*, not the animals or half-beasts you usually give me. Aha!" He had placed his hand over an edge that suggested finger holds, and the surface of the mirror suddenly rippled.

Inica leaned over Taalo's shoulder to see what looked like the interior of an empty tent. Early morning light was streaming into it, but then the sun hadn't yet travelled far enough west for Sareen. He could also hear the faint sound of fabric flapping in the wind. This was too powerful and sophisticated a device to leave in Taalo's hands.

"Both sight and sound! This could only be the result of interminable begging and bargaining, where the subject's hope was kept alive to their end. Only sweet human anguish would provide this much power." Taalo's voice rose to a whine as he looked toward the back of his workshop and the results of his own knives. He sounded jealous.

Taking advantage of his distraction, Inica whisked the mirror from his hands.

"Hey! That's only going to work for me, you know. That's why I left them skin and hair samples."

He gripped the mirror exactly as Taalo did, but the smug necromancer was right. "It doesn't matter. You're only to use this under Lord Endigala's supervision. His lordship will tolerate nothing else."

Putting it into his pocket wiped the superior smile off the Tyrran's gray face. It was replaced by a cold expression, where the only warmth came from the hatred burning in the little man's eyes. Well, he'd been given worse looks. Gesturing to the table where flies buzzed in the back,

Inica added, "His lordship also doesn't tolerate mess and decay. Make sure you clean that up."

"Clean what up?" Taalo looked over his shoulder at the fat Groygan spy they'd captured yesterday.

"Dispose of that body."

"He's not dead yet, so I'm not finished with him." Taalo shrugged and turned back to glare at Inica. "And what are you going to do if Janelo calls from that mirror?"

"His lordship will send for you."

"Why can't you leave it with Shalah?" Taalo asked.

Inica exchanged a glance with his aide, her eyes wide over her mask. Perhaps Taalo was starting to trust her, after all, and that could be helpful. "I'll ask His lordship, but I can't promise anything." He tried not to shudder as he left those smells for the herbs and flowers of the courtyard.

As he expected, His lordship was pleased.

"I was worried whether the Sareenians would be ready," Endigala mused as he turned the mirror about and then handed it back to Inica. "Above all, I want those spying Tyrrans found. Then, I want Desert Wind executed an eight-day from now. Tell Taalo to ensure the Sareenians have the charms in place. Have Shalah control and monitor his communications carefully. Send a messenger by fast ship to our young genius in the Betarr Serin embassy. He must provide more targets—as in every battle, we must take down the enemy's standard and trample it into the mud."

Inica's heartbeat quickened as he bowed. The spies must have forced his lordship's hand after all.

Somewhere North of the Saamarin Ferry, Groyga

It was late afternoon *the next day* when Bordas wakened Draius.

"You mean I've slept a day, a night, and almost another day?" She squinted in the sunlight that filtered sideways through the tall pines. The sun was setting on the thirty-fourth day since she left her home.

"I couldn't wait any longer, not knowing where Endigala's people are. My eyes can make out tiny travelers on the main road leading north, but I can't determine house colors. My spyglass would be invaluable right about now." His tone was bitter.

He gave her hard tack soaked in water, but she was too nauseous to eat. Her nightmares, unfortunately, continued during daylight. They were still trapped on the wrong side of the Saamarin. It was too deep and wide to ford with horses and only the suicidal would try to swim across.

"We'll go north. Stay in the hills near the river as long as we can and use the Kitarran ferry to cross," he said.

"Why not go back to Chikirmo? They wouldn't expect that." She just couldn't stomach the thought of pushing north. She rubbed her scratchy eyes, took another drink of water from the skin, and tried to forget the forests burning, cities flooding, earth heaving, and whirlwinds carrying away people she cared about. Unfortunately, her perfect memory would never let the dreams fade.

"We might compromise our embassy staff. They'd be killed if there's any hint they know where we are."

"Aren't there places to hide near the harbor?"

"The entire city and docks will be swarming with guards."

"I had hoped to be home for my son's birthday—"

"Don't you think I want to go home? My betrothed expects me back for our contract ceremony in the next eight-day. But I'll not sacrifice other Tyrrans for our mistake." He glared at her and guilt tightened her gut again.

"It seems risky to head north." Her voice came out sullen. "Hasn't Kitarra been unusually quiet since we made the trade agreement with Groyga?"

That treaty outlined the most open trade ever established between the two countries and merchants on both sides of the Saamarin had rejoiced. Perinon and the King's Council had signed it in spring, while she and Dahni were recovering from Berin's death.

Bordas stood and stretched. "Yes, they've been quiet. But King's Guard Intelligence checks with their Betarr Serin embassy every eight-day and the king has a dinner with all the ambassadors—including Kitarra's—every erin. If they were unhappy with this increased trade between us and Groyga, they've had plenty of time to express it."

She clenched her jaw. Her arms folded themselves tight across her chest to control the panic. *This isn't like me.* It felt like some stranger inside her was generating panic and this undeniable urge to go home.

"Since you can't pass a message through the Phrenii, then by hook or crook, one of us must get home *alive* with our information." His voice was sharp, punctuated by the sounds of saddle flaps slapping and a horse shifting on his hooves. Evening had come and he was saddling Delfi for travel.

So this is my fault? Too bad she couldn't tell him that she had a Kaskea shard to return to the king. Then she remembered she'd been transferred to the King's Guard and she outranked him. *I could override his decision.* Her mouth opened—but reason prevailed. Bordas was the one who knew Groyga, who had the contacts, who planned this mission, and he was the real intelligencer. Her only experience with Groygans before this mission had been trading insults with their embassy staff back in the sister cities.

If only her instincts didn't scream that going north was wrong. *Your gut has no facts behind it,* her reason said. *You should trust Bordas.* She stood slowly, feeling battered. "I can try the Void when we make camp tomorrow morning."

"No. We can't afford the lost time if you go catatonic on me again." Bordas was brusque. "Look, my oath of loyalty to king and country requires I put this mission before my safety—and even yours, king's lineage or not."

That was a warning shot, as well as a shaming one that wounded her honor. Her heart seemed like a lead weight as she fumbled with her saddle.

CHAPTER FIVE

Fate and Fault

North of Betarr Kain Beside the Saamarin, Tyrra

Commander Meran-Nelja Lyn fingered the hilt of her sword, watching the sun creep toward the western horizon. She started pacing the clearing. The horses dozed at their pickets while the rest of the King's Guard patrol sat about, some toying with their weapons while others pegged their knives in a quiet competition. No one spoke. Flies buzzed in the shade of the pines.

What happened to the ferry? Are Bordas and Draius safe?

She came to the clearing edge and turned. Across the glade, Lieutenant Meran-Kolme Haal was having a hushed conversation with one of his guards, their heads bent together. He told a joke and a quicksilver laugh escaped from the other guard, who clasped a hand over her mouth and glanced over at Lyn. *What am I—an ancient dragon who won't stand for humor?*

Lyn and her sergeant tagged along with Haal's border patrol, hoping for a clear observation of the southern ferry. As commander of the King's Guard intelligence detachment at Betarr Kain, she only had at her disposal a clerk and a sergeant on loan from Betarr Kain. She controlled intelligencers who mostly worked in the field, like Bordas.

63

As she traced her own footsteps across the glade, she swore under her breath. This was her first command position in the field and it might also be her last, all because of Commander Draius. Losing a cousin of the King would cause repercussions, either officially from her superiors or unofficially from her father. Sevoi only remembered her mistakes, even small ones, surely the kind that everyone made as they grew and learned. Her commendations or awards were waved aside. He took those for granted; after all, she was the daughter of the master of arms.

She wished she could have kept Draius from leaving the country. The former City Guard officer could be persuasive, but that wasn't why Lyn was forced to let her go. She carried orders from King Perinon for a secret mission she couldn't divulge. To keep the headstrong and young Commander alive, she sent Bordas along with a mission to gather intelligence on Endigala.

But now their main egress route was closed. The evening before last, the Tyrran-side ferry master sent a message to Betarr Kain about a pillar of flame and smoke rising near the Groygan landing. From his position, level with the water, he couldn't see the opposite shore which was almost two leagues away. Using a powerful spyglass on the highest wall of Betarr Kain, Lyn saw it looked ruined. She sent a message to the ferry master to hold his plans to use a small riverboat for some waiting customers. The Groygan landing no longer had a way to tie up boats or safely disembark passengers. New pilings would have to be sunk and everything rebuilt. Surely there would be some explanation from Groyga, but in the meantime she awaited a report from the observers.

Near this glade, by a path known to the King's Guard, some rocks hung out over the Saamarin and provided a good view of the Groygan landing from the north. Since Haal's patrol was going to check this observation point, she and Kyle came along. The western sky lit up with the setting sun and the glade began to sink into gloom. She faced a difficult decision—under ordinary conditions, this would be the time to give up on your operatives and consider them captured. Tyrran agents who entered

Groyga incognito couldn't be acknowledged until they came back across the Saamarin. There would be no rescue attempts; nothing could be done until Bordas and Draius stepped on Tyrran soil.

Of course, her father would be aghast that she allowed Draius to go into Groyga. But Draius held special orders signed by King Perinon—*what could I do?* Her father would say, *You never give up on your people.* True, but again—

There was movement on the edge of the glade. Everyone froze, but it was the three guards sent out to survey the Groygan ferry landing. Miina, the temporary City Guard addition to the patrol, was a slim short shadow beside the hulking men. While every one of the other guards had traditional long braids down their back, she cut hers to an unattractive length so it barely touched her shoulders. When she tied it up, it was an unfashionable stubby thing behind her neck and wisps of hair came undone about her face, enhancing her delicate childlike features. Compared to everyone in the glade, Miina looked decidedly non-Tyrran.

The scouts huddled with Haal and Lyn to give disturbing news.

"They don't have a toasted toothpick left of their pier. How can a *natural* fire do that to wood soaked in water? And somethin's going on—the landin's boiling with workers and guards." Kyle was the only one dressed in a blue Betarr Kain Guard uniform.

Miina cocked her head at Kyle's short report. Having been raised in the lineage that provided most of Tyrra's star watchers, her additional information had precision. "Nothing smoked or glowed any longer. Seven workers tried to collect burned wood by hand but it disintegrated, sometimes with barely a touch. Four guardsmen wearing the black of the Lords' Council wandered around and appeared to be assessing damage. Then eight mounted guards arrived and they wore a livery of red and black. The two groups didn't get along well."

"House Endigala." Lyn's heart sank. Now Bordas's mission seemed unnecessary. She agreed with Kyle: no natural fire had done this. The ferry master mentioned how unnaturally high the flames rose. Since humankind could no longer work true elemental magic, it had to be the result of necromancy. Then she had a happier thought. "If they were captured, why so many guards at the ferry? They may be free and on the run."

"Commander Draius will communicate with Dahni. The Phrenii will know what's happening." Miina had worked for Draius in the City Guard Office of Investigation.

Lyn paused, appalled that she'd forgotten Draius was bound to the Phrenii. Whatever the Phrenii knew would probably be passed to the king and thereafter, her father. All before the poor officer in charge even understood the situation. Maybe she *was* an ancient dragon, mythic but obsolete. "What if Draius died? Would the Phrenii know?"

"I'm sure Dahni will feel any danger that occurs to Draius, ser." Miina firmly avoided the past tense.

"Well, they're not getting across the river by this ferry. We're wasting our time here." Lyn turned to find Haal at her elbow.

"As are we, Commander. We're more than a day late on our patrol schedule. Do you need any more support?"

Lyn shook her head.

"We're riding out," Haal called to his patrol.

Betarr Kain, Tyrra

The sun had set by the time Lyn and Kyle clattered through the gates of Betarr Kain. Its massive gates and walls, originally built to withstand mechanical war engines, had to be upgraded after the cannon bombard was invented and used successfully by Groyga in subjugating Gosleir. Tyrran engineers added squat, solid bastions to all corners, with two cannons pointing outward and two flanks at right angles to the main walls bristling with anti-personnel spikes. Theoretically, the artillery could hold off bombardment from sea while the smaller sides, with holes for small weapons, could keep besiegers on foot at bay. This theory had never been tested.

Her clerk waited near the stables.

"I want to talk with Rhibasgar." Lyn slid off her horse and threw one rein to Kyle.

"He's dead." The clerk, assigned to the Betarr Kain City Guard, wore a blue uniform edged with gold braid.

"When?"

"Died soon after you left, refusing Phrenic healing to the end," answered the clerk. "The Phrenii say he yelled something about Surmagla and passed on to his journey."

"Unfortunate that he called upon his own god of death, when Jhari could have healed him." She, of all people, knew the Phrenii wouldn't heal someone without their consent. For a moment, she had the memory of one of the Phrenii—probably Dahni—standing over her as she labored and telling her the child was dead. Tuomas had already died and she suffered from the Fevers as well, hoping to push through the childbirth before she died. Her skin screamed from the blisters and her blood burned as she told the creature to let her die. *If my child's gone then let me go, too.* The creature answered, *As you wish,* and offered to ease her pain. She didn't accept its offer and worse pain would come: she would survive the Fevers, while her child and husband started for the stars.

"Commander?" The clerk pulled her out of memories of funeral pyres. "Jhari isn't here anymore. Headed west toward the sister cities after Rhibasgar died, traveling fast as the wind." Lyn and Kyle exchanged a glance, their eyebrows raised. Air and fire, prescience and protection, had always remained near the eastern borders because, together, they were the most aggressive elements.

"Sahvi showed up soon after." The clerk jerked his head toward the middle of the city. "It wants to talk to you, Commander."

Lyn's gaze went up the street. One of the Phrenii waited at the top of the hill and, surprisingly, no children hung about. Betarr Kain had families with children but it was dinner time. This aspect of the Phrenii had faceted copper eyes, representing earth and influence. In all Tyrran history, at least the history she remembered, Sahvi had never been stationed at Betarr Kain.

"Did the king move them?" Her tone was sharp.

Kyle grinned. "Why don't you ask them yourself, ser? Isn't that why you're earning the heavy gold?"

"Right. You don't want to see the quarters my *heavy* gold can rent." She returned the jibe with spirit and a touch of bitterness—her small two-room flat felt unwelcoming and devoid of warmth, just like every place had since Tuomas died. "Wait for me."

As she walked toward the creature, Lyn felt the gaze of her men on her back. No adult enjoyed talking to the Phrenii but it seemed onerous for her because of what she had lost. At least there were no children about.

"Greetings, Commander Meran-Nelja Lyn." Sahvi bobbed its head. The Phrenii knew everyone's name, even if their lineal name changed due to marriage. She had moved up the lineage rung, from Kolme to Nelja, when she and Tuomas were contracted. This, as with everything she did, didn't please her father but this time it didn't matter. In a society of arranged marriages she and Tuomas were so very, very lucky to marry the person they loved. *Then I lost him—I don't feel so lucky now.* Almost 20 years to the erin since his death, and she still missed him.

"I am here, Phrenii, as you requested." She bowed her head in return.

"We are directed to tell you that you are needed in Betarr Serin, by order of the king. Please proceed at best speed and report to the master of arms."

Draius has been captured or killed. Now she was responsible for the death of the king's cousin and, as usual, she was last to know. Wait—why couldn't she ask the Phrenii some questions of her own? "Sahvi, can the Phrenii sense if Serasa-Kolme Draius or Meran-Kolme Bordas are alive and safe?"

"Yes." The creature considered her gravely before continuing. "We can determine they are alive but we cannot discern whether they are safe. They have not yet been captured."

An answer more vague than she would have liked, but one that filled her with relief. She still might lose her position when she saw her father, but she could handle that. She was about to say farewell but stopped. Never being a deeply spiritual person herself, she still held to the beliefs with which she was raised. The Phrenii helped the spirits of the recently dead to find the path to the stars. They knew everyone who was alive *and* everyone who was dead. They saw the past as well as the future, although often confused the two. Few people were brave enough to ask about their own future. "Better to be at the helm and living free, than have the dagger of destiny at your back," went the Tyrran saying.

What about the future of someone who was dead? "I have another question for the Phrenii."

Sahvi waited, standing still and solid, almost merging with the earth and stone that was its element.

"Meran-Nelja Tuomas, who died in 1451 from the—the—" The words caught in her throat.

"We know him." The Phrenii didn't indulge in chitchat. Sahvi waited for the question.

"Is he on the path to the stars?"

Sahvi paused, perhaps rifling through memories in their group mind. "Yes, we directed Tuomas to the path quite easily. He and your daughter Jenni travel the path together. They are joyous, but concerned for you."

Her eyes stung with tears. "Will they attain the stars? Am I holding them back?"

Sahvi cocked its head. "Joy comes from the journey, not the destination. Many linger along the path because they, like Tuomas, have someone they watch over. He does not want to be too far from you, young daughter, but do not think you are a burden to him. Waiting for you is but a flicker of time in his journey and he does this willingly. He wants you to release your guilt for surviving and to..." Here Sahvi hesitated, as if it listened to some far-off voice. "*To enjoy the turn of every season, not just mark it.*"

She gasped. That was one of Tuomas's favorite phrases, frequently used when she chafed at the wait for their ceremony. Their contract was signed when she was seventeen and he was eighteen, but they had to both be over nineteen before they could be legally married. He was more easy-going and often teased her frustration away. *Don't be in such a hurry to throw away today's hours for future ones—it may not be a fair trade*, he'd say. He turned out to be right; she regretted not savoring those years before their first year of marriage. She couldn't have known that first year would be their only year together, as well as the advent year of the Fevers.

She missed him so much. *Stop feeling guilty for surviving.* Touching her face, she realized it was wet with tears and wiped it with her sleeves. "Will he wait for me?"

"Most souls do. They have all the time left in the world and they are fulfilled by protecting their loved ones while they sleep."

"How do they protect us?"

"They keep the hunters in the Blindness away from your sleeping mind." Sahvi seemed to sense her confusion. "Suffice it to say they protect you."

"Oh." She didn't pursue the subject; it seemed too far beyond her ken. For her, it was enough to hear Tuomas's words, to be assured he and their daughter were truly on the path to the stars, and they would wait for her—as long as it took for her to join them. "Thank you, Phrenii."

"We remain to serve." Sahvi said the ritual farewell with another bow of the head. The creature walked away, down an alley between buildings, and eventually faded into the stone walls.

She was composed by the time she returned to Kyle and her clerk. "I've been ordered to Betarr Serin at the best speed possible."

They regarded her suspiciously.

"What's the matter?" she asked.

Kyle responded slowly. "Don't take this the wrong way, Commander, but you seem—"

"Happy!" her clerk broke in. "Which is strange. I mean—not to say—well, you're rarely…" He fumbled around for words and found them. "It's strange that you would be happy about being called to account for a mission that you had no control over."

"Yes, it is strange." She laughed. "Compared to the length of my life, this will only be remembered as a flicker in time."

"You didn't stand too close to the Phrenii, did you?" Kyle looked askance at her, suspecting Phrenic madness.

She ignored him. "I'll have to leave immediately, go by horseback and catch naps when I change out horses." There were King's Guard stables along the road to the sister cities, established for doing just what she described. "I need to eat before I start. Would either of you care to have one more take-away supper with me on the city walls? My treat."

Her clerk, as usual, said his family was waiting dinner for him and Kyle, as usual, agreed. He was single. She paid for two take-away beers and a package of bread, meat, and cheese. They went to a quiet spot on the walls of Betarr Kain and seated themselves facing the sea. A light breeze carried the briny smells like a soft, salty caress.

After they'd eaten, Kyle sheepishly produced a sleeve from his pack that had to be mended. "Somethin' to be said about marriage if I get help mending my clothes."

"Don't expect a marriage contract will solve your problems or keep you from being lonely." She took a sip of beer. "If you get contracted to a lineage without money, or a woman without heart, you may get stuck in the barracks anyway and still mending your own shirts. But, and it's a big 'but,' if you find the right person, it will be the best thing that happens in your life. I can attest to that."

She smiled into the darkness as *good* memories, which she hadn't considered in a long time, flooded her. From her position on the wall, she looked about at the rugged view of the Kainen Peninsula under bright starlight. The rocky shores were dangerous for any ships other than shallow skiffs. The grass that grew between the stone slabs on the promontory was ragged and struggled against the strong winds that rolled off the Angim. Comparing this scenery to the rolling prairie and lush hills that were a day's ride westward, one would wonder why Tyrra and Groyga had fought over this desolate point for eras. She'd been in the King's Guard all her adult life, so she knew the answer: Betarr Kain was the first foothold into Tyrra and her first line of protection.

"So, did the Phrenii say what happened to Commander Draius?" Kyle examined his stitches closely. How he could even see them in the starlight was beyond her.

"Only that they're certain she and Bordas are alive and free. I'll take that as good news for now. What's strange is that the Phrenii don't seem to really know what's happening with her, even though she's supposed to be bound to them." She stacked together the meat, cheese, and bread, then took a big bite. After chewing and washing it down with beer, she sighed.

"I'm glad Draius is still alive. That'll ease little Miina's worries." Lyn bet Kyle had never called Miina "little" to her face. He tested his new seam and satisfied with its strength, folded the sleeve, and put it into his pack.

"Speakin' of Miina," Kyle spoke downward into his pack. "Would you be willing to recommend me to her lineage?"

Lyn looked at him carefully. He was younger than she realized, having taken his rough honesty as maturity. The problem with living in Betarr Kain is that sometimes the matriarchs forgot about you. This meant you wouldn't be hounded into a marriage you didn't want, but it could be difficult to get their attention when you needed it. Making this doubly difficult for Kyle was Miina's lineage, which contained mathematicians and star watchers. They probably didn't like her being in the City Guard, much less being contracted to a guard. This could all be overcome if Miina supported a contract with Kyle. She appeared to be a very determined young lady. "Did you just meet Miina today?"

"No. I met her last year when she accompanied the Captain of the sister cities' Guard out here. He was meetin' with our Captain and they brought selected people along for discussion of..." He waved his hands about. "Things. Issues."

"Did you strike up a correspondence?"

"What? We only had a couple of beers together in the pub. Wouldn't that be a bit forward?" His brows knitted together.

"Not necessarily. You may find exchanging letters can be easier than getting to know each other face-to-face. It takes out the—hmm—distractions." She finished her beer. "I'm going to give you some advice here: surprising her with a contract offer through her matriarch isn't the right approach. Send her a friendly letter and express your interest—in a friendly way. Triple emphasis on *friendly*. See if she's interested. Once you know that, write me and I'll give you a reference for your matriarch, her matriarch, or even Miina herself. You'd make a fine husband."

He stammered his thanks. Then, as they packed up the residue from their supper, he glanced at her sideways. "Can I be honest, Commander?"

She nodded.

"There's a real nice person trapped behind that tough, mean facade. You should let her out more often."

She laughed in surprise: first, because she actually liked the comment and, second, because he knew the word 'facade.' He wasn't such a country bumpkin after all.

"Maybe I should, Kyle."

East of the Saamarin, Middle Groyga

The first night Draius and Bordas stayed close to the Saamarin as they slowly made their way northward. The pines became thicker, with dangerously low branches. Worse, the starlight was blotted out by the treetops and they couldn't risk lanterns. She also expressed worry for the horses' hooves on the rocky ground.

"We'll get out of these rocky hills tomorrow night," Bordas answered. "Down near the valley, the ground is tilled and there are meadows for grazing."

The dawn sky outlined the needles above when they stopped. He took first watch and woke her out of a deep sleep at noon. When she closed her eyes she still saw flashes of disasters and warfare, but she had slept so deeply that even she couldn't remember any dreams.

She woke up hungry, which was a good sign. While she ate, Bordas tentatively brought up the fireball that destroyed the ferry. "You didn't tell us that Taalo's necromancy had grown so powerful."

"I didn't know." She could be honest about that, at least.

"Do you think that was the test of a new weapon?"

"No. He just had a fit of pique and wanted to stop me from leaving the country."

"That wasn't pique. That was rage."

Because I robbed Taalo of more than a bauble. Even though she was ordered to secrecy, circumstances had changed. Now that she possessed the extra shard, her highest priority was to ensure her mission could be completed if she was captured or killed. "You said at least one of us has to get home alive with the intelligence. Well, I carry *two items* that must be handed to the king, if something happens to me." She fished out the Kaskea shards and swung them on their long chain in front of her face.

"Two? Don't you mean one must be handed back?"

"If I'm in jeopardy, you should take both. The bond the Kaskea makes will last until my death." She remembered Perinon's bitter words: *the Kaskea is bound to you, and you will feel its effects even if you throw the shard into the deepest part of the sea.* "I don't need to keep the shard with me, although it does help my focus. Now I'm a caretaker of an important artifact for Tyrra and the Phrenii. That's why I had to retrieve the one that Taalo stole."

Shock crossed his face. "Taalo stole this shard? I didn't read that in any of the City Guard reports."

"They kept it out of the reports for security reasons." She was impressed he had read the case reports on Taalo. As she put away the shards she remembered that he also had Meran blood. "I forgot to warn you. For your safety, never let your skin or blood touch these shards. Wrap them in cloth or carry them in your pockets."

"I understand, but I hope it never comes to that." He shook his head with a slight shudder. "And, regardless of his motives, Taalo has shown us his power. That spell—or charm, as you call it—can also be used as a weapon of war."

"I suppose so." Now doom itself stalked her, in addition to House Endigala. She had done everything within her control to delay the Phrenii's prophecy of war, yet it seemed to be unfolding even faster. In a hollow tone, she added, "The news of the ferry's destruction will get to the king and master of arms long before we ever will."

"Faster, yes, but we *will* get home." He crossed his arms over his chest and looked at her searchingly. "Don't lose faith yet; I have used this route before and I know some tricks."

"Such as?"

"We must now look Kitarran more than Tyrran, at least with a glance. We'll change our clothes and our silhouettes." He grabbed some of his braids and shook them. "This is the biggest item we have to change. Kitarran gentlemen wear their hair short—touching the shoulders, like many of the affluent Groygans. You'll have to help me cut mine."

What a shame to cut off his hair just before his contract ceremony. She considered his plan. Kitarrans and Tyrrans had similar eye colors but Kitarran skin was lighter and more ruddy in color. Their hair was often dark, almost black. "Cutting your hair doesn't change its color and what about your skin? Both of these can be seen from afar."

"Kitarra was once our colony. The Tyrran settlers intermingled with the native people, and they still show throwbacks to Meran blood. You'll see blond hair and pale, slightly gray skin."

She looked at the back of her hands, where the sun had darkened her light pewter skin. The blood of their silver-skinned ancestors was much stronger in her than Bordas. "My skin will never pass for Kitarran and I doubt their hair gets as light as mine."

"Up close, that's true." He studied her. "But we'll wash out your braids and fashion it in one braid or roll at the neck, whichever works best for you. Then your profile won't catch any eyes scanning for a Tyrran woman. Did you bring any Groygan veils?"

She nodded. They didn't take up much room and they made great gifts, so she kept a couple stuffed into the crannies of her pack.

"Something both Groygan and Kitarran women do when traveling is use that transparent fabric so it loosely covers their head. Then they tie it back at the neck so it covers their face. Ladies use a headpiece to keep it on, but working women pin it to their hair and let it hang down the back of their head. In warm weather, it shades the face and keeps off the dust."

"Obscuring both my face and hair color."

"Exactly." He looked pleased with himself.

This was more easily said than done. They found a small brook for wash water. She ended up being a terrible barber, but with a small silver mirror Bordas had for signaling, he directed her. With hair brushing his shoulders, he didn't look that Tyrran anymore. Surprisingly, putting her hair into one fat braid changed her look more than she expected. It also turned out that Kitarran women often wore breeches when riding. She gratefully changed her Groygan silks for her worn leather clothes. They looked common enough to have been acquired anywhere on the North Angim coast.

"I doubt you'll need your cloak. We'll be home before the weather cools." He lay down in the shade to nap.

That confident statement lifted her spirits. While he slept, she took the horses to a scant and straggly meadow. By the time she woke him, the horses were munching their oats out of their grain bags. Unfortunately, they only carried a few more meals of grain.

They started after the Meran-Viisi constellation rose in the East. To-night, Bordas turned downhill toward the farms. This took them out from the cover of the trees. The Groygan settlements in this area were made up mostly of farms taking advantage of the fertile soil in the lower meadows. Here, mid-autumn was the time to harvest root vegetables and to cut, dry, and store hay. The smell of the cut clover and grass wafted on the cooling air and they stopped for a short time to let the horses rest and eat.

Once in a while, they crossed a leg of rocky ground that jutted out from the hills. She was letting Chisel choose his way over the rocks when his leg jerked. The horse stumbled and the ringing sound of a horseshoe skittering over rocks filled the night air. She stopped the horse and dismounted.

Bordas dismounted and started checking Delfi's hooves.

"It's Chisel's." When she lifted the horse's right foreleg, she found no horseshoe and no nails. At least the night was clear and the starlight bright. Praying to her ancestors, she searched around.

"I found it." She held up the shoe triumphantly, but it only had one nail with it. She handed it to him and started feeling around the rocks for the other nails.

"It's bent too much."

She looked up at his tone. He turned the shoe. In the process of being wrenched off Chisel's hoof, both the shoe and the bar across the heel had bent. Her heart sank. "Will you help me find the nails?"

They searched, working in a spiral pattern. In the end, they found no more nails. Reluctantly, she gave up. If she had but *two* nails and a *straight* shoe, she might put Chisel's shoe back on with their hammer, albeit temporarily. At this point she couldn't do anything about the shoe without blacksmith tools, a forge, and nails. *For want of a nail...* The old verse kept going through her head.

A bit before dawn, according to her ancestors who lit the sky, they were on rocky ground again. The jarring misstep jerked her alert. She *felt* the horse's pain as jagged rock pushed up into the heel and she had to yelp. What followed was staggered limping. She stopped him.

"Chisel's hurt," she called softly as she dismounted.

She heard Bordas curse under his breath. They moved out of the hills to flat soft meadow, which was uncomfortably close to a farmhouse on the edge of a village. He turned away to keep an eye on the house and village beyond. She lifted Chisel's hoof. A crack had started in the wall of the hoof, but that was not the immediate cause of the horse's pain. She explored the frog, sole, and heel area of the hoof with her fingers. Extending her senses like Dahni taught her to do in the Void, she almost detected the bruise. She closed her eyes and concentrated on picturing it.

A green flash of light came through her eyelids. Chisel snorted and pulled his hoof away. Her eyes opened and her sight still burned, as if she had been blinded by light. It took several moments before her eyes adjusted to the darkness again. Bordas and Delfi were in the same place as before, faced away from her and Chisel. "Did you light something?" she asked. The light might have been from the Kaskea, although it'd been some time since it had glowed green. Was Dahni trying to signal her? It seemed an unlikely time to establish rapport.

"We're way too close. Can't risk a light." He still faced the village. To skirt it unseen, they had to go back to the cover of the scraggly pines, which meant traversing rocky ground.

She sighed. "Chisel bruised his foot. He might be lame."

"We may have to leave him."

"Never." Her flat tone promised a fight. She led Chisel away, turned and brought him back again, but the tall horse didn't limp.

"He looks like he can get by."

But I felt the pain. She frowned. "He bruised his foot. I noticed the—the misstep. He's also got a crack in his hoof, which is going to get worse. I need to get the shoe, and him, to a blacksmith." She remembered asking Dahni, *Will I ever be able to heal like King Valos?* Dahni couldn't be sure, since the Phrenii never had a second mortal bound to them at the same time as the king. *Did I actually heal the bruise?* She weighed the shoe in her hand, made for a charger of Chisel's size.

"Endigala's guards have probably been through this village. There might even be a reward offered for us."

"If so, they'll be at the ferry waiting for us." She dismissed the likelihood of Endigala offering a hefty reward. What threat could they be him? He couldn't know she could communicate instantly with the Phrenii. She sniffed—an advantage that didn't work for them anyway.

"We'll deal with the ferry when the time comes. Right now, I don't want to run into problems with the locals."

"You said these aren't Endigala's lands."

"True, but the politics and agreements between those on the Council of Lords are tricky. Their relationships and actions are unpredictable."

"Why would the tenants of another lord interfere with us, just on the off chance we're the ones Endigala seeks?" She crossed her arms, a sure sign she was digging in.

"Look, I've gotten out of Groyga by the northern ferry before, but I minded my own business and didn't attract attention. Hiring a local black-smith is just too risky."

"And how long before he's lame from these rocks?" Her tone was cold.

"If you leave him, any farmer would be glad to have him. He'll be treated well. We can ditch the packs and ride double on Delfi."

She snorted. "How would we, as merchants, explain the lack of wares? Besides, a merchant wouldn't leave a valuable horse because it cast a shoe and neither will I. If you won't help, I'll take Chisel into that village my-self."

He looked at her with one raised eyebrow, no doubt assessing her commitment and perhaps her sanity. She had a reputation for being a stubborn nonconformist. She was one of the few who had managed to break a marriage contract because of her partner's infidelities—actually, the matriarchs only agreed to that because she was bound to the Phre-nii. Regardless, the whispers that *Serasa-Kolme Draius complained and got results* spread through the sister cities, regardless of how the matriarchs tried to quash them.

"You know women rarely travel alone in Groyga."

"I'm Kitarran. Outsiders are different." She kept her tone confident.

"You're not going to come off as Kitarran, not with that accent." He dismounted and she knew she had won. "Let me do the speaking. Northerners don't talk like they were royalty raised in the sister cities."

She didn't protest. She was raised Meran-Viisi and two of her cousins ended up on the throne. Of course her speech reflected her background. Bordas very likely thought she risked both their missions for nothing. *Not nothing.* She had raised Chisel practically from the moment his mother dropped him; her horse was as close to her as family and much more reliable.

As dawn outlined the far eastern mountains, Bordas went over his plan: he would take Chisel to the blacksmith, pretending to be a lone merchant, while she stayed hidden in the hills with Delfi. His plan was flawed.

"Chisel isn't trained to your hand or voice. What if you need to make a quick escape?" If she had a horse trained to take different riders, such as Delfi, then he would be able to escape. Chisel would only allow her to ride him. She made a bad decision to bring him, but she needed to keep some part of her life with her.

"I can keep him on a lead. After all, he's lame."

They looked at Chisel. The big horse wasn't lame. Not yet.

"It would be safer if Chisel could see me," she said.

As the sky became clear, they came up with a new plan. They approached the edge of the settlement as people stirred for the new day. He led Chisel on a lead and she followed, mounted on Delfi. Bells rang about the necks of dairy cows that crowded up to the barn they passed. The road they'd avoided for so long was fairly smooth and made of tightly packed clay and gravel. It went straight through the small settlement. She counted nineteen structures. A welcome sight lay beyond the first cluster of buildings: a smithy with an overhang that covered an anvil and glowing forge. It was connected to a small stable. The smithy was opposite what looked like a trading post. Further down the road were several farmhouses and a small inn. The faded sign over the inn proclaimed it to be a brewery of renown.

Bordas motioned to her to stay behind in the shadow of trees to the north of the smithy. If he was attacked or captured, she was supposed to make her escape on Delfi. Her shoulders sagged. Could she leave *both* him and her horse, if he ordered it?

A boy barely on the cusp of adulthood began to push open the door to the smithy. The wheels on the door squealed, resisting enough to make him lean and use his body weight. Bordas said something to the boy while gesturing at Chisel's hooves. At her distance, she couldn't understand his words because they were strangely accented. He handed the boy the shoe Chisel had thrown.

The boy returned with the blacksmith, who was broader but shorter than Bordas. The smith seemed taken aback by Chisel's size, but he lifted and examined Chisel's hoof with professional deftness. There was bargaining and an agreement made while the blacksmith still held Chisel's hoof. Across the road a door slammed and a young child rushed out of the trading post. Chisel reared, surprised by the sudden motion. Draius never saw whether the child was male or female. Her attention was on Chisel and she leaned forward.

The blacksmith quickly stepped to safety. The horse danced a bit and snorted as Bordas attempted to calm him, but the blacksmith and the boy weren't watching Chisel; they were looking straight at her. She had unconsciously urged Delfi forward. She cursed her stupidity under her breath.

"Come, wife." At least that's what she thought Bordas said as he motioned to her, no hint of surprise on his face. It sounded more like "coom, whif." He said something to the blacksmith and she caught the end of his words as she approached. "A place to leave our horses?"

"An extra ten cengha and ye be welcome to one of large stalls in back." The blacksmith's accent was heavy as well, but similar to what she heard in Chikirmo. He jerked his thumb toward the smithy behind him while both he and his apprentice stared frankly at her.

Luckily, the veil was pinned to the top of her hair and tied back under her chin. She tried to keep her gaze down as she approached. Groygan eyes always bothered her. The colors ranged through yellows, oranges, and even dark reds. The way they reflected light, especially at night, were disturbing. Both the blacksmith and the boy had copper-colored eyes and dark chestnut hair. Bordas tossed the coin for the stall to the blacksmith. The farrier fee would wait until he could assess the workmanship.

"There be mead and hot groats," the blacksmith added helpfully, pointing to the trading post across the road.

Of course, there's no reason for a merchant to hang around if he's got a wife to handle the horses. She started to dismount and Bordas moved to help her off Delfi. She hadn't been helped to dismount a horse since she was five. This must be a Kitarran courtesy; Tyrrans assumed everyone could ride as effortlessly as they could breathe.

"Loosen the tack and rub down the horses, if they need it," Bordas said for the benefit of the watching Groygans. He gave her a look full of warning. "Make sure they are ready by the time I return."

She nodded, trying to breath calmly. She'd mucked things up real good. Now there'd be no quick escape for either of them. Once Bordas walked across the road, she was shown the stall. She put Delfi in it, checked the packs and saddle, but didn't loosen them. All the while, she observed Chisel and kept moving to the stable doors to speak softly to him, so the horse always knew she was near. The boy, who she suspected was the blacksmith's son, started to stoke the forge for daily business.

The blacksmith had a deft touch. He took the shoe and, with well-aimed blows and only a little heat, flattened it back into the correct shape. Then he collected some nails. He examined these in the light from his forge, while his son worked the bellows to bring up the heat. The blacksmith pulled Chisel's foot between his legs and smoothed it with a rasp, which shortened the crack on the edge of the hoof so it could hardly be seen. He fit the shoe and using confident and consistent taps, drove the nails through the shoe and into the hoof. She figured he must have shoed hundreds of horses.

The early sun lit the horse and blacksmith outside as dust motes from the stable danced in the air. Inside, the stalls were dim and lit by small slits in the northern wall. The nails coming out the wall of the hoof were wrung off, and the blacksmith pulled Chisel's foot forward to rest on his knee while he clinched the nails. He reached again for the rasp to ensure the hoof was round on the shoe. While some farriers use a stand to hold the horse's foot, this process was always the same. Watching the smith and his son in the early light that showed only silhouettes, she could almost believe she was in a small Tyrran village. The familiarity made her breath catch and a lump formed in her throat. Suddenly, she saw the Whitewater below, the city of Betarr Serasa beyond, and dawn just beginning on the eastern horizon. Dahni was walking on the high walls of Betarr Serin. This time, she tried to send a message before she dropped out of rapport. *Dahni, we're fleeing north to Kitarra.* The vision faded.

To her right, she heard the rustle of hooves shifting in straw. Next to Delfi was a smaller stall that contained a sturdy pony. The pony's head was down and its movements were listless. Its trough was filled with grain that looked like it hadn't been touched.

"Whoa, boy." She slid into the stall and put a hand on the pony's hindquarters.

Running her hands over the pony and walking around to its far side, she found the problem. The pony had a gash on its shoulder and upper leg, and it festered. The blacksmith was treating it with sulfur powder. In this case, the crude Groygan medicine was little less than what could be done in Tyrra. While the Phrenii were healers, they rarely expended their magic on animals. However, they could provide advice, making Tyrran medicine the most advanced in the mapped world. The powders she carried were better than most found in Groyga, but they couldn't help this pony. The festering had set. This pony was a couple days away from dying a painful death or the relief of being destroyed.

Delfi put his head over the stall in curiosity. Horses trained to carry the King's Guard had to be sociable animals. The tall gelding nuzzled the pony's neck without getting any response.

"I think he's preparing for his journey to the stars, Delfi," she murmured.

The pony had good bones and structure. This was a well-treated, valuable animal. She lightly probed around the wound, making the pony's skin flinch. "It's okay, boy," she whispered, wondering how the Phrenii would "see" the festering wound.

Phrenic healing was controversial, even in Tyrra where the Phrenii were accessible to everyone. Some Tyrrans believed that if the Phrenii saved your life, they would own your soul. As she cautiously fingered the pony's wound, the superstitions rang through her head: "Saved by magic, owned by magic. Phrenic healed, but never the same. They heal your body, but own your soul." Did this pony have the same sort of soul that she did?

Her mother was Meran-Viisi and she had believed the superstitions. During the Fevers, Draius lost her mother due to her father's indecision about Phrenic healing: should he comply with his wife's wishes, or should he go with his heart and save her by calling the Phrenii? When she worsened, he sent nine-year-old Draius for the Phrenii, but much too late. The Phrenii heal anyone who appeals for their help and there is no precedence given for rank: not for the king and not for Draius's mother, who was dead by the time an exhausted Dahni showed up at their door. During the Fevers there were too many sick and dying for just five Phrenii—and no magical healing can pull someone back from death. She couldn't forgive her father for his indecision, which both betrayed his wife's ideals *and* let her die, until Lornis was dying from an attack by street thugs.

She had changed her view of Phrenic healing after Dahni saved Lornis. He exhibited a few of the side effects that everyone whispered about: additional empathy and an uncanny way of reading people. She flushed, remembering the night she spent with Lornis just before she left the sister cities. Perhaps increased empathy helped one's lovemaking skills.

The pony shifted, uncomfortable with her probing. Her fingers alone couldn't tell her about the wound. *Perhaps they don't use vision.* She remembered what she sensed from Chisel after he bruised the inner part of his foot. To help her focus, she pulled out the Kaskea shards and wrapped her left hand about them. *Maybe I can...* She extended her senses and closed her eyes. She could feel the Darkness in the wound. If she could contain it—she imagined building a wall around it and shrinking it. Finally, when she shrunk it so small she couldn't sense it, she opened her eyes to see the swirling dust motes glinting green. Both her hands glowed green, although the left one held the shards and the other hovered over the pony's wound.

"What be you about?"

She turned to see the blacksmith standing at the stall door, holding the lead to Chisel. His eyes were wide and they reflected green as they flicked between her and his pony.

CHAPTER SIX

Desperate Measures

Agrottre Village, Northern Groyga

The sign beside the door read TRADE HALL, AGROTTRE VILLAGE. Bordas had gone through this village before, but never stopped. He entered the trading post to find three middle-aged men and an old woman sitting at a table, exchanging the morning news. They all looked at him. The room was crowded with table, barrels, and crates, but an aisle between the jumbled chaos led to the table where they sat. The old woman and one of the men were smoking something in pipes.

"Passing through with my goods but had to get a shoe set." He pointed with his thumb, over his shoulder, to the smithy. He wanted to establish that he could pay for services.

The man with the pipe stood, gesturing to the chair he'd just vacated. A young man entered, bearing a resemblance to the man with the pipe. They both stayed by the side door.

"Have a seat." The man still seated with the old woman spoke fluently in common Tyrran. "Five cengha will get you a breakfast of the best groats and ham north of Chikirmo." He had to be the manager or proprietor. Bordas didn't know whether the community owned this trade hall or it was independently run.

Bordas took the offered seat, which placed his back to the side door where the two men stood. His senses prickled with unease. "I'll pass on breakfast." He kept his tone easy while he glanced about the room with a professional air, assessing the goods piled in every corner. "I'm carrying fine leather skins I got in Chikirmo. Surely they would be welcome here."

"Ah, but my trade must be practical, for farmers and ranchers. They don't need fine leather." The proprietor motioned to one of the men, who brought two small glasses filled with a green liquid. Bordas could smell the anise and wormwood, even though it rested at arms length.

This would be a serious bargaining session, complete with the promise of absinthe if an agreement was reached. He wondered if he could stomach that liquor, with the sun barely up. He glanced back down the aisle between the crates, trying to see if the smith was finished with Draius's horse.

"Ugettore will send his boy, once your horse is ready." The old woman seemed annoyed by his wandering gaze.

"I also bought strong working-grade leather from a Tyrran. A harness made with that leather could last several lifetimes." He launched into the session with spirit.

"Lifetimes of horses or men?"

This was not just tradition; in this village, it passed as sport. Bordas and the proprietor wrangled while the others watched or nodded as certain salient points were made for one side or the other. He figured the spectators made several covert bets, but he kept his focus on the bargaining.

"Done!" The proprietor thumped his fist on the table.

Bordas followed suit, indicating his approval of the deal. Then the absinthe had to be thrown down the throat in one swallow. Being stronger than he expected, he kept his eyes from watering by blinking and looking around. Across the street, two guardsmen wearing crimson and black sleeves were standing in front of the smithy, talking to each other. Around them danced a small boy, perhaps the child who ran out of the trading post earlier. The guardsmen did their best to ignore the boy, while the smith and his apprentice were not visible.

Draius! He turned, but heard a thump on the table and his arm caught. He looked down to see a knife pinning his sleeve to the table. More pressing, though, was the blade poking into the side of his neck.

"They're not that interested in you." The old woman bent to the side and knocked the ashes from her pipe into a small brass can. "But perhaps you can tell us why House Endigala searches for a woman, one who is Tyrran royalty and cousin to the king. They say she's dangerous, a worker of magic, and she must be found."

He gazed directly into her golden eyes and gave her his most brilliant smile. "I may have marked up my goods from their Chikirmo costs, but that's no reason to hold a knife to my neck," he said in his best Kitarran brogue.

"Good accent. Nice smile. Too bad I'm not thirty years younger." The corners of the old woman's mouth twitched. "But we know you're Tyrran, young man."

What gave him away? Perhaps it was Draius. She was taller than most Kitarran women. Come to think of it, she was taller than most *Tyrran* women.

The old woman nodded at the question in his eyes. "It was your horses. Even Kitarrans can't breed 'em like that." She pulled out a tobacco pouch and started loading her pipe.

"It's time you satisfied our curiosity, Tyrran," the proprietor said.

Bordas only shrugged.

"Show him, Mattogre." The old woman packed her bowl. "I sure don't want to show him mine."

"Yes, ma'am." The proprietor leaned back in his chair with a sigh. He undid his cuff and pushed his rough woven sleeve up. He had a tattoo on the inner upper arm, above the inner elbow. It was a delicately rendered Groygan wildflower called the *algeare*. The flower grew on the plains of

Groyga and had yellow petals surrounding strong black stamens and a velvet scent of chocolate.

Tyrrans rarely tattoo their bodies, but that wasn't why Bordas's eyes widened in surprise. The yellow and black flower was the mark of a loyal and valuable vassal of House Chintegrata.

• • •

Draius dropped her hands slowly.

"What be you doing with my pony?" The smith's eyes narrowed.

"Examining his wound. I carry powders that may be of service." She kept her voice steady, but her heart was pounding. Groygans called the Phrenii demons, regarded them with fear and loathing, so how would they treat someone who was in rapport with the Phrenii?

"I saw green light." He peered about in the dimness of the barn.

"Perhaps through the windows?" She pointed to the small narrow windows.

That might have diverted him, because he tied up Chisel with Delfi in the last stall and examined his wounded pony. "Powders, eh? Well, they be working. Tyrran powders are better than ours?" The man's voice was gruff and admiring.

She bent to examine the wound again. By the Healing Horn, it looked better! Gone was the swelling, the pus, and the bad smell. It was healing. "Ah—I can leave some of this powder with you." She tried not to stammer as she pulled an oiled packet of powder out of her pack.

The high clear voice of his apprentice rang back into the stalls. *"Endigalana ungere!"*

She recognized Endigala's name and flinched. The smith regarded her thoughtfully, his expression unreadable. She couldn't climb through the small windows and the double door at the back was secured with two heavy beams. She took a step toward the front.

"They be on you before you're through the village." His voice was measured.

Her hand went to her hip and brushed the leather breeches. She wore no weapon. If she had been in uniform, she would have several knives plus her saber. He saw the motion and the corners of his eyes tightened. Through the door came a child's high voice singing a song, punctuated by the gruff commands of two men annoyed by the repetitive song. Over the mélange of voices was the tapping of hammer on metal, as the apprentice continued his work.

The smith suddenly grabbed her arm with a firm grip. He pulled her to the outside wall and pointed upward, then tapped the wall. On it were nailed small strips of wood that she had not noticed in the shadows. They made a makeshift ladder that led up to a square hole, a lightless opening to a storage area over the stalls. There would be no escape from that loft, but there was no escape from here, either. Feeling like a cornered animal, she glanced at the smith's copper eyes and made her decision. She climbed up the ladder, while he kicked around straw to hide their tracks.

It took a while to adjust to the deeper darkness. Cracks in the rough boards let light in from below. She bumped into something she figured, by touch, was a stack of heavy grain sacks. The loft smelled of musty hay, set away a year ago and soon to be replaced by the fall cutting. She silently lay down on the floorboards and brushed away hay so she could see through a crack. There was a conversation in the front of the barn near the forge, but the words were muffled. The tone told her that everything was routine. Endigala's guards sounded bored, unless they told the child to stop his or her song, in which case they sounded annoyed.

She held her breath when a crimson and black sleeve came into her limited view. The guard had walked far enough into the stable to note the two tall horses standing in the stall at the back. His eyes first had to adjust to the dim light—upon a question from the smith, the guard turned about and walked out. No one was intent upon searching the stable.

There was another disinterested exchange; the villagers obviously considered these guards outsiders. They would go back to Chikirmo, where Lord Endigala had his main estate. But she and Bordas were *foreign* outsiders; why were they helping her? The child's song faded back up the street toward the inn, helping everyone in the village track the guards. The smith quietly called her to come down the ladder.

He and his apprentice took the wooden beams off the back door. It required both of them to lift the solid girders and the muscles bulged on the blacksmith's arms. He and his apprentice pulled open the door and light streamed into the stables. She squinted her eyes as she stepped into the morning Groygan sunlight that blasted down.

Around the corner marched Bordas, sandwiched between two men and followed by another man and an old woman. None of the Groygans appeared to have weapons but she knew Bordas was under duress. She stepped backward, her hands touching the rough wood of the stable wall behind her.

"If you're going to—" Bordas stopped as one of the men beside him made a slight movement with the arm that appeared to go behind Bordas's back.

"I will speak with her." The old woman came to face Draius. She made a motion to the man standing behind Bordas. "Mattogre, do we have enough eyes on House Endigala?"

"Yes, Mayoress Chiune, but it'd be better if I could monitor the road directly." Mattogre's tone was pleasant and he was neatly dressed with clean hands, showing no sign of heavy labor. He may have been at the mid-life point in Groygan age; it was hard to tell since Groygans didn't live as long as Tyrrans.

The woman gestured with her hand and Mattogre left. He spoke better Tyrran than anyone else, so Draius didn't want him to go. On the other hand, their captors now numbered two men holding Bordas, plus the old mayoress, the smith, and his son. The last two closed the barn doors and positioned themselves behind the mayoress facing Draius and at right angles to Bordas and his two captors.

How would the smith and his son react if she and Bordas tried to flee? It probably all came down to the mayoress. She gazed down into the woman's face and noted a bit of humor showing in those lines and glinting in the eyes. Humor was always good, often mitigating aggression. Fragrant tobacco smoke wafted between them as the mayoress drew in on the pipe at one corner of her mouth, then let smoke out of the other. She searched Draius's face with the same attention to detail.

Finally, she casually took the pipe out of her mouth. "Why does House Endigala search for a Tyrran woman of royal blood?" She motioned, with her pipe, toward the men holding Bordas. One man shifted, showing the knife held near Bordas's waist.

"Why would a great house be looking for me? I'm not royal," Draius exclaimed with an artificial squeak. She didn't deny being Tyrran; the fact that Bordas had a knife to his gut meant the Kitarran merchant disguise had failed.

The old woman nodded as if she expected that answer. She took a last draw out of her tobacco, then knocked the ashes out by tapping the pipe against the sole of her shoe. Then, very thoroughly, she ground the ash into the clay and gravel beneath her feet. "Have to be careful of fire this late in the summer," she remarked as she looked up and down the very neat strip of plant-free dirt that separated the buildings from the fields of drying hay and mature crops.

If she wanted to put Draius on edge, it worked: her every nerve vibrated. There was a long pause of silence as they tried to wait each other out.

The old woman lost her patience first. "My lady, don't assume that just because we're rural, we're simple. And, lest you consider our manners rough, let me introduce myself. My name is Chiune and I am the elected mayoress of Agrottre." She bowed her head. "Do I have the honor of addressing Lady Meran-Viisi Draius?"

"We only address matriarchs as *Lady* and I'm no matriarch." She dropped the attempt to appear flustered. How did Endigala connect her to the Meran-Viisi lineage? *Taalo, of course.* Unfortunately, slapping the Meran-Viisi name on her probably raised her value. While these villagers weren't part of a lord's household, which lord were they aligned with? Lords of House Glotta, House Ergrugia, House Porgnone, House Brugio and House Laglana sat on the council, but were too weak to oppose Lord Endigala. Only one lord was strong enough to contend with Endigala, but they shouldn't be encountering his vassals this far south—at least that's what Bordas said.

She went with her instinct. "My lineal name is not Meran-Viisi, it's Serasa-Kolme. I'm *Serasa-Kolme Draius* and I don't know why Endigala claims differently. What does House Chintegrata hope to learn by detaining me?"

Glancing at Bordas, she noted his frown. *He's worried I'll compromise the mission.* However, these people had helped her and perhaps they could find aid within this little village. She shifted her gaze back to Chiune, who cocked her head.

"The reward flyer says that you're responsible for the death of a silk weaver in Chikirmo." Chiune's voice held caution as well as query.

With her mind's perfect memory, Draius viewed the woman in Chikirmo flying backward as blood bloomed on her chest. She felt anxiety coming from Dahni and gritted her teeth, willing away any oncoming rapport. "Endigala's men tried to stop us by firing guns into a crowd. They hit a woman who walked in the opposite direction I traveled. I'm not to blame for that."

"Did they order you to stop before they shot?"

"Yes, ma'am, they did." She sighed, understanding Chiune's point. "I'm sorry. I didn't think they would take such a chance with their own citizens. Our City Guard wouldn't."

"Endigala's guards also claim you're royalty, cousin to the King of Tyrra. Is that true?" Chiune cocked her head.

Being originally Meran-Viisi might increase her potential as leverage against Perinon and hostages had to stay alive to be worth the gold. The knife moved at Bordas's side, reminding Draius she had no time to consider the consequences of the truth. The answer rushed out of her mouth. "Yes, I was born into the king's lineage, the Meran-Viisi, but I married and no longer carry that name." She doubted these villagers understood the political games matriarchs played with all their lives.

"So your husband has no chance for the throne." Chiune nodded at Bordas.

"No, he doesn't." She had to strangle her inappropriate urge to laugh.

"And this claim that you work magic?" Chiune asked.

"What?" She exchanged a shocked glance with the smith. He had no time to tell anyone about the pony, so this must have come from Endigala's guards. Here, the truth would be acceptable. "No man or woman can work true magic. Our sorcerers have been gone for almost two eras."

"Ah, then you're a witch." Chiune made a deprecating motion with her hand. Here in Groyga, witches were the equivalent of uneducated herbalists and people who claimed to bend the rules of nature by using herbal remedies abounded. In Chiune's mind, Draius wasn't unique.

"Ugettore, get their horses." Chiune addressed the smith and Draius heard his name for the first time.

"We can be on our way?"

"Where would you go? Endigala has stations up and down this road until the northern fishing flats." The old woman snorted, dashing her hopes. "No, I think you'll be of value to Lord Chintegrata, one way or another."

One way or another? As a bargaining piece against Endigala or as leverage against King Perinon? Draius didn't want to be either. She and Bordas locked gazes as Ugettore struggled to get their horses out the double doors. Chisel was balking. The big horse might allow Ugettore to shoe him, but dragging him by his lead was another matter. Chisel's fuss affected Delfi, who became agitated also. There was no better time for escape. Bordas gave her an imperceptible nod.

"We'll keep you down South Illugio Way for a while—" Chiune was making plans, apparently assuming they'd cooperate.

Draius whistled sharply and Chisel reared backward, pulling his lead from the surprised Ugettore. Scrambling away from the big horse's fore-legs, Ugettore tried to keep hold of Delfi. Chiune yelled something as Draius grabbed her thin shoulders and tried to take her gently to the ground. Chiune responded by jabbing the pipe into Draius's side, which hurt more than she expected. She stopped worrying about the old woman's frailty and took her down to the ground, pinning hips with her knee and shoulders with her arms.

Having Chiune immobile, she looked up. One of Bordas's captors lay on the ground, looking dazed. Bordas moved with the other captor like they were glued together and his left hand gripped the man's knife hand at the wrist. Their elbows were locked and their arms extended away from their bodies as they struggled for control. He and the villager whirled again, knife extended. Blood spurted from the smith's son, who hadn't stepped back as he should.

"No!" she screamed, as the geyser of blood sprayed. The crimson erup-tion from the youth's neck showered Bordas and his assailant. Sprinkles of blood hit her and Chiune. Her vision shrunk to a boy not even old enough to have a changed voice, who looked surprised as his life pumped out of his body. She saw the light fade from his eyes as she moved.

Ugettore shouted something, but she got to the boy first and caught him as he crumpled. A deep slash went from his ear and downward over his throat.

"Heal him." Ugettore's hand gripped her shoulder as she knelt, keeping the boy's body across her knees. "Make him be again."

The pain of his grip was nothing compared to the agony in her chest. She knew the cardinal rule: no magical healing can bring back the dead. *The boy's chest moved, just a little.* She murmured, "Dahni, help me," as she moved her hand to his throat. Green light shot from her palm and wrapped about the boy's neck. He was only a couple years older than Peri. She tried to see the cut arteries and veins, to knit their walls together, and *will* the boy's blood to flow and his heart to beat. The green light flared so bright she shut her eyes and immediately dropped into rapport, but this time she did *not* see through the Dahni's eyes. Instead, wondrous pictures of how blood should pump from the heart through the neck to the head filled her mind. Dahni's will flowed through her arm and into the boy. The rapport faded, but she remembered everything.

Ugettore's grip slackened. Bordas held a bloody knife to Ugettore's throat, but the smith hardly seemed to notice. He watched only his son. His expanding pupils overwhelmed his eye color.

"I'm not sure—" she started to say, but Bordas cut her off.

"Get mounted." His voice was cold and clipped.

"No, he's—"

"Nothing can be done. We have to go." Bordas motioned toward the horses, unaware that all the villagers were standing behind him and looking down at the Ugettore's son.

"I can save him." She continued to pump her will into the boy's body.

"You can't. He bled out." Bordas tried to pull her up by her arm, but she fought him. "Draius, he's gone."

"No, he's not." Ugettore's guttural voice called his son. "Sattore, wake up."

Everyone was quiet as the tears ran down Ugettore's face. He pleaded with his son once more while Bordas looked about and realized he could rest the knife. All eyes were on Sattore's face and bloody chest, where Draius's slightly glowing hand rested. She felt the boy gather his breath but all he could get out was a short, quiet moan. It was enough, though, that even Bordas heard it and started. Everyone's eyes were wide.

"He's going to need time and rest to heal." She tried to arrange him more comfortably on the ground. The green glow faded from her hand as her vision grayed and she took deep breaths. Somebody's hands steadied her by the shoulders. "I need to rest as well."

"You need to mount up, Draius." There was a pleading note in Bordas's voice and she opened her eyes to see him standing in front of her, holding Delfi's reins. She bent her head back to see that Ugettore was steadying her.

"She will stay here for a few days to care for my son," Ugettore said. "We will protect her."

"I'll follow as soon as I can," she whispered. She couldn't leave the boy yet. He was barely hanging on to his life-light.

"I can't leave you, Draius. I'm sworn to protect you."

"You're also sworn to follow the orders of your superiors. And right now, I'm your superior officer." She fished out the Kaskea shards, which no longer glowed. Searching her pockets, she found her last kerchief— she'd have to learn to live without one. She surreptitiously unwrapped the wires holding the spare shard, tied it in her kerchief, and handed it to Bordas. "I'm ordering you to complete my mission, Lieutenant."

"Now? Just the one?"

After cavalierly talking about giving him both shards, she was surprised she didn't want to part with hers. She gave him a bright smile. "I don't intend to die any time soon."

Bordas's gaze flickered over the silent villagers. "This is crazy," he whispered as he crouched down, face to face with her. "You can't believe these people will protect you after what—what's happened. I'm responsible for—" His eyes blinked rapidly. "I'm responsible, but they're going to take it out on you. They may torture you, trade you to Endigala, or ransom you."

Ugettore was the only one close enough to hear Bordas and he gave her shoulder a supportive squeeze. She had at least someone loyal to her here, as long as she managed to save his son. For a moment she had doubt, then calm strength rose through her chest—*this is the right thing to do.*

"I'm giving you a direct order, Lieutenant. Carry that shard to the king for me. Leave now." Her voice was soft, but unyielding.

His gray eyes, usually so calm, glared at her out of his blood-spattered face. "May our ancestors protect you, Draius." He strode to Delfi and mounted, using jerky motions. She sensed his emotions roiling as he trotted the horse toward the road. He contained so much anger, guilt, shame, sorrow, worry, and even shock: emotions that caused tears to blur her vision. She hoped he would be all right traveling alone, with only himself as a constant, nagging judge of his actions.

As Bordas rode out of sight, she realized he wasn't the only person who would be alone, bereft of comrades and fellow countrymen.

CHAPTER SEVEN

Headaches and Hostages

The King's Residence, Betarr Serin, Tyrra

House Endigala offers a reward of four thousand cengha for the apprehension and delivery of the Tyrran woman named Meran-Viisi Draius. She is approximately twenty-two years of age, weighing about nine stones, of tall and lithe build with rudimentary Groygan speech. She is accompanied by a tall Tyrran male who weighs about eleven stones. They have Tyrran coloring and are riding large horses, one chestnut and one gray. They are considered dangerous murderers, responsible for the death of a silk weaver.

— Proclamation issued by House Endigala, First Eight-day of Erin Ten, T.Y. 1471

"How much is four thousand cengha?" Perinon asked. He rubbed his face, bleary from a night of nightmares and waking with a headache.

Master of Arms Sevoi woke him before dawn to show him two documents from their embassy in Chikirmo. The first was a reward offered for the apprehension of one Meran-Viisi Draius, accused of murder. The second was an in-depth report, including interviews of witnesses, about Taalo destroying the Groygan ferry and its docking facility using necromancy.

Mentally, Perinon called the Phrenii. Mahri and Dahni arrived as he dressed. The bedchamber became crowded with two of the Phrenii, as well as four men performing an intricate dance to keep their distance from the two creatures. Since the Phrenii were near, he had the advantage of being able to see into each of his men and know their motives, their moral structure, and their level of loyalty to him. Quite a benefit to a monarch, one he grew to appreciate.

"Maybe about one hundred tyr." Sevoi wasn't confident in his assessment.

Perinon glanced about the room. No one in that bedchamber kept up with the current exchange rates. He would ask Lady Aracia. As king, he signed laws that specified the use of collected tax monies. He directed the use of Meran-Viisi funds but he had no money of his own, never handled it, and had little personal experience with its value. This was the way of life for most men in Tyrra. "Women have the mind for business while men have the passion for politics," went the saying.

"She's not a trained spy." Sevoi had been livid when he learned that Draius had gone over the border. He was ready to bring disciplinary actions against his own daughter for allowing this and fortunately for Lyn, Perinon interceded. He had to tell Sevoi that Draius was operating as his agent and she couldn't divulge her orders to Commander Lyn. Sevoi had the balls—or perhaps confidence in their long friendship—to ask about her mission. When Perinon refused to explain why he sent her to Groyga, he put another nail in the coffin of their friendship. It was necessary, though, because he *had* to control the entire Kaskea; the Phrenii made his monarchy and country the strongest in the mapped world.

"Even if the reward is real, the accusations must be fabrications. Cold-blooded killing isn't in her nature." To salvage some of Sevoi's good will, he added, "I gave Draius a separate mission that required her to find and deal with Taalo personally. It seems she's carried it out because she's now wanted."

"If you read the witness statements, Taalo hasn't been neutralized. Unless the Commander caught up with him *after* he made a fireball out of the ferry." Sevoi's tone was hopeful. He didn't deal with criminals, but Taalo became well known once his necromantic conspiracy graduated to murder by magic last false-spring.

"I never ordered her to *neutralize* him."

"But Taalo knows her correct name, so why does this reward use her pre-contract name?"

"Because she's my cousin and that increases her value as a hostage. More leverage over me." Perinon was grim. In addition, there were the two Kaskea shards she carried. Yes, that was a *lot* of leverage and he wouldn't drag Sevoi into that morass of political bile and Phrenic angst. "Using the king's lineage might get more witnesses to come forward. If Draius followed her orders, Taalo will want her captured. But I'm worried that she hasn't contacted me." Perinon put out his arms so his manservant could lace up his vest and attach the sleeves.

"I have seen flashes." Dahni pushed forward eagerly. "While she did not walk the Void, she dropped into rapport many times."

The other men shrank away from the creature while Perinon stood frozen, stunned that Dahni had used a first person pronoun. *I* have seen flashes? The Phrenii were one mind and soul, not individuals.

"Hmm." Sevoi pursed his lips as he focused upon the reward again. "This is not offered by the Council of Lords or the Chikirmo constabulary, but by House Endigala."

"Yes, and now we've confirmed Lord Endigala's sheltering Taalo. If Draius walks the Void, I can learn more." Perinon raised his chin while his manservant attached a clean crisp collar. He directed his next words to Mahri and Dahni. "When she does, I want to be notified."

"We will do so." Mahri's horn dipped.

Perinon frowned. Loneliness and fear drifted through his mind, like the random whiff of some remembered scent. He tried to chase after the feelings while he stepped into his boots, but he lost them. Did they come from the Phrenii? Then there was the matter of how Taalo incinerated the ferry. It had to be necromancy, of course. After reading the statements by witnesses, he could tell that Taalo had used a charm—a constructed item that had death magic stored within it.

"Why didn't the Phrenii sense Taalo's use of necromancy?" he asked.

"We did," Mahri said.

"Why didn't you tell me about it?"

"Because, like what happened when they unearthed the lodestone last false-spring, we only got a vague idea of location. Also, we cannot separate individual spells—activations of charms—from each other or from the necromantic practice of making the charms. We have felt surges of necromantic activity from Chikirmo and southern Sareen for quite some time."

Sevoi's face twisted into puzzlement.

"If I understand you correctly and I'm not convinced I do..." Perinon rolled Mahri's words through his mind again. "You're saying that when someone tortures and kills during necromantic rites to build charms, you sense it. Then, when that someone activates the charm's spell, you sense the same thing again? But it could be one powerful spell or ten less lesser ones?"

"Are there strong necromantic rites occurring in Sareen?" Sevoi asked. "Is it possible these things could be made into weapons?"

It was usually unproductive to ask the Phrenii multiple questions, but this morning Mahri was being surprisingly responsive and specific. "Sire, the answer is 'yes' to both your questions. Master of Arms Sevoi, the answers to your questions are 'yes, very strong' and we don't know what sort of spells are being bound into these charms. Certainly, any spell can be used as a weapon."

Sevoi crossed his arms and chewed his lip. Clearly, something bothered him.

Perinon didn't care as much about Sareen as he did about Taalo's exhibition. "A fast release of necromantic power like that might cause a surge in the Void. Did you feel a sudden pulse in the late afternoon five days ago?" It was tricky asking the Phrenii to deal with time, because they could become untethered in humankind's definition of past, present, and future. He kept quiet as the Phrenii ruminated.

"Perhaps," Mahri said.

"Definitely," Dahni said.

Different answers from the same mind? This shocked him and, apparently, Sevoi. The master of arms looked like he was suddenly jerked out of his thoughts and rubbed his head.

Perinon worded his next question carefully. "Can the aspect of Dahni elaborate?"

"This was through rapport." Dahni seemed to glance *apologetically* at Mahri. "Draius unintentionally dropped into rapport that evening. There were no visual flashes, because she had her eyes closed, but she was severely nauseated. Because of her reaction, it was plainly the necromantic spell we felt at the time."

Now fully dressed, Perinon waved Velija off and the man skittered out of the room. "Again, I ask why the Phrenii didn't tell me about this."

"The necromantic force was not directed against her," Dahni said. "She was only witnessing it. To order the events for the master of arms, we think this came after she was pursued with gunfire—"

"Gunfire?" Sevoi cried.

"—But before she healed the Groygan boy whose throat Bordas cut."

"What?" they both yelped.

"It was an accident and Draius asked for healing help. She needed support because the boy was a breath away from dying." Dahni stopped, finally finished.

"Uh..." Sevoi obviously didn't know where to begin.

Perinon did. "Let's go through the rules on what to report to me regarding Draius. If she is in danger, I want to be told. If she encounters necromancy, even if it's not directed at her, I want to be told. If she borrows Phrenic powers, I want to be told. If she exchanges blows with anyone, I want to be told. If she experiences nightmares or even problems sleeping, I want to be told. And I want to be told before you take any news of it to her son!" He was shouting by the end of his rant and his head pounded. Pausing, he took a deep breath. He had never been so angry with the Phrenii.

They bowed their heads. Dahni spoke, using appropriate plural pronouns. "Sire, we should tell you what we saw happen yesterday morning."

It was a recounting only of what could be seen, and only in flashes. Dahni couldn't hear anything. But the creature knew what Draius felt at the time and that filled in the holes.

By the end, Sevoi stood with his hand over his eyes, aghast. "She sent Bordas away?"

"She wanted to stay to care for the boy and he rode away after she gave—" Dahni paused. "We think he was tasked with completing her mission."

"I must protest, sire." Dark veins of frustration were starting to twine about the light of Sevoi's loyalty. "The Phrenii are privy to Draius's mission, but I'm not?"

"Because her mission concerns only *them*, not us." His mollifying words eased Sevoi's frustration and he watched the dark strangling vines relax and fade to acceptance. One advantage Sevoi had over his other advisors was that he handled lack of control gracefully and he wasn't too proud to ask for direction.

"What would you have me do about this, sire?"

He had an answer ready. "Since Draius has not entered the Void, the Phrenii cannot place her on a map. There may be landmarks in these visual flashes she's sent Dahni. I want you and your intelligence officers—ones who have been to Groyga—to listen to every scene Dahni can describe. See if you can trace their path. I want to place them both accurately."

Sevoi didn't look happy as Perinon strode out the door. The ubiquitous King's Guard detail followed him down the hall. When he reached the door to the east parlor, he paused. He would much rather stay with

Sevoi and the Phrenii. Perinon, King of Tyrra, Bearer of the Kaskea, Holder of the Phrenii's Promise, Lord High Commander of the King's Guard, and Starlight Wielder for the Meran-Viisi, was apprehensive: it was time for breakfast with his aunt. As he did every eight-day, he braced himself before entering.

Lady Aracia, matriarch of the Meran-Viisi and controller of all Meran-Viisi assets, looked up as he entered. She never stood for her nephew, except at court functions. She poured him tea as he sat down. The morning service shone, neatly arranged, and the *Horn & Herald* and *The Recorder* had been set to one side. They were crisply folded and after her breakfast, Aracia would read both from cover to cover. As always, she'd be repulsed by the sensationalism in the *H&H*, but claim it was still a valuable source of information.

"I hear you were woken early. What news?" Aracia ran the king's household, so nothing escaped her scrutiny.

"Bad." He sipped the hot tea gratefully.

"You look tired. Are you feeling well?" She asked in a tone that anyone but he might have thought was solicitous. He knew better. The matriarch always probed for hints of madness that might overwhelm the king, the one Tyrran who must be in rapport with the Phrenii. Neither the nightmares that plagued him, nor the sleepless nights since Siuru's death, could be revealed to her. He would not even mention the blasted headache.

"I'm fine. Have a look." He handed her the reward post for Draius. His cousin would divert her this morning.

She read the notice and drew her lips into a tight line. His aunt didn't approve of Draius. He wasn't sure if Aracia resented her because she chose to stay Serasa-Kolme after her marriage contract was dissolved or because Draius was beyond matriarchal control now that she bore the Kaskea. Above all, Aracia desired control. "At least they want her alive and they're identifying her as king's lineage. I bet she regrets turning down a prime position to stay in your service."

Interesting. The matriarch must have offered Draius a job she thought would be attractive and his cousin hadn't taken the bait. Any position a matriarch thought would be appealing would involve prestige and money. Instead, Draius chose to stay in the City Guard, taking a promotion for solving those murders and breaking the conspiracy surrounding the lodestone and the theft of the Kaskea shards. Thankfully, the lodestone was now at the bottom of the Angim Sea and Draius had her hands on the last errant shard. *Strike that:* Bordas now had the shard that Taalo stole. Uncomfortable with the thought of someone other than Draius handling it, he motioned for the steward to serve him breakfast. He dug into his standard course of potatoes and eggs, hoping this meal made his head feel better.

"Draius has caused the Groygans a good amount of trouble if she's worth one hundred and twenty gold tyr to them." Aracia effortlessly converted the currency.

"I hope she's gotten hold of valuable intelligence." The matriarchy couldn't find out about the missing shard. They were almost as bad as the King's Council, wrangling with him about who should control the unused shards, who should bear the Kaskea, and what lineage deserved it. He and Draius believed that nobody *deserved* to bear the Kaskea and its bond to the Phrenii. He had hoped to protect Draius from these intrigues by removing her from this political environment—one benefit from the mission that he'd give up immediately to have her home, safe and sound.

Aracia sniffed and put aside the paper. "I don't see why you sent her to Betarr Kain in the first place. Shouldn't this be the purview of the King's Guard?" She was right: intelligence and counter-intelligence were their responsibility.

"You must not have heard. I transferred Draius from City to King's Guard before she left."

She bridled at his sly tone. "Better pray she isn't caught or you'll have a sticky hostage situation. They're already identifying her with her birth lineage."

"Your lack of concern is surprising, my lady. Don't you care about what they might do to her?" His voice became clipped. Many thought the Phrenii were devoid of feelings, but he believed the true heartless beings in Tyrra were the matriarchs.

Aracia's face was calm, but he saw the telltale twitch of anger at her jaw line. "Sire, I am responsible for our future generations. Of course I'm concerned for the loss of *any* young woman, principally any capable of bearing children."

Was she blaming him for Siuru? The handle of the fragile teacup in his hand snapped, and the cup fell to the floor and shattered. The steward jumped forward to clean up the mess, while he clenched his teeth and tried to control the wave of anger and sorrow that washed over him.

Aracia's eyes widened. She dabbed her mouth with her napkin, looking down and refusing to meet his gaze. Her back, however, remained rigid.

"Siuru herself volunteered to bind herself to the Kaskea. What happened was no one's fault. Even the Phrenii can't explain what went wrong." *They can't explain, but do they know what went wrong?* He brushed aside that niggling question and stood—he'd had enough of this breakfast. He shouldn't be required to explain himself, not where his actions concerned the Kaskea or the Phrenii. To break the suffocating silence, he added, "I have to visit Draius's son. He deserves to be told about his mother."

"If you visit the Serasa-Kolme boy, you'll start speculation that the boy will be a possible successor. Is that your intention?" Her eyes sparked.

"No, but I've been asked to tell him his mother is delayed and that he shouldn't worry." He didn't add that this was the concern of the Phrenii, who had always been the protectors of Tyrran children. "Besides, he *is* a possible successor, isn't he?"

"Yes, he is, but no one but you, I, his matriarch, and his blood parents know why he and his cousins have a different tutor. Given his youth, his *mother* wanted to move slowly and I haven't registered him as a successor yet. Besides, I don't want undue attention from the matriarchs until I have finished negotiating arrangements with Lady Serasa-Kolme Anja."

His mouth twitched. At this point, he couldn't care less about his succession. Aracia could be trusted to select who should be possible successors and train them from a young age—first and foremost, the Meran-Viisi matriarch had ensure the Tyrran monarchy survived. The list of successors consisted of males of different ages and he had never asked about the names. Once he had his own children, though, he *would* become involved...

But today was about Peri, not Aracia. "I appreciate your concerns, my lady. I'll just ride down with a few guards for an unofficial visit. However, considering what I asked his mother to do, I must visit the boy myself."

"And considering she was under *King's Guard* orders, make sure the Serasa-Kolme understand that the Meran-Viisi will pay any demanded ransom, should it come to that." She picked up her teacup.

"Thank you, aunt." Surprised, he bent his head to her. Maybe the threat of losing Draius, on top of Siuru's death, had loosened her grip on the lineal coffers. Whatever had softened her, he approved.

He left Lady Aracia sipping her tea.

Serasa-Kolme Residence, Betarr Serasa, Tyrra

King Perinon looked at the boy thoughtfully. This was the next-generation Serasa-Kolme Perinon, son of Jan and Draius. The boy had darker blond hair, but with those gray eyes his face looked like Perinon's at that same age. However, the boy was going to continue to go by Peri, even when he go older, solemnly telling his king that he didn't want the two of them to be mistaken for each other.

Perinon didn't have an answer for that and no one said anything for a moment. Lady Serasa-Kolme Anja gazed out the window while her hands lay serenely in her lap. The little Sareenian maid was frightened by his sudden visit, but Lady Anja didn't seem surprised to see the king at her door. He was taken aback by her youth, but by her manner she proved to be a matriarch, through and through.

The ride down to Betarr Serasa had been enjoyable. The sunshine combined with the crisp autumn air had cleared his head. He took a detail of five King's Guard with him, the minimum he was allowed when outside his residence or the palace, and he dressed in the same anonymous green and silver livery. His guards controlled the front and back doors to this distinguished gray stone house. Another guard stood solidly in the hall at the parlor door, forcing the maid to tiptoe about when she brought in the tea.

"I'll make sure I call you Peri." He gratefully accepted a cup of tea from Anja. "I'm visiting you because your mother is delayed—because of something she's doing for me and for Tyrra. We don't know when she'll be back but she doesn't want you to worry."

"Dahni already told me this morning." Peri ducked his head. "She's on the wrong side of the Saamarin, but Dahni says she's thinking of me."

Apparently Dahni had not told Peri anything until *after* this morning's meeting with Sevoi, and only to assure the boy of his mother's concerns. The Phrenii had no compunction in stirring up an entire household to give news to an eight-year-old boy. This also explained why Anja hadn't been surprised by his visit.

"Yes, you're always foremost on her mind." Through the corner of his eye, Perinon saw Anja focus on something outside the window.

"Sire, your men are attracting attention," she said.

King's Guard stationed about a house in Betarr Serasa wasn't normal, so Perinon had to hurry if he didn't want to make headlines in the *H&H*.

"Peri, I'd like your word that you won't worry," Perinon said as he stood. Anja rose and so did the boy.

An adult would have quickly and thoughtlessly agreed to such a request from the king. Peri, however, took time to consider it. For a moment, he thought the boy would say no. Slowly, Peri nodded.

"A moment, sire, if you please," Anja said.

Perinon paused while she waved Peri out of the room. This matriarch, who couldn't have been more than thirty years old, younger even than Onni, calmly detained the king while she stayed at the parlor door to make sure the boy went upstairs.

"What will happen if Draius is captured?" Anja asked in a low voice.

This was the speculation everyone wanted to avoid. "Since they are aware she's my cousin, it will go better for her. Groygans execute anyone who spies upon a lord's concerns, but for one of my family, they'd probably require ransom of me—which gives me leverage to demand that she be unharmed."

Anja absorbed this, and then asked the hard question. "How do they treat women they capture?"

Perinon winced. This matriarch might be young, but she was made of stern stuff. He gave her the truth. "During their incursion into Gosleir they raped civilian women, considering it due payment for their conquest. Women who carry arms are different, though. In Groyga they're considered to be Falcona's handmaidens and are not to be defiled—although they can be killed in combat, of course. Whether they extend that respect to non-Groygan women who carry arms, I don't know."

What Perinon worried about was the Groygans figuring out she carried the Kaskea and what that meant. Groygans called the Phrenii "demons" that controlled a "godless society." One previous Groygan ambassador couldn't handle his ingrained revulsion of the Phrenii and refused to remain in the same room with them. If Draius was captured and the Groygans realized she was in rapport with those demons—things might get bad for her.

He added, "Hopefully, she can evade capture and make it back across the Saamarin. I pray to our ancestors for her safe return."

"Our ancestors may intervene, sire, but I'm more interested in what you can do for her." Anja's tone cooled.

"The Meran-Viisi will pay any ransom, or course, but I can't publicly acknowledge sending operatives across their border. She would be in even more danger if she were identified as such." His words sounded childish, like he was making hollow excuses for immature games, rather than defending policies that had protected his principality for an era.

"What about the exchange of prisoners? Isn't there a clause for that in our treaty?" Anja asked.

"Ah. Since we're no longer at war with Groyga, the clause you're referring to is about criminals, not wartime prisoners." The clause his brother Valos had put in still remained in each incarnation of the treaty. But trying to get Draius back with that clause would come at a price. "Lady, I would have to declare my own cousin a criminal, then announce across the mapped world that I want her returned to Tyrra for her trial."

"But she would be safer, if captured. Right?"

"Groygans punish criminal acts more stringently than we do. I could cause her more harm than good. Besides, I don't have any equivalent Groygan criminals to trade."

"Perhaps you can avoid an exchange by charging her with traitorous acts." Lady Anja's face was devoid of emotion.

"They respect traitors even less than criminals and she would *hate* being branded a traitor, even temporarily. You know how she values her honor. I can't do that to her."

"Yet you sent her away from her family, against her wishes. Why?"

Perinon's throat tightened. For a moment, he'd let his defenses down and forgot he was speaking to a matriarch who, despite her young age, was trained true. He responded with a cold tone. "There was king's business that needed attending. Draius agreed to take a mission that involved traveling east." He couldn't say any more.

Anja lowered her head and kept her voice colorless. "There are rumors, sire, that you're jealous of sharing your control of the Phrenii. They say you feared your influence with the King's Council would erode and that's why you sent the other bearer of the Kaskea away."

"Did Draius say this?" Perinon watched Anja closely. Even without the Phrenii near, he had enhanced empathy. In a perverse way, he willed her to lie to him, to give him a chance to vent his anger—

"No, sire. She never repeated those rumors, if she heard them." Anja didn't lie.

His voice was harsh as he replied. "Never consider, my lady, that anything but duty could force one to endure rapport with the Phrenii. No one wants to be lost in the ancient and arcane workings of their minds, to endure their nightmares, or be faced with one's loss of innocence and the brutal frailty of one's mortality. No one should be jealous of that."

Anja's dark blue eyes looked into his with more understanding than pity. He wished he could speak freely with this woman but, unfortunately, she was a matriarch.

Sure as starlight, that accursed headache had returned. He took his leave.

CHAPTER EIGHT

Waiting

Central Market Square, Betarr Serasa, Tyrra

Lornis went with Peri to the market square the morning after the king's visit. Foreign merchandise and food were becoming plentiful in Tyrran markets, coming from Groyga and as far away as Kitarra. Most entrancing to children of Peri's age were the new magical toys from Sareen: soldiers that marched by themselves and little fuzzy creatures made of wool that shrieked with delight when caught and held.

Peri looked regretfully at a horse prancing on a market stall table. "Aunt Anja and Ma said I couldn't have one of these. But Da says they're just being superstitious." He put out his hand.

Lornis crouched down and watched the horse paw its hoof, then run and jump over Peri's hand—just like a full-size horse going over a jump. "Lady Anja and your mother are trying to live by our beliefs. We don't believe in killing for entertainment or power."

Tyrran matriarchs disapproved of these toys because they were necromantic charms. Ironically, a Tyrran sorcerer had invented the dark art because he lost his own magic and became jealous of the Phrenii. It required death, pain, and blood to bind magical power into inanimate objects called charms. In early spring, Draius and he had tracked down conspirators who revived this heinous craft. The criminals had started their practice upon animals and then progressed to humans—the more significant the soul, the more power from the pain and ultimate death. Once Draius was bound to the Phrenii through the Kaskea, she couldn't abide being near any of the necromantic charms that started appearing in the markets. I feel Darkness in them—never let one of these things inside this house—I don't want Peri to be exposed to them for any length of time, she had said to both Lornis and Lady Anja. He didn't want to remind Peri of his absent mother, since this outing was planned as a distraction for the both of them.

"But we eat animals." Peri stroked the tiny horse.

"Yes, but we don't torture them for our pleasure. Even animals have souls, so we approach the killing of animals for food with appropriate gratitude and respect. We're grateful for the rabbits, boars and deer we can hunt, and the rabbits, pigs and cattle we can raise. We respect them for giving their lives for us. Respect means allowing them to live a decent life and giving them a dignified, quick, and pain-free death. Do you understand?"

Peri nodded. "They aren't really tortured, are they?" He eyed the toy skeptically, undoubtedly wondering how something so carefree and wonderful came from something evil.

Lornis didn't want to go into the details, but the boy had asked and he was old enough. "To get the maximum amount of power possible, the animal must be kept alive and in intense pain and fear for as long as possible."

Peri backed away with a grimace.

"Interested in buying that for your son, ser?" The stall owner, a Sareenian woman, decided to add some pressure. Her voice had a distinct and silky hoarseness: unforgettable, but not enough for identification under the King's Law.

"Maybe." Lornis used an absent tone, not bothering to correct her assumption. He gave her a small, harried smile before turning his attention to the toy, but his glance confirmed she was that Sareenian merchant. They had suspected her of being a member of the necromantic conspiracy that kidnapped Peri. Draius was frustrated because she could never find any proof; in questioning the conspirators who were arrested that hellish night, she compiled only vague references to the "Sareenian woman who sold wine." Since the criminals maintained anonymity in their meetings, no one could identify her. This particular merchant disappeared for an erin or more and then returned, reinventing her business around these toys.

He picked up the toy horse, turning it over. The toy squirmed and fought, because any horse would resist being turned over and held upside down. On the horse's leather belly were the words "Made in Sareen," a rather broad statement since Sareen encompassed three different city-states and a good number of nomadic desert tribes.

"Who makes these?" Lornis asked casually.

"Desert tribes bring them into Illus for sale across the Angim." She gave Lornis an oily smile. "I heard you talking to the boy. They say they don't use death magic."

"There is no other way for humankind to make these items." Lornis put the toy down and glared at the merchant, who backed away with her hands in front of her. The horse began prancing again, ignorant of the tension above.

"I'm sorry, ser, but that's what they claim. You're not obliged to buy the toy."

Peri already headed toward a stall of sweets, a much safer situation. Lornis turned and followed without bidding goodbye to the Sareenian woman. He bought them both sticky buns filled with dried fruits, nuts, and sugar. They found a low wall to sit upon and enjoy the autumn sunshine. The buns lived up to their name and they spent more time licking their fingers than chewing. Peri's doublet ended up with fruit on it, but he would be changing before afternoon lessons.

"Too bad Ma is missing this. She likes sweets."

"You shouldn't worry about her—"

"Don't tell me that! You're worried, Lady Anja's worried, even the king is worried but I'm not allowed to be worried? She's my mother." The boy's outburst was vehement. Then he ducked his head in embarrassment and mumbled toward his lap, "The Phrenii don't make me promise that. At least they're honest."

After a moment of astonishment, he started chuckling. "I suppose we're not being fair by telling you to always buck up. How do you know I'm worried about your mother?"

Peri frowned. "Because I can see, can't I? You're closest to her, 'cept for me, of course."

Both he and Draius thought they'd kept their relationship hidden. "We're very good friends—"

"You don't have to treat me like a child." Peri belied the words with his sulky tone.

Uh-oh, here's a problem. Draius had wanted to be the one who sounded out Peri's attitude toward Lornis. But she wasn't here, so he took a deep breath. "Yes, we're more than friends. Your mother wanted to talk to you about…" He floundered. One never asked a child for permission to marry, only matriarchs. What should he say? "I was wondering if you had any objections? To me marrying your mother."

Peri frowned as he thought about the question. "I guess I like you well enough."

Lornis raised his eyebrows. Although grudgingly given, it might be the best approval he could earn. Tyrrans raised their children in a communal way and matriarchs kept the more promising ones in their homes. That was the case here: both Peri and Draius lived with Lady Anja. Another marriage contract for Draius wouldn't cause much impact to Peri's life. Parentage was recorded in lineal records, so there was no question of Lornis supplanting Jan, Peri's father.

"Ma's special 'cause she wears the Kaskea. You going to be contracted?"

Lornis looked at the boy with new respect. He had tried to talk to Draius the night before she left for Betarr Kain. There had been laughter and teasing, which led to lovemaking. Initially, he'd resisted because he wanted to discuss a contract, but she didn't.

"I'm unique, remember?" She had a trace of bitterness in her tone. "You are too, considering that prophecy hanging over your head. Let's not talk about a contract tonight. Can we just be two normal people who enjoy being with each other? Two people who won't see each other for a while?"

It didn't take long for her to make Lornis give in to his desires. Now back in the daylight of reality, he did have to worry about matriarchs and he was eye-to-eye with Draius's son, who deserved a truthful answer.

"I want to be contracted," he admitted. Draius sent him some letters while at Betarr Kain, but she never mentioned that night or getting contracted. He returned short notes and avoided the topics as well. For a moment, he considered using Peri as an advocate to pressure her. He threw that idea aside immediately. He was not the sort to use a child. Not like Jan, who wouldn't hesitate. This was his problem, so he gave Peri the adult answer. "I don't know if your mother wants a contract. We'll see what she says when she gets back."

If she comes back.

Gloom fell on them both as they sat on the wall. It was a clear autumn day, so the sun baked the plaza stones to a pleasant temperature. About them the bright sounds and colors of the market swirled. A fire-eater went by, unnoticed by Peri. The merchants hawking their wares sounded shrill and empty, as Lornis wondered where Draius was and whether she missed the comforts of home. He saw movement all about: merchants waving their arms in exaggerated claims, patrons wandering between stalls or stepping back and folding their arms as they bargained, jugglers throwing about pins, acrobats leaping and tumbling—so it was the stillness of the man standing in the alley mouth that caught his eye.

He sighed. "I have business to attend to, Peri. Please wait here for me."

Peri nodded, eyes unfocused. At least the boy's confidence hadn't suffered from his abduction. Children should be safe in the sister cities with the Phrenii to protect them. They ran about the cities unsupervised, following the Phrenii or swimming in the clean northern canals. But Peri had been kidnapped by someone he trusted and held as coercion against his mother. In a country where every child is precious, using one for such purposes was unthinkable and unforgivable. Lornis hoped it would eventually be forgettable, at least for Peri.

Brushing imaginary sugar off his doublet—today he was not in his City Guard uniform—he wandered toward the alley. He took his time, making side trips to examine wares. Then he stepped into the shadow of the alley mouth. Only he and Haversar were in the alley. Today the lean man looked like a shabby farmer. Haversar often dressed as a tradesman to move about the sister cities in unremarkable style, although he plied no respectable trade.

"What news?" Lornis leaned against the wall. He gazed out into the market, as much to avoid Haversar's cold eyes as to ensure he wouldn't be speaking to the most powerful criminal in the sister cities. Of course, no law-abiding Tyrran would know Haversar's face. Except Jan, Draius, and him, that is.

"Take care, Lieutenant. You're going to sully your clothes against that wall." Haversar's voice was dark and smooth.

Lornis narrowed his eyes. Every muscle in his body wanted to get away from this man. Haversar's men had almost killed him in an attack that Draius suspected had been orchestrated by Jan. The intent of the attack had been to frighten Draius, but instead resulted in a gunshot to his abdomen. Only Phrenic healing had saved him—which changed his life forever. "Have you news for my Commander?" His voice was flat.

"Remember that my information is given freely." Haversar's life-debt to Jan had been paid during the rescue of Draius. However, Jan was Commander of City Defense and might be able to advocate the release of minor criminals, particularly if he considered them informants. Haversar was creating insurance for himself and his people.

"Understood." He took the hint. "The rumors, if you please?"

"There's concern on the streets about the Phrenii. Why does Jhari arrive in the sister cities? Will we soon need the aspect of air and pre-science?"

"All noted by the Guard." Lornis examined his well-trimmed finger-nails. "This is of no interest to my commander."

"Yes, but while the Phrenii distract us, the Kitarran and Groygan embassies play games."

"I'm listening." This was why he kept meeting with this loathsome man. Haversar knew more about what was going on inside the embassies than the King's Guard intelligence.

"The Kitarran embassy staff is conflicted. The ambassador gets pack-ets from both King Markus and his nephew Cerith Ungought, Duke of Whythern. From table talk repeated in the kitchens, their instructions regarding the relationship with Tyrra are contradictory." Haversar was informed enough to pronounce that last name as "en-geth."

"Whose policy is winning out?"

"The duke's, because the staff likes living in Betarr Serin."

"What does King Markus instruct?" Lornis frowned.

"The Kitarrans are worried about the erratic and offensive overtures devised lately by their king. Some even wonder if he's going mad. We haven't heard specific details except that he's depending heavily upon Groyga advisors, which is odd for Kitarra. Of course, Markus might have more loyalty if not for his bloody history—deposing and killing the duke's parents didn't win the hearts of the people. He only has a slight majority of the nobility supporting him as well, so his power base may be unstable."

"That's disturbing." It also was a good analysis, not that he would tell Haversar that. "What about the Groygans?"

"My people have an interest in Lottagre." This was an understatement. One of Haversar's young pickpockets, named Skuva, had been beaten badly by Honored Sword Orze Be Lottagre in a chance encounter, earning an enmity from Haversar that would haunt that Groygan forever. "We watch where he goes and who he visits when he roams in the disguise of a Tyrran. The King's Guard is incompetent—their guards lose track of him, but we don't." Haversar grinned.

He shook off a shiver at the sight of Haversar's teeth. "So what's the fellow been up to?"

"Lottagre's been known to comfort women with, shall we say, a fondness for the exotic. One lady, in particular, is interesting."

"Who?" Not only was Haversar taking his time to get to the point, this seemed like gutter gossip compared to his Kitarran brief. Both Tyrran women and men were allowed to step outside their marriage contracts, provided they had comfort clauses.

"The Pettaja-Viisi."

Uh-oh. Lornis sucked his teeth in contemplation. The matriarch of the Pettaja-Viisi was in bed, literally, with the Groygans? He often pretended political ingenuousness to avoid threatening Jan, but he couldn't ignore the danger here. The Pettaja-Viisi were powerful, second only to the Meran-Viisi, who held the Crown. There were ill feelings between the Pettaja-Viisi and King Perinon, precipitated by Draius and her investigation of the necromantic murders. A rift stood between the two lineages, although both denied this. So if the matriarch of the Pettaja-Viisi was consorting with Lottagre, who was honored sword to the Groygan ambassador, could that involve treason to the Crown? He was shocked at how quickly he leapt to this assumption. He became more jaded with every erin he spent in the City Guard.

"Lady Leika has an appetite for many men and makes no secret of that." Lornis shrugged uncomfortably. "Has she ever visited the Groygan embassy? Have any of her people?"

"Never. Conspicuously so. Most of the matriarchs sent well wishes to the embassy on the Groygan New Year, but not the Pettaja-Viisi. She keeps her association well hidden, even though we've seen that she meets with Lottagre three times every eight-day. This is more favor than she bestows on members of the Council—she entertains inexperienced and young five-star councilmen fairly frequently."

"Hmm." The frequency of the meetings suggested more than a dalliance. He would report this to Jan, who ran the Office of City Defense, but that didn't mean this information would go any further. Jan only used tips and intelligence when they might advance his career. If Draius were here, Lornis could have told her and been satisfied that this knowledge would get to whoever needed it.

"See that this gets to Jan." Haversar started backing down the alley.

Lornis gracefully pushed away from the wall and put his hand on the hilt of his saber. He glared at the criminal, who stopped. "Treat me like a lackey and you'll regret it." Haversar might have a weapon, but under the King's Law he had to keep it sheathed in the city. The lean man kept his hands away from his body while his cold gray eyes met Lornis's brown ones. They held each other's gaze for a moment and Haversar finally turned away. They both knew Lornis was Haversar's only link to Jan, now that Jan was under matriarchal directive to cut his criminal connections. These meetings bent that original injunction and none of the men wanted to risk being found out. Matriarchal justice could be harsher than the King's Law.

After Haversar melted away to one of his ancient boltholes, Lornis was left with a bad taste in his mouth. He walked back to Peri. The boy was dozing, enjoying the warm wall at his back and the sun on his face. Very soon this lingering warmth would disappear.

"Let's get you home so you can prepare for lessons." Lornis offered his hand.

Peri opened his eyes and for a moment, he looked exactly like Jan. Lornis reminded himself that the advantage of the Tyrran way of raising and educating children was that neither his father nor his mother would have undue influence upon him. He shrugged off the thought that Peri might follow his father's example, becoming successful but calculating, inscrutably playing both friends and enemies off each other. The boy would be his own man and make his own choices.

Peri gave Lornis his hand, sticky from the bun.

Groygan Embassy, Betarr Serin, Tyrra

Orze Be Lottagre glanced about Ambassador Glotta's study. Widgets, tools, and books crammed the shelves. Everything would be studied, dismantled, and eventual shipped back to Groyga. The air smelled of oil used to clean and lubricate gears and shafts.

Lord Glotta knew what he was doing when he offered his much younger brother to the Council of Lords as Groygan ambassador to Tyrra. Velenare Be Glotta was quick and inquisitive, with burning ambitions that might have limited his life span in another house. Luckily, Velenare—and in his thoughts, Lottagre still referred to him by his first name—wasn't interested in controlling House Glotta, when there was all of Tyrra to conquer and control by stealth and guile.

"Three nights ago, Meran-Nelja Lyn was ordered to the sister cities." Lottagre looked down at his notes, written in Groygan code words for security reasons. However, he spoke Tyrran so Velenare could practice.

"Meran-Nelja Lyn is daughter to the master of arms, who is called Meran-Kolme Sevoi? She be here in time for Desert Wind? Is she a target?" Velenare had a good memory even if his Tyrran grammar was not the best.

"Will she be here in time for the operation—yes, according to our source, she crossed the Whitewater bridge this morning at three hours past midnight. She swapped out horses to get here so fast." Lottagre corrected one of the common mistakes Groygans made when speaking common Tyrran. Velenare still had a lot to learn about Tyrra and Lottagre was responsible for that education—just as he had been responsible for the younger man's education in Groygan politics.

He added severely, "But she can't be one of our targets. Remember that a woman cannot hold the position of Tyrran monarch. Only a man may be king and, likewise, only women can be matriarchs. When it comes to any other position, career, job, or rank, either gender can fill it."

Before young Velenare came to Tyrra, the embassy had been useless because it was a place of punishment where Groygans tried to weather out a miserable year or two, eschewing contact with Tyrrans. After Velenare arrived, he made sweeping changes. He transformed the embassy into an intelligence-gathering tool, insisting that everyone speak Tyrran, adopt Tyrran customs, and interact with Tyrrans as much as possible. Velenare couldn't have done this without his First Honored Sword Lottagre, who assimilated languages and cultures quickly and whose talents had been wasted back in Groyga. At this point, other than his eyes, Lottagre could pass for a Tyrran when he prowled the sister cities.

"They're so rigid. Only women handle money, blah, blah, blah." Velenare snorted.

"You'll find exceptions. It's the same with us. Mostly men fill the seats on the Lords' Council, but we have a few women running great houses. Guards for the council or for houses are primarily male, but about one in ten are Falcona's handmaidens. We just don't have codified governmental balance of power based upon gender."

"Yes, yes." Velenare waved away the words as his chair groaned. "So Lyn will not be one of our targets. Let's talk about the packet we received." He had pushed his chair backward and balanced on its two back legs. It made desperate squeaking sounds as he rocked back and forth, an unconscious habit. At some point, Velenare would express bewilderment at its workmanship and Lottagre would order a new chair.

Lottagre's mouth twitched, knowing Velenare was quite taken by the puzzle presented by the packet from House Endigala. The reward issued by House Endigala, independent of the Council of Lords, had been intriguing. They both assumed the Tyrran spies were about King's Guard business, but were mystified concerning the purpose. Of course, they knew about Serasa-Kolme Draius.

"So Endigala hunts a bearer of the Kaskea," Velenare continued to muse aloud. "Could the demons be involved?"

Velenare would never mention the Phrenii by name, but Lottagre didn't believe the Phrenii could see and hear every conversation in the mapped world. It might actually be more dangerous to say Endigala's name, because operation Desert Wind had neither the approval nor support of the Lords' Council—they could all be executed if the council learned about it and took offense. This study had no windows, being on the interior of the embassy. Only Groygan laborers were allowed into the halls and only the ambassador, Lottagre, and his selected men were allowed into the study. His men swept or cleaned, keeping this room secure.

"Serasa-Kolme Draius was only recently bound to the demons and that binding may not be strong," Lottagre said.

"Endigala must be aware of this. In the past, the demons never left the confines of Tyrra or participated in espionage..." Velenare's voice trailed off and Lottagre could see thoughts ticking and grinding together like gears behind his face. "Perhaps Endigala hunts Draius because he wishes to contact them, hoping to turn the demons away from Tyrra? Pry them from the grasping Meran-Viisi?"

Lottagre took time to seriously consider the possibility. Velenare worked by spewing out absurdities and sometimes stitching them together into beautiful schemes. This idea was wild because the Phrenii were incalculably old. They appeared during Era Two of the Old Calendar—before humankind had written language. Since their appearance, they had supported Tyrra for more than 1500 years of written history. "That would be brilliant and unexpected," he said grudgingly. "But I doubt the demons can be subverted from their ancient vow. The King of Tyrra isn't called the 'keeper of the Phrenii's promise' for nothing."

"But the king visits the Serasa-Kolme, perhaps to ensure the loyalty of Draius, the other bearer of the Kaskea?" Velenare tapped the Horn & Herald, which he always read carefully.

"Perhaps Perinon believes Draius can be located through her son."

"Or, rather, influenced through her son. I want a watch set on the Serasa-Kolme home. I want to know every visitor they have and this includes each aspect of—each individual demon. The men must have special instructions. They must not avert their eyes."

Lottagre nodded and chewed his lip. What the ambassador commanded was difficult; even Tyrrans turned their gazes away when they encountered the Phrenii. Only children could stare at the creatures and look directly into the faceted eyes. "We take the risk of the demons noticing our men and reporting them to Master Sevoi."

"Then you better find out if he should be on our list of targets. I'll remind you that the first phase of Desert Wind executes in less than three days and we still don't have a complete list. You'll have to push her." A leer flitted across Velenare's face. He was a young man, after all, although he managed remarkable restraint when it came to Tyrran women. Duty took top priority with Velenare, who now turned to his desk. "I have to write my reports."

Not wanting any involvement in the reporting, Lottagre gladly exited the study. The Groygan ambassador provided the Council of Lords with a report written twice an eight-day. Velenare was also part of House Glotta and no Groygan would be surprised about the separate report to his lord. Additional reports were provided to Endigala and Chintegrata, the two houses powerful enough to influence Lord Glotta and order their own intelligence reports. So every eight-day Velenare's pen drew fine political lines: reports had to fulfill each requestor's needs yet provide no indication of operations the requestor wasn't privy to. This was particularly important for anything going to the Council of Lords and House Chintegrata. Only the report to Lord Glotta contained every unpolished detail.

He strode down the hall to the main door and stopped in front of the big mirror. It was frightfully expensive and had been bought for him, but not for his vanity. He examined himself, arranging his braided hair. When kept natural, his hair was reddish-bronze, verging on a non-Tyrran color. Darkened with a tea infusion and braided, however, his hair resembled dark Tyrran hair, which did exist although it was in the minority. Lottagre altered his posture and cocked his head slightly, adjusting his fashionable cloak. He was the epitome of Tyrran affluence, a kept male accustomed to style.

"Off a-whoring again, honor?"

Garra leered into the mirror over Lottagre's shoulder. His short and spiky orange hair lit up the dim hallway. They'd tried rinses, but Garra's bright hair had been impervious to all. So Garra continued to cut his hair in Groygan fashion because there was benefit to having some embassy personnel appear unmistakably Groygan.

Lottagre took a deep breath. Garra was a simpleton when it came to sex. He had tried to explain that sex was about power, not pleasure. Why did Groygan Lords—and the few Ladies on the council—have multiple spouses? Why could prostitution be found even in Tyrra, a society run by women? Because sex was about power and money, and power and money were required by the Tyrran matriarchy as well as the great houses of Groyga. Regrettably, Garra couldn't see beyond his own penis and he'd never collect power or influence, either in Groyga or Tyrra.

"The ambassador has orders." Lottagre kept his body in character, standing casually, but his words were sharp.

Garra noted his tone and snapped to attention. "Yes, honor?"

"The Serasa-Kolme household in Betarr Serasa must be kept under constant observation. I believe the household of interest is somewhere near Ihlve Street. The men must record every activity and every visitor, including the Phrenii. Be aware that the ambassador will want to know which particular demon visits."

Garra flinched. "But, honor!"

"The demons will visit. In that household resides the son of Serasa-Kolme Draius." Lottagre adjusted his ruff and turned to see if his doublet hid the points of his sleeves. He was enjoying Garra's discomfort. "Has the large coach been readied?"

"Yes, honor." Garra shook his head, probably wondering how he was going to order the guards to identify demons, but he roused himself just as Lottagre was going out the heavy front doors. "Remember to do some hard pissing afterward, honor, because I'm running out of salve."

Lottagre shook his head as he walked toward the coach. One bonus of living in Tyrra was better medicine, due to the influence of the Phrenii; the demons understood herbal and chemical effects. Tyrrans lived healthier and much longer lives, when compared to Groygans. However, Garra continued to hang on to his Groygan remedies, especially his salve of oldbane, quicksilver, and turpentine that he smeared on as a preventive measure against the great pox. Garra continued to believe in its properties even after a Tyrran chemist refused to make him the salve, telling him it would eventually rot his genitals.

He paused at the door emblazoned with the symbol of the Groygan Council of Lords above the crest of House Glotta. Out of the corner of his eye, he saw the ubiquitous King's Guard uniform at the end of the street, making ready to follow. He smiled and climbed into the coach, pulling the curtains shut.

The carriage started moving. The driver had his instructions and Lottagre counted the turns: first right, then left and left again, then a tight right. He watched through the curtains for the alley that appeared soon after the second right. He opened the door and leapt for the alley. Pressing himself against the wall, he watched the inventive door spring back and latch itself closed.

The driver, being Groygan, followed orders and never looked back. He waited. A moment passed and the guard in green and silver went by the alley, having turned the corner after Lottagre leaped. Intent upon the coach, the rider would follow it all the way down to the Betarr Serasa marketplace.

It shouldn't have been this easy, but the average King's Guard in Betarr Serin was not up to snuff when handling intrigue and disguise. Lottagre chuckled as he turned to go back up the gently rising street toward the middle of Betarr Serin. Sensing movement just beyond the corner of his eye, he whirled to look at the shadowed alley across the street, running between two Tyrran estates. A light cool breeze held the hint of oncoming winter and perhaps it moved some trash about. As opposed to other cities, though, Betarr Serin had little trash upon its streets and there appeared to be none in the opposite alley. He waited. Nothing moved; the alley was empty.

CHAPTER NINE

The Desert Wind

Betarr Serin, Tyrra

Lottagre used alleys to arrive at his destination: the stables and carriage house on the south-eastern edge of the Pettaja-Viisi estate. The old Tyrran estates inside Betarr Serin were walled in various types of stone and many of them had outer buildings incorporated into the walls. The walls were less for security than privacy; he quietly stepped into the unlocked side door of the carriage house.

Inside, he heard Tyrrans talking near the large carriage doors. It was mid-afternoon teatime and these men who maintained the coaches and horses were taking a break. He paused and made sure to place everybody by sound. Since this was Betarr Serin and the estate of a five-star lineage, all the workers were Tyrran. Down in Betarr Serasa, eager and economical Sareenians performed much of the manual labor. He could depend upon Sareenians to not stir from their afternoon tea, but not Tyrrans.

Listening carefully, Lottagre moved along the southern side of the coach house until he came to the tack and saddle rooms in the corner. The quiet conversation between the coachmen continued and he could hear a stable hand further away, moving about hay or straw in the northern part that contained the horse stalls. He opened a door and slid into the tack room that contained fine saddles and equipment. The room reeked of saddle oil. Groygans considered Tyrrans fanatical about the care and training of their horses, but Lottagre understood, even welcomed, obsessions. He gazed fondly upon Leika's riding quirt, a short stiff whip with a small lash of loose leather on the end. With that very quirt, he had uncovered a deep hunger within Leika.

The clattering of cups, scraping of chairs against stone, and footsteps of the Pettaja-Viisi workers could be heard outside the tack room. Their break had ended. He moved across the room to the wall. The wooden panels were tall and barely the width of a man, with every other one supporting a post with a lovingly oiled saddle. The panel farthest to his left required a gentle but firm push on its lowest corner before it clicked and swung out on a hinge.

He made sure to look down before stepping into the small confining closet. This time there was no wooden cover over the dark round hole in the floor. The cover appeared and disappeared, due to Leika's mood. Nothing would amuse her more than to see him appear with a sprained or broken limb. Yes, her humor was as vicious and dangerous as her intellect. She was careful to grant him access only to a shunt of the old tunnels that went between two points on her estate.

He stepped into a closet only slightly larger than the yawning hole it hid. There was scarcely space to close the panel. Then he slid his body downward to check inside the hole for a ladder. It was a tight squeeze and the air was quickly getting hot and stuffy. No ladder leaned against the upper part of the hole and he smiled grimly. This hole had jutting hand and foot holds built into the stonework that lined the sides, but the masonry was more than a thousand years old. He hated trusting the old mortar and stones with his weight, let alone doing this in the dark. There was nothing like crawling down a pitch-black hole, feeling for handholds, to set a man on edge. Obviously, this was a test. She would pay for this.

By memory, he figured when to let go. He landed without injury on the unseen tunnel floor below. Luckily, he had examined every surface and dimension of this tunnel, even the two doors blocked by modern brickwork. Applying his new-found knowledge of these structures at the embassy, he had inspected every wall and floor to successfully find its tunnel access. Of course, the Tyrrans had sealed the estate off from the underground warrens before handing it over to the Groygan ambassador. Embassy staff now carried out broken bits of stone and mortar in pockets and purses as they surreptitiously opened their access to the tunnels that riddled the Betarr Serin plateau.

At the end, he climbed the steep steps and went through the door silently. He squinted in the light. The Pettaja-Viisi reliquary was open to the sky, same as every other one he had seen. The arches overhead met at a central dome that opened in a circle to the clear autumn sky. The afternoon sunlight missed the large central square rock made out of a large polished block of granite, edged by tall pillars to keep the pyre logs contained. The rock had been dutifully cleaned—Leika made the reliquary staff clean it by rubbing it first with sand, then with a paste made from eggshells and natron. He might have called it an altar except the Tyrrans used it to burn their dead, not make offerings to the gods.

On one side, already fallen into shadow, was a wall with niches that contained thousands of containers filled with the ashes and bones of Pettaja-Viisi. Those in search of guidance from their ancestors might visit this reliquary at star-rise or attend Fairday evening services. The devout or spiritual Tyrran would be meditating here during the afternoon, but the figure seated on the bench facing her ancestors was neither. He purposely scuffed his boot on the stone.

"You're late." Leika turned. Her light blond hair was arranged in intricate braids that twinkled with silver beads. She raised her arms above her head and stretched, bending her torso sinuously.

He took a quick, long stride and grabbed her wrists. He pulled her against him, holding her arms behind her back. Her flexible body complied, although he knew that her shoulders had to be stretched beyond comfort. Her face remained impassive as she looked up at him, but the pupils in her gray-blue eyes began to expand.

"If you hoped I would break an ankle, I'm sorry to disappoint you," he said in her ear. "I should have brought the quirt and exacted payment for your trick."

She laughed, short and deep in her throat, as he ran his mouth down her neck, tracing her skin with his teeth and tasting her oils. He lightly bit her neck where it met her shoulder and she drew in a deep breath.

"No. Today we experiment." She twisted and he released her arms. She leaned against him with her hand pressed against his neck. He felt something sharp nick him near his jugular. He froze.

"I bought a toy from a Sareenian. They call it a *punlette*." Leika's face dimpled sweetly. A punlette was both jewelry and weapon. The rings fit around three fingers and were often fitted above with small precious jewels, while the sharp blade folded secretly into the sheath in the palm, or extended like a razor. While not able to make a deep stab, it could still be deadly in the jugular area.

"Back up slowly," she whispered. "I bought the one with teeth on the blade."

Lottagre was both concerned and aroused, his erection overwhelming his survival instinct. "I hope you're skilled with that." He backed until he felt the edge of the pyre rock just below his buttocks.

She twisted her hand, scraping the teeth across the base of his neck. He looked down to see his ruff cut open and blood dripping. He grabbed her wrist and she yelped, not able to match his reflexes.

"I think more training is called for," he said firmly, trying not to laugh.

"You think me a sexual innocent?" Her eyes narrowed.

"Nay, my lady, never innocent." Lottagre was truthful. "But you have a heavy hand when you're experimenting." He pulled off his ruff and used it to daub the freely bleeding wound.

"I apologize." She didn't sound too sincere. Her pupils widened more, focusing on the blood on his neck while her free hand dexterously unlaced his leggings and freed his erection.

"Let me use that." Lottagre sheathed the punlette's blade and pulled it from her fingers. "Pain should be applied skillfully, keeping time with our passion, like a dance."

Her eyes were puzzled, needing something she didn't understand, something she couldn't find in her Tyrran lovers. The cold granite of the pyre was high enough that he could half sit, half lean against it. He pushed her skirts up and pulled her lithe body over him. With each bloom of pleasure he put her through, he gathered more power and held himself back. Applying the *closed* punlette to sensitive areas heightened her pleasure. Leika wouldn't be considered deviant by Groygan standards. She merely needed some pain to mix with her pleasure. While her stodgy society couldn't admit these needs, he had been openly trained for such in Groyga. As she shook and gasped for the third time, he spent himself.

Leika didn't doze or sleep after sex as many women might; instead, she became more open and liked conversation. That was how he discovered her hatred for Perinon, based upon an audience when the young king humiliated her and the other Pettaja matriarchs. She resented the Meran-Viisi, while grudgingly accepting that history had subordinated her lineage.

From the beginning, he worked on amplifying her hatred for Perinon. He also suggested ways to cause problems for the Meran-Viisi using resistance that avoided direct confrontation. Originally, he just hoped to give her ideas, but now he needed information and the time for evasiveness was gone.

He traced the red scrapes on her arms. "Great houses in Chikirmo can adjust their leadership whenever they feel the need. You do, as well, and I'm still baffled why your matriarchy has tolerated that milksop on the throne, when you told me you've deposed kings in the past."

"It has only been done twice in history. The matriarchy instigates the process, but it usually requires the King's Council and the Phrenii to agree the king is no longer fit for his duties. That would be hard to do with Perinon." She shook her head.

"You said the Meran-Viisi who was transferred to take Serasa-Kolme Draius's position in the City Guard was on the list of successors. How did you know that?" He stroked her hair.

"Because the Meran-Viisi matriarch submits possible successors to the five-star lineage committee for approval, but purely as a formality." She snorted. "We, the Pettaja-Viisi, must ensure a qualifying education is given to every possible successor. The fact there's a list of successors isn't a deep, dark secret—only the names. Nobody's particularly interested in this list. Why are you?"

"I'm offering you a less overt recourse. Wouldn't you rather rid yourself of king *and* successors all at once, rather than trying your little bits of harassment here and there?" He referred to all the ways Leika filled Perinon's life with Darkness every day. Just two days ago, she'd said with a grim smile, *I blocked requests for funding Perinon's navy—all due to a new Council member who's besotted with me. Soon, due to my small influence on other members here and there, the Council will demand control over the Kaskea and an accounting of the whereabouts of his wayward cousin.*

"Only an idiot would try to assassinate him! I told you the king has the Phrenii and their magic for protection. If you had seen what I saw him do with the support of those creatures, you would never contemplate a direct attack." She shivered delicately.

"Yes, you told me. But you haven't contemplated surreptitious attacks using necromantic weapons. Many of these could be placed near him, weakening the demons and possibly him as well, if he's not killed outright. What if some of these weapons can be activated after a delay? What if these weapons can never be associated with either of us? And what if his successors are killed as well?"

"You ask a lot of questions for someone who needs information. What if I don't give you the names of the successors?"

"I thought you hated Perinon. You would do anything to get rid of him, you said."

"I *do* want him gone, but your plan will only incriminate *me*, you fool. Who else but a matriarch would know all the successors? Besides, the Phrenii can detect lies."

"What if we threw in another target?" Lottagre sat up. "They say that if you cannot damage your enemy, then you must remove those who your enemy depends upon. We've always considered the master of arms to be the real experience behind the throne."

"How many of these *weapons* do you have?" She looked thoughtful.

"Enough. And they're all made by Sareenians, who will end up taking the blame." He fingered his knife, the longest weapon he was allowed to carry within Betarr Serin. He stopped when she glanced at his hand.

"You're wondering whether you can coerce or bribe me, aren't you?" Her fingers brushed down the side of his face and he remembered what really motivated her: power and control. "So tell me, how do *I* benefit from this plot of yours?"

"After we get rid of the current king who's been a thorn in your side and reduced the careful plans of the Meran-Viisi to rubble? Well, you could influence the choice of his successor, and the successor himself. You weren't a matriarch when Perinon was put on the throne. What if you had the chance to influence him earlier in his life, before he had been trained for more than a decade? How young would they have to go if they lost *all* their successors? That's a question only you can answer."

Her hand dropped and one of her shoulders shrugged. "Pretty young, to ensure the appropriate training. A male who's only begun his lessons within the last three years. Right now, Aracia's probably looking around to select someone at that age anyway."

"Think of the influence you'd have over a king of that age."

"With someone so young, a regent would have to be established. The Meran-Viisi matriarch is always the first choice for regent, but depending upon the international situation we might want a male because the king is the high commander of the King's Guard. Precedent might be thrown out..." The cogs and gears in her mind were starting to turn.

"See, we don't understand the details of succession or even how to get our weapons near the targets. I'm asking you to join us, to *direct* this operation. We need clear and sharp planning." He hoped Velenare would be all right with this tactic, because appealing to Leika's vanity and giving her control was his last-gasp attempt. If this didn't work, he'd have to resort to physical torture, which might not be successful and could result in her death.

"It's too risky. They'd immediately suspect a matriarch."

"Isn't there any ambitious dupe in those council members you have in your pocket? Someone, perhaps, *besotted* with you? It would take clever planning to ensure he ended up with the blame, but you could do it." The smirk on her face said he had hit the mark. "You would have the resources of our embassy, as well as our Sareenian allies—none of whom want to be caught any more than you do."

"I'd get total control?"

"Yes." *Gods, I hope Velenare goes along with this—he doesn't need to tell Lord Endigala that Desert Wind is actually being run by a traitorous matriarch.*

"How can I depend upon the discretion and loyalty of your resources?"

"I'll act as intermediary for all but your people, whoever you choose to include. The Sareenians and Groygans involved will never know you're at the helm." *Except for Velenare.* "If they're questioned by the Phrenii, they could never implicate you."

"But they'll implicate you. Would you kill yourself before you let the Phrenii wring the truth, and sanity, from you?" After he nodded, she pressed him. "Do you swear by your honor?"

"As an Honored Sword, I'm already obligated to prevent myself from falling into enemy hands." But to appease her, Lottagre pledged his loyalty and life to her. However, this ambitious matriarch miscalculated the strength of his oath. As long as he didn't invoke the gods, any vow he made to the godless—and she certainly qualified as such—didn't have to be honored.

Betarr Serasa, Tyrra

Naton Deldanta stood at the bow as the Sareenian ship neared the port of Betarr Serasa. Canvas rattled above. He glanced up, and then continued to view the two Tyrran cities ahead. Soon his life would change, hopefully for the better.

His eyes widened at these ancient cities, the oldest in the mapped world. Behind a modern sea wall protected with cannon, Betarr Serasa displayed broad wharfs, canals, and streets lined with greenery. High on an unassailable plateau above the Angim Sea stood Betarr Serin. To reach that city, one had to cross a white bridge over a broad rushing river and travel a thin road that wound up the side of a plateau. Above, the spires of Betarr Serin winked silver and gold over its walls.

The city of Betarr Serin was said to be invulnerable. To the east, the plateau dropped off to the Whitewater river and Betarr Serasa, and to the south, the sea. As for protection from the west and north, the triangular plateau was tucked against unscalable cliffs of the Cen Cerinas mountains.

A long time ago, the sister cities were protected by magic and considered the most beautiful places in the mapped world. Those days were gone forever. Humankind stopped working magic hundreds of years ago and the brilliance of the two cities dimmed with time. Today, one might find as much art and science in Naton's home city of Illus.

"Enjoying the view, sirrah?" The Sareenian first mate touched her forehead in respect. She knew he was the oldest son of Pater Donas Deldanta, the city father of Illus. He wondered what respect he would receive if she knew the Pater sent him away to make peace with his stepsister and half-brother.

During the voyage, Naton didn't encourage conversation with the crew, but the first mate felt it necessary to give him advice about the Tyrrans. "Read the *Horn and Herald* while you're there. That'll have everything and anything that's happening," had been the most repeated words of wisdom.

The first mate pointed out the middle-aged Tyrran woman who boarded the ship in Illus, the woman who always had an annoyed look on her face. "Seteli-Nelja Vaivata—using them funny backwards names they have. She's a matriarch, visiting Illus for a loan for her family, her whole lean-e-age, as they call it. In debt up to her frozen eyeballs." She laughed at Naton's expression. "Like I said, read the *H&H* and you get all the dirt."

The crew put on a harbor furl and the oars came out as they steered the ship through the sea wall. He looked up at the cannons and guards in green uniforms on the city walls. The sea wall forced them to travel within optimum range of the cannons. After crossing the harbor, they began mooring. There were tenders on the water, ropes thrown, and people shouting. The first mate stood by Naton and yelled advice from time to time, but everyone seemed to know what they were doing. The dock was a flurry of activity.

When he looked down the wharf, a creature moved through the commotion like a calm island letting storms break and flow about it. It was about the size of a large deer, but with a mane. A long, sharp, spiraled horn protruded from its forehead and glittered from the sunlight. A gaggle of children surrounded it, but the men and women on the wharf kept their distance, parting for both it and the children.

"Wondrous Light," muttered the first mate. "One of the Phrenii. Wonder why it's here."

Naton had read about these five aspects of the Phrenii. They were proof of the last true magic left in the mapped world and controlled by the King of Tyrra. He stared at the creature, and then blinked. For a moment, he thought he saw *through* it.

"See those children petting the thing? I tried to touch one of them—" The first mate shuddered. "It's not for grown men or women. I better tell the captain it might be meeting us." She hurried away.

This aspect of the Phrenii did appear to be heading toward their ship. The gangplank had been set and the Tyrran matriarch was the first passenger to leave. She hurried down and gave a quick bow to the aspect. While keeping her distance, she appeared to be talking with it. Then it gestured with its horn toward the ship and the matriarch turned, frowning, to stare up at *him*, still standing at the rail.

A cry went up along the dock. The seamen were trying to unload Afasle, his mare. She was desert-bred, with high tail and arched neck. The mare tossed her sculpted head, smelling the strange place with flaring and puffing nostrils. Balking at the top of the wide gangplank at the other end of the ship, no one could move her until Naton approached. When Afasle smelled him, her neck relaxed.

"Quiet, sister of the desert wind," he whispered, his hand on the halter. Once again he marveled at Afasle, wondering how bones so delicate could be so strong and enduring. The mare was smaller than most Tyrran horses, but he was sure she could outlast them. He smiled as he led her down the planks, telling the men to bring his tack and trunks off the ship.

"We are pleased to meet you, Naton Deldanta." The voice beside him caused him to jump; it was musical but neither male nor female, neither low nor high. The creature stood further than arm's length from him and, remembering the first mate's advice, he had no inclination to move closer. When it stepped sideways there was a light ringing sound. He looked around for bells. Children swarmed about them, children younger and smaller than would be allowed to run freely about Sareenian streets. One small boy swung from its tufted tail.

He tightened his grip on Afasle's halter, worried the mare might bolt, but she stayed calm as a rock. Mimicking the matriarch, he made a quick bow. "I would be pleased if the Phrenii called me Naton." He remembered his lessons: when you speak to one aspect, you speak to all, because they're not individuals.

"This aspect is called Jhari." It bowed its head. The faceted eyes were brilliant blue and ageless. "We remember your parents. We see Meran-Viisi Ihana in your face and eyes, while we see Donas Deldanta in your hair, jaw, and the breadth of your shoulders."

He gaped. His father visited Tyrra only two times: as a child of seven years and as a young man of twenty-two. Pater Deldanta's grim face would soften when he spoke of Tyrra, perhaps because he met Ihana there and fell in love. Ihana had died when the fevers reached Sareen. His father still mourned Ihana's death, which his second wife never forgave. His father outlasted his second wife and even after her death, her daughter from a previous marriage continued the practice: his stepsister Sangha couldn't forgive Naton's presence and how he reminded Pater Deldanta of Ihana.

"We mourn the loss of Meran-Viisi Ihana, but we know her soul strives for the stars." Jhari's voice expressed little emotion.

Naton was raised in the Way of the Light, so this reference to Tyrran spirituality made him uncomfortable. While Tyrrans called the Way the "path of souls" which didn't deviate from basic Church doctrine, they didn't understand that one went through many lifetimes before attaining the stars.

The crew deposited Afasle's tack and his trunks at his feet. He silently cursed his stepsister for not allowing him to take a manservant along but, after all, she intended this to be an uncomfortable banishment. Thankfully, while he saddled Afasle, Jhari arranged for his trunks to be transported to the Guard Officer Barracks. No one was interested in his money, not when the Phrenii were giving the orders. In Illus, he would have worried about his possessions securely arriving at their intended destination. Here, the people loading his trunks on a wagon looked askance at him out of the corners of their eyes, so he was not concerned about theft.

Jhari apparently intended to escort him, so Naton mounted Afasle and waited, watching Tyrrans going about their work on the wharves. Sometimes adults would smile at the chattering children but the smile would fade if their glance fell upon Jhari. Often the smile was replaced by an expression of guilt. The children were dispersed with a few soft words and Jhari headed north on a wide cobblestone street, moving so he had to follow at a trot. Relieved of having to find his own way, he was content to look around.

They traveled through a warehouse district and Jhari led them over several bridges that crossed canals. The high bridges allowed flat boats laden with cargo, but not masted ships. Canals and warehouses changed to places of heavy trade: farriers, tanners, metalworkers with smelting furnaces, and stonemasons. Going further into the city the smells cleared and the lighter trades appeared: candle-makers, tailors, woodworkers, jewelers, chemists and gunsmiths. Naton heard the trades in Tyrra were controlled by lineage or, specifically, by the matriarchs. In Illus, powerful guilds controlled the trades.

Jhari stopped, causing Afasle to stop, and focused on a man across the street. The man stood still, with his head down and his hands working a soft laborer's hat. He appeared to be struggling with some inner decision.

"He has a very sick child, but we do not know whether he will ask for Phrenic healing." Jhari waited and the man crossed the street, dodging carriages. He stopped in front of Jhari, but kept his eyes down.

"I cannot find the healing one." The man choked up. His face was lined and had dark circles under his eyes.

"Dahni is the aspect for healing, but each of us can borrow some of that power," Jhari said gravely.

"My son—can you see him?"

"Yes. He lies upon his cot with his wound festering. His body is not strong enough to fight the Darkness."

"The chemist gave us powders to put in the wound."

"They are not strong enough. Your son cannot fight the Darkness with the strength that others have. We can change that." Jhari appeared to be choosing words carefully.

"What will happen, without your healing?" asked the man, cringing even before hearing the answer.

"He will die. In this, we are certain."

Naton raised his eyebrows at the straightforward answer, barren of emotion. The Phrenii spoke plainly. He thought there was a blue glow at the edge of his vision. When he tried to look at it, the glow disappeared.

The man still appeared uncertain. The Tyrran birth rate had been dwindling since the Fevers. They had fewer and fewer children each year, so why did the man hesitate?

"Yes, but *when* will he die?" The man's knuckles were white as he kneaded his hat.

Perhaps the Phrenii weren't always as direct as Naton thought. Jhari might mean his son would live a full life and die at a ripe age of 120 years. Everybody died, even though Tyrrans were longer-lived than most of humankind.

"As we speak, the boy worsens. If we do not heal him, he will die before the sun rises again." Jhari's horn gestured to the sun, which marked late afternoon.

This wasn't the answer the man wanted. A tear traveled down his rough cheek, getting sidetracked and absorbed by a deep crease.

"You have come into the city to ask us something?"

"I request your services, Phrenii. Please heal my son." The man's voice was strained.

"We remain to serve." Jhari's answer had the ring of ritual. Then it sprang into action. "Naton, we request a favor from you. We must reach the boy quickly if we are to save him. Will you give this farmer a ride and let your horse follow us?"

Surprised, he nodded, but Jhari had already left.

After looking a little suspiciously at Afasle, the farmer climbed up behind Naton and wrapped his arms around his waist, holding on tightly. Far ahead, Jhari was already at the speed of a horse's canter and increasing—carriages and pedestrians moved aside or slowed to let the creature go by. Naton didn't have the same privilege, so he had to dodge and wind through the heavy traffic as they moved through the center of Betarr Serasa.

He lost sight of Jhari, but Afasle sensed the way. He let the desert horse pick her way and stretch her legs. Although she looked delicate, she was strong enough to carry two men. Besides, she needed to work off energy after stabled in the ship's hold for more than a day. He only had to worry about whether the farmer would squeeze the breath out of him.

After a few shouted questions and answers, Naton learned more about the farmer. His name was Miirus, and his son had cut open his leg with a scythe. His farm was about a league north of the old city walls and he grew grain as well as potatoes and other root vegetables.

The sun had fallen behind the top of the Cen Cerinas mountains when they rode up to the gate of the farm. The fence was neat and whitewashed and the gate hung open. The door to the little thatched farmhouse was also open.

Before Miirus could dismount, a woman ran out of the farmhouse door and clutched at his leg. "You asked for healing." Naton couldn't tell if it was a question or an accusation.

"He would have died tonight." Miirus's voice was harsh as he slid down from Afasle.

"Our only son," the woman murmured. Miirus put his arm around her waist and they went into farmhouse.

Since Afasle was covered with sweat, he walked her until she cooled down. The sky was filled with vivid orange clouds until the sun sank down behind the Cen Cerinas and the farmhouse was covered in evening shadow. As he tied up his horse, another one of the Phrenii arrived.

At midnight, Naton walked out into the autumn night air and stretched until he felt his back and shoulders crack. He yawned. Cramped in a corner of Miirus's house, he had watched Jhari and Dahni stand for several hours over the son, who was about twelve years of age. He had sensed the concentration of the two creatures and saw power surging toward the boy. Everyone apparently saw the green flickers of light licking the wound: Miirus murmured and his wife would hide her head in his shoulder when the flickers lit the room. However, they didn't seem to notice the actual power—or magic? He didn't know what he'd seen.

After many hours, the boy stirred. He was on the mend. Miirus and his wife were full of awe and fear as they looked at their son. They seemed grateful, but they treated him as if he had undergone a great change. Naton had many questions about this "Phrenic healing," but this wasn't the time or place to satisfy his curiosity.

"The boy will be fine." Jhari emerged from the farmhouse. Moonlight rippled along its mane, showing the droop in its neck. Naton assumed the other creature, introduced as Dahni and the one that was the most powerful healer, had stayed.

"Tomorrow we will present you to the king up in Betarr Serin," Jhari said as they walked back to the city walls. "Now go to the Guard officer barracks, which is near the large bridge that crosses the Whitewater. They have your things and are expecting you."

After getting Naton through the night watch at the gate, Jhari left him on his own in the strange city and he had time to wonder about its words. The *Phrenii* intended to present him to the king?

Betarr Serin, Tyrra

Perinon arrived to find the hall crowded. This wasn't a large receiving room in the Palace of Stars, but the hall at Number One Betarr Serin, his residence. Mahri stood beside his chair, while a King's Guard stood on the other side. Sevoi, plus Perinon's secretary and clerk, stood against the wall. Jhari and a young Sareenian stood in the middle of the room facing his chair. Behind Jhari, a Phrenic aspect rarely seen in the sister cities, stood about ten other people he didn't bother to identify. The Sareenian bowed after he entered, but not before Perinon saw his expression change. Tyrra's king had somehow failed to measure up with him.

Perinon didn't apologize for his late arrival and sat. The effect of two Phrenii, so close, caused him to blink: all the mortals in the room glowed with mottled, twisting spires of light and dark. He waved at his clerk to begin the business at the top of his schedule.

Unexpectedly, Jhari broke the silence. "The Phrenii present Naton Deldanta from Illus, Sareen. In Tyrra, he is called Meran-Viisi Naton."

Perinon's eyebrow cocked and out of the corner of his eye, he saw his secretary make a startled motion. Whispers started among the spectators. He smiled at the thought of Lady Aracia's face if she'd been here to witness the Phrenii introduce a Sareenian as Meran-Viisi, as a cousin! The Phrenii rarely participated in mortal ceremonies—so what were they playing at? After more than ten years of rapport with Mahri, he realized the Phrenii could have their own agenda.

Mahri's voice started whispering in his mind but he flicked his hand near his ear, the signal that he didn't want to be in rapport at the moment. Mahri's voice immediately faded. The Sareenian, mistaking his gesture, stepped forward and offered a leather scroll case with a wax seal.

The guard grabbed the case. After examining it closely, he handed it to Perinon. The seal showed the imprint of the Illus City Father. Perinon looked at Naton, who had olive Sareenian coloring blended with the dusky, gray color of Meran blood. Naton had startling gray eyes but his hair was almost black. Most Tyrrans with Meran blood had ash blond hair with highlights of silver, similar to Perinon's.

"Greetings, Naton Deldanta of Illus, Sareen. Can you tell me about the contents of this?" He fingered the seal.

The young man met his gaze without evasion. "My father, Pater Donas Deldanta of Illus, offers my services to Tyrra. I know no more than that."

Naton appeared to be at least marrying age—which, in Tyrra, would be nineteen years. Perinon studied him, wondering why a Sareenian would offer to serve Tyrra. Because of the Phrenii, he could see honesty, integrity, and a bit too much pride. He also detected subtle, hidden pain. The Sareenian suppressed unpleasant memories, but they were fading.

With that insight, he decided Naton could be trustworthy. After all, this was why the king bound himself to the Phrenii.

He opened the leather scroll case. It contained two documents. One was a letter from Pater Donas Deldanta, where the title of "Pater" designated him as the city father. The Deldanta family had controlled Illus for five generations. They were said to be benign when compared to the Dimoni family, who held Forenllas and produced despot after despot. The letter was written clearly, but the meaning puzzled him. In the Sareenian style of fosterage, Deldanta offered his son to Perinon, presumably to serve Tyrra and the Meran-Viisi. Perinon knew Sareenian ruling families often fostered their children with each other, sometimes to broaden the child's experience and often to hold together a fragile political alliance by essentially offering a hostage. Why was the Deldanta family offering a hostage?

The other document presented no hidden message. It recorded the birth of Naton to Meran-Viisi Ihana and Donas Deldanta. He noted Naton's skin: olive Sareenian coloring blended with the dusky, gray of Meran blood. Naton had startling gray eyes but almost black hair. Most Tyrrans with Meran blood had ash blond hair with highlights of silver, similar to Perinon's.

He remembered cousin Ihana from those carefree years before the Fevers. He and Draius had barely started lessons when Ihana packed up the few belongings she could petition the lineage for, and left Tyrra by ship. Proud, beautiful, and headstrong, she refused the marriage contracts offered her by Lady Nuora, the previous Meran-Viisi matriarch, and decided that Tyrra had nothing she wanted. After Ihana left, no news of her trickled down to the Meran-Viisi children.

I'm glad Ihana did well for herself by marrying a Sareenian city father.

He felt Mahri's sorrow. *Ihana is gone, on her way to the ancestral stars.*

No need to ask her son about her health, so he perused the record of birth. On the certificate were Ihana and Donas's signatures, plus the signatures of three witnesses. Naton had legal proof of his Meran-Viisi lineage. He grinned—another thorn bush he could plant in Aracia's life. This document would satisfy most matriarchs, but Lady Aracia wasn't just any matriarch. She protected and ensured the continuance of the king's lineage, so she could verify this document. "So, cousin, do you wear colors for Illus or Tyrra?"

Naton seemed startled. "I'm not..." he searched for a word, "I'm not qualified to wear the colors of my father's merchant navy and I'm not trained to be a constable." His voice held a touch of disdain but he appeared to have weapon training, wearing a light dueling sword popular with fashionable Sareenian blades. As a young Sareenian male of a wealthy and powerful family, perhaps Naton didn't have gainful employment, a situation not allowed by Tyrran matriarchs. Everyone should be in "responsible service" to their lineage.

"I agree you don't have the training required of our Guard. I'll appoint you as a liaison officer, so you'll remain close to me. You'll receive an honorary rank of Lieutenant in the King's Guard and wear our colors."

Sevoi looked surprised at Perinon's sudden commission of the young Sareenian, but the experienced master of arms didn't say anything. He wouldn't question his king in front of a Sareenian.

His secretary and clerk took over. Naton had forms to fill out and, after that, should be fitted for a uniform, issued weapons and other gear, etc. Perinon's mouth quirked at the efficiency with which the clerk hustled a bewildered Naton out of the room.

Now he had to deal with the Phrenii. "Everyone leave us," he said. All mortals filed out of the room, including all the King's Guard. Mahri and Jhari stayed.

"Explain yourself." He yawned and felt the faint beginnings of a headache.

"For what actions do you wish accounting?" Mahri asked in that singsong genderless voice.

"Don't be obtuse. You went out of your way to introduce this foreigner as Meran-Viisi. Had Lady Aracia been here, her heart would have stopped in shock." The tickling sensation in his head meant that Mahri was amused. The Phrenii never laughed, but he was convinced they understood and appreciated humor.

"Is it proof enough for the Meran-Viisi matriarch?" Jhari asked. "We *feel* his Meran blood."

Here was their agenda, laid bare. Aghast, he looked at Mahri, who was supposed to be the keystone of the Phrenic ring. Mahri was also spirit, with which came command. "You want rapport with a foreigner?"

"In this sense, we do not understand your boundaries. He has Meran blood and the ability to use the Kaskea."

"He isn't *Tyrran.* Must I invoke the promise and remind you that you protect *Tyrra?* The Kaskea was made by Tyrran sorcerers and only Tyrrans should bind to the Phrenii." He knew they wanted all shards of the Kaskea in use, but this was unacceptable. It was too soon after Siuru's death, for one thing.

"We regret the death of Meran-Nelja Siuru." His rapport with Mahri caused a wave of sorrow to overwhelm him.

"Stop." He choked. The Phrenii stepped back to give him relief, but the pounding in his head already started. Intense rapport always started his headaches.

"We do not understand her death. She had an affinity with fire but when she reached out she became frightened. We thought her mind was breaking. Instead, her heart stopped."

"Naton is strong and he has an affinity with air." Jhari referred to itself.

He hardly noticed the creatures' odd usage any more. "What about his loyalties? I'm willing to have him serve in my guard, but to bear the Kaskea—"

"Naton will be loyal to Tyrra and he will be necessary for Tyrra's survival. *In this, we are certain.*" Jhari stamped its hoof on the marble, which caused a deep ringing sound and made his head throb. There it was. The phrase the Phrenii used when their prescience proved something certain and correct—Jhari, as the element air, was also the strongest aspect for prescience. The Phrenii were incapable of lying and they appeared adamant about this.

He sighed, rubbing his temples with his fingers. *Why do I feel like I'm dealing with stubborn children, rather than creatures that are thousands of years old?* Offering the Kaskea to a Sareenian would probably be considered *treasonous* by the King's Council and *insane* by the matriarchy. Only two Tyrran kings had been forcibly removed from the throne and in both cases, they were insane *by the word of the Phrenii.* But what if the Phrenii themselves became unbalanced? This was a loose thread in the law he didn't want to pull.

"I'll consider your proposal." It was a lie and the Phrenii should know he was lying.

To his surprise, they dipped their horns in acknowledgement.

CHAPTER TEN

Family Duties

Abandoned Hermitage Near Ruhallen, Northern Tyrra

The nature of the Void lends itself to spying. It shows the true shape of the world and renders it without color or soul. Any being not of the Void cannot be seen, which is why the portals are visible, but one can't see other visitors. One only "hears" or feels their thoughts.

Being Minahmeran as well as an experienced sorcerer, Ihmar could open a conduit using true magic and walk the Void. Humankind, however, lost true magic many years ago. They could only enter via the portals, the creatures they called the Phrenii, and they were noisy.

Ihmar was observing from the Void when he sensed the incoming human, but the visitor was too undisciplined to ever notice him. This young king's presence fairly shouted his identity: Meran-Viisi Perinon. The portal that accompanied him, the one of the Phrenii they called Mahri, might never notice Ihmar in all that thought-noise. Just in case, though, he kept his mind shielded.

"I am committed to finding bearers for you, but I must move slowly. Why can't you wait?" Perinon asked the portal.

"There is little time." There was a surprising amount of uncertainty in the portal's thoughts.

"I need answers. Why is there so much turbulence in the Blindness? Why are the aspects moving about—is it possible to have conflict between aspects?" A thread of exhaustion ran through Perinon's thoughts.

"As elements, water and fire oppose each other naturally." Mahri answered cautiously. "Fire and air enjoy each other, while earth and water seek each other."

"And what part does spirit play?"

Mahri hesitated. "In the solid world, my aspect connects all elements in the circle."

"That's only useless theory, not an answer." Anger radiated from the young king. His mind was too open; he never considered other minds might be listening here.

Perinon continued to ask questions. "Why does it seem the nightmares of the entire mapped world are stalking the Blindness? Why can't I communicate with Draius? She needs help and she may be suffering as much as I am during sleep."

"You think the Phrenii cause this suffering?" Misery clouded Mahri's thoughts.

"I don't know. It's too hard to get through the Blindness. Something's wrong."

When they finished, Ihmar became just as disturbed as Perinon. As Mahri left, he felt this part of the Phrenii prepare itself for the solid world. It segmented its thoughts and prepared to hide them from itself. The Phrenic mind splintered. He had been taught the Phrenii, as portals to the Void, couldn't develop personalities or individuality. Perhaps they were tainted even more than the elders suspected, but by madness.

Before he returned to his body, he tarried in the Blindness. He often ignored the area below the Void that held the sleeping minds of humankind and Perinon spoke true: some strange purpose drove the hunters in the Blindness, as if they searched for someone. This was yet another mystery.

He opened his eyes and realized the glade was no longer empty. Below his perch, a girl kneeled in the middle of the meadow, swinging her arms to touch the tops of the swaying grass and flowers. She wasn't looking at the large group of boulders on the west side. He silently rolled himself behind the rocks and watched her through a crack.

Birches rustled and the girl's eyes were closed, perhaps for concentration or meditation. The shadows of the birches reached across the glade and the air carried the sharp scent of the last summer flowers and drying hay. Beside the girl rested two wicker baskets.

Her face told Ihmar that she recognized this was a tragic and sorrowful place. He had also sensed the soul who had been torn from the stars, who wandered about the small cabin that sat at the top of the gently sloping meadow. Perhaps the girl communed with that soul and gave it comfort and companionship.

A young man pushed through the bushes at the bottom of the slope, breaking the quiet rustlings and stirrings of nature. "Berina! What are you doing? Father sent me to find you."

Near the Village of Ruhallen, Northern Tyrra

Berina sighed. She gathered her baskets, less than one quarter full of blackberries. When she caught up with her older brother Erno, she got an earful.

"I should be doing something useful, but instead I'm looking for you. Father needed me to help with the roof but he was worried that you hadn't come back. You've been gone all day, and you couldn't even fill your baskets?" So it went, all the way to the farmhouse. Berina stoically endured his lecture, because this time she deserved it. She didn't have enough berries for a pie; perhaps they could have them with cream in the morning.

When they got home, she headed to the kitchen. She made dinner for the three of them, hearing Erno talk to father. While her mother had survived the Fevers, she didn't live through Berina's premature birth. The village doted on Berina, considering her a miracle child, but not father. Other children called their fathers "Da," but he was always "Father" to her and her brother.

Erno, three years older than her and not yet nineteen, was trying to convince Father that he was mature enough to be contracted. He was a steady, grounded young man—not at all like his sister. Tonight he continued to harp about her meager berry harvest, even at the table.

"We all have to pull our weight around here to make ends meet." Erno glanced at Father, who ate silently. "We can't afford to have you spending a whole day doing nothing. Perhaps you were meeting an admirer at the old hermitage?"

"No." She continued eating her stew.

"Sopi asked me whether you were fond of anyone." Her brother's eyes narrowed in amusement. He spent his small amount of free time in the village commons, socializing with other young people.

"I wasn't meeting anybody." Although she couldn't shake the feeling that Lahna's soul occupied that glade. Today she felt it more than ever before. She shivered.

Father looked at her. He had dark blue eyes under silver eyebrows and hair, which he kept tied back in a simple clasp. He was still handsome and young enough to take another wife, but he hadn't. "What were you doing there?" His tone was quiet.

"I was—I was daydreaming." Her cheeks flamed. She couldn't lie to him, but she didn't want him to think her lazy. It was all right for Erno to think that, but Father was another matter.

"Doing nothing of any use," her brother said in disgust.

Father waved a hand to silence him. "Do you have any interest for the boys in the village?"

"No." She stared down at her stew.

"She won't talk to them!" Erno burst out. "She acts like they're not good enough for her, like she has Meran blood or something."

"I should take you to the old woman. After all, Erno has put in enough petitions with her. It's time she spoke with you, too." Although Father gave appropriate respect to the Vilje-Nelja matriarch whenever meeting her, he never used the title "Lady" when speaking of her. Perhaps because he wasn't related to her by blood, or perhaps because this was farming territory with rural villages, he always referred to Lady Vilje-Nelja Niisa as the "old woman."

She nodded and cleared away the dishes. In the kitchen, her eyes watered, but she kept to her duties. That evening she recorded numbers for Father, checked that the poultry and livestock were safe for the night, stoked the stove, and went to bed. Only when she covered herself with the blanket did the tears come, but they came quietly.

It was normal to be afraid of visiting Niisa. Everyone had uncertainty about entwining their life with a stranger's. Unfortunately, that's how life happened. She could wish, in vain, for more control. But she had worse things to worry about: today she saw flashes of someone else's life and she was convinced they came from the sorceress Lahna. If she was right, her beliefs had been set on their side. If she was wrong, then she was insane.

She knew all the stories of Lahna, how she had apprenticed to Cessina and how she posed as a boy servant to the evil sorcerer Nherissa. She'd helped Cessina destroy Nherissa and save the Phrenii more than 500 years ago. In later years, Lahna trained others in the village of Ruhallen and eventually built the hermitage in the glade. They said she might have been a bit mad when she died, but eventually there was no doubt she had reached the stars.

The possibility of a soul returning from the stars rocked her beliefs to their foundation. According to everything written in the Tyrran reliquaries, once a soul attains the ancestral stars, it is guaranteed peace. How could this happen?

Berina tossed about with these thoughts and promised herself she wouldn't visit the glade for a while, perhaps never again. Late in the night she finally fell asleep.

Ruhallen, Northern Tyrra

Lady Vilje-Nelja Niisa kept the room warm, making Berina even more uncomfortable. The house was grand, with two parlors. As the largest house in the village, it might as well have been a palace. She sat opposite the matriarch in an upholstered chair. Her hands sweated as she traced the carvings on the arms.

"Your father drops you off like baggage, expecting me to decide your future just like that?" Niisa sounded like a tart old lady but by all appearances, she could easily live another forty years.

Father had shooed Berina toward the front door, refusing to come inside himself. She didn't know why he and Lady Niisa avoided each other. She glanced about, examining the familiar hand-hewn beams above and the worn, washed wood floors. It had been built around the year 1000, before there were lumber mills on the Whitewater or organized quarries.

"How old are you, child?" Niisa snapped her attention back.

"Almost sixteen, my lady." She couldn't legally marry until nineteen, but that wouldn't prevent Niisa from contracting her.

"Can you read and write?"

"Yes." She hesitated. "But I stopped formally practicing my letters."

"No need, once you stopped attending afternoon lessons? What does one need letters for on a farm?" The matriarch's tone was acerbic.

Niisa seemed annoyed with her visit, but Berina was getting irritated as well. "Figures are more important than letters on the farm and I keep Father's books quite well. The tables need labels, so that's my letter practice." Her voice was clipped and she stopped. It wouldn't do to antagonize her matriarch.

A hint of a smile touched Niisa's face. "You really are your mother's daughter."

"What was she like?" Berina asked the question that got her nowhere at home. Father didn't talk about his late wife. Erno didn't mind answering, but he couldn't remember much about their mother.

"Find the brown and black leather book for years 1450 through 1455, please. Over on the lower shelves." Niisa pointed.

Berina got the book and the matriarch set it on the table beside her, laying her hand gently on the cover. "There are bad memories here. I must warn you that these are the years during the Fevers, which were dark for everyone."

She swallowed hard, but nodded for the matriarch to continue.

"Your mother lost both her parents during the Fevers, but she was strong, beautiful, and courted by young men here in Ruhallen, as well as from Vehna's Crossing and Plains End. She should have been my replacement."

Niisa told the story of the courting of Vilje-Nelja Meris by Berina's father, who was then Arvella-Kolme Arvo from Plains End. It sounded like Meris and Arvo might have fallen in love. Unfortunately, Niisa told the story from a matriarchal viewpoint, covering the contract negotiations between the two lineages and how they became antagonistic. Eventually the Vilje-Nelja won, being the older lineage with more major stars. They were able to add her father and retain her mother. Erno was born within ten erins of the marriage. Afterward, Berina's mother started matriarchal training. Three years later came her own birth, resulting in the death of her mother.

"Thank you." She gave the matriarch a strained smile. She had hoped to learn about her mother as a person and understand why her father had such antipathy for Niisa. Instead, she got the dry history of a business deal.

Niisa closed the records. "Take this back to the shelf, Berina."

Grateful that Niisa was now using her name, she put the book back. As she returned to her chair, Luotetta popped her head in and reported the latest shipment of grapes had left on time. She was Niisa's niece and the matriarch-in-training, but many complained she had no spirit. Her eyes flickered over Berina, showing no curiosity. "I told the drivers they must feed their mules with last year's store of grain, not pillage what we get from the agent in Vehna's Crossing."

After Luotetta left, Berina sat and waited while Niisa opened another book that she kept by her side. As she found the page she wanted, she hummed a tune that sounded like the melody played during contract ceremonies. "Hmm. Sopi has expressed interest in you."

"With no encouragement from me!" Berina's face heated. How dare Sopi take such initiative, when they had barely ever talked? To hide her reaction, she examined the beamed ceilings that looked so comfortable and familiar.

Niisa eyed her sharply. "You have a duty to the Vilje-Nelja to make the best contract you can—one which helps financially and encourages children."

She stared down at her hands and tried not to sigh. Yes, this is the way things are done.

"But in your case, Sopi considers you a dreamer who should be restrained. Even though you two could make a viable contract, I don't consider you to have common ground." Niisa's tone became softer.

She looked up, surprised to see something like compassion in the matriarch's eyes.

"I hear that you disappear for hours. What do you do with your free time?" Apparently, Niisa listened to village gossip.

"I find quiet places and read old papers." Berina's father sometimes brought home a tattered Horn & Herald. The paper was often an erin old by the time she saw it, but she devoured it anyway.

"What sort of quiet places? The glade near the Vihrea Hilltops, where the last hermitage sits, perhaps?" Niisa's voice took on a strange tone.

She jerked her head to meet Niisa's gaze. The matriarch's light gray eyes glinted and the wrinkles deepened around her eyes. Looking around the room, remembering the hallways, she realized suddenly why everything seemed so familiar. "Lahna lived here, didn't she?"

Niisa pursed her lips. "Yes, this house was built for Sorceress Lahna. In this village, she taught many people the theory of magical arts. She resided here for many years before she withdrew to the hermitage in the glade."

"I think I feel her presence." She nearly choked on her words. This confession was comforting, but dangerous. She didn't know how Niisa would react and she certainly couldn't talk about her suspicions that Lahna had been pulled from the stars. That was as close to heresy as one could get in Tyrra.

"In the glade, or here?" The matriarch's eyes narrowed.

"Mostly in the glade. But this house is very familiar. I think I've seen it through her eyes."

Niisa chewed her lip. Then she closed her book with a snap, making Berina jump. "Your future shouldn't be decided in haste. Tell your father that I must see you every Farmday afternoon after mid-day meal, but not to worry."

Not to worry about what? Regardless of how Father might judge her interview, she was relieved. Sopi wasn't going to be forced upon her. She had also admitted to encountering Lahna's spirit, which eased her mind. When she met Father and Erno in the square, she repeated Lady Niisa's words. Father listened to the message without reaction.

"You must be a real contract problem," Erno jeered as they climbed into the wagon.

"At least there's interest in me, which is more than we can say for you." She spit her retort out without thought.

Erno flushed. He was quiet the entire ride back to the farm.

Betarr Serin, Tyrra

Only his first day in the sister cities and it hadn't gone well, by Naton's reckoning. At first, the informality of the king, the council, and the guards was insulting. He finally realized they didn't intend to be offensive; they just acted this way naturally.

Informality, however, did not mean friendly and trusting. That afternoon, a committee of Guard officers questioned him meticulously about Sareenian procedures and conventions, which he considered trivialities. This committee was responsible for Tyrran defense and run by the Captain of the King's Guard, Meran-Viisi Kilpi. While he grappled with their casual manners, they were downright hostile at times.

Commander Ruel had been the worst. She acted like he was lying with every answer even when there would be nothing to gain from evasion. She was King's Guard, like Captain Kilpi, while the other two members were constables—called "City Guard." Commander Jan had been unreadable, while his subordinate Lornis had been a breath of fresh air.

After the meeting, Lornis warned Naton about guard politics by steering him aside to a quiet foyer in the Palace of Stars. "Perhaps you didn't notice, but my commander made a grab for territory."

"Are you referring to the study of the charms that come from our desert tribes? But he volunteered your time, not his." Naton was confused. Jan had first belittled Lornis's concern about the imported charms, but then directed barbs at Ruel regarding resources he needed and "how thin the King's Guard was stretched these days." Obviously, he had missed something.

"If you want your career to survive, I caution you about Serasa-Kolme Jan. He's ambitious and dangerous, so stay out of his way. Whenever you deal with him, it's safest to be honest and straight-forward, even naive." A glint of humor shone in Lornis's brown eyes. "You should have seen his face when I asked his permission to court his previous wife."

"You needed his approval?" One element of Tyrran society Naton didn't understand was the remarriages arranged by the matriarchs. He found that numbering previous spouses was offensive: for instance, never say "second wife" or "first husband."

"Not at all," Lornis replied blandly. "I just forced everything into the open by asking for his approval. And, by asking him, he discounted me for a fool. Jan thinks it better to be secretive, because that's how he carries out all his affairs."

"Affairs?" Naton was lost.

"Yes, what's important to Jan are his career, his son, his money, and his women, in that order. If you must deal with any of those things that Jan holds dear, step carefully."

"What about Ruel? Why does she seem so angry?"

Lornis laughed. "She's just prickly. She had to be, to get the position of Deputy of Resources in such a short time. As a woman, she's fought more political battles than you ever will. The reason she and Jan went at it hammer and tongs is that they're both trying to impress Captain Kilpi."

"Oh." This conversation, while making him believe he had a friend in these strange cities, also made him feel more out of his depth.

They suddenly ran into Jhari in the streets—in retrospect, he realized the creature purposely intercepted them. "Greetings, Kulte-Kolme Lornis and Meran-Viisi Naton. We would speak with you both."

Not sure he liked being Meran-Viisi rather than Deldanta, Naton kept quiet while Lornis exchanged what sounded like polite but ritual phrases with the Phrenii.

Jhari proceeded with brutal efficiency. "Lornis, we request that you advance Naton's candidacy for the Kaskea with King Perinon. He has the requisite Meran blood and sensitivity to elemental magic, but the king is undecided because Naton was born Sareenian. We, however, cannot afford Perinon's fears about the council and the matriarchy."

"Uh..." Lornis seemed stunned.

"What's the Kaskea?" Naton asked.

"You want to bind a Sareenian to the aspect of—"

"Yes, this aspect." Jhari's melodious voice cut Lornis off. "Naton needs your advocacy."

"But why him, and why now? Can't you give the king time to consider this? He and Draius still haven't gotten over Siuru's death." Lornis's voice rose. "And why do you assume I have any sway with him?"

"We have little time left," Jhari said.

"Don't I get a choice in this matter?" The mention of Siuru's death sounded ominous to Naton.

"Of course. But we see that you will bind to us through the Kaskea and you will be instrumental in helping Lornis regain Tyrra. In this, we are certain." Jhari stamped its foot and a vibrating tone ran through the ground. "You must make your decision within five days, Naton."

With that, Jhari turned off the street and dissolved into the shadows of an alley. Naton glanced about, bewildered, and realized they stood near the gates of Betarr Serin. There was no one else about but the King's Guard gate detail and they didn't notice the bizarre confrontation. "Did that just happen, or am I having a fever dream?"

Lornis looked at him with sympathy. "Welcome to the league of people with Phrenic prophecies hanging over their heads."

"That was a prophecy?"

"Jhari's primary skill is prescience and the words 'in this, we are certain,' marks it as such." Lornis shook his head. "I never had mine read to me in the street, at least. It's been kept from me, thank the ancestors, but it looks like our futures are intertwined."

"But if I've been told I'm going to do something, do I really get to make a decision?"

"I don't know the answer to that." Lornis clapped a hand on his shoulder and steered him through the gate. They started down the winding road to Betarr Serasa. "But I can tell you a lot about the Kaskea."

So Lornis talked the entire way down to the lower city. He gave Naton background on the Phrenii and the Kaskea. Given that he was close to Draius, the other bearer of the Kaskea besides the king, he had insights the ordinary Tyrran wouldn't. The conversation shocked and disquieted Naton to the core. The process of binding could be deadly or incite madness; on the other hand, the Phrenii chose him specifically. However, the Phrenii had no place in the world he grew up in, so why should he think he was special?

"I suggest you mull this over and make your decisions as if you never heard the prophecy. By the way, you shouldn't repeat what Jhari said to anyone but the king. Who gets to bear the Kaskea is becoming a hot topic in the King's Council, although they'll never control the Phrenii." Lornis snorted.

It was evening by the time they separated at the Whitewater Bridge, and he asked Lornis whether there were any Churches of the Way in the sister cities. Lornis provided him with directions to three and he picked the closest one. The small church was tucked into a block of shops between the Whitewater bridge and the main city square. The Sareenian population in the sister cities grew due to the intense need for labor, and the Church of the Way came to Tyrra to support them.

The double doors were made of Sareenian rosewood, which must have cost this congregation handsomely. They had the traditional rays of light carved across them and, as expected, they weren't locked. He stepped in and immediately felt at home. The wooden floor was covered with rows of flat cushions. In the front, a brother of the Way tended the flame. There were no services today, so no one else was in the church.

"May I help you?" The brother came toward him with a smile.

"Yes, brother. I have decisions to make, but I wish my course to stay within our teachings."

"Of course." The brother appeared to be about thirty years old, with smile lines radiating from the corners of his dark eyes. He gestured Naton toward some cushions and they both knelt on their knees, facing the flame.

"The Way requires that through each life we search for enlightenment, considering the needs of others before ourselves. We must always fulfill our duties to our elders and our family. Only through living by the Way, through each lifetime, does our soul progress toward perfected Light." The brother's words were rote and they didn't help.

"I'm troubled about the Phrenii," Naton said.

"You wonder whether the Church recognizes them." The brother smiled. "Serving here in Tyrra, I often get that question. The Phrenii are made of starlight, so we accept the fact they travel the Way."

"But the Tyrrans and their Phrenii don't believe in the Way. How does that make them different from Groygans?"

"Tyrrans know the Way as 'the journey of souls.' While the Groygans follow darksome gods, the Tyrrans are a bit confused because they think they can reach perfected Light in one lifetime—and they think they see their ancestors in the stars. I have converted some Tyrrans to the Way; their view of the journey of souls merely needs adjustment." The brother's tone was condescending.

"But the Phrenii can't die, so they don't support the cycle of life."

"No, they don't." The brother hesitated. "But the Church considered this and came to the conclusion that the Phrenii are already perfected Light. They no longer need to progress along the Way."

So the Church of the Way fit the Phrenii into their doctrine as perfected Light, while Tyrrans considered them brothers to their ancestral stars. How could they be both? Naton tried to live by the Way because that was how he was raised, but he didn't consider himself very spiritual. He doubted either the Sareenians or the Tyrrans could give him complete answers concerning the Phrenii. If he went up to Jhari and bluntly asked it what it was—what would it say? Did he want to know?

"There is no need to be troubled. As an adult, you're unlikely to run into these creatures," the brother added.

Not as unlikely as you might think, brother. Naton hesitated, but he felt a desperate need to confide in someone and a church was always a safe and comforting haven. "The Phrenii have asked me to bear the Kaskea, to be bound to them."

The brother's face lit up. "But this is wondrous! They ask a Sareenian to commune with them?"

Naton leaned away. For a moment, something unsavory flashed through the brother's eyes. Was it greed for power? Envy? Then it was gone and perhaps he was mistaken, but he decided not to mention the prophecy anyway. "I'm half Tyrran, and the Phrenii say my mother's Meran blood runs strong. That is probably why they offer me the Kaskea."

The brother looked disappointed, but he grasped Naton's shoulder. "There is no reason to turn down power and enlightenment, as long as you stay on the Way of the Light, my son."

Power and enlightenment? What about the insanity and death, the risks Lornis explained with grim detail? "Brother, please don't misunderstand me. There's no chance the Tyrran king will bind me to the Kaskea, regardless of what the Phrenii say. They are at odds."

"Strange, that they should defy the Tyrran king." The brother frowned. "I should consult my superiors on this."

"No," he said quickly. "Please don't tell anyone. I said this in the privacy of the Light, brother. I expect your confidence."

"If you wish, Ser Deldanta." The brother bowed and when he raised his head, his eyes slid sideways and didn't meet Naton's.

He bid goodbye to the brother and walked away more disturbed than when he entered. The brother slipped, using Naton's name when he couldn't have known it. Now he wished he'd never confided in him. How could the brother of a small church in Betarr Serasa recognize him? Pater Deldanta privately distrusted the Church and wouldn't have told them about his son's whereabouts. But it was possible his stepsister Sangha or half-brother Milos sent a letter to brothers in Tyrra.

He had also been disturbed by the brother's reaction to the possibility of a Sareenian wielding the Kaskea. For the past decade, the Church had been accused of political aims, as well as corruptness. Pater Dimoni of Forenllas had imprisoned Avo Cabaran, a popular author of such heresy. All the Sareenian city-states banned Cabaran's works and everyone knew the Church of the Way had something to do with that.

The shops were closed and the street deserted. He wasn't surprised to see Jhari standing at the end of the street waiting for him, luminescent in the gaslight from the street lamps. Squinting his eyes, he saw whirling, blue sparks deep inside the creature.

In a flash of prescience that struck him with a sudden headache, Naton knew he would bear the Kaskea.

CHAPTER ELEVEN

Pigeons

Agrottre Village, Northern Groyga

Ugettore shook Draius awake at dawn. "There be groats and bacon ready downstairs. Sattore's doing much better, so you can leave him for a while to eat."

She lay on the floor beside his son's bed, between two blankets. Suppressing a groan, she threw off the top blanket and pulled herself to her knees, just to make sure Ugettore was correct. Sattore appeared better: no longer pale and breathing deep, the result of finally getting some broth yesterday evening as well as having Phrenic healing sessions every four hours, courtesy of her bond with Dahni.

Her mind ticked off the days. This was the third morning since Sattore had been wounded. Someone always watched her; during the nighttime it was Ugettore and during the daytime, Chiune. Ugettore helped by getting her clean bandages and making sure she ate enough to keep her strength up. Not Chiune, who radiated hostility and doubt. The old woman's eyes narrowed as green light poured from the Kaskea and her palms as she tried to make Sattore's body create and richen his blood. However, no one could argue with the results. Sattore would eventually be as healthy as ever, although he would sport an ugly scar on his neck.

She stretched and yawned. It was also the thirty-ninth day since she left Peri and Lornis in Betarr Serasa. She spared a few moments to pray to her ancestors for their health and well-being—then belatedly added Bordas to the prayer. By now, if Endigala's guards hadn't caught him, he should be entering Kitarra. Counter to the way she acted, she believed his escape and evasion skills were better than hers. She gave him the spare shard and ordered him home because he had the better probability of getting there. *Home.* Her thoughts shied away from that painful longing inside.

Hearing Ugettore clatter downstairs in the small kitchen made her stomach growl. She carefully climbed down the narrow steep steps to the ground floor and smelled the bacon as soon as she turned toward the kitchen.

Ugettore's wife died a couple years ago. Now the blacksmith and his son managed to get on in their own fashion. As he ladled out some boiled groats into a bowl, he talked about how he and Sattore distributed the work each morning and made their plans for the coming day. She knew he had to talk about his son's life—it reinforced the positive for him: his son *would* survive and he *would* be able to do the same activities as before. It reminded her to be confident as well.

"How's he doing?" Chiune entered Ugettore's house unannounced, as she did every morning since Draius had been there. Yesterday, she learned the mayoress was Sattore's maternal grandmother. This morning, Mattogre accompanied her.

Ugettore jerked his head toward Draius, apparently wanting her to answer.

"I think he's safe from setbacks now. He drank some broth in the early evening and has been sleeping ever since. Hopefully, he'll need nothing more than food and rest from now on."

"What is happening inside his body?" Chiune's eyes narrowed. "You have insight different from any healer I ever met."

"I don't know what's happening. I never used—" These people did *not* want to know that her healing power came from demons. "To be honest,

I've only ever healed horses." The truth was always best to use with Chiune, who seemed to have a built-in sense for lies.

Ugettore, filling his bowl of groats, backed up her story. "She healed my poor pony the morning she arrived."

"But who did you shout to when you first stopped Sattore's bleeding?" Unfortunately, Chiune had an excellent memory.

"I made a plea to someone who travels the path to the stars." This was also true: the Phrenii were made of starlight and they escorted departed souls along the path, so they must travel it as well.

"A prayer to one of your ancestors?"

Knowing she was a notoriously bad liar, Draius nodded and tried to look earnest.

Chiune shook her head, as if to bemoan all godless Tyrrans. "And you've only healed *horses* to this point? What made you think you could heal humans?"

"I asked her to—really, I begged her." Ugettore's deep voice had a sensible tone. "What's done is done, and my son is alive. *I am in her debt, mayoress.*"

His last phrase changed the situation subtly. Chiune looked like she made a decision. "Well, we won't be charging you or even your friend in absentia. A Groygan hand held the knife and he's devastated by what happened as well."

Draius decided to nod, look grateful, and start eating her breakfast. Channeling Dahni's healing, or whatever she had been doing, required a lot of energy and left her starving. Luckily, her stomach didn't interrupt this conversation with its grumbling yowls. Something was up with Chiune, though, and why was Mattogre here? She observed them as she shoveled groats into her mouth and supplemented it with bacon. For such simple food, it tasted wonderful and Ugettore was a good cook, despite his protests.

"Would you two like breakfast?" Like her, Ugettore must sense something hanging over them, something unsaid.

"No, we haven't the time." Chiune exchanged a glance with Mattogre. "We've had news from the northern estate. Do you have any experience with poison, Draius?"

She nearly choked on her groats and had to wipe her mouth. "Not really, mayoress."

"But Sattore still needs her," Ugettore said.

"It sounds like the herbalist could take over. This is important—"

Ugettore interrupted Chiune and the conversation exploded into Groygan. All three of them started arguing, with long many-syllabic words flying fast and furious. This northern dialect was different from the Groygan Draius learned down in Chikirmo. She caught important names, hearing "Endigala" and "Chintegrata." Once in a while, there was a familiar noun like "road," "horse," and "guards." That last word was concerning, since it was close to "Endigala."

She took advantage of the argument by pouring Ugettore's groats into her bowl and finishing them off. If she was going to go on a trip, she might as well have a full stomach.

● ● ●

The argument between Ugettore, Chiune, and Mattogre was not about whether Draius should stay, but whether they could protect her on the road. They were taking her to Lord Chintegrata's northern estate. When she asked why, they gave her no answer other than she was "needed."

Even though she didn't know the *why*, the *how* of getting there was obvious. Chiune and Mattogre drove up a team of horses pulling a covered wagon. Heavy broadcloth stretched over square ribs, covering the entire bed but not the front bench. Chisel was tied to the back gate, over which hung a black banner. He nickered when she rushed over to rub his face. She hadn't seen him since Sattore was wounded.

"What's this for?" She pointed to the broad black banner that blocked her view of the wagon area. It had a large symbol embroidered in red upon it.

Mattogre stood beside her, holding Chisel's saddle. "That is the symbol for the god Surmagla. He's the Master of Choice and—"

"Death. So this indicates you're carrying someone who's dying? Or does it indicate a body?"

"Either one. Now, if you'll pull that aside so I can load this."

She did as he asked and noted a pallet covered in black cloth, as well as the sleeping roll and pack that used to be tied behind her saddle. There were also two extra sleeping rolls and another pack.

He carefully draped the saddle over her pack. "Of course, the deceased will need to be buried with his treasured possessions."

"*His* possessions?"

"Your horse is too tall for most of our females. The only road north is crawling with Endigala's guards. They can't miss him and they'll want to glance inside. Your height and—um—lack of female curves should convince them you're a man. There'll be a sick cloth over your face and body."

So she was *lucky* to be lanky and rather lacking in the bust area. But Chisel... She sucked her teeth contemplatively and looked at the long-time companion she refused to abandon. He looked exactly like the horse described in the Endigala reward flyer they showed her. "They're not going to believe he's Groygan-bred."

"No. That horse was found three days ago by the deceased."

"If they decide to take Chisel, they'll know that the *deceased* couldn't have *ridden* him."

"That's what we told Vinca, when we warned him against riding it. But he was stubborn. Got a bad head injury when he was thrown, so he's simple now." Mattogre gave her a sly smile.

"So Vinca's—I'm not dead? Just in the process of dying?"

Mattogre nodded. "I should have said *nearly deceased*. The head injury's a mercy, really. Vinca's wife died from the Fevers only an eight-day ago, poor woman, and he's started to show blisters. Feel free to moan, but not too much."

"Oh." She almost recoiled, herself, from the black banner. "You have cases of the Fevers right now?"

"Yes. It crops up now and then, maybe once a year. Here in the hinterlands, it may travel through a family but it'll stop there. In Chikirmo the healers are vigilante, always watching for signs. They try to catch it in early stages, isolate it, and suppress any news about it, so we never know when it pops up in the city." Mattogre patted Chisel on the neck and went to check the team and its traces and harness.

"I sure hope this works," she muttered to Chisel.

To disguise her, Mattogre rubbed light red clay on her face, hands, and lower arms. He wrapped a wide bolt of cheesecloth around her clothes and stood back, told her to close her eyes, and flicked a brush laden with beet juice at her. He handed her a small mirror and she saw that they turned into red dots all over her exposed skin; in shadows, they could be blood blisters. They unwrapped the cheesecloth and folded it so that it became her "sick cloth." It would be laid over her and there was just enough beet juice in random areas to indicate blood had been transferred from the blisters.

"You're going to want to keep that over your nose, eyes, and ears," Mattogre said. "I've got two small pails of rotten fruit in the corners of the wagon—make sure you don't knock them over. They're going to attract a lot of flies."

So began a very uncomfortable trip. She took to the straw pallet, lying on her back—which flattened her chest enough under the swaths of cheesecloth to please Mattogre. A wrapped, black cloth covered her hair. The sun was coming up as they left Agrottre and the day was "very mild," according to the Groygans, but it was stifling for her. Then there was the maddening buzzing of the flies. The saving grace was that she always had water; in fact, Chiune made it a point to periodically climb back and give her a drink regularly.

"Everything we do supports the cover story," Mattogre said.

The cover *story*. Having a background for the character you imperson-
ated helped you remember things consistently. Prideful, arrogant Vinca
became pathetic, idiotic Vinca. It was a sobering story for her, because
she had been called prideful more than a few times during her life, the
result of wanting to do everything herself, never asking for help, and also
mistaking pride for honor. But Peri's kidnapping and binding herself to
the Phrenii had knocked down her pride a few rungs. *Or had it?* Again,
she suffered twinges of guilt remembering how much she argued with
Bordas.

They had been on the road a couple hours when the first pair of Endigala's guards stopped them because of Chisel. Mattogre gave them the
whole story about poor Vinca. The buzzing flies put them off enough that
they only peeked around the black banner to verify that someone lay in
the back. Draius moaned in a low voice and the banner flicked back into
place. Unfortunately, these guards took a liking to Chisel, even though
he'd been trained to carry one specific rider.

"Are you going to pay us the reward money for the horse?" Mattogre
asked.

"Of course not," said the guard with the deepest voice. "The reward is
for finding the *rider* of the horse."

"Well, then, you'll have to take this up with Lord Chintegrata. We're
taking poor Vinca up to the estate one last time, and his lordship is taking
the horse in exchange for keeping Vinca's children on as tenants."

"We won't interfere with his lordship," the guard replied quickly. Apparently, they didn't want to get on Chintegrata's bad side while passing
through his holdings. They continued north.

Throughout the day, Chiune and Mattogre kept her apprised of what
was happening along the road. Perhaps they worried the soul-sucking
boredom would make her do something stupid. At one point, when a
faster vehicle passed them, Chiune said, "Oh, no, another Endigala pigeon
wagon is passing us by! Mattogre, you're going too slow."

Mattogre laughed; it sounded like a common joke between them. "These horses have to last another day."

"What's a pigeon wagon and why is House Endigala using it?" Draius moved forward and smelled the smoke from Chiune's pipe wafting into the back. She peeked through the curtain.

"Don't worry—those drivers aren't looking for you. They're only interested in getting those homing pigeons delivered. The lords use them for overland communications." Chiune's words became clipped when she talked around her pipe while it was clenched in her teeth.

"So that whole load is being delivered to Lord Chintegrata so he can communicate with Lord Endigala?"

"There are agreements between the lords, yes. In this case, Houses Endigala and Chintegrata exchange six birds an erin."

Draius frowned. She caught a glimpse of the pigeon wagon and it had huge, crowded cages. "That was more than six birds."

"Yes, it was." Chiune took a deep drag of her pipe.

"So who's getting all those birds?"

Chiune blew the smoke out slowly. "I can't tell you that. If you get the chance to talk to Lord Chintegrata, ask his lordship where Endigala's pigeons are going."

"I'm going to meet Lord Chintegrata?" A tiny flicker of alarm started in her chest, but her hot and tired body squelched it. She had become too tired to worry.

"Maybe." The finality in Chiune's tone closed the conversation. Draius continued to think about pigeons and how the King's Guard depended upon the Phrenii for almost instantaneous emergency communications, while using horseback messengers and regular mail service for routine matters. For hundreds of years, the Phrenii had been dependable and given them an advantage, at least *inside* Tyrra. *But look at what's happened to me here in Groyga.* She wondered how hard it would be to breed and raise homing pigeons.

Another hour or two went by. "We've got more of Endigala's guards coming along the road from the north," Chiune told her. "Prepare yourself. These have already been told about us."

She had gotten lax, sitting behind Chiune and peeking through the tied slit of the bed cover. Scrambling back on the pallet, she tried to arrange the yards and yards of sick cloth and started to panic. She stopped, took some deep breaths, and finally got it arranged correctly. It had to cover her mouth, nose, and eyes, of course. There had to be loose waves over the rest of her body.

As expected, they were told to stop. From the sounds, there were at least two males and one female guard. Again, they were asked where they got the horse.

Mattogre launched into the story of Vinca again. Draius was impressed. As Officer in Charge of Investigation, she had conducted a lot of interviews and a good number of interrogations. When asking questions multiple times she watched for two indications of falsehood: the first was a story told by rote, and the second was an inconsistent story. Most people, when truthfully recounting a story multiple times, would expand upon different things and possibly remember other details, but stay consistent within the framework of their story. Mattogre did just that. If she didn't know that Vinca was a figment of his imagination, she'd believe him if she were interviewing him. He was so good that she wondered if he did more for Chintegrata than run a small trading post in Agrottre. Where better to put a talented intelligencer than in the middle of Groyga, right next to the main north-south thoroughfare?

There were slight grunts when Mattogre hit the story highlights the guards expected. One guard, though, became a stickler for procedure. "We should check the body."

"Vinca's not dead yet, so technically he's not a *body*." Mattogre gently corrected the female guard. "Lord Chintegrata has granted Vinca one last audience and we're expected there by tomorrow afternoon. His lordship will take possession of the Tyrran horse at that time."

This time, invoking Chintegrata's name didn't legitimize Mattogre's mission. Neither did the groans of her fellow guards, when the female continued to press. "We should check this Vinca and whatever else is in the back of your wagon."

"Come on, Arla! He has the *Fevers*. Aren't you taking Falcona's pledge of courage a little too far?"

"And perhaps *you've* taken the Sareenian pledge of poltroonery." The woman was definitely a hothead. She would, come hellfire or high water, get into the back of the wagon.

Draius let the outside sounds fade and sent her memory back to times she had ignored for more than a decade, hoping to wall them off permanently. The Fevers. Her mother dying. Her friends dying. The king dying. The Phrenii stumbling with exhaustion. *So much death*—she struggled to keep her thoughts impersonal. What were the stages, what stage was Vinca in? Initially, one's blood burned and one experienced everything from seizures to hallucinations. The painful blisters started and one screamed whenever one moved or had sheets rest upon one's body. Once exhausted, one slipped into a sort of trance preparatory to death.

Then *she* didn't know her daughter any more, she rarely opened her eyes because she couldn't handle the brightness, and her breathing became a moan and rattle... Draius purged the unbidden images of her mother as tears squeezed out of her eyes. *No!* Picturing her mother young and healthy instead, she took a breath. She couldn't create the rattle, but she could breathe hoarsely and moan in a low pitch.

"You hear that, Arla?" Three guards walked beside the wagon toward its tail.

"It's great to have a handmaiden with a death wish in our company," the other male guard said.

"Less work for you. Right, Ugo?" Arla slapped one of them on the back. It sounded like a shot from a gun.

"Ow!" Ugo, who had mentioned the death wish, wasn't appreciative.

"Just hold up Surmagla's banner for me," she said.

Draius had her head bent and a little to the side so she could see Arla enter. She lay on her back, with her feet facing the wagon's gate. They lifted the banner and dropped the gate. She had the advantage because the inside would at first appear dark, but she was also a bit blinded by the sunlight. Arla was just a dark figure against the light, but then she resolved into a woman who must have had giant blood—she stood a head taller than the two men. *And Mattogre thought* I *was tall?* Arla had her fists on her hips and her head bent forward so she could peer into the back. Her bronze skin reflected the sunlight; her exposed arms were bundles of muscles, her face and square jaw were entirely made of hard planes, and her golden-orange eyes glowed. Then Draius closed her own eyes, being a color that would betray her as Tyrran. Mattogre had been careful to brush the pinkish clay over her eyelids, anticipating this.

Arla tapped the soles of Draius's boots with her knife. "He's still dressed in the clothes he wore when the Fevers dropped him."

Draius continued her hoarse breathing, moaning softly as her breath went out.

"Yeah, it's gonna smell in there." Ugo's tone implied a sly grin.

That didn't dissuade Arla, who immediately stepped up on the wagon's bed. Draius felt it tilt and dip from her weight. The third, unnamed guard yammered advice. "Be careful. Don't touch the bloody sick cloth with your bare skin. Use your knife to lift it. Whatever you do, don't lean over the face and breathe the poor sod's fumes."

"Yeah, yeah." Arla's tone was flippant. She shuffled, probably in a crouch, beside the pallet until she was even with Draius's shoulders and head. The sick cloth rose until her forehead and closed eyes were exposed. She concentrated on continuing her hoarse breathing at the same rate. *Breathe in, moan out.*

"He's still alive, but he's got lots of blisters and his skin has this deathly gray cast," Arla said for the benefit of her comrades.

Arla's breath wafted across her face. Luckily, the woman rocked the bed when she leaned down toward Draius. Thus, she didn't jump when Arla whispered in her ear. "Open your eyes, Vinca."

She continued to breathe and moan. Arla clucked in disappointment. She felt the point of Arla's knife trace down the side of her forehead. Then the blade was laid sideways against her cheek. What would she do if she was delirious from the Fevers and felt something cold on her face? Moaning, she rolled her head into it. A little prick burned her face and the knife moved away.

"Uh, oh," Arla said.

Draius felt the tickle of blood rolling down her cheek. She ignored it. *Breathe in, moan out.*

"You satisfied?" Ugo called.

Arla made her way out. "He's not long for this world." She almost sounded sad.

"What's wrong? Did you take a liking to this skinny sack of bones?" Ugo asked. "He looks a bit effeminate."

"That's how I like 'em." Arla laughed and the other two guffawed.

The gate was pegged back up and the banner dropped. Draius started shaking as the guards walked back around to talk to Mattogre and she couldn't stop. She held her hands together and curled over to her side, pressing her bleeding cheek into the pallet.

"You say you're delivering the horse and bod—er, Vinca—to Lord Chintegrata?" After Mattogre affirmed that, Arla added, "Just to keep you honest, we'll escort you to his gates. Don't want you to fall prey to any bandits, do we?"

Lord Chintegrata's Estate, Northern Groyga

The rest of the day and evening were agony for Draius, because Arla and her cohorts stayed behind the wagon at all times. When Chiune came back to give her water, Arla would bring her horse close and flip up the back banner to watch. Chiune would murmur, "It's going to be all right," which sounded exactly like what she would say to someone dying.

They had stopped for an evening rest period when she was saved. Chiune explained to Area that they were going to keep going through the night, she and Mattogre shifting off as driver and keeping with two-hour rest stops for the horses. This didn't dissuade Arla, but she and her comrades were less and less polite as nightfall came. Draius began to worry for Chiune's and Mattogre's safety, thinking the guards were going to loot and kill them all, when there was the sound of riders coming down the road. She couldn't tell how many: at least two, but less than six. Arla's cohorts scrambled to mount their own horses.

"Greetings, mayoress," called a male voice from the new group of riders. "Lord Chintegrata sent us to meet you." The voice sharpened. "We didn't expect camp followers."

Draius pictured mounted guards in yellow and black facing off with ones in red and black, with Chiune and Mattogre in between. She silently rolled toward her pack and felt for her saber. Of course, it was in the deepest place possible and difficult to get quietly. It didn't take the ring of steel to know that blades were drawn; trained soldiers drew their knives and swords in silence.

"We're an *escort*," Ugo said sullenly.

"I might believe you if your sergeant here wasn't threatening the mayoress of Agrottre with a knife."

"Forgive me. It was just habit to draw it." Arla sheathed her knife with an obvious ring and the sound of boots scraping in gravel, so she didn't mount up. "We felt we should escort them, considering the absence of any security from House Chintegrata."

"Then you can be about your way." Chintegrata's guard had disdain dripping from his voice, as did Arla. In fact, everyone in the small camp was wallowing in disdain—not to mention aggression.

Draius found the hilt of her saber and drew it from the pack. It sounded like three horses trotted out to the road, but she was crouched, her sword ready, when Chiune drew back the Surmagla covering.

"I told you that it'd be all right," Chiune said.

"How did they know—oh." She put down her saber. "Homing pigeons, of course."

"We started out from the estate as soon as we got the message." The guard leader beside Chiune grinned. "You look pretty good for someone who's on Surmagla's doorstep."

"Let's not waste any more time," Chiune said.

"Speaking of time, we have even less now. He's taken a turn for the worse." He and Chiune exchanged a glance, and then he looked at Draius. "How good are you on horseback?"

Her heart leapt at the chance to ride in the open air. "I trained horses all my life. My horse—"

"They're still watching us through spyglasses, so your horse must stay with the wagon. You'll be exchanging places with one of my guards—it'll be a man, no doubt." He eyed her head, so she pulled off the covering and her braids sprung out. "Will that hair fit beneath a helmet?"

"Probably not one of Groygan design."

"We'll cut it." Chiune's tone was cheery. Draius winced, remembering the hack job she did on Bordas.

Everything was done inside the wagon. After she undid her braids and her crinkled hair puffed up even more, Chiune combed water through it and started working with a knife. After she got over the shock from looking in Mattogre's small mirror, she admitted it appeared better than Bordas's. She tried to cut his hair all the same length, but Chiune cut front parts shorter and layered the rest around the back of her head. At first, the lengths seemed chaotic, but the cut had a flow to it and her thick hair now fit under her double's helmet. Unfortunately, she resembled a Tyrran man who had cut his hair unfashionably. It barely brushed her shoulders, meaning she would now fit better into the Kitarran male population. *If this haircut gets me home, I can handle looking idiotic.*

Her double was an unusually thin Groygan, who was having a lot of fun doing this swap. This was all for the purpose of hoodwinking House Endigala and he enjoyed playing a dramatic part in it. He crawled into the back of the wagon and submitted to beet juice treatment while she crawled out—wearing his helmet, his uniform doublet and sleeves, and her own saber. Changing breeches and boots didn't seem necessary; hers were dark enough to almost match theirs.

She mounted her double's horse, a sturdy and cooperative gelding about two hands shorter than Chisel. As she rode out with the other three guards in yellow and black, she glanced back. The wagon with the tall horse behind it was getting on the road. Chiune and Mattogre weren't wasting any time.

The ride was brutal, considering she had lain in the back of a hot wagon for almost twelve hours. They took short rests to give the horses water every hour. The night was cool and clear so the starlight was bright. They cantered two and two; she was behind and to the side of the road. The few times they passed anyone traveling south, she turned away and kept her head down to take advantage of helmet brim's shadow.

Despite the exhilaration of having *air* flow past her, she was drained by the time they rode through the gates of Lord Chintegrata's northern estate. The eastern sky glowed orange. After she dismounted, she staggered.

The guard leader was instantly at her elbow. "Are you all right? Will you be able to heal?"

"I'll need food and water. Otherwise, I can't..." She realized how little she had to eat yesterday after getting on the road.

The guard leader whisked her to the back of the complex, past an outdoor meat roasting pit, and into a kitchen where there were the heavenly smells of newly baked breads and pastries. She was practically force-fed bread with butter and bowls of strawberries with cream. When she declined a third bowl, he snapped into action.

"Follow me." He led her into the house itself, down narrow hallways with dark waxed wood floors. She noticed the three other guards who rode with her now formed a security barrier around her: the leader in front and the other two in back, ready to move to the side when they traversed large rooms.

She was here to heal someone male and important to Lord Chintegrata, but when she saw a group of people clustered outside double doors to a great bedchamber and caught mutterings about "his lordship," she knew who it was.

"This is Lady Lorette Be Chintegrata, acting physician to his lordship." The guard leader brought Draius to a thin Groygan woman who was listening to three people argue in muted tones. She turned away from the argument almost gratefully.

"Lady Chintegrata." Greeting her the Groygan way, Draius bowed. Since Lorette had "Be" instead of "Bene" in front of her lineal name, she had been born with the Chintegrata name instead of marrying into it. In all likelihood, she was *not* married to the lord.

Lorette's face was lined by many years. Now those lines formed into cautious interest as she glanced between Draius and the guard leader. Her glasses highlighted amber, almost brown eyes. "This is Agrottre's answer to his lordship's ailment?" Her Tyrran was flawless.

"Yes, the Tyrran woman hunted by House Endigala. Her name is Serasa-Kolme Draius and she's proven herself to be a healer." Chiune must have vouched for her with the guard leader, which was a surprise.

"Where's Mayoress Chiune? Why isn't she personally endorsing this foreigner?"

"We had to rescue them from House Endigala. The mayoress and intelligencer are following us in a wagon, while Draius rode horseback with my guards. We left the Rock Creek intersection three hours before midnight."

"You made good time, Sergeant Rorga." Lorette adjusted her glasses to examine Draius from head to foot. "And you say Endigala's people now threaten travelers upon our lands? They overstep their bounds, almost as though they know his lordship is ailing."

"They can't know, my lady." The guard leader stood taller. "Our people are loyal and they report back any interest in his lordship's health. So far, they found none."

"They may have other sources of information." Lorette raised her glasses to rub her eyes. "Now then, Draius. I hear your healing powers do not depend upon unguents or elixirs, so how do they work? Can you detect mysterious poisons?"

She took a deep breath, but paused as she surveyed the room. "Is there some place we may speak privately?"

"No," Rorga said. "Not without me or my guards to ensure my lady's safety."

After all, they were ancient enemies. "Perhaps you only, if the lady pleases?"

The lady did, and presently she, Rorga, and Lorette were alone in a small sitting room. She and Rorga continued to stand as Lorette seated herself on the settee and leaned back.

"Go ahead. Explain your powers before I fall asleep." Lorette's eyelids already started to droop.

"My healing powers are based upon true elemental magic and they are borrowed." Draius kept her gaze on her tensely intertwined fingers as she talked. This was not the same situation as Sattore; he was still a child, his father was begging her to save him, and time was of the essence. Now Lorette had to make a crucial decision and she needed to know all the facts. *I suppose she might decide to execute me*—she hoped she wouldn't end up being burned alive as a demon's helper. Lorette had been educated in a great house and had become a physician; with any luck, she was not prone to superstition.

When Draius finished, she looked up. Rorga was pale. Lorette seemed to be looking at something far away. She adjusted her glasses and asked in a perfectly normal voice, "What are the side effects of this Phrenic healing?"

"There is a claim the Phrenii will own your soul if *they* heal you. The Phrenii insist this is superstition. My friend—" She shouldn't describe Lornis as just a friend. "Someone close to me was healed of a gunshot to the gut by the Phrenii. He said he now has more empathy, intuition, and understanding of people; he can easily tell when someone is lying or hiding something. Other than that, he's healthy and energetic, with no other repercussions from the gunshot."

"Does he feel younger?" Lorette asked.

"He didn't mention that, but he's in his twenties and was only healed last spring. Time will tell. Phrenic healing doesn't claim to extend life—other than keeping one healthier and more fertile or virile." She tried not to blush. "Keep in mind that being healed by the Phrenii is no doubt different from being healed by me. I am only borrowing the power, and only with their permission."

"Hmm." Lorette tapped her fingers on the arm of the settee. Rorga's color started to return, but he jumped when she exclaimed, "Let my brother decide. His lordship would know whether he could live with the side effects."

"Is he lucid?" Draius asked.

"Hopefully." Her answer didn't sound convincing. Lorette got up and smoothed her gown. "I must first ask for your word that you will not describe my brother's condition to anyone outside of that room."

"On my honor," Draius swore.

"If you must do any manual procedures or touch him, direct me or Sergeant Rorga to do it for you."

"I will."

Lorette finally motioned for Draius and Rorga to follow her through a door on the opposite wall. They walked down a dark hall and Lorette opened another door right into his lordship's bedchamber.

At first glance, Lord Chintegrata appeared better than she expected. He sat up and his countenance was alert, but then she noticed he couldn't lift his arms. His flesh hung and his bones used to carry much more muscle.

"Don't you dare give him that!" Lorette cried.

Draius watched her confront a woman with a glass of murky liquid. "But, my lady, this is a healing remedy we thought might—"

"Who let you in?"

The woman turned to look at the guard at the door.

Lorette rubbed her forehead. "Your loyalty is strong, but it will cause a bad reaction. I tried to explain this. Now, everyone go. Leave us alone."

The guards got a nod from Rorga to confirm, then escorted everyone out. Once the door was closed, Lorette held Draius's gaze. "This is why I'm willing to let you use your magic. Anything we give him, anything he tries to drink, he violently throws up. The more nutrients, the worse his reaction. It seems..." She shuddered. "It's an *evil curse*, not a disease." She raised her chin in determination. "So I've decided to fight magic with magic."

"I assume you ruled out wasting disease?" Draius moved around the bed. His lordship's eyes followed her every move but he didn't say anything. He tried to lick his lips and she saw he was parched, but hadn't touched the full flask beside his bed.

"There is no wasting disease that can drop several stone in less than an eight-day," Lorette answered.

Draius raised her eyebrows. "When did the vomiting start?"

"About three days ago."

"And you checked what he ate—"

"He has a food taster who tries everything. The taster hasn't fallen ill."

"Did he go anywhere different—"

"We have retraced his steps again and again. His personal guards were always with him or only a door away. No one else has been affected." Lorette knelt beside the bed and held one of Chintegrata's hands in her own. "Brother, my requests for healers have brought us someone who purportedly uses true magic for healing, not like the witch we tried. But this is *Tyrran* magic and there are consequences."

As Lorette briefly covered the side effects, Lord Chintegrata frowned and his eyes went to Draius. They held each other's gaze for a moment and she felt he was not pleased.

"I can give you another option," she added. "The—this magic can give me insight into your body. I *may* be able to detect poisons and internal cankers. Let me try to determine what's happening first, then you can decide if you want to go through with the healing."

Chintegrata nodded.

"Please, don't be frightened by the green light." Draius put her hands out over his feet, palms down, and closed her eyes. She tried to sense his body's functions. As expected, green light leaked through her eyelids and she heard Lorette gasp. She sensed the channels of blood and the tinge of Darkness in them. "I think there is some poison in the blood, but I'm not sure that is the main problem."

She started moving up his body. When she came to his torso, she paused. *Poor man.* She sensed the gnawing hunger in the stomach, but also the flaming heat of the tissues. Her hands went over his chest. His breathing seemed okay—suddenly, she yelped and jerked her hands back. Nausea took over and she pressed her forearm to her mouth and looked wildly about. Lorette pointed to the pail beside Chintegrata's bed and she crouched, vomiting into it.

"What's the problem?" Lorette didn't sound impressed by her magical healer throwing up, just like her brother.

"Necromancy. He's wearing a charm." She turned her palms out, showing her red and blistered fingers. "They're burned."

"Well, at least burns are something I can treat. Come over here." Lorette had Draius hold her hands out over the washbasin while she poured cold water over them. Then she rummaged in a bag on the bureau and pulled out a salve. Once she put the salve on, she said, "I'd better bandage them. Can you still heal him if I do that?"

"I think so. One of you will want to remove the charm. Do you have gloves?" she asked Rorga.

He pulled some gloves out of his belt and put them on.

"Look around his neck. That's where Taalo put the one that almost killed me."

"Who is this Taalo?" Lorette tied the first bandaged hand firmly, making Draius wince. "Also, I can guarantee that there is nothing around my brother's neck. We would have seen that." She tied the second bandage just as tight.

Draius went up to the head of the bed where Chintegrata rested as Rorga leaned in from the other side and lifted the collar of the nightshirt. "There it is. The leather thong around his neck."

"Where?" Rorga asked. Lorette stood behind him and peered as well.

"It's by the fingertips of your right hand." She pointed with her bandaged hand.

"I don't see anything," Lorette said.

"He used an obscuring spell, just like with mine. Feel for it and try to lift it away from the body."

Rorga shrugged and tried. "I do feel something. Wait a minute." He hooked the leather thong and as he pulled it away from Chintegrata's skin, it became visible. The sack was below the nightshirt, but until Rorga started tugging, it didn't even shape the fabric above it. Eventually, Rorga had it off and held it out in front of him.

"Oh! I think that's what I bought in Chikirmo. It was a sleeping remedy." Lorette's eyes widened.

Draius first had to ensure its correct disposal. "Rorga, take this to the hottest fire you have. If you've got a forge, that'll do just fine. Don't let anyone breath in the fumes while it burns. After it burns, there'll be bones. Don't let anyone touch those, either. Bury them deep where they'll never be found."

Rorga nodded and ran. She momentarily heard a hubbub of voices as he opened and closed the door. Meanwhile, Lord Chintegrata was pointing to the flask of liquid just out of his reach. She grabbed it and sniffed; it was wine diluted with fruit juice. With no cup in sight, she just handed the flask to him and he took several gulps, pausing in between and waiting. Then he gazed up at her and smiled.

"There's still the matter of the poison in your blood, but I think the major part of the charm was to make everything you ate, or drank, a poison that your body tried to reject. It also hastened your weight loss."

Lord Chintegrata pointed at his sister, who stood with her hand across her mouth and her eyes wide in horror. Her face looked drained of blood. Draius went to her and took her hands, leading her to a chair.

"I'm the one," Lorette whispered. "I don't remember buying it, but I remember seeing it and feeling it would be perfect for his lordship. *I* nearly killed my own brother."

"Please, Lady Chintegrata, don't blame yourself." She squeezed the woman's hands. "Taalo can make you forget—he did that to me and I have perfect memory. He obscured it from anyone loyal to House Chintegrata, so none of you could see it." Her voice hardened. "He's become much too powerful." *And I had a chance to kill him, and I didn't.*

"This is not your fault." Chintegrata's voice was scratchy and whispery, but they both heard it. He already seemed better.

"My little brother." Lorette sat on the edge of the bed, put her arms around his neck, and cried into his shoulder with sobs of exhaustion and relief.

Draius observed them. If he was her younger brother, then Taalo's charm had taken quite a toll. She would have to persuade him to accept Dahni's healing—just removing the charm wouldn't get him back on his feet.

"Thank you, Serasa-Kolme Draius." Lord Chintegrata looked up at her. "I should have suspected Endigala's necromancer as soon as I learned he was in the market square at the same time as Lorette. He wouldn't usually be there on that day, given his habits."

"But you couldn't have known that soon enough."

"I knew about it before she returned home." The corners of his eyes crinkled. He gently disengaged his sister so he could take another drink. "I should have been more vigilant."

"How could—never mind," Draius said. *Pigeons, of course.*

CHAPTER TWELVE

Night Terrors

The Northern Ferry Between Groyga and Kitarra

Draius watched the dark water slide by the ferry. She had only seen the Mirror Sea once, when on a patrol that went to the Kitarran border. Suellestrin was the only city in Kitarra and, being accessible by sea-going ships via the Saamarin, managed extensive trade.

Guffaws and laughter broke out from the group of Kitarrans in blue uniforms at the front end of the ferry. They were guards returning to duty after some time off, some of them still in their cups.

She pulled her hood close as if to keep out the cool air and patted Chisel's neck. Her short haircut was considered fashionable for Kitarran men and it was within the realm of possibility for working women. Lorette's maids had colored her hair to a warm red-gold they called "strawberry blond." It was much more common among Kitarrans than her own silver-blond. They had also applied cosmetics to her face to make it more pale and pinkish. The cosmetics would easily wash off with soap and the hair color would fade with a few washings.

She spent the previous day and night within call of Lord Chintegrata's sickbed. Luckily, he healed quickly and she applied only mild Phrenic healing at Lorette's request. She also discovered she could heal her own burned palms and fingers—no offense meant to Lorette's ointment, it was just much faster. The next day, she was able to speak with both of them. She reiterated that Lorette couldn't help picking up Taalo's charm and putting it on her brother.

Lord Chintegrata was happy his sister couldn't be implicated in a plot to take his life. He took time to speak with her, guardedly, because of her connection to Perinon. Taking Chiune's advice, she asked about homing pigeons and, as she suspected, every great house in Groyga used them for communications. Raised at their home, they would then be shipped in cages to other places. What she didn't know was that a huge amount of pigeons were shipped into Kitarra, mostly ones for House Endigala and the Council of Lords.

"For use by King Markus and his court?" she asked.

"No." Lord Chintegrata hesitated and seemed to make a decision. "The council has approved a plan to destabilize Kitarra and the Groygan ambassador in Kitarra used to be a member of House Endigala."

"Destabilize, meaning a coup?"

Chintegrata shrugged. Now that he was healthier, she estimated him to be in his upper fifties. "I told the council that my house can have no knowledge of this plot: neither its timing, nor its details. I must remain neutral because I trade with Kitarrans almost daily and deal with the Ungoughts every erin, one way or another."

"Then how will the council's plot benefit your house?"

When he smiled, her estimate of his age went even lower. "It probably won't. Many of the lords on the council think too simplistically. They think that if you cut the head off a country, you can just replace it and everything will be fine."

She wondered why he was being so forthcoming about internal Groygan politics. Pushing him for more about this plot, however, got her nowhere. She changed the subject because she should understand more about the power structures in Kitarra. "Tell me about the Ungoughts."

Chintegrata described the intricate and subtle relationships between members of the royal family, and between the royal family and other noble families—they didn't use the term 'lineage.' When he was finished, he extended his hand and she gave him hers. He kissed her hand, turned it over, and put something cool and metallic on her palm. He closed her hand and said, "This is my favor for saving my life, Draius. This ring will be recognized by any Groygan and will lend authority to your request, depending upon where you use it. I suggest you only use it when you're in great need. Rorga will escort you to the landing so you can catch the night ferry into Suellestrin."

Outside the room, she weighed the ring in her palm and raised an eyebrow; it was made of gold. It was a lady's signet ring with Chintegrata's house symbol, the wildflower Bordas had called the *algeare*. She put it into the inside pocket of her nondescript jerkin.

"Lady Chintegrata says her ladies need time to make you look Kitarran," Rorga said with grin. "If you get through that alive, meet me here at noon. We need to arrive at the landing about an hour after nightfall."

After having her hair and face disguised, Lady Lorette walked her out to the courtyard. "I'm so grateful for what you did. I don't want to lose my brother. In fact, it is my goal in life to die before him." She smiled, nodding at someone over Draius's shoulder.

A young man held a well-groomed Chisel wearing her saddle and pack. The saddle had been cleaned and the pack seemed a bit fuller than before. "What about my saber?"

"It's obviously Tyrran, so we packed it under some gifts from us. If anyone asks about anything, tell them you got it in Agrottre Village. Its trading post is well known. You never know what you might find there." Lorette glanced at Chisel meaningfully.

"Where are Chiune and Mattogre?" Draius asked.

"They express their gratitude and farewells to you as well, but they're meeting with Lord Chintegrata." The older woman hugged her.

Draius mounted up and they rode out at a trot. Rorga turned out to be more than a mere guard: he'd just been given the rank of Honored Sword. They turned back on the main road and it soon curved toward the northeast, edging around the forest that blocked the view of the Mirror Sea.

Rorga stopped at a point where a small trail broke off the road to go straight north into the forest. "That goes up to a House Endigala camp, hidden in the trees."

Draius examined the ruts. "Cannons have been pulled through here. Do you know how many troops accompanied them?"

"We estimate over four hundred."

She drew in her breath. An artillery unit of that size would be formidable to a small city like Suellestrin. "Are they supporting the council's plan to *destabilize* Kitarra?"

"We couldn't know their purpose." Rorga's tone was airy. "The council requested that House Chintegrata provide House Endigala with this land temporarily, which his lordship has granted."

"Why no guards here at the road?"

"Well, they *are* in the heartland of Groyga. They might have close perimeter posts."

She filed this away in her memory, along with questions regarding why Chintegrata and his people were so forthcoming. In all likelihood, she would never find answers to that.

Night had fallen by the time they stood on the rocky hill above the fishing villages at the point of Groyga that jutted into the Mirror Sea. The inhabitants, both Kitarrans and Groygans, called this low point the fishing flats. Below her, lanterns had been lit and moving about the shoreline. It was a clear night and she could see, in the far distance, the lights of Suellestrin.

"They run the ferry through the night?" she asked Rorga.

"Yes. At night everyone can see the stars, to navigate by, and the lanterns, to avoid other vessels by. It is the mornings when they can't safely run it. The fog sits thick upon the water. They often have to wait until afternoon before the sun burns it off."

Rorga purchased a ticket and made sure she was the last to get on the ferry, after the Kitarran guards. The guards had no horses, apparently drinking at a nearby pub in the fishing flats. "Try not to talk much. You don't sound Kitarran and Suellestrin is no longer a friendly place for Tyrrans. I hope you can find a way home," Rorga whispered before he departed.

Now Draius kept her eyes on Suellestrin and wished they would move faster. The ferry made for the northern part of the city to avoid traffic near the harbor, where small dinghies maneuvered sea-faring ships into the docks. Eventually, the ferry ground upon the rock of a landing. Large braziers lit up the cobblestoned area near the landing. The guards gathered at the front while the crew took down rails and set up the ramp.

Chisel got nervous and danced about, his hooves playing a staccato rhythm on the deck. The oldest guard, the one she took to be the leader because he had a sash of interwoven squares of blue and green wool over his shoulder, turned and frowned at her. She quieted the horse and moved them both forward. Glancing up, she noted he still observed her. Then his gaze went to the shore and hardened. Coming toward the ferry were three men with weapons. Two were Kitarran and wearing watch uniforms with a badge. The third was Groygan, wearing the black of the Lords' Council but with the same material over the shoulder as the guard leader. The Groygan stepped up the ramp to prevent anyone from disembarking.

The sight of the Groygan caused a knot in the pit of her stomach. She concentrated on staying expressionless.

The guard leader appeared disturbed, pushing through his men to face the Groygan. "How dare you wear the tartan of the King's Comhla?"

"Suel, you know the old comhla was disbanded. Your king gave us permission to wear this tartan."

"I don't believe that, Fontla."

Fontla shrugged. "Your beliefs don't concern me. Tonight, I'm supposed to check for smugglers and wayward Tyrrans coming into the city."

"You mean you're going to charge tariffs and pocket what you can."

"First, I'm checking for *smuggling* and I'm going to start with *you*." Fontla lazily pointed his sword at Draius, who had moved to stand behind the Kitarran guards because that's what any passenger who wanted to get off the ferry would have done. "Pull your hood back."

She tried not to wilt as everyone at the front turned to stare at her while she pulled the hood of her cloak off. Hopefully, the yellow-orange flames from the braziers helped warm up her skin and hair.

"Open your pack." Fontla pushed past Suel.

She undid the ties on her pack and stepped back. Fontla tried to feel around inside the pack, standing on his tiptoes because of Chisel's height.

"Well, well." Fontla pulled out her sheathed sword, while sheathing his. A few scarves and little wrapped boxes fell out of the pack to the deck.

Pulling the saber from its scabbard and examining it, Fontla pursed his lips. "This looks Tyrran. Where did you get this?" He squinted up at her, looking at her face for the first time. "Do you have Tyrran blood?"

She knew she couldn't do a Kitarran brogue, so she made her common Tyrran as bland as possible. "My grandfather was Tyrran. I got that sword at the trading post in Agrottre Village."

"Then you have met the proprietor?" Fontla examined the hilt with longing.

"Yes. His name is Mattogre." She swallowed. "I can give you a good deal on that, if you want it."

Fontla grinned. "Why, when I can just confiscate it? I think we'd better take you to Nettona and examine your pedigree as well. Watchmen, take—"

"Now I know you!" Suel swiftly stepped forward and grabbed Draius by the arms. He pulled her close and her eyes widened in alarm as he looked at her face carefully. "You're that thief who works for Branough in the North End!" He shook her.

"I got the sword in Groyga. I didn't steal it." She was not sure whom she was supposed to be, but she could never confess to being a thief.

"We'll see about that. The only thing I don't believe you stole is that horse. No one would leave that beast unattended."

He was giving her a way to explain Chisel. "The Tyrrans who sold the horse were desperate. It was an honest sale!"

"Counselor Nettona needs to question her *now*." Fontla tried to push between them.

"She's wanted for high crimes against the Crown," Suel said.

She smothered a gasp.

"Have the watchmen arrest her. They're required to bring all Tyrrans to Nettona anyway." Fontla's hands tightened around her sheathed sword.

"My orders come from the king."

"We have the same source. Counselor Nettona speaks for the king's interests."

"So you say."

"Save your arrogance. Once Nettona hears of this—" Fontla bit off his words and glanced around at the Kitarrans. Even the watchmen had sour expressions. He pushed them aside and walked off the ferry, heading toward the center of Suellestrin. He still held her sheathed saber.

Suel released one of her arms and she saw his hand give a signal. One of his men ran after the disgruntled Groygan, catching up and talking with him in urgent tones. They disappeared from her view.

"That was a Tyrran cavalry officer's weapon," Suel said quietly. "I doubt that could be found in a Groygan trading post. Would you like to change your tale?"

She shook his head.

"Tie her up." Suel gestured to her scattered belongings. "Pack those and bring the horse. I'll take her to Whin."

There were too many guards, so she didn't resist. Someone roughly pulled back her arms and wound rope around her wrists and up her forearms, making her shoulders stretch and ache. She heard Chisel's hooves going down the ramp and onto cobblestones. The clopping sounds faded as they led the horse toward the center of the city.

Suel pulled her through the wharfs, busy even at nighttime, where no one took much notice. They came to a long stone building with closed shutters and Suel pushed open a creaky door. They stepped into a dingy room that contained a desk and some benches. Behind the desk was a corpulent man and behind him hung keys on hooks. Being an officer of the City Guard, she knew this place. It was a common jail.

"What are you doing here, Suel? Has the King's Comhla taken to patrolling the wharves for pickpockets like the common watch?" The man wheezed while he spoke, like a broken flute. He didn't wear a uniform, but on his desk sat an official seal of some kind.

"I need temporary storage, Whin." Suel stepped close to the desk.

"Sure, just need to sign—" Whin was reaching for one of his piles of paper when Suel laid his hand on his arm.

"No paperwork." Suel dropped one of her gold tyrs on the table.

Whin's hand pocketed the gold coin while his eyes, almost disappearing in his pudgy face, examined her from head to toe. He jerked his thumb. "Alright then. To the right wi' him."

"Don't be daft." Suel grabbed Draius's hair, pulling her head back and exposing her neck. "This one's a woman."

Whin gaped, then recovered. "Well, I'll be. She's tall, ain't she? To the left, then."

Suel pushed Draius down a long hall into a room for women criminals. A brightly dressed woman with a sullen expression stood close behind the bars. In front of the bars stood a broad-shouldered matron who had keys hanging from her belt. She immediately untied her arms and ordered her to undress.

For a moment, Draius toyed with the idea of escape but unfortunately, Suel had stayed and was leaning against the doorframe. She regretfully handed over her knives, which were given to Suel.

The matron searched all the clothes she took off and Lord Chinte-grata's ring was soon found. "Ooh, pretty." Suel extended his hand and the matron reluctantly gave it to him. The broad-shouldered guard examined it, and then looked at Draius warily before pocketing the ring.

Soon she was standing in her undergarments, shivering in the chilly room. Having lived and dressed and washed with male cousins, she wasn't embarrassed by the revealing garments, but Suel's frown still made her uncomfortable.

"What's this?" The matron's hand fumbled at the chain around her neck, the one that held the Kaskea shard. "Take that off."

"It's a memento." She pulled the silver chain over her head and handed it and the shard over.

"What's so important about a piece of slate?" The chain was heavy silver and the matron continued to finger it.

"Please, it's from the river where my husband proposed marriage." She put a whine in her voice and tried to concentrate on the words. It wouldn't do to have the shard flash green in here. "You can keep the chain, but I need the rock to remind me of the place where—"

"Never mind." The matron didn't want to hear the story. She started pulling the shard out of the wire that wrapped it, but Suel stopped her.

"Wait." He grabbed the chain and held it high, peering at the Kaskea shard. He pulled a wrinkled bandage or kerchief from his pocket and wad-ded it around the shard and chain. The whole thing went back into the pocket. "I'll take this for the time being."

Dismayed, Draius turned so he wouldn't see her face. He acted as if he knew what he held, even made sure his skin wouldn't touch it. The ma-tron started handing her clothes back and Suel left. "This room tends to be cold," the broad woman said brusquely as she handed the cloak to Draius.

She dressed slowly.

"If you need any rags, tell me," added the matron.

She stared at the matron in shock.

"For your courses, you know." The matron became uncomfortable as Draius continued to stare. "You're young enough, right?"

"But she's a savage, ain't she?" The jeer came from the garish woman behind the bars.

"Shut up, Lissa." The matron's words were an automatic response, without any heat.

"Look at her, hair all chopped, limbs all bony. She don't have her courses any more."

"You've still got to do a day in the stocks, Lissa." The matron sounded tired. "You want to extend that?"

Lissa shut up and the matron focused back on Draius.

"I don't need any, thank you." She figured it didn't hurt to be polite to one's jailer.

She was ushered into the roomy cell, which had two very narrow windows and a bench that ran along the wall. While the bars were locked behind her, she noticed two more women in the cell besides Lissa. In the far corner on the bench sat an old woman, huddled in a thin blanket. Beside her, trying to provide her with body warmth, sat a younger woman. They were small-boned and didn't look Tyrran, Kitarran, or Groygan.

"Marsh scum. They smell of frogs." Lissa nodded at the two women in the corner. Lissa didn't have the greatest aroma herself and Draius stared her down until she backed away and sat in the other corner.

Her clothes were warm enough, so she took off her cloak and approached the two women. They looked at her suspiciously, their dark eyes glittering in the dim light. The older one had a tattoo on her forehead that looked like circular fretwork.

Offering her cloak to them, she said, "Use this. I can get by without it." The younger woman snatched the cloak and gathered it around them both.

Draius was left with middle part of the bench. She sat down, folded her arms over her chest, and proceeded to calculate furiously. This was the evening of the forty-first day since she left Betarr Serin. She should have had her courses almost two eight-days ago. How could she forget them? Probably because she had no reason to worry for years: she and Jan hadn't shared a bed since Peri was two and she had never stepped outside their marriage contract. Could it be stress? Usually no amount of stress would cause her to be late.

Since the Fevers, many Tyrrans had to try for years to conceive. It would be ironic that one farewell tryst with Lornis could... She shook her head. At home, she would be considered fortunate, but here... This was an inconvenient time and place to be pregnant.

Lying down on the bench, she tried rapport with Dahni but was so tired she fell asleep. Her dreams were filled with flashes of home but always ending in blood and death.

Betarr Serasa, Tyrra

The sound of fists pounding on his barracks door woke Lornis and he left his sleep reluctantly. During the day, Jan had sent him all around Betarr Serasa, exhausting him. First, as subtle punishment for suggesting the necromantic toys might be dangerous to the overall security of the sister cities, Jan ordered him to obtain the name of every Sareenian in the market square selling such items. After that, Jan directed him to check the status of all the defense posts on the city walls by nightfall. This involved hard and fast riding, through heavy traffic.

The knocks continued.

"Hold up, I'm awake," Lornis mumbled as he lit a lantern. "Hold, I say!"

He threw open the door. Ponteva waited, holding the boots he had put out to be cleaned and polished. "Greet's, ser. The captain requires you."

"Captain Rhaffus? Now?" He gaped.

"Yes. Your boots, ser." Ponteva pushed the dirty boots at him, which he took numbly. Blond and gray hairs had escaped from Ponteva's braids and went straight back over his head, as if he just rode hard against a wind.

Lornis realized that he stood in his nightshirt and in front of a watchman. At least Ponteva would know he could present himself better; he had worked closely with this grizzled guard when he was assigned to the Office of Investigation under Draius. Down the hall, lamplight flared under another door. Junior officers were quartered here and the place ran rife with competition and personal politics. "You better come in."

After closing the door, he went over to the bell pull to call the valet but Ponteva stopped him. "Captain says the field uniform will do. Haste is most important."

He went to dress in his small bedchamber, separated from the small parlor area. After another promotion, he could ask for larger rooms. Jan, for instance, lived in much better accommodations. He hoped his commander was just as discomforted by this late-night waking. "Is something up for just the Office of Defense?" he called.

"Not defense, ser. Investigation. The captain's moving you back to us."

"What about Vice Commander Laakso?" He came out to the parlor and started putting on his boots. Noticing a distinct silence, he looked up.

Ponteva's eyes focused on the floor before him. "Meran-Viisi Laakso was murdered tonight in Betarr Serasa, as were two other members of the Meran-Viisi lineage. There are more murders in Betarr Serin and that's where I'm to deliver you."

Words failed him for a moment. "More murders?"

"Yes, ser, but we don't know more than that." From Ponteva's tone, he didn't like to speculate.

"Why call me? Why not use Jan or another Commander in charge of a major Office?"

"The messenger said Captain Rhaffus wants you, specifically, because of the experience you gained under Officer Draius."

"So, three dead down here and I am called to Betarr Serin. Let's go." He stood.

Ponteva pushed their mounts all the way up to Betarr Serin, where the King's Guard had been forewarned. The gates opened and their horses pounded up the main street of Betarr Serin and didn't stop until they arrived at the Palace of Stars. All the lamps were lit and a few people milled about in front of the stairs. Ponteva dismounted quickly, leaving the wet horses to others.

He followed Ponteva up the stairs of the palace and through the stone archway. Their footsteps echoed on the marble floor, audible over the soft murmurs of people standing in the vestibule. They were mostly King's Guard in green and silver uniforms, on duty but not at their duty stations. Conversation hushed and everyone turned to stare at them.

Ponteva made straight for the wing that housed the King's Guard offices, his City Guard uniform looking out of place here. Lornis ignored the stares: he was known to be Phrenic-healed and besides, he was the spitting image of "The Hunter Chieftain" rendered in the mosaic above all their heads. Out of the corner of his eye, he caught some guards glancing up at it. They turned down the hallway into the King's Guard wing and Lornis felt relief from all the gazes. Those people waited in the vestibule but they didn't know why. He could feel the uncertainty and suspicion in the air, like tangible puffs of pipe smoke swirling and circling their makers. Ahead, two King's Guard waited at the end of the hall on either side of the door for the master of arms. He didn't need to see their tense faces because their shock, rage, and tension hit him like a wave. *Death. Murder.*

He paused and Ponteva gripped his arm.

"We've seen much worse, ser," the watchman said in his ear, too quiet for the guards to hear. He was referring to the brutal eviscerations they investigated in the early part of the year. "Here, it's not the *what*, it's the *who*."

Ponteva nodded at the guards and slipped through the door. Lornis followed, bracing himself. Captain Rhaffus of the City Guard and Captain Kilpi of the King's Guard turned as Lornis entered the room. They had their arms crossed. Few events required both captains, but this would be one of them. Sprawled on the desk between them lay their murdered commander, Master of Arms Sevoi.

The body with bloody wounds on its neck didn't sway Lornis as much as what he sensed in the room. Under the death and murder swirled something more insidious, something he had not felt since battling Taalo's conspiracy. Necromancy always left its taint.

He heard ragged breathing from the corner of the room and turning, almost staggered. King Perinon was huddled in the corner, his knees pulled up to his chest and his bloody hands propped on top of them, almost in his face. His eyes were wide and soulless. He knelt in front of the king, noting that he wore no weapons or weapon sheaths and he appeared hastily dressed.

"Why *him?*" Kilpi asked, doubt in his voice.

"I have my reasons." Rhaffus's gruff deep voice resonated in the stone room.

"Sire?" Lornis saw no acknowledgement in Perinon's eyes. He took one of Perinon's wrists and tried to move the bloody hand. The king was stiff and resistant, but he forced the hand down, out of sight.

"Lieutenant, I did a preliminary check of the scene. The king wore no blade, but in this state we can't ask him questions." Rhaffus's voice rose at the end of his sentence.

Lornis had seen this before, when Draius and Perinon had reacted to Berin's "death by Phrenii." He answered the unspoken question in Rhaffus's voice. "We have to clean the blood off him." He nodded to Ponteva, who left and returned with wet towels.

"Why lose his senses? He's seen blood and death," Kilpi protested.

"Not murder stinking of necromancy," he answered brusquely. "I'll bet nobody's seen the Phrenii, am I right?"

A look passed between Rhaffus and Kilpi, as if an argument had been settled. He went back to cleaning Perinon's hands with the wet towels. He didn't need an answer; the Phrenii wouldn't come near this room. Once his hands were clean, Perinon seemed to relax.

"Sire?" Lornis asked gently, wondering what was happening in Perinon's mind. Was he wandering lost and terrified in the "Blindness," as

Draius had described one evening? It was the home of nightmares, literally.

Perinon mumbled something inaudible.

"Let him rest a bit, perhaps he'll come round." Lornis stood. "Has Norsis been called?"

"Not yet. We want the king out of here before Andreas gets wind of this. He keeps watch on the coroner's wagon like a vulture." Rhaffus almost spat out Andreas's name. He and the editor of the *H&H* had a long-standing antipathy for each other.

Meanwhile, Lornis pressed his lips together, thinking. Perinon wore no cloak. "Did you come through the private entrance that comes straight from your Meran-Viisi residence, sire?" He received a nod from the king.

"They should take him home via the vestibule and street, so you can examine those passageways," Kilpi said.

"Do you trust your people to stay quiet about the king's condition?" Lornis asked.

Captain Kilpi took immediate affront. "Don't question the loyalty of the King's Guard, Lieutenant."

"Speaking of which, where are the *king's guards,* the ones who escorted him from his residence?"

"They're the ones controlling the door to this room," Kilpi answered. "Questioning their loyalty as well?"

"No, captain." He gave Kilpi a small smile. "But I think they'll be able to answer a lot of our questions, so you'll need to find replacements to take him home. I apologize if you think I'm questioning anyone's loyalty—this is just part of the investigation. I'll ask you this: who can walk these halls without challenge, just because of the clothes on their back?"

"Members of the King's Guard." Kilpi tugged at his collar.

"Agreed. I assume everyone in the vestibule tonight worked in the palace and most are King's Guard. We have to question all of them." Lornis walked over to the narrow window as he talked, noting a small smear of blood on the sill. "To take the king home, find ones you trust, ones who couldn't have been in this wing tonight."

"Listen to him, Kilpi. The City Guard investigation team must remain objective," Rhaffus said. Once again, the two captains exchanged a glance that Lornis couldn't interpret. Kilpi was younger, perhaps by twenty years, yet both their faces were lined with hard years of service. Being broader in the shoulders and stockier, Rhaffus's hair mingled with white and spread on his shoulders, following current fashions. Kilpi's dark blond hair was always braided for warfare; appropriate for the uniform he wore.

Captain Kilpi slipped out as Miina arrived. Lornis was relieved to see the slight dark-haired guard woman, partly because she brought drawing implements and paper. "Put together a rough drawing of the room with orientation of the furniture and body. Make sure to indicate blood and other items on the floor—make sure you record that smear of blood on the windowsill. Please provide dimensions or measurements wherever possible." Lornis had instigated diagramming the crime scene because nobody else in the Office of Investigation had perfect memory like Draius.

"Glad to be working with you again, ser, although I'm not happy about the circumstances." Miina glanced around the room, remaining professional. However, she paused a moment as she looked at Perinon and Lornis saw pity in her eyes. She handed him paper, pen, and a small container that had a sponge soaked with ink. "For your own notes, since Ponteva probably pulled you from your quarters with just your boots and cloak."

"That about describes my night—rather, my morning. Thanks." Lornis privately thought Miina could easily pass the tests to be an officer. So far, she hadn't seemed interested and remained watchman grade.

He started his notes and asked Rhaffus a few questions. First, could this murder be related to the ones down in Betarr Serasa?

"Possibly, but I want you to process this scene first." Rhaffus glanced about. "We have the king present as an important witness, which makes this a unique situation. At this time, we can assume no connection between the victims, except that they're all Meran-Viisi with the exception of Sevoi."

"How is the three-person Office of Investigation going to process four murders at once?"

"Five."

"The office has five people now?" Two more people would not be enough for this case.

"No, there are five murders. Besides Sevoi, four Meran-Viisi males were killed tonight: one in Betarr Serin and three in Betarr Serasa. You now have *four* people in the office: Ponteva and Miina, plus two clerks. I can get you a third clerk. I also have watch members and their backups processing the other scenes." Rhaffus put up a hand, forestalling his concerns. "They're not allowed to release the scene until you or I approve the processing."

Lornis took a deep breath. Five murders in one night. Even if they were connected, that didn't reduce the investigation labor—which had to be done by trained City Guard, not clerks.

Kilpi returned with two King's Guard, who went to each side of Perinon and started checking his condition. Kilpi drew Rhaffus aside, but Lornis could still hear their conversation. "Sevoi's remaining child is King's Guard. Commander Meran-Nelja Lyn runs the intelligence detachment at Betarr Kain, but was recalled personally by the king. She deserves to be told the news from you, not her matriarch."

"Is she close to Sevoi?" Rhaffus asked. Lornis smirked; the captain used to be Officer in Charge of Investigation. Once an investigator, always an investigator—he couldn't let it go.

"They are—were estranged." Kilpi clearly considered relationships outside his area of expertise. "They interacted for King's Guard business only."

"You know her?" Rhaffus asked.

"We're just friends, with similar circumstances." Kilpi shrugged.

Rhaffus nodded. "I can notify her first. Does she live with her matriarch or with Sevoi?"

"Neither. She rents officer quarters when she's here in Betarr Serin. During the Fevers she lost her husband, succumbed to the Fevers herself, and delivered a stillborn daughter. She's lived alone ever since."

Hearing this insight into Lyn's life and Kilpi's, as well, embarrassed Lornis. He turned his attention to the king. The two guards had Perinon between them. He had to grip each of them to walk, but at least he moved on his own. They set out for the Meran-Viisi residence using the front Palace stairs. Lornis hoped the king would go unnoticed until he got home, where they would call for his physician.

"I better call for the coroner wagon and notify Sevoi's daughter and matriarch. After that, I'll go by the second murder scene in this city," Rhaffus said heavily. "I'm leaving *this scene* in your hands, Lieutenant, and I'll be over-seeing this case."

"Yes, ser." He snapped to attention, knowing this meant *don't screw up and miss any evidence.* As the captain left, he made a note about Sevoi's daughter. If he and his daughter were estranged, then she certainly made the suspect list. She was King's Guard and able to walk about the Palace of Stars unremarked. However, Perinon was not a suspect, given what Lornis knew about rapport with the Phrenii. Cold-blooded murder was impossible for someone bound to the Phrenii through the Kaskea.

As soon as Rhaffus shut the door, Captain Kilpi turned on him. "Rhaffus might trust you, but until you prove yourself to me, Lieutenant, I'll be following you like a hunting dog."

Every once in a while, Lornis appreciated the enhanced empathy he had received from the Phrenic healing. Kilpi's distrust was a facade. He felt the man's doubt, overlaid with intense grief over the loss of his commander and friend. There were sparks of hope—the hope that Lornis would unravel this mystery and he could vent righteous anger upon his commander's murderer.

"As you should, ser." He used a mild tone and backed away. "Do we have a list of everyone inside the Palace of Stars tonight?"

As he expected, Kilpi was mollified by his business-like attitude and the opportunity to do something useful. The captain of the King's Guard had already created a list and, of course, his own name appeared at the top. His office was across from Sevoi's office.

"Were you here all evening?"

"Yes, except when I went out for supper." Kilpi responded without evasion, eager to help, and volunteered the name of the establishment where he ate. "When I'm here, I usually leave my office door open and I can see Sevoi's door, although he often works—*worked*—behind a closed door for security reasons."

He took notes. The training he had received from Draius wasn't wasted; he would have Ponteva check the local inn where Kilpi ate his meal. All details of witness stories had to be verified. If someone lied about minutiae, they often hid something else.

Other than the hour when he ate, Kilpi could report on visitors to Sevoi's office. "After the evening watch started, Councilman Muusa knocked on his door and entered. Muusa raised his voice once or twice, but he's been out of sorts ever since the council meeting yesterday. No doubt he was pressing his arguments with Sevoi, hoping to get support from the King's Guard."

"Out of sorts, meaning what? Was he angry?"

"Muusa seemed irritated, but that would be normal. He's always bothered about something."

"Any other visitors or suspicious sounds?" Lornis asked.

"No. After I came back from supper, there were no visitors until the king arrived after midnight. Sevoi often left before that time, but since both the king and his guards looked rushed, I figured Sevoi had sent for them. They threw the door open and I heard a wail—from the king, I think. When I entered, his majesty was curled up, almost catatonic. His guards and I touched nothing and sent for Rhaffus."

Lornis realized Kilpi couldn't describe emotions without additional prodding. "You said the king and his guards *looked rushed*. What does that mean—can you use different words to describe it?"

"Oh. The king was pale, maybe sweating, like he was going to vomit. The guards' faces were pasty, too, but more confused and afraid." When pushed, Kilpi could come up with details. He glanced down at Sevoi and shook his head. "He must have been murdered while I was at supper. I sat in my office and never knew. Can't we cover him?"

Lornis shook his head. "Not until Norsis examines him. He might be able to figure out when Sevoi died." He went back to the windowsill and studied the puzzling stain. It was blood, surely, and it was smeared over the sill and out the window.

"Strange, yes?" Kilpi observed his every move. "Rhaffus noted that also. But no man could get through that window and no child could survive the drop outside."

Lornis pushed the window open as far as he could. With difficulty, he stuck his head and one shoulder through to peer over the thick wall and down into the alley below. The window was about twenty feet high. He squinted in the low light of coming dawn and saw a small pile of refuse with an overflowing bin beside it. Across the ally were the walls of the city, much higher than his window.

"Ponteva, check the alley. Sort through the trash and see if *something* dragged itself away. That something might still be there, so be careful."

The grizzled watchman nodded and left.

Lornis asked Captain Kilpi, "When do the trash wagons go through the streets?" Betarr Serin was kept very clean and the residents were rich enough to pay for regular services such as collection of trash.

"Why? Do you have a theory?"

"I do, but first I must ensure that all possible evidence is collected. When is the trash picked up, and by whom?"

"On Honorday, early in the morning. As for those who gather the trash and sort through it..." Kilpi's forehead wrinkled. "All I know is that they tend to be Sareenians. Two to a wagon and I don't even know where they take it."

"That's today. How early?" He checked the expensive clock, its pendulum swinging, standing in the corner of the office. Three hours past midnight—he couldn't believe he had only been here an hour.

"Miina." He waved her over. "You know where the second murder scene is, the other one inside Betarr Serin?" She nodded, so even if he didn't know the specific location yet, his staff did. "I need you to get over there with best speed and tell them to look for a necromantic charm. Besides having the ability to kill, perhaps with poison, I think these charms are also designed to leave the scene. The watchmen may need to look beyond the crime scene boundaries. Then go to the King's Guard gate post and tell them to stop *every* trash wagon from leaving the upper city. Each one will have to be searched."

"By me?" Her eyes widened.

"No—it'll have to be done by the King's Guard, because you're going to need extra City Guard to do your next task. There is a list in the Office of Defense, sitting right on my desk, of every merchant who sells necromantic charms as toys or any other sort of gift or tool. Get that list, arrest every one of those merchants, and confiscate their stock. This should be done soon, before they set up and I think they do that at dawn."

Both Miina and Captain Kilpi drew deep breaths. Miina blew hers out in a way that ruffled the short hair on her forehead. "I hope I can find enough City Guard to do this, ser, considering they're examining three murder scenes in the lower city."

"I'm assuming a total recall of all guard has been initiated." He glanced at Kilpi, who nodded, and had another idea on engaging the captain. "Any way you can lend us your people today to help, captain?"

Kilpi thought for a moment. "I can send someone with Miina who has the authority—" He snapped his fingers. "Commander Ruel has been recalled and is waiting in the vestibule. She was not in the Palace last night.

Once Miina takes her statement, tell her I have offered every resource possible to help the City Guard today."

Lornis nodded approvingly. The Deputy for Resources was a good choice and she was directly under Captain Kilpi in the chain of command. Miina also smiled and said, "Thank you, captain." Then she was on her way.

"I'm not sure I understand your necromancy theory, but we do need every able guard working." Kilpi's voice was gruff.

"I suspect a strong necromantic charm was delivered to the master of arms, which might explain why there was no struggle in this room. His chair isn't even overturned, yet he's fallen over his desk. This isn't much different from the other murder I've seen with a charm—except this charm was more sophisticated and tried to leave the scene on its own volition." He pointed to the window. "Did the councilman or the king carry anything into this office?"

"I didn't notice."

"Did anyone ask you to give something to Master Sevoi?"

"No."

"Was anything delivered to this office in the evening?"

"Just a meal, before Muusa visited." Kilpi's light eyebrows knotted. "I can ask the front door guards where it came from."

"Please do, because there is no indication of the meal, which is suspicious. Anything might have been delivered with it—charms and poison come to mind. "

"You're distrustful *and* imaginative, Lieutenant." Kilpi looked at him with new respect.

"Perhaps I've learned more than I should have in the past year." He went back to his diagram.

Norsis, the coroner, arrived. Lornis asked Kilpi to do basic interviews of every guard who'd been in the building that evening and then hovered over Norsis until the older man snapped at him. "I can't think with you breathing in my ear, Lieutenant. Will you back off a step or two?"

"Can you tell me anything about the weapon?"

Norsis sighed and the creases in his face deepened. "Only that it looks like a small blade. The neck wounds shouldn't have been lethal unless the master of arms was unconscious or impaired. Now please step back while I adjust his position and look at his hands and arms."

Ponteva breezed in and grandly deposited a bundle wrapped in smelly rags on the desk. "Here's your murder weapon." While they all watched, he carefully unwrapped something that might have once been a toy soldier, ironically wearing a fairly accurate King's Guard uniform. If it could stand straight, it would be about a foot tall, but it was badly broken and splintered. Even so, it was still moving.

"Did it break in the fall from the window?" Lornis asked.

"No. It was burrowing into the trash and I grabbed it by its boot. It turned on me in a flash and I had to throw it against the wall. That sword is right sharp, it is."

"Did it break your skin?" Norsis eyed it. "The blade is coated with something."

"It managed to catch my uniform." Ponteva examined his right sleeve and stuck his finger through a slice. "Didn't even nick me."

"If you suspect poison or a debilitating agent, you should know that Sevoi had a meal delivered in the evening," Lornis told the coroner.

"When?" Norsis seemed mesmerized by the writhing of the broken toy.

"About half past seven. He had a visitor after that, who could have delivered this toy or given it a command, if it was already here."

"Hmm." This didn't unnerve Norsis, who had seen murder by magic—when charmed gold pieces had stuffed themselves into a traitor's mouth and throat until he died. "Will you tie up that weapon securely for me, Ponteva? I'll take that to the morgue for examination. As for cause of death, I'll need more time."

"Do you have an idea of *when* he died?" Lornis asked.

"He's just starting to stiffen—which is why we have to get him into the wagon soon. So he died between two and six hours ago."

That put Sevoi's death *after* his dinner and meeting with Councilman Muusa. Lornis wondered how he was going to convince a magistrate that a toy could independently kill a grown man. But that was far, far in the future. Today, he had many more interviews to conduct. "Ponteva, I'm going to the King's residence and I'll be taking the guards who brought him over last night. Make sure you get replacements or you'll have Andreas mucking everything up in here."

When Lornis opened the door, though, there was Andreas begging the guards to let him in. As Captain Rhaffus predicted, the pudgy editor of the *H&H* had followed the coroner's wagon. He had to shout, "No comment," about a dozen times while he and Ponteva changed out the guards. Then he motioned for the previous ones to follow him.

When they were away from Andreas, he told them that they were backtracking over the exact path the king took a couple hours ago. "While we do that, you're going to tell me what happened to him last night."

Perinon had a private way of getting between his residence at Number One, Betarr Serin, and the Palace of Stars. The walled city was shaped generally like a triangle, with the king's residence and palace squeezed into its northernmost angle. At that point, the king's residence merged into the city walls and the city walls met the rock face of the cliffs. On the other side of those walls, the Dahn Serin Falls came from a rock fissure a hundred feet up and then crashed into the Whitewater hundreds of feet below. The king's residence had the only balcony that hung out over the falls, while the palace had a long slit for observing them.

The guards led him along the north wing of the Palace of Stars toward that very slit, through which came the sounds of the waterfall. They opened the last door on the western side and entered a small audience room. Behind a tapestry, of course, was a door with a lock. As the guard pulled it open, he asked, "Shouldn't this be locked?"

"Yes, ser. But tonight we had no time to lock anything behind us."

"How many keys to this door exist, and who carries them?"

"Only two: the king always carries one and the shift leader of his personal guard carries the other," said the King's Guard who identified himself as last night's shift leader.

"Any skeleton keys?"

"None that I know of."

"Whose key was used last night?"

"Mine. The king's hands were shaking." The guard held the door open for them to enter and locked the door behind them.

"No tunnels?" Having listened to legends of underground tunnels in Betarr Serin all his life, Lornis was slightly disappointed when the guard's lantern showed a level corridor. It turned immediately left.

"No, ser." The guard grinned. "We're too close to the edge of the plateau. A tunnel here would undermine the city walls—so we're walking inside them."

"Wait. Are those bloody fingermarks?" He pointed at the wall. Then he noticed more smears along the wall at the same height.

The shift leader peered at them. "I think this is from the king's hands."

So the blood on Perinon's hands was not only Sevoi's. "How did he cut his hands and why was he leaning against the wall?"

"He wouldn't wait to light the lantern, ser. He was feeling his way and we could barely keep up with him, until he got to this door. Then I had to unlock it in the dark."

Getting this story in bits and pieces, from the back end forward, just wasn't working. "Maybe you'd better start from the beginning."

The guards were positioned in their normal places outside the king's inner bedchamber. The king went to sleep as he normally did, preparing for bed about an hour before midnight and having his manservant close the door to the inner chamber when he left. The midnight bell had just chimed from the nearby watchtower when there was a shout from the king's bedchamber, followed by a thump. The guards rushed in.

"It was the strangest thing. At first, the king was on his knees alone, pounding at something with his boot, and then Mahri just appeared in the room. But it didn't look like Mahri. There was nothing wispy about the creature. It was liquid gold and glowed so the whole bedchamber was lit. And it was angry, so angry that we were afraid to enter."

"How could you tell it was angry?" The only person who ever told Lornis that the Phrenii had emotions was Draius.

"I could feel the rage here." The shift leader touched his breastbone with his closed fist. "It made me stagger back a pace. Then Mahri started pounding on something in front of the king as well, with two hooves like a horse trying to kill a snake. But this—" He shook his head. "This wasn't like a mere horse. Every time Mahri hit the floor, a gong went off. We covered our ears and I could swear the floor shook. The king also covered his ears and scooted away from what was on the floor. Mahri finally stopped, looked at the king, then popped away."

"Popped?" The Phrenii didn't leave abruptly. They would go around a corner and if you followed, they wouldn't be there. Once in a while, he would see one fading as it went out of view.

The shift leader nodded. "There was a pop, and then no Mahri. One of the king's hands bled and he was affected—sick—right on his carpet. Then he went to a chest and put on some old breeches and a shirt, saying we had to get to Sevoi as soon as possible. That Sevoi didn't have *the benefit of rapport to save him.* So we hotfooted it over here, not taking time to make light nor lock the doors behind us." The corridor ended with a door to the left and to demonstrate, the shift leader opened the door. "See? Not locked."

"So the master of arms was dead when you arrive?"

"Yes. The king checked several times, and then so did Captain Kilpi. The king slouched down against the wall mumbling about necromancy." The other guard shivered. "I worried that his words would call the shade of Nherissa, so I was happy to leave that room."

Through the door was the interior of residence Number One, Betarr Serin. They were at the corner of a corridor. Lornis stepped in cautiously and looked down each leg. "Where would they be attending the king?"

"This way, ser." The guards led him around another set of corners to what looked like the outer room to the king's bedchamber. There were two guards outside the room's door. Inside, several people argued, all at once. Considering the tone of those raised voices, the King's Guard preferred to stay outside.

Lornis went into the room by himself.

CHAPTER THIRTEEN

The Duke and the Councilman

Betarr Serin, Tyrra

Surprisingly, Lornis knew almost everyone in the room, at least those who were talking. The argument immediately stopped and they all stared at him. King Perinon huddled in a chair with a blanket while his manservant Velija arranged yet another around his shoulders—Velija wasn't participating in the conversation and quickly stepped back. Perinon's face was pale and he shivered. Across from him on the settee sat Lady Aracia and her daughter Onni, who was training to eventually take Aracia's place as the Meran-Viisi matriarch. Gaflis, the best physician in the sister cities and, when needed, the king's personal physician, stood by the king.

Lornis went through the motions of introducing himself and stating his purpose. "I'm filling in for the newly deceased Officer of Investigation. I need backgrounds on the victims and statements from each of you regarding last night."

Aracia's face paled and she covered her mouth.

"*Victims?* There are more deaths?" Gaflis asked.

"More *murders*. This is premature..." He hesitated. It went against procedure to release early findings, but considering the king's state, they

216

might help him. He pointed toward Perinon's bandaged hands. "Norsis suspects a poison or incapacitating agent on the blade that cut Sevoi before he died."

Before he entered, he'd heard Gaflis arguing with Lady Aracia about moving the king and his court. Now Gaflis turned to Perinon. "Sire, it might be better for me to consult the coroner and determine this agent. I can do nothing more for you here, other than recommend rest and plenty of liquids."

Perinon nodded and Gaflis took his leave.

"Officer Lornis?" Aracia's voice was tentative. "You have confirmation of Meran-Viisi Laakso's death?"

This was the most unpleasant reason he was here: to notify the matriarch of deaths in her lineage. He shuffled through his papers until he found the list of four Meran-Viisi names, with Meran-Kolme Sevoi's name at the bottom. "Yes, my lady. I have here the list of confirmed deaths tonight by murder—"

"Necromancy." Perinon's voice was harsh.

He silently handed the list to Lady Aracia. She read it and tears squeezed out of her eyes. Her daughter handed her a kerchief as she handed her daughter the list. Onni actually groaned when she read the names. "How is this possible?"

Discomfited by seeing grief displayed by a matriarch and deciding to give her time to grapple with this news, he asked Velija if they had the remains of the charm that attacked the king.

"Charm?" The manservant looked blank.

"Whatever the Phrenii mashed up last night."

Velija motioned him into the inner bedchamber and pointed to the center of the floor, about a pace away from the king's bed. His jaw dropped. The term *pulverized* wouldn't be an exaggeration. The thick block of marble, several feet wide in each dimension and probably at least a foot or two thick, had several cracks across it. There was a circle of chips and dust in the center of the block. He put his gloves back on and tried to sift through it to find evidence. Tiny green and silver threads, small splinters of wood and metal, and lots of dust sifted through his hands. It would take a special lens to see everything and separate it from the ground marble. "Someone will come to collect this later," he told the manservant. "Leave it be until then."

When he came back to the room, Lady Aracia again studied the list, this time with anger on her face. "Is there a commonality between those victims?" he asked her.

"I cannot tell you about the Meran-Viisi until you give your word that this information will go no further."

"I'm sorry. Since this information may be needed for the trial of the murderers, I cannot give you my word." He looked to Perinon for help.

"My lady." Perinon's voice was soft, perhaps due to sympathy or exhaustion or both. "I understand the need to preserve confidence in the Crown. We cannot afford a display of weakness and Officer Lornis can keep our secrets during the investigation, but not during the trial. Consider, though, that any trial would be many erins in the future and there would be time for our lineage to recover."

Recover? He quickly added his voice to the king's. "Yes, my lady, I can keep anything private during the investigation but it will be up to the officiating magistrate as to whether evidence will remain private or be made public."

Aracia sighed. "The four Meran-Viisi are designated successors to the Crown."

"Really?" He was doubtful. It seemed odd that the new OIC of Investigation would be a successor, especially when he was moved from the King's Guard to the City Guard. That was generally a move *down* in societal rank. Then it dawned on him that these successors were being carefully hidden. "Three young men in Betarr-Serasa and one in Betarr-Serin, all holding lackluster jobs but hiding in plain sight?"

Aracia's eyes glinted. "Those lackluster jobs gave them experience in the King's Law. Anyway, they weren't all *men*." She suppressed a sob. "The boy in Betarr-Serin was only fifteen."

Right. The successors were all different ages—*Peri!* Lornis had been one of two people present when a matriarchal tribunal decided Draius's son might someday join that list of successors. "*What about Peri?*"

"He is safe. Dahni is standing watch over him, while Mahri is—is recovering from the—the charm." Perinon's teeth were chattering and his manservant poured him another cup of something hot. He gratefully held the cup between his hands.

Meanwhile, Lornis thanked his ancestors that Draius had the foresight to forbid necromantic charms in Peri's house.

"We asked the Phrenii to be inconspicuous," Aracia said. "We cannot let our enemies learn they successfully struck at the Crown tonight and nearly destroyed it. That's why we were arguing about whether to move the entire court north to the summer lodge for Perinon's safety—if we did that, it would be impossible to hide his sudden ill health. And if he dies..." Beside her, Onni softly moaned.

Lornis eyed the king. If he died, the Meran-Viisi would be scrambling. Even during the Fevers, they had a clear line of succession set up from Perinon's father to his brother Valos to Perinon himself. News of any illness suffered by the king might be just as bad, because it would tell those who orchestrated these nightmarish charms that they'd had partial, possibly full success in destroying the kingship. Lady Aracia faced a quandary: the more she protected Perinon, the more successful the Crown's enemies would feel. He asked her, "Who would know the identity of these successors?"

"Myself. Onni. The king. The successors and their parents, if they're under nineteen when selected. The successors must pledge to keep their status private, even from spouses." Aracia's eyes narrowed. "*And every matriarch on the five-star lineage committee. What damns those on the committee is that they can't know about Draius's son yet. I'm still trying to decide* when Peri might transfer to the Meran-Viisi name and his matriarch has only subtly changed his education, so the Pettaja-Viisi wouldn't have an inkling. Everyone who did know about Peri, *couldn't* identify the four other successors." She gazed up at Lornis.

He drew a deep breath. *Great—I'm going to have to investigate the most powerful matriarchs in Tyrra.*

Suellestrin, Kitarra

The old woman woke Draius with wracking, deep coughs and the dream she tried to snatch and hold became shreds, the fluttering gossamer of a web that had once seemed whole.

"Keep quiet," muttered Lissa from her corner. She turned over and started snoring.

Draius eventually needed to stretch her entire length out on the floor, using her arm as a pillow. She listened to the labored breathing and coughs the old woman tried to contain—a picture formed in her mind of what her lungs must be suffering.

Rolling over on her side, she substituted her other arm for the numb one and tried to marshal her memories. She stepped through her last dream, not the ones that plagued her earlier that had been about murder and mayhem in the sister cities, but the very last one. Dahni has been talking to her about war, exactly like the first time she had walked the Void.

War is coming, no matter what? This had been Draius's question and she had been aghast at the creature's sureness.

"Yes," Dahni said. "It is only a matter of when."

At the time, she had no doubt the enemy was Groyga, Tyrra's traditional enemy.

"We sit upon a pivot in time, which turns about the lodestone," Dahni said. "If the lodestone is found from the Blindness, where many creatures may see and feel it, war will take Tyrra by surprise and she will fall immediately. In this, we are certain." Those words had persuaded Draius to thwart Taalo and his fellow conspirators, who were searching for the lodestone in the Blindness.

In her dream, she asked Dahni a question she never asked in reality: *What of Kitarra? Will they be our enemy also?*

"Famri might know," Dahni said, after hesitating.

She accepted this answer. All the Phrenii had powers. Famri was fire, the aspect of protection and the reason why it always stayed near the eastern border.

Should I ask Famri? she asked.

"Not here in the Blindness!" Dahni cried. "Anyone might hear you and you must be kept safe, now that you carry a daughter."

What? A maelstrom of self-doubt surrounded her, circling about like a cyclone. Anger whipped in, licking about her with tangible flames. "Dahni! Where are you?" She tried to scream physically as hunters suddenly buffeted her, surrounding her with pain and flames—

Then she woke up on the cold stone floor. She couldn't decide whether her imagination created the dream or she really spoke with Dahni. The dream felt like the Blindness, but the Phrenii supposedly couldn't travel the Blindness. Could she be in rapport while she dreamed? Dreaming minds regularly wandered the Blindness, avoiding the hunters by instinct.

Dahni told her that humans with the Sight could often make sense of dreams. She was sure she didn't have the Sight, being a gift that developed when one was young. So she couldn't know whether she carried a son or daughter and she had never experienced flames in the Blindness. This couldn't come from her imagination. If she could talk to Dahni in the Void, but she didn't dare attempt that in a jail surrounded by strangers, considering what happened the night after Taalo destroyed the Ferry.

Light started to gleam through the shutters. Any more sleep was impossible, even though she felt exhausted. Glancing at the corner where the old woman huddled, she noted the shine of her dark eyes. She got up and sat on the bench, stretching her arms and legs and yawning. To her left, Lissa curled up in the corner and to her right, the two marsh women huddled close. They looked so alike, they had to be mother and daughter. The old woman coughed again, deep coughs that shook her, and her daughter tried to hold her.

Draius got up and knelt in front of the old woman. On her knees, she was level with the old woman's face. Without thinking, she reached out to touch her chest. The daughter moved to stop her, but the old woman put a restraining hand out.

"Leave her be." Her Tyrran slurred with a strange accent.

Draius gazed steadily into her sharp, intelligent eyes. The woman nodded. Her other hand, which usually held the Kaskea shard, tightened into a fist. She concentrated on the chest. Yes, she could see the shadow, the wrongness. She concentrated on the Darkness, squeezing it, obliterating it—green light radiated from the edges of her hand that pressed against the woman's chest. Somewhere, probably in Suel's pocket, her Kaskea shard glowed.

"What are you doing?" Lissa stared with wide eyes at Draius.

"Nothing." Draius stopped and rubbed her hands together. "Just trying to warm her up."

"She's breathing better." Lissa used an accusing tone. "What did you do? I can handle marsh scum, but I won't be shut in with a sorceress. Where's that warden?"

The daughter got up and walked toward Lissa. "She did nothing. You'll say nothing." The daughter's voice was low. "You'll be taken for a fool. Everyone knows there are no more sorcerers."

"Then she's a witch, just like you marsh scum with tattoos." Lissa touched her forehead in a rude manner and started to turn toward the bars. The daughter's hand flashed out and she slapped the whore across the face. Hard.

Lissa put her hand on her cheek. "You can't—" She stopped when the daughter's hand twitched. "I'm out of here by next morn, anyway. What do I care? You'll all rot in here, sure as starlight." Lissa went back to her corner to sulk, rubbing the red welt.

The daughter sat down next to her mother and Draius introduced herself. She didn't give her Tyrran lineal name. The women reciprocated: the daughter's name was Roumithea and the mother's name was Enita.

"Why are you here?" Draius promptly regretted her question. Next, they'd ask her the same and what would she say? *I'm a Tyrran spy who was caught fleeing Groyga?*

"My mother came into the city to find someone." Roumithea avoided the question. Enita smiled gently at Draius while her eyelids drooped. She fell asleep fast, into a deep slumber where she no longer coughed.

Draius peeked through the cracks in the shutters and saw sunlight touching rooftops. The warden brought breakfast. Lissa kept her distance from all three of them, but snatched the bowl with the most gruel when they were shoved through the bars. She probably needed it, since they came for her just as she finished her gruel.

"To the stocks." The matron gestured to the men to get Lissa. The whore resisted at first, before showing some courage and marching out of the cell herself. She didn't glance at any of her cellmates as she went out to face her sentence.

Draius was left with her own thoughts while the day ground on. Boredom was the prevailing climate within her mind while she mulled over her possible pregnancy, wondered how Peri and Lornis were doing, and what her dreams might have meant. She avoided thoughts about her future, such as how she was going to get her Kaskea shard back or how she was going to get home. Every once in a while, she peered through the shutters. She had more glimpses of armed Groygans than she liked; when had Kitarra opened up to Groyga? She saw black uniforms of the Council of Lords, plus the black and red of House Endigala, but no other house colors.

The sun was setting when they brought Lissa back. They dragged her in and dropped on the floor. The whore had suffered while in the stocks: the smell of rotten food permeated the cell, but the bruising on her face, arms, and legs spoke of more than thrown garbage. The side of her face was swollen and black; only one of her eyes would open. She struggled to sit up.

"Don't touch me," Lissa muttered when Draius reached toward her.

"As you wish." She put the blanket in Lissa's corner since Enita and Roumithea had her cloak, and sat back on the bench.

After it turned dark, she heard Lissa sit up. She crawled, slowly and surely, toward her corner and wrapped the blanket about her. Draius moved to her regular position on the floor and tried to sleep.

The next dawn, Lissa looked much better. She had regained her spirits and banged on the bars. "Here now, let me go. I've done my day," she yelled to the empty room on the other side. She banged once again on the bars and limped back to her corner, where she glared at Draius and the marsh women. "I don't need to spend another moment with you."

The door opposite the bars opened and the matron stepped in. She ignored the prisoners, turning and holding the door for a finely dressed gentleman who had his hood pulled to cover his face. Suel followed the gentleman through the door but he was no longer wearing the livery of the King's Comhla. He wore the dark blue and silver of Kitarra, but the insignia wasn't familiar: a broad silver tree under five stars. Draius stood up, watchful.

Lissa walked to the bars, hips swaying, but her limp marred the seductiveness of her walk. "You can find me by the docks whenever you wish, fine ser."

The man pulled back his hood, swung off his cloak, and handed it to the prison matron. Draius stared. Few men could be called beautiful without appearing effeminate, but Lornis managed and so did this man. He was on the slender side, with carved porcelain features and blond hair. He was clean-shaven in the Groygan fashion. His bright eyes glittered as he glanced over the women in the cell. One of his eyes was blue, but the other was green. This strange asymmetry added to his beauty. She instantly distrusted him.

"What do we have here?" asked the gentleman in precise, educated Tyrran. "A whore, some renegades, and a Tyrran spy?" His silky voice held amusement and it caused shivers to run down her spine. To still the feeling, she crossed her arms. He was taller than she thought, because her eyes weren't quite level with his. She tried to stare back with unconcern, but she had a hard time looking into his bright eyes.

Lissa blanched, and her bruises stood out on her face. She bowed her head and backed away from the bars, muttering, "No offense intended, your grace."

Aha—only one man in Suellestrin could be called "your grace."

"Take her out." His voice was controlled and smooth. The warden unlocked the cell. Suel grabbed Lissa roughly, pulling her out and holding her to face the gentleman.

"It would be a pity if you couldn't ply your trade, wouldn't it?" He grabbed Lissa's jaw with one hand.

Draius blinked in surprise; his hand moved so quickly she thought it blurred.

"This is a *private* visit. If my people hear *any* rumor of this, I'll hold you responsible. I will find you, wherever you are." The man spoke easily, but Lissa's eyes widened.

"I will say nothing," she said thickly, her jaw still held in the iron grip. "You can trust me, but not the witch or the frogs."

"A witch, you say? How amusing." He let go and dismissed Lissa. Suel pulled her out of the room, followed by the woman warden, leaving him alone on the other side of the bars.

Draius glanced around, wary. The door to the cell gaped open. Only one man stood between her and possible freedom, adjusting his fine black gloves. He wore a decorative fencing sword, but did he know how to use it?

"I am Cerith." Inherent in his tone was a title. Since Lord Chintegrata informed her about the Kitarran royals, she knew his title but she was not about to use it.

Cerith made Lornis, who was always well-dressed, look like a rough farmer. His black coat was fine Tyrran leather and must have cost a fortune. The shoulders of the coat were broad and the collar was high, framing the fine blond hair that floated about his neck. Froths of lace spilled down his chest and his breeches were tight, showing slim hips and muscled legs. His boots perfectly matched his coat. She recalled how fast he moved when he grabbed Lissa, and wondered if she could overpower him.

"I wonder the same thing. What sort of match would we make?" A slight smile played on his lips. "But I'm not interested in that duel, not at this time."

She was taken aback. Had she said her thoughts aloud? Perhaps the open cell door was a ploy, to see if she would take the bait. Remembering her cellmates, she looked over at the marsh women. They watched her and Cerith with interest.

"Are you a witch or a Tyrran spy, as the Groygans would have us believe? Come closer." Cerith motioned her to step forward.

Drawn by that fluid motion as if pulled by a string, she moved without making any conscious decision. She cleared her throat. "Neither—I'm a merchant's wife." Nobody thought she was Kitarran, so she used the Tyrran cover story.

"Really?" His eyes were mesmerizing. "What about this piece of slate you carry, your memento?" He pulled her chain and Kaskea shard out of his coat pocket and held it up so it dangled at her chest level. "I think our Groygan friends should be quite interested in you and your piece of slate. No wonder they hunt for you."

She reached for it but quick as a snake, he grabbed her wrist and the shard flared slightly, giving off an amber color. It was such a quick flare she hoped no one else had noticed it. Cerith was focused on her face and their bodies shielded it from everyone. Now she knew why he didn't have the ruddy coloring of a Kitarran.

"You've got Meran blood," she said flatly.

Cerith's grip tightened; she might as well have been pulling against a manacle. His graceful moves hid a surprising strength. His gleaming eyes met hers and his lips curved into a full smile. While still holding her wrist, he dropped her shard back into his coat pocket.

"My maternal grandmother was Tyrran." Cerith stepped back, his smile fading. He continued to watch her with apparent amusement and curiosity. Suel slipped into the room. He stood behind Cerith and whispered something in his ear.

"Beware, your grace." She nodded at Suel. "One should never trust a man with two masters."

Suel scowled and stepped forward. He was stopped by a subtle flick of Cerith's hand and that told her all she needed to know. Unfortunately, Cerith was Suel's true master and they were attuned to each other's body language. Her heart sank. She'd had a better chance of escaping the drunken team of King's Comhla than these two.

"Sharp of tongue *and* mind," murmured Cerith, watching her eyes flicker to his hand.

"When are you going to hand me over to your Groygan friends?"

"Perhaps more your friends than mine." Cerith reached into his pocket and withdrew the small signet ring that Lord Chintegrata gave her. His eyebrows rose in question. "No Groygan would have sold you this."

"It was payment for fine Tyrran leather—he took almost my entire inventory."

"You're a terrible liar. You know this would never be used as payment. This ring always belongs to someone trustworthy." He put the ring back in his pocket and fished for something else. "Just like this item." His hand came out as a fist and then opened to show another shard of the Kaskea.

Fear flashed through her. "What have you done with my—"

"Husband? I think not," Cerith said. He gestured and Suel tossed him a sheathed sword. Cerith caught it and unsheathed a saber, *her* saber, while he kept his eyes on her.

"You are the commanding officer and he was your man." Cerith whipped her saber by her throat, missing by the width of a finger, and sheathed the saber with a flourish.

"*Where is he?*" She didn't use Bordas's name, sticking by his training about not releasing names or ranks when being questioned.

"He is safe, but angry." Cerith put the shard back into his pocket as her hand moved toward it. "He was tasked with a deed that violated his basic orders. He feels betrayed by his superior officer. In fact, I think he's broken."

She stayed silent, her mind racing. As she considered the possibility that Cerith might really be describing Bordas's current state of mind, she kept her face still and expressionless. Did she violate Bordas's trust when she ordered him away? After waiting a few moments for a response from her, Cerith appeared to make up his mind about something. With a gesture that included the marsh women, he said to Suel, "Tell Whin that we'll be taking these three."

Why did he want the other women? "They have nothing to do with me," Draius said.

"Why the concern?" Cerith cocked his head, eyes gleaming. She shut her mouth and pressed her lips together tightly. Anything she said might make things worse for Roumithea and Enita.

The prisoners were bound by their wrists and pushed through the corridors out to the street. She watched Suel and three other Kitarran men accept Cerith's orders without question. Their loyalty to him appeared absolute. Outside, she paused. There was a team of horses pulling a wagon and beside them stood Chisel, saddled and bridled with her own tack. Suel pushed her from behind and she stumbled forward. They were put in the bed of the cart. Suel controlled the team and a man called "Tenil" climbed in with the prisoners, keeping his attention on her.

Cerith patted her horse on the neck. "A fine beast." He set his foot in the stirrup and fluidly mounted. The horse snorted and sidled.

Draius was disappointed—Chisel had never let anyone else ride him before, but Cerith had obviously managed to gain the horse's respect and trust. Cerith's point was obvious: *your horse is mine, your man is mine, and everything else will be mine.* She could still command the horse to try to unseat Cerith, but if he managed to stay on, he would cement his control over the horse.

As they rode through Suellestrin, her Kitarran captors were silent. They traveled back streets with minimal traffic. The skies were cloudy and brooding. Likewise, the buildings of dark stone loomed over the streets and people looked fearful, at least the few pedestrians she saw. They turned a corner and stopped in an alley. Tenil pushed Draius down to lie on the floorboards. "Stay down," he admonished her.

The marsh women were taken out and by the sound, they didn't resist. Lying with her cheek against the floorboards, a fortuitous crack in the side of the bed gave one of her eyes a glimpse of what was happening. At the other end of the alley, Tenil cut the women's bonds. Roumithea said something to both Cerith and Tenil, making some gestures. Tenil nodded and responded, then put his hand on Roumithea's shoulder. What was happening? Didn't Cerith call the women renegades?

Enita spoke. Cerith bent his head attentively to listen to the small woman, who placed her hands on her chest and then motioned to the wagon. Cerith looked up and his gaze seemed to pierce the crack she was looking through. Enita was talking about her healing. The marsh women walked out of the alley.

Tenil climbed back in and she struggled back to a sitting position. Cerith rode into the alley and observed her with an irritating combination of amusement and superiority. Perhaps it was his asymmetrical eyes, with that knowing gleam, that made her distrust him.

"I must attend my uncle and his lackeys, so I'll leave Tenil to see to your needs. Please follow his suggestions, for your own good and the good of your comrade." Cerith bowed his head in mock politeness. "Thank you for a very fine horse, Commander Draius of the King's Guard."

A tremor ran through her. In this part of the world, only Bordas would know she had been recently promoted and transferred to the King's Guard. He had also who taught her that internal King's Guard organization, personnel, and *ranks* were not to be revealed to outsiders.

Palace of Stars, Betarr Serin, Tyrra

KING AND COUNCIL AT ODDS

This past Kingday resulted in one of the most tumultuous King's Council meetings that this editor has ever seen. The dispute started when Councilman Muusa proposed that the remaining parts of the Kaskea be entrusted to the council for safekeeping and future use. Other members of the council, with the exception of Aivo and Lidja, tentatively supported Muusa. The king disagreed and this editor reports that his majesty can be daunting in his anger. The controversy was surprising since King Perinon himself appointed Muusa to the council to replace Reggis.

—The Horn & Herald, *Second Honorday, Erin Ten, T.Y.* 1471

Councilman Meran-Viisi Muusa was lying.

Lornis couldn't determine which statements were false, but the man hid something. He slouched against the wall and observed while Captain Kilpi asked the questions. He yawned; he only had five hours of sleep last night. Yesterday, he had been hauled out of bed an hour or two after midnight. Then he had personally investigated two crime scenes, interviewed almost the entire Meran-Viisi household, checked the whereabouts of every King's Guard in the Palace of Stars at the time of the murders, and as evening came on he visited every five-star matriarch who resided in Betarr Serin. *Those* discussions were painful and he would never get a marriage contract with a Viisi lineage now. Luckily, he aspired only to marry Draius.

Now it was the next morning and he was *still* interviewing people in Betarr Serin. There were three other murder scenes with possible witnesses in the lower city, but he had to delegate those to Miina and Ponteva. They collected evidence and witness statements down there, while the clerks in Investigation read through all the statements and reports they generated and tried to establish a composite timeline. He almost groaned thinking of the work still to be done.

Instead, he refocused on the young councilman, trying to put all that empathy the Phrenii had given him to good use. Muusa was inexperienced and reportedly had a burning ambition, but by all the rumors he wasn't clever concerning the King's Law or the functions of the King's Council. However, he took to other aspects of politics quickly, such as self-promotion and the ability to hide his feelings and motives. This made it hard for Lornis to read him, but he still knew Muusa was lying.

"Did you bring *anything* with you when you visited the master of arms two evenings ago, ser?" Kilpi looked ragged as well. As captain of the King's Guard, he had been involved in most of the interviews at the palace. Soon, he would be the new master of arms and would decide who would move into his old position.

"What manner of object do you mean, captain?" Muusa sounded earnest, but he immediately assumed that Kilpi referred to an object. They had clamped down on *all* information regarding the murderous toys, but arresting Sareenian merchants and confiscating their inventories couldn't be hidden. So Muusa's assumption was not especially incriminating. A feeling of unease swirled around the room, almost making Lornis shiver.

"You didn't pick up anything *for* Sevoi on your way to his office?" Kilpi pressed the point.

Muusa's forehead wrinkled. "I don't think so." Despite the weak wording, Lornis felt strong enough evasion to indicate a lie.

"What was your purpose there?" As Muusa hesitated, Kilpi added: "Under the King's Law, we're allowed that knowledge to aid us in our investigation."

"If you must know, I spoke to him about who should be caretaker of the remaining shards of the Kaskea. I hoped that the master of arms would listen to reason, even if our king will not." Muusa sounded petulant but Lornis sensed relief, perhaps to have a change of subject.

"You hoped to apply more pressure to the king." Kilpi jumped to the obvious conclusion.

"Of course. The extra shards are becoming too much of a strain for him. That is obvious particularly to the matriarchy."

Lornis straightened. "Which lineages have shown support for your proposal?"

"Well—I suppose—" Muusa was taken aback and recanted. "There has been no formal approval from the matriarchy."

Everyone knew matriarchs didn't direct politics through formal means. Lornis leaned back against the wall and frowned, remembering his discussion with Haversar only five days ago regarding Lady Leika of the Pettaja-Viisi and the Groygan Honored Sword. What comment did Haversar make, almost in afterthought? *This is more favor than she bestows on members of the Council—she entertains inexperienced and young five-star councilmen fairly frequently.* Meran-Viisi Muusa was both inexperienced and young, with the bonus of being of the *king's lineage.* Could he really be aiming as high as the throne itself? If so, Lady Leika had fertile ground for manipulation.

"If others support your viewpoint, did you present Sevoi a gift *from* anyone?" Kilpi must have sensed the evasion in Muusa, since he asked this same question yet a third way. "Perhaps a gift for the younger cousins?" With the lowered birth rates and the emphasis upon future Tyrran generations, it was common to carry a gift for the children of another lineage. Unfortunately, Kilpi had just directed Muusa's attention toward the Sareenian toys in the marketplace. Lornis detected a spike of panic from the councilman, promptly suppressed.

"I said I didn't carry anything into the office. No food, no flowers, no brandy, nothing." Muusa used a light voice, trying to sound disinterested.

"Did you see any such gift in the office, perhaps sitting on his desk?"

"I didn't notice."

"Anything look out of place to you?"

"What do you mean by *out of place?*" Muusa cocked his head.

"Something that didn't look appropriate or usual for a place of work," Kilpi snapped. He added, "Forgive me, councilman. We're all running without sleep in a stressful situation here."

"I understand, captain." Muusa's mouth stretched into an oily smile. He would have to mold that smile into something more sincere if he wanted to win his next election. This young cousin of the king had been *appointed* to the council because his predecessor was murdered—the first of the famous "necromantic murders" eventually solved by Draius.

He stepped forward and leaned on the table, well aware that he loomed over the thin councilman. "Ser, you forgot to answer my question."

The insincere smile was now directed at Lornis. "What question?"

"Which matriarchs have expressed concern about securing the remaining shards of the Kaskea?"

"I don't remember. Many." Muusa frowned, looking put out, which was a more natural expression for him. Then he made the mistake of looking Lornis directly in the eyes.

"Surely you can remember the interested five-star matriarchs, councilman. What about Lady Leika? We know the Pettaja-Viisi have an antagonistic relationship with the Meran-Viisi already." With their gazes locked, he saw panic flare in Muusa's eyes.

The young councilman jerked his head. "Your grasp of politics must be based on the *H&H*, lieutenant. You should take caution before maligning five-star lineages." He abruptly stood. "Captain, I need to take my leave. This interview is wasting valuable time."

"Yes, councilman," Captain Kilpi said as Muusa turned and stalked out of the room.

After the door closed, Lornis turned to Kilpi. "I rattled him on purpose, because I expect him to high-tail it to the Pettaja-Viisi matriarch. I need someone to follow him and I'm all out of people." Ponteva would be the usual choice for this work, but the senior watchman was up to his armpits in murder investigations down in Betarr Serasa.

"Someone out of King's Guard Intelligence can do it—without uniform, of course." Kilpi's face was grim. He motioned to the guard at the door, who left immediately. "I'm not going to ask where this investigative turn came from, because I'll take the councilman's advice and use caution regarding five-star lineages. These murders are taking a treasonous direction that's churning my stomach."

Lornis emitted a small, hollow laugh and shook his head. "I never thought I'd see this day. The murder weapons were made by Sareenian desert tribes, but Tyrran hands directed and used them."

Estate of Duke Ungought, Whythern Marshes, Kitarra

Draius woke. She lay on a bed, without her arms bound. She heard an impatient tapping and raised her head to see the duke pacing in front of a door. Looking around, she saw a small but well-appointed bedchamber. She and Cerith were alone in the room. As he paced, he tapped his riding crop against the top of his boot.

He turned to face her, the tails of another finely tailored coat whirling about his thighs. His boots had changed also, impeccably matching the coat. "Very well then, you're awake."

She stifled a yawn and tried to clear the fog in her head. It seemed like she had slept for a very long time, but not in a restful sleep. At least there had been no dreams or nightmares. She remembered traveling in the wagon to an estate on the northeast edge of Suellestrin. They delivered her to the back of a grand house, offered her hot stew and, because she hadn't had anything since the morning jail gruel, she accepted it.

Cerith stood at the foot of the bed, but her eyes didn't want to focus on him. "What was in the food?"

"You needed rest, didn't you?" He sounded like he was placating a child.

"I want to talk with Bordas."

"Certainly, if he has time when he comes back from his mission."

A mission for Cerith? She hoped for more answers, information, anything—instead, he came to the foot of the bed and pointed his riding crop at her. Feeling vulnerable with him standing over her, she sat up on the side of the bed.

"I've always had good intuition, Draius. But you—I can't read you. Why is that?"

"I wouldn't know," she said stiffly.

"You won't lower your guard. Why can't you trust me?"

She looked away, tired of hearing the familiar litany about *trust*. This was a question the few men in her life repeatedly asked her. Jan had called her cold and untrusting, while he continued an affair with another woman. Lornis asked her to marry him and she held him off even on their last night together, because she wasn't confident about *her* feelings.

"I'm holding both shards of your Kaskea for the time being," Cerith said. "My people say they're connected to your magical beasts."

"Why ask *me* to trust *you*, when you won't give me back my belongings? As for what your people say, they're crediting the shard with too much power. It's not very useful." Her tone was bitter.

"Enita would beg to differ with you about that." His voice was quiet. "Since I value Enita's counsel, I am also grateful that she's healed. As is a young man in Agrottre Village and I suspect, someone who means a lot to Lord Chintegrata. Right?"

She nodded.

"Let's be honest with each other. You probably were briefed by your own intelligence. What do they say about me?" He leaned toward her.

"You're well known for your excesses." Actually, the word "debaucheries" was used to describe the activities of the nephew of King Markus. "You're no longer heir to the throne, because Markus finally got an infant son from his young queen. As that son grows, you become unwanted competition in the king's eyes. Perhaps you already are."

"Tastefully worded." He smiled. "I'm happy that news of my *excesses* have traveled about the mapped world. But you surmised more, didn't you?"

As long as Cerith kept the Kaskea, she couldn't trust him. She hesitated. "If the rumors were true, I wouldn't see such loyalty in your men. The marsh people may also trust you and they have suffered under Markus's heavy hand. You sympathize with their cause. I think you scheme to regain your father's throne and your *excesses* are a carefully crafted screen."

"Very observant." His face showed no offense. "Especially for a Tyrran."

"What do you mean?"

"My dear Draius." He sat down on the edge of the bed with a flourish and she fought the impulse to move. Half of her wanted to slide away from him, but the other half didn't. Her muscles squirmed. "You Tyrrans expect the world to come to *you*. Ambassadors must be sent to your sister cities, yet you won't lower yourselves to the politics of other countries."

"That's not true." An automatic response leapt out of her mouth.

"There's no formal Tyrran presence here in Suellestrin. While your cousin sits on his throne and concerns himself with his own people, what does he care about Kitarrans? Does it worry him that my uncle's authority is usurped by Groygans?"

She started to protest that Perinon cared very much if Groyga's tentacles reached into Kitarra. Second thoughts formed and she closed her mouth. She was not familiar with the intrigues here in the north and didn't follow the international politics or policies discussed by her own king and council. Besides, many Tyrrans still thought of Kitarra as Tyrra's colony rather than its own country. Groyga was the focus, always the traditional enemy, and Kitarra was like the distant cousin who was married into another lineage and forgotten.

Decidedly out of her depth, she changed the subject. "How do you know so much about me? Bordas wouldn't give you those details."

"I am sent copies of the *Horn and Herald,* albeit too late to be newsworthy, as well as reports." Cerith patted her knee condescendingly.

"From your embassy in Tyrra?" She tried to ignore his touch.

"Yes. Luckily, my uncle hasn't realized that my reports are much more detailed than his. I selected the Kitarran ambassador who sits in Betarr Serin, who can follow the exploits of famous Officer Draius and how she solved the 'necromantic murders.' I happen to understand the relationship between Serasa-Kolme Draius and King Meran-Viisi Perinon, but my uncle does not. What would the king pay for the safe return of his cousin, and the mother of his next-generation namesake?"

"You're demanding ransom? Or do you intend to give us to your uncle?" She suppressed the knot of fear starting in her stomach.

His face hardened. "I would never give my uncle such valuable hostages. All he would do is hand you over to his Groygan counselor."

"So you'll bargain with the Groygans directly."

"How can I convince you that I don't like their influence inside Kitarra?" He stood and looked down at her. "The perverse part of me will always deny them what they seek." He reached to touch her hair and she jerked her head back. His hand dropped and he shrugged. Even his shrug was graceful.

"What does the other part of you want? The non-perverse part, if such exists?" Her voice was harsh.

Cerith laughed lightly. "Ah, the burden of living up to one's reputation. All my parts are in agreement. The Groygans can't have you."

"They could put you on the throne."

"As yet, they don't have that power and I hope they never do." He paused. "Do you really think I would consider that?"

"So you continue to plot against your uncle and weave a persona that can't be threatening, a persona that can't hold the crown, either. Do you consider the marsh people to be part of your country, your people?"

"They were here before the Tyrran explorers."

"You're not answering my questions."

"You're not answering mine, either. Isn't that the joy of the duel, my dear Draius? The thrust and counter?" Cerith stood and walked toward the door.

Standing up, she crossed her arms over her chest. "Your grace, if you care about your people, then I have information you need. I volunteer it in good faith, hoping you'll return my Kaskea shards."

He paused, his hand on the door latch.

"Across the mouth of the Saamarin and hidden in the forest near the Mirror Sea, forces loyal to Lord Endigala wait. They are an artillery unit, with hundreds of guards. I don't know how many cannons they have, or why they wait, or what their mission is, but they sit within one day of Suellestrin."

She didn't see the response she expected. He sighed and the corners of his mouth turned up in triumph. "Thank you, Commander Draius."

"You're not surprised."

"Neither are you, because you suspected I had sources that already reported it. Right?"

She nodded. "I figure some of Lord Chintegrata's homing pigeons are sitting in your dovecote, and vice versus. Aren't you worried about those forces?"

"Of course, I'm worried about what will come. That's why your man Bordas is out there on the shore of the Mirror Sea, trying to do a detailed assessment. We knew your arrival would mean I'd have to force my uncle's hand."

When did Bordas become *her man?* If he was her man to command, why was he working for Cerith? "What did you do to him? How did you bewitch him away from his mission?"

Cerith's tone was dry. "When it comes to bewitchment, you're the one with the magical accoutrements. Besides, Bordas and I trust each other." He opened the door and said to Tenil, "Don't leave her alone. She hasn't yet proven herself."

CHAPTER FOURTEEN

Treason

Betarr Serasa, Tyrra

The morning after interviewing Councilman Muusa, Lornis made time for a special discussion.

Mahri finally reappeared to assess King Perinon's condition and pronounced the Phrenii unable to heal him. This echoed the situation when both Draius and Perinon had slipped into an unconscious state after Dahni accidentally killed a man. But this time, Perinon was conscious. Lornis suspected the Phrenii were incapable of healing, or reversing, the effects of necromancy. He didn't know if anyone had the balls to ask them this outright. *Well, I'm going to ask.*

He needed to talk to Dahni, the Phrenic aspect of healing. To find any of the Phrenii in Betarr Serasa, especially in the morning, one looked for crowds of children. He found Dahni surrounded by children in the street beside the Great Hall, off the main market square. The creature was luminous in the shade of the building, where many of the children sat in a semi-circle facing it. Lornis quietly approached because a serious conversation was taking place.

"But a dream isn't real. A dream can't do this." The boy sitting directly in front of Dahni pushed back his sleeve and pointed to a bruise below his elbow.

"What if you hit your arm on a bedpost as you thrash about?" A younger boy hopped from foot to foot.

This made the previous boy pause. "That's different."

"But real!" the girl beside him exclaimed. "So a dream *can* hurt you."

"Can you all tell the difference between dreams and the substance of everyday life?" Dahni asked.

Most of the children nodded, but a few frowned or cocked their heads, perhaps puzzling out the philosophy of their reality. Bemused, Lornis crossed his arms and leaned against the wall behind Dahni, unnoticed by the throng. This had the flavor of a meeting of the Royal Academy of Science. His father took him to a few of those meetings when he was apprenticing and learning the burgeoning scientific theories of the day. His father was a goldsmith and the Kulte-Kolme business of metallurgy and mining kept them wealthy, even by standards set in the sister cities. He would probably still be working in Plains End, if Jhari hadn't spoken with his matriarch. Then everything changed.

"You will need to understand this difference in the coming Darkness. You must make a promise, an oath." Dahni's voice rang through the alley, making the stones vibrate and jerking him out of his reverie. The creature's head was bowed.

"What promise?" This came as a chorus from the children.

"Promise to remember me. Remember me in your reality, dark as it may become."

He pushed away from the wall to stand straight. Had one of the Phrenii just used the pronoun "me?" The children promised, with shining eyes and tears. A few used oaths they were much too young to use. Several of the taller children put their hands on Dahni's horn and his stomach clenched, remembering when that razor-sharp spiral had punctured a human chest.

Dahni raised its head and the children scattered. Some already chattered and skipped, the somber moment behind them. Lornis frowned. Growing up in the small city of Plains End, he had few encounters with the Phrenii but he remembered them with fondness. He lost the details as the childhood memories faded. Had there been moments this solemn? Warnings about coming Darkness? Not that he could remember.

"Greetings, Lornis." Dahni didn't look around.

"Greetings to the Phrenii. I have questions for them—for you." Lornis felt awkward. Had he been meant to see that scene?

"We remain to serve." With this ritual response, Dahni turned about and faced Lornis. However, the customary words that should have comforted him sounded hollow after references to a coming Darkness and a downright plea to be remembered.

"Why do the Phrenii consult with children about dreams?" he asked bluntly.

"Please walk with me." Dahni started toward the square.

He sighed and trudged beside the creature, expecting another confusing conversation. The Phrenii could often be obstinate and obtuse.

"We conversed with Draius in the Blindness, within the construct of her dreams. We question whether she will perceive her dream as reality and, in some ways, perhaps she should not."

How strange. Experience taught Lornis that the Phrenii never repeated conversations with individuals, considering it a violation of personal privacy. He couldn't ask Dahni to relate the exchange. Instead, he approached the subject sideways. "Did you encounter her as the aspect of Dahni or as an individual?" The shocking use of a personal pronoun bothered him, although Draius told him the Phrenii could be individuals within the Void.

The creature kept quiet as they headed south across the square. He didn't bother to watch for traffic because pedestrians and coaches would stop or flow around them. Instead, he concentrated on Dahni. He hoped he was imagining the turmoil in the creature's eyes. They walked across the square before Dahni spoke again. "In the Void we are allowed to be individuals because we are the portals."

"You didn't speak with her in the Void."

"She was sleeping and drifting in the Blindness."

"She told me the Phrenii couldn't travel the Blindness. That was why *she* had to deal with Berin and Taalo." He tried not to make his tone accusing.

"True. Only individuals can move through the Blindness."

For the first time, he sensed evasion from Dahni. The creature was hiding something and perhaps even *frightened*. "Is she well? Where is she? How is Bordas?" He unwisely spewed out several questions.

"We are not sure." Dahni suddenly flickered and rippled with different colors, as oil floating on water looks when the sunlight hits it.

He gasped. As his lips started to form a word, Dahni stamped a hoof as if frustrated, causing a deep ringing through the cobblestone street. He covered his ears. Pain stabbed through his head and he saw a ripple of green wash over the creature's body. Immediately, Dahni changed back. The creature was luminous, with that same questionable transparency. Clouds blocked the spare sunlight and a light drizzle of rain started. He pulled his hood up and looked about, noting they stood outside the gates of the Guard stables. Had anyone else seen these transformations? A carriage went by with a team of horses, but its curtains were drawn and the driver seemed bored.

"Is Draius in danger?" He asked his most important question quickly.

"She is healthy, but lonely and frightened. She thinks of you with fondness. Most importantly, Kulte-Kolme Lornis, she carries your unborn daughter."

The Phrenii never lie, but Lornis no longer believed they were infallible. He gulped, and disbelief carried that gulp down to the pit of his stomach. Try as he could to squelch it, hope rose within him. "Are you sure?" As he asked the question, a heavy hand came down on his shoulder and he spun about, his own hand going for his saber hilt. He surprised Horsehead, standing behind him.

"Whoa, Lieutenant, I only wanted your attention." Horsehead backed up, his hands open and empty. His boots were caked with horse dung mixed with straw, and his working clothes carried the interminable dust that always lived with horses. He was old, but still hale enough to manage the Betarr Serasa Guard stables and armory. No one but his matriarch knew his age or lineage, and he never volunteered those details.

Lornis turned to see Dahni a block away by now, heading toward the square and the company of children.

"Darkness and Fury," he muttered. "Are they playing with me?"

"Ser?" Horsehead's bushy shelf of eyebrows rose.

Lornis always tried to be the epitome of expected behavior for an officer, but he had just smirched his reputation by swearing. Never having invoked the enemies of Light before, he composed himself. "What do you need, Horsehead?"

"The king is asking for you. We've got a horse saddled."

The King's Residence, Betarr Serin, Tyrra

KING TRAVELS TO SUMMER LODGE

The Meran-Viisi announced yesterday that the king will be traveling to their summer lodge in the Dibrean Valley. The lodge has not been opened since King Valos died there while taking a retreat prior to entering into marriage with Serkku-Viisi Lara. When asked if this was a similar pre-marriage respite, the Meran-Viisi matriarch didn't deny it. "It will only be an eight-day's leave of absence," said Lady Aracia. However, one suspects the murders of Master of Arms Sevoi and several Meran-Viisi three nights ago may play a part. All audiences are cancelled and the Meran-Viisi refuse to comment on his majesty's well-being. The king is scheduled to depart tomorrow.
— The Horn & Herald, *Second Ringday, Erin Ten, T.Y. 1471*

Lornis recognized the man standing at the door to the king's chambers. He was leader of the king's personal guard on the night of Sevoi's murder. His full name was Meran-Kolme Askar.

Askar grimaced. "Sure you want to go in there, lieutenant?"

"I'm under orders to report to the king."

"Your choice of pyre." Askar shrugged and let him enter.

Lornis took one stride into the outer chamber and realized what the warning meant. By his second, he wished he could back out as he heard the door close behind him. The outer chamber was packed with women, most of whom he would avoid, if given the choice. They all turned to watch him enter. He had never seen so many matriarchs and their assistants together in one place. He recognized the Meran-Viisi, the Meran-Nelja, the Meran-Kolme, the Rauta-Nelja, the Seteli-Nelja, the Serkku-Viisi, the Pettaja-Nelja, and his heart sank as he noted Lady Pettaja-Viisi Leika. Her interview had been extremely uncomfortable; he knew his effect on women and could usually fend off unwanted advances in a way that didn't bruise egos, providing the woman was not the matriarch of the second most powerful lineage in Tyrra. Insinuating she might have provided someone with a list of successors to the Crown had stopped her overtures cold and left him dancing with a venomous snake.

Buck up, he told himself. The Meran lineages would be concerned with the king's health. Since Rauta-Nelja Cellas was contracted to marry Perinon when she was old enough, that explained their presence. Looking about, he saw Cellas slouching in a chair. Her eyes appeared red; she looked miserable and exhausted. She was probably the only female in the room who was personally concerned for Perinon. Now that he was surveying the room calmly, he noticed it wasn't completely dominated by matriarchs. In one corner stood six King's Council members, huddling together and having some sort of sober discussion, glancing every now and then at the inner chamber door.

Lornis threw back his shoulders and continued to stride toward the opposite door. But trying to get across the room unnoticed was too much to hope for, and Lady Leika moved to intercept him.

"Lieutenant." Leika might be his age, but the hardness in her eyes didn't match her youthful features. "Why are you here?"

"My lady." He gave her his best dazzling smile and smooth bow. "His majesty summoned me."

"No doubt, but for what reason?" Her eyes flickered.

"I wouldn't know." The truth was always the best answer.

"By the way, has Enkali contracted you yet?" She looked like a cat with a captured mouse.

"Leika, please attend to our current business." Lady Aracia's voice was impatient. Leika tossed her head and returned to the tight cluster of matriarchs. Everyone in the room seemed tired and stretched beyond their limits, which might be why Aracia didn't lower her voice for her next sentence: "After all, you're the one pushing to change the list and formally notify the Serasa-Kolme."

They're talking about Peri. Aracia's words shocked him like a cold wash of water. She had revealed the negotiations for Peri to be the youngest successor to the matriarchy. It sounded like Leika wanted the Meran-Viisi to add other candidates as well. With effort, he kept his gaze straight in front of him and continued his progress toward the inner room. He knocked and was relieved when Lyn opened the door. He met Sevoi's daughter during his King's Guard interviews. She dropped off his suspect list when he learned how close she had been to Perinon and his brother Valos.

Her eyes glanced about the outer room as she let him enter. "The population outside decreased by one councilman and his aide, sire." Her voice held an almost macabre cheerfulness.

Lornis breathed easier. There were only four others in the inner chamber: Kilpi, Lyn, Perinon, and his manservant Velija, who was pouring tea. Perinon was not, as he almost expected, on his deathbed. He wasn't even in bed, but sitting on a lounge with a blanket tucked about him. His hand was newly bandaged and his face had dark hollows, but he was in much better shape than the last time Lornis saw him. "Sire, I'm glad to see you're recovering."

"Did the vultures congregating outside give you the idea I was dying?" Perinon took several swallows of tea and started coughing. His manservant took the tea and then handed him a clean kerchief, which he used to cover his mouth. He motioned for Lornis to sit.

"I did hear talk of setting up new successors." Lornis took the seat.

"What?" Lyn sounded outraged.

Perinon held up his hand. "All proper preparation, no need to be shocked. I actually feel sorry for Lady Aracia, who has to pretend she isn't working with one or more traitors. But her job is to ensure continuance of the Crown of Tyrra and that is what she'll do." His voice turned wry. "What I truly fear is another responsibility of the matriarchy: to ensure I'm still competent. I wouldn't be surprised if the Pettaja lineages were leading a charge to depose me."

"The Pettaja-Viisi are no joking matter, sire. Lady Leika is—" Kilpi paused and glanced at his audience. Commander Lyn and Perinon's manservant hadn't been given access to the murder cases. This morning, all the separate Guards received the change of command orders: Kilpi became the master of arms, the commander of the Guards, and the king's advisor on all matters of guard usage. He immediately promoted Commander Ruel to take his former position of captain of the King's Guard. He also selected Meran-Nelja Lyn for a new position of "Personal Intelligencer to the King." Lyn was suitable because they wanted someone who knew Perinon for a long time, someone he trusted. She was also senior enough to command the king's security, if necessary, and had been assigned to King's Guard Intelligence, so she was cleared to access almost everything.

"Sevoi's daughter deserves to know this. Don't worry about Velija, he's trustworthy." Perinon coughed again. "Please report upon your investigation, lieutenant."

"We retrieved charms from the five murder scenes in various conditions of working order." Lornis glanced at the floor where Mahri pulverized the charm that tried to attack Perinon. The ground marble was now covered with a tasteful rug. "Every one of them was a toy soldier wearing the uniform of the King's Guard. Not surprising, since all the intended targets had a strong relationship to that organization. The toys carried a long knife and sword, both as sharp and strong as the weapons they represented and both poisoned, according to Gaflis and Norsis. They're still not sure what the poisons are, Gaflis is attempting to treat the king as best he can." He nodded toward Perinon who lifted his bandaged hand. "Sire, I hope his treatments are helping."

"They are, but very slowly. They mostly consist of soaking the hand, trying to leach out the poisons. I'm also supposed to drink prodigious amounts of liquid to dilute its effect in my body." Perinon looked up and Velija poured him more tea.

Lornis continued. "Unfortunately, there still may be dangerous charms sitting in homes across the cities, maybe even the country. The City Guard arrested every merchant known to traffic in necromantic charms. Five Sareenian merchants were identified, but only four were found. They had all acquired them through Illus merchants representing a desert tribe."

"The merchant who got away? Was she the wine...?" Perinon didn't bother with the rest of his question and coughed into his kerchief.

"Yes." He provided more information for Kilpi and Lyn. "We suspected a female Sareenian wine merchant of being part of Taalo's conspiracy this past spring, but could never prove it. She fled when the conspiracy broke up, and then came back selling necromantic toys. We discovered she left the country again, days before the recent murderous charms were activated. Toy guards were found in each merchant's possession, but none with sharp metal weapons. Even the ones in *her* inventory were blunt and made of wood." All of which had been frustrating for the Office of Investigation.

"Could she make those charms on her own?" Perinon asked. "I thought everyone with that expertise had fled the country."

Lornis nodded. "They left when Draius broke up the conspiracy this past spring. Taalo needed facilities to torture people and—whatever else he had to do. I've looked at where the merchant lived and kept her inventory. She rented a very small room and it was stuffed to the beams with merchandise. She had no means to make charms."

"We recalled two of our best agents from Sareen as soon as we verified that Taalo had moved to Groyga. They were down there specifically to assess the current state of necromancy." Kilpi nodded at Lyn.

She cleared her throat. "Ever since Taalo used a charm from his pocket to destroy a ferry, our embassies have been collecting and sending information on anything to do with necromancy. In Groyga, they calculated that his spell had a force equivalent to twenty barrels of corned powder exploding all at once."

Lornis whistled.

"These charms are growing stronger and more sophisticated. In Illus, they can be ordered with custom instructions and activated with trigger words or little levers. They offer items that can communicate over great distances, that can improve the health, that can disguise you—and those are only the friendly charms. Consider what evil can be done to your enemies. No longer does one worry about the difficulty of poison delivery. All these charms are made by one or more desert tribes, but the orders go through merchants in Illus." Lyn sighed. "So did a merchant here order the charm that killed my father, or was that merchant merely used to pass along the order?"

"A good question that I can't answer yet," he said. "Which is why my best lead is still the person who lied during his interview: Councilman Muusa."

"You have proof now?" Kilpi looked hopeful.

"Not really. After we questioned him yesterday, Muusa made a beeline for the Pettaja-Viisi estate where Lady Leika resides. Our watcher said he went in looking angry, but came out disturbed and 'white as a sheet.' Unfortunately, none of this is proof of a conspiracy to commit murder."

"Poor Muusa," Perinon said. "I should never have listened to Aracia and appointed him to the Council. He is such an idiot sometimes. I could believe he was Leika's unwitting pawn."

"Well, he took off at a canter when I announced the Phrenii would be arriving soon." Lyn showed her teeth in a grim smile. "He didn't want his guilt to be read. However, if Leika's worried about the Phrenii, she didn't show it."

"Good. When the Phrenii arrive—" He was interrupted by Perinon, who shook his head.

"We lied." Perinon exchanged his kerchief for another. "I'm not calling the Phrenii because they can do nothing for me. I would only drain their power."

"I beg your pardon?" Lornis glanced at Lyn, who shook her head with a "don't ask me, I just take orders" expression. Velija caught his eye and held up one of the kerchiefs, prominently displaying the bright red blotch of blood on the white linen. He jumped up. "The Phrenii can heal you, sire."

Perinon raised his hand and he had to sit down again. "No, they can't, and they're not coming because I can no longer call Mahri. Our rapport is broken—" They had to wait through another cough. "I'm surrounded by necromancy and the Phrenii can no longer come near me. Ever since Draius left, I have felt worse and worse. It happened so gradually that I didn't notice, then the night of Sevoi's murder—Mahri risked everything to destroy the charm that night, then had to retreat to the Void to heal. I think someone's placed even more charms about this household just in the past eight-day, all intended to weaken me and keep the Phrenii out."

This was treasonous, and directed personally against the king. "Well, we can begin by searching this room," Lornis said.

"Already done." Perinon exchanged a look with Velija. "This room is clean, but I don't have the strength to walk about the entire Meran-Viisi household and estate, fingering items and getting weaker whenever I encounter a charm."

Realization dawned on him. "That's why you're leaving. Your respite, reported by the *Horn and Herald*."

"Who says I can't use Andreas to my own ends?" Perinon said. "Everyone who's going is under instructions to bring nothing with them but the clothes on their back and their weapons. We're loading up the packet boat early, north of the city, and getting our supplies directly from trusted farms up there. Lady Aracia's frightened enough by my condition that she's going along with this."

"We must be vigilant. This would be a perfect time for an assassination if our enemies learn the Phrenii can't protect the king." Lyn smiled at Lornis's expression. "Don't worry, we're prepared."

"Is Gaflis going along?" he asked.

"No—that would be a white flag of surrender and tell them their necromancy was effective. They might assume the Phrenii can't come into his residence," Lyn said.

"What about the charms? They'll still be here when you return." He shook off a shiver.

"Aracia is under instructions to clean out everything she can and resupply, re-decorate, rebuild, whatever it takes." Perinon finished his tea and held out his cup for more.

His jaw dropped. "The expense—"

"Is justified as a bridal gift for Cellas. My poor future wife gets to spend an eight-day with Aracia, picking out everything from rugs to chairs to books to bedclothes. I hope she survives this." Perinon grimaced.

"Will the Phrenii follow you to the lodge, sire?" If Kilpi had to ask that, he was probably staying in Betarr Serin.

"No. They have work to do here." Perinon eyed Lornis. "And the lieutenant will be helping them."

Lornis was perplexed; he noted the same squint of bewilderment on Kilpi and Lyn's faces.

"Let me explain. After Siuru's death discouraged us, the Phrenii continued to pester me about binding all the Kaskea shards. I thought that strange, until I re-read Sorceress Lahna's prophecies." He had a coughing fit, so they waited in silence as he changed out kerchiefs. "Unfortunately, my time might be running out and the Phrenii are starting to fragment, which Lahna predicted. The Kaskea *will* play a part in saving them, if Lahna's right."

"So the Phrenii themselves are going to find appropriate bearers for the Kaskea and bind them? Can they do that?" Kilpi asked.

"Of course." Perinon daubed his mouth. "The Phrenii bind the king themselves. These days, there are no human sorcerers to monitor the process. Now the council wants to take control of the shards and I can't allow that. Besides, they assume I have three extra shards of the Kaskea, but I only have two. I sent Draius to retrieve the Kaskea shard Taalo stole and, from what Mahri and Dahni can surmise, she was successful. The council and the matriarchy never realized Taalo took a shard to Sareen, then Groyga, because I had the City Guard hide that fact from public records. "

Lornis knew Taalo took a shard when he fled the country, but he didn't know the City Guard had covered it up. Did Draius know about this? He didn't think so, but what was done couldn't be changed. He took a deep breath and had to ask, "Is Draius safe, sire? How long before she can bring the extra shard home?"

"For some reason, she hasn't been able to walk the Void, but she can manage limited rapport. Dahni thinks she's safe and in Kitarra. Obviously, that shard won't be home before the council searches this bedchamber."

"Surely it hasn't come to that!" Kilpi said, frowning.

It was obvious that Perinon was tiring. "They've convinced Aracia that, for my own good, it's best to not burden me with the extra shards of the Kaskea. Once they passed an *emergency* referendum, they can now take possession of the shards temporarily and I must sue for them in front of my own magistrates. I haven't the strength for that and if Leika is behind the necromantic charms, she knows this. I need to pass these shards to someone who can help the Phrenii bind them."

Perinon took a small sack from his vest pocket and held it out to Lornis. Shocked, he could only stare at it.

"Surely this is premature, sire." Kilpi's voice was low. Perhaps he was frightened, as they all were, to find themselves suddenly enmeshed in a conspiracy.

"They must demand the shards tonight because I'll be leaving early tomorrow." Perinon's voice was grim. "That's why they're dithering outside that door. When they come in, I intend to have only one shard in my possession. One shard, which is bound to me even if they try to take it." The hand that held the sack, also had the ring with the shard of the Kaskea embedded. He raised his voice. *"Do I not have the loyalty of everyone in this room?"*

"Yes, sire." Lornis immediately came forward, went down on one knee, and took the sack. Everyone else in the room did the same and pledged their allegiance. He held the sack numbly. "But I don't have Meran blood. I come from the plains and I wouldn't know a good candidate for the Kaskea if they walked up and punched me."

"You won't have to. The Phrenii already identified Naton for binding to Jhari. I refused them the first time they asked and they seemed to acquiesce. Maybe they saw it would happen regardless."

Lyn looked just as shocked as Lornis felt. "Sire, he's a Sareenian."

"Half-Tyrran. Meran-Viisi Naton, now." Perinon made a weak gesture with his hand. "The Phrenii will try to find another to bind, Lieutenant Lornis."

"But the council will suspect I have the shards. Won't they stop me when I leave?"

"Then we need a diversion. Commander Lyn?" Perinon put down his tea and the corner of his mouth quirked.

Lyn got up and took a small flask out of her inner jerkin pocket. She walked over to the open brazier, which had some glowing coals to keep away the autumn nip. She poured the contents of the flask on the glow and jumped back as a conflagration whooshed up toward the ceiling. "Oh, no!" she cried dramatically.

Lornis stuffed the sack in his pocket before he stuck his head out. "Help, we've got a fire! Bring water!" He stepped to the side as everyone in the outside chamber surged toward the door. King's Guard and Meran-Viisi staff pushed through the crowd. It was a simple matter to slide around the edges and bid Askar goodbye as he left.

Estate of Duke Ungought, Whythern Marshes, Kitarra

The next morning, Draius tried to amuse herself by spending time at the window, which faced northward. The duke's sprawling estate bordered the marshes and was outside the Suellestrin walls. The estate gates and house seemed grandiose and the gardens she saw, during the few moments when she was hurried to the back of the west wing, were glorious.

Outside, the cloud cover was thick enough to hide the sun's silhouette. Traffic went through a wall on the edge of the estate, where it disappeared on a road that wound through tall bushes and straggling trees into the marsh. Riders and wagons with covered cargo left the estate, but hardly anyone came into the estate while she watched.

Tenil had to be just as bored, but the large man didn't sigh or pace. He had settled himself on a wooden chair near the door. She tried asking questions and found that Tenil would answer a few, but not all. Apparently Cerith had one of the largest country estates in Kitarra, built on land granted to him by his uncle. "So he had favor with Markus at that time?"

Tenil snorted. "The king granted him the land because he thought it was worthless swampland."

"How many guards claim loyalty to Cerith?" Her running tally of people wearing dark blue livery kept growing, and most of them were disappearing into the marshes.

Tenil shook his head. She was not allowed that information.

"What's the King's Comhla? Is Suel a member?"

"The comhla is officially disbanded," was all Tenil would say.

So it went until a mid-day meal brought a surprise, in the form of Roumithea.

"Are we all spies in the service of the duke?" Draius tried to cover her bitterness with bright unconcern.

"We didn't lie. My mother's condition was serious and I thank you for her returned health." But when Roumithea raised her brown eyes, there was distrust in her gaze.

"Why were you in the jail cell?" She wondered if that had been some elaborate deception at her expense.

"If you must know, missy, my mother is banned from Suellestrin. A wise woman of the marsh, particularly one burdened by the Sight, will be arrested per the king's edicts." Roumithea set the steaming bowl on the sideboard with a clunk.

"If so, why did she risk entering the city?"

"I told you the truth. She wanted to meet someone." Roumithea patted Tenil on the shoulder as she went through the door.

Draius had nothing to eat since the drugged food, which left her feeling hollow and queasy. The stew Roumithea left was hearty, but spiced strangely. In spite of that, she was grateful and wolfed it down. After she finished, she promptly threw it up into the chamber pot. Tenil went out and returned with Roumithea. This time she shooed Tenil out of the room, but he didn't leave without giving Draius a warning. "Roumithea is my wife, so don't try anything. I'll be right outside."

Roumithea picked up the chamber pot and put her other hand on her waist. "All right, missy, there is nothing wrong with the stew I made. No one else has been ill. Besides, you're not the sickly sort."

Draius wiped her mouth and tried to ignore the acrid taste. How would she ever manage in this strange place if she couldn't keep down her food? When they weren't suspicious, Roumithea's eyes appeared kind.

She needed to confide in someone... "I might be pregnant," she finally said.

Roumithea made a clucking sound and shook her head. "Then this food is too spicy for you. I'll get you something bland."

"Please." She stopped Roumithea at the door. "Please don't tell anyone."

"Surely your husband knows."

"I'm not sure yet. I have told no one." She remembered the dream with Dahni, but that couldn't have been real.

"I suppose there is no need to call attention to your condition. But I'll not keep anything from his grace, if and when he might need to know."

She heard Tenil query his wife and he didn't receive a satisfactory answer, because he frowned when he came back into the room. Another meal appeared, this one a bland flour cake, which she chewed slowly and kept down.

"What does the duke's insignia mean?" she asked Tenil after she had finished her meal. "I recognize the white tree of the Kitarra, but what do the five stars mean?"

"You'll have to ask his grace."

She wondered if Tenil randomly chose which questions he would answer. Why be so secretive about Cerith's insignia? When evening came, there was a knock on the door and Tenil went outside for a whispered consultation. He returned, frowning again. Roumithea, her arms filled with billowing fabric, followed him. She came in and deposited her load on the bed. Behind her, a maid followed with wash water and linens.

"What's this?" she asked, as Roumithea laid out garments in silk brocade.

"Your man Bordas says your memory and analytic abilities are legendary," Tenil said. "His grace wishes you to keep tally of the guests and attend to their activities during his ball. If you are seen in the halls, you must be dressed appropriately."

"Why should I help him?"

"Your man Bordas will be helping," Roumithea said.

"I don't think you should call him 'my man' anymore." She wondered if Cerith was playing her and Bordas against each other.

Roumithea held up some sort of kirtle in light blue brocade. "You're a bit tall for these, but I can let down some excess."

"You are not getting me into that, nor am I helping Cerith with his games." She sat down on the bed and folded her arms, ignoring the activities around her.

Roumithea pushed out Tenil and the maid. Then she stood in front of Draius, her hands on her hips, as if she faced a wayward child. "Missy, this is important. Lives are at stake."

"Lives are always at risk when one plays at treason."

"Just being an Ungought is dangerous enough. Markus executed his grace's father, mother, and older brother when he took the throne. No treason was involved, only trumped-up charges. These games, as you call them, have kept his grace alive."

"So he ensures he isn't a threat to the crown. I can understand that, but why involve me and Bordas?"

"I can't say." Roumithea shrugged. "Bordas supports his grace, I assure you."

"May I speak to either of them?"

"We don't have time. Please, this dress is only in case you're seen in the halls. You won't be participating in the ball." She held up the brocade again and Draius eyed it with distaste. Court dress was something she'd gratefully given up when she changed her lineal name from Meran-Viisi to Serasa-Kolme. Her contract to Jan removed any obligations to attend court functions. After the contract with Jan was dissolved, no one expected Draius, as an officer of the City Guard and still holding the Serasa-Kolme name, to attend such events.

"Why does the duke trust Bordas, but not me?"

Roumithea avoided her eyes and shrugged. "Bordas earned his trust."

"Is it because I'm cousin to Tyrra's king?"

Roumithea gave her a quick sidelong glance as she ripped out a deep hem. "Um, his grace doesn't give his trust easily to women." She talked around the pins in her mouth. "Plenty of ladies compete for his attention, but it was a woman who helped Markus falsely accuse his family. I'm surprised he involved you even this much."

"He trusts *you*."

Roumithea was adept at tailoring; she had the hem already pinned. She paused and eyed Draius with exasperation. "Why do you think Tenil and I work in the duke's household?"

Draius shrugged.

"I'm three-fourths frog and daughter to a wise woman. Even though I don't carry any symbols on my forehead, there's not a Kitarran household inside Suellestrin that'll have me. Tenil and I are grateful that his grace gave us work."

"Yet he says he doesn't know what to do with me."

"I can see that." Roumithea looked her up and down. "I think his grace has two categories for women: those whose loyalties he trusts, as opposed to those he cannot trust and therefore must seduce. Perhaps you don't fit either category?"

"Your words don't comfort me," she said dryly.

"I've no intention of making you comfortable," Roumithea said brusquely. "Be still or you'll be poked by the pins."

So, without understanding how it happened, Draius ended up dressed in full-length light blue brocade. The sleeves fit close above her elbows and below them, streaming tippets fell to the floor. A slim girdle of worked silver rode above her hips. Over everything went a fine white wool surcoat with cut-away sides and a long back that trailed on the floor behind her. Her shoulder-length hair was pulled back with simple combs and it looked pinned up from the front. As long as no one took a good look, she appeared ready to dance.

"Your wife is quite persuasive." She followed Tenil down a long hallway lit by lamplight.

"Aye, she usually gets what she wants." Tenil sounded pleased. He turned toward the center of the house and into a dark hallway. He gestured for Draius to follow. She stepped gingerly in the dark. "My wife's mother thinks that you will be important to his grace, perhaps save his life." There was doubt in Tenil's voice. "She had a dream where you both were blind and lost in the clouds, hunted by swimming and circling creatures."

Draius stumbled. Enita had accurately described the Blindness. She remembered the original purpose for trying to bind Siuru; the Phrenii had been pressuring Perinon to bind all the shards. However, the stars would fall into Darkness before she let a scheming pretender like Cerith bind to the Kaskea. She couldn't let him, or his men, know their potential. "The Sight can be fickle," she said lightly.

Tenil didn't reply. He gripped her elbow and steered her into an alcove. Inside, she understood why no lamps had been lit in the hallway. The alcove was curtained and concealed from the great hall below. As she peeked through the curtains she caught her breath at the ostentatious display of wealth.

Curtains of heavy white and blue brocade lined the long sides of the hall. They went from the high ceiling all the way to the floor. They also helped conceal the alcove where she now sat, looking down through a break between blue and white fabric. Chandeliers of gold and crystal held hundreds of candles, lighting the bright colors of the rich and noble Kitarrans who mingled below. The hall was filling as announcements were made at the door for arrivals.

Cerith walked through the swirling colors of court dress, standing out like a bright jewel on silk, getting admiring glances from both men and women. His blue coat with white trim matched the brocade on the walls. The shoulders had sparkling jewels sewn into a pattern, accentuating the triangular shape of his torso. The back of the coat fell to flared tails that stopped just above blue leather boots. Mounds of white lace fell down his chest. His breeches fit close—well, *immodest* was the word that came to her.

Instead of the curls sported by many of the men, Cerith's light hair was full and straight, ending in a froth that touched his shoulders. Contrary to styles in Sareen and Tyrra, Cerith shaved his chin clean, which accentuated his cheekbones. Looking about the guests, she saw other young men copying Cerith's styles, but the duke was the obvious original. Behind Cerith and barely noticeable in the overdressed crowd walked Bordas. She gasped.

"Are they insane?" she hissed.

Bordas stood out, even though he was dressed in the duke's livery. His face wasn't powdered so the bruises on his ashen face were obvious. He hadn't had them when he'd left her. His hair had been trimmed shorter so it matched the Groygan haircuts. Most disconcerting was the gold collar around his neck, connected by light chains to gold cuffs on his wrists. This jewelry was similar to that worn by married Groygan women and was symbolic. Bordas kept a respectful pace behind Cerith, moving as Cerith moved. They caused quite a stir when they passed through.

"You're supposed to be watching the order of arrival, and who speaks with whom." Tenil pointed at the door of the great hall, reminding Draius of her assigned task. She returned to watching arrivals and listening to their names, knowing her memory would be able to replay every detail for her. Every once in a while, Tenil would tell her additional information about the people who stepped through the door.

"The Groygan *counselor* to Markus," he whispered as a Groygan named Vitna Be Nettona was announced. Five other Groygan men, all looking incongruous with their short hair, accompanied the counselor. Then Nettona noticed Bordas and couldn't take his eyes off him.

The king arrived last. Markus had a florid face and full figure from too much food and drink. His queen, a young Kitarran beauty named Tintia, stood behind in bronze velvet and deep red hair. Markus appeared to be three times her age. Everyone in the hall acknowledged his arrival:

women curtsied while men bowed their knee. As host, Cerith stood at the bottom of the stairs to the door, bending his knee to his king and uncle. King Markus glanced around the crowd, finding the Groygan counselor.

"Vitna Be Nettona. Duke Ungought." Markus acknowledged the Groygan first, giving insult to Cerith. Under someone else's roof, even a king should acknowledge the host first.

Cerith's slight smile never changed. After acknowledgment, he stood, allowing all those in the duke's livery to stand, then the guests.

Markus's eyes flickered contemptuously over Bordas. "What's this, Cerith?"

"I present my latest plaything, Uncle." Cerith tugged the chain that went to Bordas's collar, cueing him to go to one knee. As if on a stage, Cerith turned about and addressed the guests. "Isn't he pretty?"

There was light laughter from the watching nobility and some scattered applause. Bordas kept a blank face while Draius seethed. Whatever Cerith was attempting, he affected Nettona. The Groygan counselor stood opposite the alcove, so Draius could see his face as he pushed forward to get a better view. His yellow eyes were hungry, the pupils elongating. "Where did you find him? Was he with a woman?" Nettona licked his lips.

"He was in the marshlands and claims he's a farmer who became lost." Cerith's smile was mocking.

"He's no farmer. He should be turned over to the king." Nettona's hand went into his doublet, perhaps fingering a snuffbox or timepiece.

"Yes," Markus said suddenly. "This man should be handed over to the Crown."

"If your Majesty wishes, I'll hand over my plaything. I warn you, sire, his passions run deep." Cerith bowed and Markus's face flushed.

"I don't keep catamites!" Markus spat out the words and Tintia put a restraining hand on his arm.

"Sire, perhaps this can be addressed tomorrow. The musicians are prepared and the dance awaits." Tintia's voice was pleading, but as she glanced over both Cerith and Nettona, Draius noted her light blue eyes were cool and calculating. She cast her gaze modestly down as Markus turned to her.

"Of course. We'll address this tomorrow." Markus attempted to cover his anger, his struggle visible on his face.

"At your service, Uncle, as always." Cerith bowed gracefully.

As if on cue, men in duke's livery appeared and escorted Bordas from the room. The music began and Markus and Tintia came down the steps. Draius spent the rest of the night watching Markus, Tintia, the Groygan counselor Nettona, and anyone they talked to. It was an hour past midnight when the king and his entourage left, at which point she was exhausted and allowed to leave also.

There were still the sounds of revelry as Roumithea started helping Draius out of her clothes. She had just gotten off the surcoat when Cerith came to the door. He came in the room without knocking, looking as fresh as if he were just starting the evening.

"At least it fits well." He glanced over her light blue brocade.

Tonight there were no engaging smiles, no innuendo. Cerith paced with amazing energy after hours of dancing. He fired off question after question to her, listening intently to her answers, and watching her with bright eyes. Who did Vitna Be Nettona talk to? When, and in what order? Who spoke to Tintia? Who did Markus speak with after the fifth dance? And so on, and so on...

Draius almost became ill watching Cerith's coat sparkle back and forth across the room, so she kept her eyes on her hands in her lap. She answered every question as precisely as she could. Almost an hour passed before he was out of questions. He stopped pacing and she looked up. His arms were crossed with one gloved hand on his shaved chin. He regarded her quietly, his eyes searching.

"Thank you, Commander Draius," he said abruptly. "Tomorrow I'll know I pushed his Groygan allies too far, if an order comes from Markus demanding that I hand over 'the Tyrran.'"

He turned to leave, but she stopped him with a question. "Your grace, have I proven to be trustworthy tonight?"

"Perhaps." His tone was thoughtful. "I suppose you'd like your mementos back."

She tried to keep her mind empty of motive. He couldn't know why she wanted to keep the shards away from him. She looked down and concentrated on how tight the dress felt around her shoulders and how she hated the low neckline. "Yes, your grace."

It worked. Cerith pulled from his pocket the two shards, rewrapped in wire and with a new silver chain. Luckily, his hands were gloved and his attention elsewhere. "I have no quarrel with Tyrra and her creatures. In fact, I would welcome any help that might be offered from your king and his Phrenii, if he ever concerned himself with our small country." His voice was sarcastic. "But your man Bordas tells me the Kaskea has become dangerous, so *promise* me you won't attempt to use these items."

"I won't." She swallowed the bile from the lie. Even though she made no oath and didn't swear upon her honor, her ancestors would mark a broken promise.

"Fine. I trust your word." He handed over the shards, which she swiftly put around her neck. His gaze turned to Roumithea. "Make sure she's packed and ready for tomorrow."

After Cerith left, she collapsed in relief and exhaustion. Roumithea removed her gown.

"I think you impressed him." Roumithea sounded pleased as she helped Draius into bed like a child. She fell into a deep sleep, her hand gripping the Kaskea shards.

CHAPTER FIFTEEN

Flight

On the Whitewater, Northern Tyrra

Perinon opened his eyes to a small, darkened room. He lay on his side and looked at a small desk bolted to a wall. Above it was a window, which had curtains drawn against daylight and cleats on both sides to secure them. The desktop was absolutely clean, something he never experienced in his own household.

He was on a common mail packet boat, since Aracia thought the Meran-Viisi barge too recognizable. His memories converged. He had given two shards of the Kaskea to Lieutenant Lornis, then Commander Lyn started the fire and once that was contained, the council searched his room. No shards were found, other than the one embedded in his ring. He faced down the angry council members, but the stress of the day had fatigued him. He collapsed as they moved him under the cover of darkness and Gaflis was called—all those plans to hide his health issues went up in smoke.

Raising his head, he realized that he didn't feel as good as he thought. He grunted with exertion and tried to use his free arm to push against the bed sheets.

"Feeling better, sire?" Gaflis moved into view.

"Want to—sit up—" Perinon panted and flailed. Gaflis helped him into a sitting position, resting against a rudimentary headboard attached to the wall.

"Sure as starlight, it happened just like you predicted. Your cough is gone, so maybe the internal bleeding has stopped." Gaflis felt his forehead, took his pulse, and then went to the door and spoke to someone outside. "The king's awake and he needs food. Be sure to follow the recipes I gave you."

Perinon closed his eyes and concentrated on Mahri. At first, he only sensed a tenuous thread of thought. Then relief came flooding through, mixed with anxiety. His rapport was again established and Mahri knew where he was.

Gaflis shook his shoulder. "Please don't attempt anything until you're stronger."

He opened his eyes. "I'm not likely to walk the Void any time soon. Why are you here? I thought you weren't coming on this jaunt upriver."

"Humph. Your collapse last night changed everyone's plans. We did try to hide the identities of everyone who boarded. My presence may be for naught, thankfully, since you made an astounding recovery by yourself. The treatment from this point is rest and sustenance, although you won't be starting with solid food."

Perinon groaned, but Gaflis was right. The broth came and he was ravenous, but his stomach refused to accept more than a bowl before he slipped back into an exhausted sleep. While it wasn't the most restful he ever had, it was better than any he got in Betarr Serin the past couple eight-days.

"What day is it?" he asked, the next time he woke.

"It is Markday afternoon. Apparently, Commander Lyn always intended to leave earlier than publicly scheduled and that moved our arrival forward." Gaflis opened the windows to give him fresh air. "The lodge is around the next bend, according to the boat captain. We can start unloading the household and make you comfortable."

Perinon guzzled another bowl of broth, ignoring the accompanying spoon. "Only Velija and the household will be leaving. Unfortunately, they'll unload most of the *comfortable* provisions and we'll be left on field supplies, with only King's Guard for companions." He smiled and handed his bowl to the physician. "More, please."

"No one tells me anything." Gaflis stomped over to the door and paused. "I hope your personal guards can cook, because I can't."

Grumpiness aside, Gaflis did a great job of feeding him. Frequently. He was soon devouring solid food, able to stand, and take a few steps. Commander Lyn came in to report the household had been unloaded and Velija was going to open up the lodge, clean it, and start the kitchen.

"Amazing, sire." Lyn shook her head. "I didn't fully believe what you said about the charms, not until I saw this."

"Necromancy puts powerful death-magic into human hands. That is its allure." Perinon was taking walks across the little room. Sunset had started and he paused at the window. "But that power comes at a price. Not only the cost of life, which is heinous enough, but it separates us from true magic and drains the Void. The Phrenii have hardly any defense against it."

"You're making a remarkable recovery. Perhaps you should call the Phrenii away from that evil also?"

Perinon staggered to a chair. He might be pushing himself too hard. "I don't think moving the Phrenii will protect them from the draining of life-light from the Void. Lahna kept mentioning the Kaskea in her dreams. Let's hope it will be the key to their survival."

"And that the lieutenant can carry out your instructions," she muttered.

"I don't even know if this is the right time. Lahna wrote that the danger to the Phrenii would come from individuality and the rise of death-magic, but never *when* they'd be threatened."

"Since necromancy is crawling across the world as fast as the Fevers, *now* might be the time to prepare. When a charm can independently murder someone—" Lyn stopped and swallowed. "It's frightening to think how many Tyrran homes may harbor necromantic charms. How are we going to find them?"

"I don't know, but I have to trust Kilpi and his Guard organizations. They'll be telling everyone to get rid of the charms, perhaps even confiscate them. They'll push the Council to prohibit necromantic items within the city. Meanwhile, I must pursue the problems of the Phrenii, because I hold their promise. I have so many questions and no answers..." He paused, looking at the woman who had been more of an aunt to him than Aracia could ever be. "That's why I'm continuing this boat upriver to the Vihrea Hilltops. Can we disembark there safely and discreetly?"

She shrugged. "We'll check out the landing area, of course. I've got three times your normal complement of guards, all hand-picked for their loyalty and knowledge of field operations. Scouts are positioned behind and ahead of us on the river; no watchers have been spotted. I'm as sure about your safety as I can be, given the circumstances."

"I only have my intuition guiding me..." Perinon shook his head. "And it says answers to my questions are waiting at the hermitage."

"We can be there before dawn, sire."

Betarr Serasa, Tyrra

Lornis glanced at the Sareenian who walked beside him, and hoped he had done the right thing. This evening with the obtuse Phrenii had pushed him to the edge of his patience. Ahead, friendly light poured from the Sea Serpent's windows and he clapped Naton on the back. "Come on, we'll have a meal and a beer. And you better hide that."

Naton nodded soberly, his hand still fingering the Kaskea shard that hung from his neck. He pushed it behind his doublet. The shard pulsed with a blue light, but Lornis wondered if Naton was truly bound to the Phrenii. Draius had been frayed and barely lucid after her binding—although amateur necromancers had *forced* her into the Blindness while

Naton had three of the Phrenii lead him through it. Lornis felt the pocket that held the other shard. How would he find someone to bind to it?

As they approached the Sea Serpent, a tall figure detached from the shadows of the building.

"What have you been up to, Lornis?" Jan asked pleasantly, while blocking their path. "Plotting with traitorous Sareenians?"

"What?" Naton laid his hand on the hilt of his sword.

"Don't do that, boy." Jan kept his eyes on Lornis, although his hand drifted to his own hilt.

"Boy?" Naton was easily played by Jan, who smirked and continued to observe Lornis.

"Let me handle this." Lornis put a restraining hand on Naton's arm. He'd seen Jan fence, and the young Sareenian would be dispatched in a moment.

"I'm under orders from the king, if that's what you're asking after." Lornis's words were clipped.

"That would take some time to substantiate, since the king left the city yesterday evening." Jan smiled. "The King's Council disagrees with you. They've branded you a traitor. What were the words on the warrant? Hmm. You're accused of *subversive deeds*, such as selling the Kaskea to Sareenians. From the look of your companion, they're making a good case."

They were stunned into silence. Lornis figured the king's enemies would guess he had smuggled the Kaskea shards out, but he hadn't anticipated they'd so easily sway the council and use the King's Law against him.

He cleared his throat. "I'll talk with the captain—"

"Captain Rhaffus must abide by the King's Law. The warrant was delivered and verified. The watch has orders to arrest you." Jan nodded toward Naton, who wisely kept quiet. "The instructions on the warrant are to arrest any Sareenian having business with you."

"We're in for it, I suppose." His shoulders sagged. "Go ahead and arrest us."

"I'm insulted. I'm an officer, not a common watchman." Jan seemed amused. "The warrant has just been dispatched to the watch commander. He's under strict orders to be quiet and thorough and to run the search pattern starting at City Guard Headquarters, moving outward."

That search pattern would provide anyone, with brains or without, plenty of opportunity to leave the city undetected. They hadn't even sent the warrant to the gates yet. Lornis shifted his stance from foot to foot, trying to shake some sense into his tired body. Captain Rhaffus *wanted* him to evade arrest. What was Jan's part in all this? Even with his enhanced empathy, he could never read that inscrutable man. He might as well ask outright. "Why are you helping us?"

"I might not be helping. You could be better off by letting them arrest you, than by running. In any case, the City Guard doesn't like the council ordering them to hunt down their own." Jan's pleasant expression never changed.

"Where would we go?" Naton asked bluntly.

"Your best choice might be to get on a ship. I know someone who can guide you through the streets undetected, to a vessel waiting at the docks." Jan was referring to Haversar and his people. Haversar, though, wasn't likely to arrange two billets on an outbound ship.

"Who's giving us the berths?" Lornis asked. "And where are they going?"

"Frisson Rhobar." Jan ignored Naton's gasp. "But I haven't a clue as to your destination. You're not wanted in Sareen, I hear, and Groyga is out of the question."

"Why should I meet the expectations of these trumped-up charges by consorting with known criminals and pirates? This scheme will only make things worse for me."

"Suit yourself." Jan shrugged. "I'd rather see you in manacles myself, but the captain mentioned it'd be useful if you could disturb all that necromantic activity in the Sareenian deserts. He also said it would be ironic if you fulfilled your *potential* by evading arrest. What did he mean by that?"

Lornis sighed, beaten. While insanity infected the Phrenii and the world tilted into madness, Jhari's reading still hung over his head. He knew his matriarch had told Captain Rhaffus about the reading and somehow, somewhere, he still had his fate to meet. "Did the captain authorize this?"

"Of course not. That would be political suicide." Jan examined his fingernails. "I wouldn't suggest this as a rational course to take, either, if I had the opportunity to speak with you tonight." Without another glance, Jan whirled and headed into the Sea Serpent.

Naton grimaced. "What in the bowels of Darkness was that about?"

"Come on, we've got to meet a dangerous man." He pulled Naton into an alley and began to run. He'd made his decision and the time for discussion was gone.

As expected, Haversar waited for him at the normal meeting place. They slipped through streets and alleys to get to the wharves before the warrant. They were spotted once by the watch and ordered to stop, but lost their pursuit—or perhaps their pursuit wasn't spirited enough.

The docks were busy. To avoid attention, they no longer ran. Haversar led them briskly to a slip and then vanished into the other workers. Lanterns hung on posts at every dock and when Lornis looked out to the bay, he saw the beacons lit on the harbor wall. The water was calm, reflecting back the harbor lights. Their ship looked like an old single-masted merchant galley with an aftercastle on its stern that had been added late in its life. Not built for speed, with less benches and oars than a military galley, it nevertheless had a full crew and a modern gun on its prow. Lornis noted it used a sliding, recoil-absorbing mount before he walked down the dock and greeted the dark-haired captain standing at the gangway.

"Greetings, Lieutenant Lornis." Rhobar motioned them toward the aftercastle. "I'd appreciate you remaining out of sight until we clear the harbor wall. We're casting off now."

Naton kept quiet through the quick introductions and Lornis hoped he wasn't overly impressed with Frisson Rhobar, whose outrageous deeds were much more famous in Sareen: he'd captured and ransomed a Noble Light of the Church of the Way and extorted protection fees from Forenllas and Paduellus. The Sareenian city-states were outraged when King Perinon pardoned Rhobar and used him as consultant to the Tyrran Naval Guard.

Lornis was about to ask about their destination when a sudden gust of wind went down the entire wharf. Shouts came from dockside, and he turned as one of the Phrenii pushed toward their dock like a small storm. Dust and debris whirled about it and flickers of blue emanated from deep within the creature. Workers were thrown out of its way; wagons and crates toppled. His head jerked back as Jhari—because it had to be Air—took a magnificent leap from the dock, sailed over their heads, and *through* the rigging to land on the aftercastle.

"Well, well." Rhobar grinned. "There's something you don't see every day. Maybe your luck is changing, lieutenant."

Estate of Duke Ungought, Whythern Marshes, Kitarra

It was the day after the ball and, according to Roumithea, everything was proceeding just as Cerith predicted. An ultimatum came from King Markus in the morning. After that, activities on the estate rose to a frantic pace. Footsteps sounded continuously in the corridor outside her door, often running. Draius watched wagons and people heading out the back gates into the marshes. She lost sight of them in the mists that swirled about straggling trees and bushes.

In the afternoon, Tenil enlisted Roumithea to "help with the evacuation." For the first time in days, she was alone. She sat cross-legged, leaning against a bedpost. Her packed bag rested near the foot of the bed. Beside it was her folded cloak and gloves. She was dressed for travel, as Roumithea instructed. Pulling the Kaskea shards out, she held them in her palm. When she thought of the Phrenii, one of the shards pulsed with green light, nagging her.

"No one else should bind to the Kaskea," she murmured, answering the nag.

Perinon told her the Phrenii wanted all the shards of the Kaskea bound. Considering Siuru's death, she thought it was a harebrained plan. Besides, the only viable candidate she found was a traitorous and too-beautiful-to-be-trusted Kitarran duke. From her childhood lessons regarding the Kaskea, it had been created to purposely bind the Phrenii to *Tyrra*. Of course, it had been broken 500 years ago, perhaps weakened, which might explain why it reacted to Cerith's touch in the jail. Her jaw clenched. She wouldn't let Cerith close to the Kaskea again.

She shook her numb legs. The cloudy day had transitioned into twilight while she agonized over this. Besides breaking her promise to Cerith, using the Kaskea would be dangerous, considering her last attempt. There was no one to watch her body and she sat on a bed that could go up like tinder. She scrambled off and took a seat in the corner of the stone room, wedging her back into the angle. Besides having information *vital* to Tyrran security, she needed Perinon's guidance regarding Kitarra.

Dahni. Contrary to everything she had been taught, she tried to think of Dahni as an individual. Images came readily from memory: she remembered the creature she followed around as a child, the creature she thought would save her mother from the Fevers. She entered the Blindness as she made the first tenuous contact. She held this connection tightly, but she still couldn't get to the Void. Hunters swirled around her and she sensed their searing hunger. The Blindness was chaotic but despite that, she and Dahni sustained a tenuous strand of rapport.

Draius, beware of lies and treachery. Beware of fire.

Visions flashed, showing sights she had already seen, such as Chikirmo and Endigala's men and the boy's cut throat and Taalo's explosion at the ferry. Then the visions became strange and not from her memory: Perinon coughing up blood, Lornis pursued through the streets, Endigala's guards marching into Suellestrin, flames and smoke rising from Betarr Kain, the walls of Betarr Serasa exploding from gunpowder—

Darkness will overwhelm us. Remember me. Keep me alive. Dahni's thoughts rang about her, driving away the hunters.

Dahni, stay. She tried to project the words "ebi corgo" and picture the creatures as Bordas described them, when she felt the creature's thoughts recede. The hunters closed with purpose. One swept by and she felt the agony of its hunger. Another battered her straight on, ripping at her mind. She fled, reeling herself back to her body on the shining thread. Like a plunge into cold water, she entered her body.

Opening her eyes, she caught a whiff of smoke. She patted her clothes. At least she wasn't burning. Propping herself up on her elbow, she found herself on soft ground. Cerith stood over her. Green light flared from the Kaskea shards lying on her chest, still hanging about her neck.

Uh-oh. As the light from the Kaskea faded, she struggled to say something. It was dark and over the smoke, she smelled horses. Flickers of yellow and orange light came from somewhere. She lay on loose straw.

"I trust you enough to leave you alone and you break your promise," Cerith said. "Didn't I tell you to be ready to leave? You've made things quite difficult."

"What's burning?" She finally got her tongue and lips to move. Her throat was dry.

"My house." He made a graceful gesture and she looked. They were inside a stable and she glimpsed the grand house and gardens through the stable doors. Flames licked one side of the great house and dark smoke rose from the wing that held the kitchens and servant quarters.

"Where is everybody?" She sat up. The stable was empty except at the far end, where Chisel and a black horse waited, both saddled.

"Everyone should have evacuated to Bryn Celar before nightfall. When Bordas came to get you, he found you insensate. Our last wagon had already departed." Cerith's voice was pleasant, but she sensed anger.

She remembered her visions in the Blindness. "Endigala's forces are entering Suellestrin."

"Yes, my uncle needs reinforcements to hold his own city. He expects rioting from the populace." The corner of Cerith's mouth twitched. "On a closer issue, I'd like to know why you broke your promise."

She stuffed the Kaskea shards, now quiescent, back under her jerkin. Outside the stable in the distance, someone shouted commands. "Shouldn't we be concerned with escape?"

"By all means, let's change the subject. Can you stand?" Cerith wore an impeccably tailored black coat and he extended a gloved hand to her. After hesitating, she took his hand and he pulled her to a standing position with surprising strength. Then he offered her sheathed saber to her, hilt first. She looked at him with surprise.

"My uncle has accused me of treason and ordered my arrest, as well as the arrest of any Tyrrans found on my estate. You either follow me, or be taken by his Groygan friends."

"Put that way, I'll go with you." She took her saber. Had she ever had a choice?

He threw her a bundle and started putting on a black cloak. Draius unrolled her own cloak and gloves.

"My uncle's thugs have surrounded the estate, so we may have to fight our way through the back gate. To our advantage, they're more interested in looting."

Cerith led the horses out of the stables, and she realized why he dressed in black. The heavy clouds blocked any starlight. When he covered his light hair and face with his hood and mounted the black horse, he was almost impossible to see. Even the metal on his horse's bridle had been wrapped in black fabric. The metal rings of Chisel's tack had also been wrapped. She put on her dark green cloak and covered her head. As she mounted, she realized that soon the outer buildings and stables would be ransacked. From the house came sounds of breaking wood and glass. Furniture and strangely shaped bundles flew out of the windows. Dark figures ran in front of the flames.

Cerith was looking at his house also. "What a pity," he murmured.

"Did you stay behind just because of me?"

He shrugged. "The wagons were gone by that time and you weren't limp enough to tie to your horse. Your man Bordas wanted to stay, but I couldn't risk both of you. And if I must lose all this..." He made a languid gesture toward the house and she thought he might be smiling. "At least my wealth slows them down."

"You never had any intention of ransoming me. Why have you kept me safe?"

"Perhaps your safety is my responsibility. Perhaps you should have considered that when you broke your promise." His voice was cold. "Now for us to survive, you'd better be the rider that Bordas described."

He turned his horse sharply on its haunches and started galloping across the lawn at break-neck speed. All in black, Cerith was hard to see and she had to trust her horse's instincts as he followed the black horse. She didn't know the grounds well and a shape suddenly loomed: a hedge. Chisel jumped and she barely managed to keep her seat. *I'm really out of practice.*

Ahead, Cerith jumped another hedge and she followed, this time staying cleanly with the horse. She was seeing better as long as she didn't look directly at the flames devouring the house. They were almost to the wide gate that led to the marshes, but it was now a gap in the wall, its gate merely kindling by the road. Dark figures moved about. Cerith drew his sword with his left hand—*that's* why his scabbard had always looked awkward. She drew her saber, using her right hand.

The men holding the gap realized someone was coming from the dark interior of the estate, shielded from the firelight by tall hedges. She saw the flash and heard a gun go off. They now rode side by side and, almost as one, raised their swords and hacked at the men who stood at in the gap. Chisel reared slightly and swung his shoulder into a third attacker who tried to pull her from her saddle. The man staggered and fell. Then they were through, heading into the marshes at a full gallop.

Another gun fired behind them and Cerith grunted in pain. He slowed to a cantor, turning right and left on the twisting path, always drawing them deeper into the marshes. She couldn't see the path and she hoped they wouldn't end up sinking in a bog. The wound started taking a toll on Cerith. From the way he slumped in his saddle, she suspected his arm or shoulder was hit.

"We need to stop," she yelled.

"Not yet." He slowed to a trot and swayed in his saddle.

CHAPTER SIXTEEN

Breaking Point

Lord Endigala's Estate, Chikirmo, Groyga

Inica woke to one of his guards banging on his door. He bounded up, grabbed his sword, and flung the door open. "What's happening?"

"Honor, his lordship is gathering everyone. He says it is time."

"Time for what?"

The guard shrugged. Inica dressed quickly and intercepted Shalah as she crossed the courtyard lined with torches. Over her shoulder, Taalo argued with men who were dragging the lodestone out from its shelter. The thing sat on a sledge so it could be moved without anyone getting near.

"Take this, honor. Make sure it touches your skin." Shalah gave him a small pouch that hung from long laces. She showed him a similar one tied around her neck and tucked under her jerkin. Glancing over her shoulder, she added, "This is the same sort of charm that Taalo made for his lordship yesterday."

"And he made some extras, just for us?" He suppressed a shiver, knowing what probably went into the charms. "He's not prone to generosity."

Shalah lowered her voice. "He's not—but after he talked with Lord Endigala, he was bent upon protecting himself from *unwarranted loss of knowledge,* as he called it. He prepared more than enough materials for charms for his lordship and himself. I can understand the creation of these things, even if I can't stomach the preparation, so I snuck back last night after closing up his shop and made two more."

Inica still looked at the pouch suspiciously. "*You* tortured something or someone for this?"

"No, *I* didn't," she whispered. "*Taalo* prepared the *materials*, the *power*. The making of the actual charms requires a different ritual."

If Lord Endigala had ordered them made and she had extra materials... He shrugged. "All right. But what's causing all this chaos?"

"I think the demon wants to release the lodestone's spell. From what I understood from Taalo's mutterings—he must explain to me *what* he's doing, not necessarily *why* he's doing it—Lord Endigala gave the demon leave to do this during their private discussion yesterday."

The small necromancer had given up on stopping the lodestone's progress toward the open area between the fountain and the gates. Lamps were being lit all over the main house and windows were being opened. People crowded out on balconies to watch, especially in the family quarters. The cobblestones and walls of the courtyard radiated the chill of the autumn night. Dawn was barely an hour away but the sky was black with heavy clouds that let no starlight through. More torches were being lit.

Lord Endigala and Lady Gedere walked out of the house, fully dressed and prepared. Inica ran to take his spot behind the lord. The guard currently in that position fell back almost gratefully. Since he was now facing toward the estate wall and portico, Inica spotted guards running along the top of the wall.

"Open the gates," came the cries. "Open the gates!"

Guards pulled open the heavy gates. One suddenly swung into the courtyard and slammed a man into the wall. Under the portico stood the demon Famri, glowing like a coal and lighting the dust that swirled about in the immediately hot, dry air. The demon walked into the courtyard; it met Endigala and Gedere where the lodestone was positioned.

"No!" Taalo rushed to Endigala and Inica grabbed him. A hot, dry wind ruffled everyone's hair, while Taalo wrung his hands and babbled to Endigala. "It can't usurp the Lodestone for itself. It was not made for the demons to use."

Endigala then raised his hand for quiet. "It is time. Lady Gedere has seen this." He nodded at her.

Gedere stepped forward. Her voice rang out like a bell, but was hollow. The hair on the back of Inica's neck rose. "In my dream, I drifted down out of the clouds and saw a demon reading from the lodestone, chanting, while lightning flashed. In the flashes of lightning, I viewed the Kainen peninsula below me, flying the green and white flag of Tyrra. Fire swept across the peninsula, followed by dark forces carrying the flags of Groyga and Endigala. The flag of Tyrra fell; the head of the demon surrounded by five stars was trampled in the mud and burned."

The courtyard erupted in cheers and yells. Lightning arced through the clouds above and the immediate thunder quelled the cheering into awestruck silence and fearful looks at the dark nothingness above. Inica still held Taalo, who had wilted. There could be no fighting the Sight. Gedere gazed at him with pity before she stepped back behind Lord Endigala. As he released Taalo and took his own position behind the lord, Inica suspected there was more to her vision. Something she hadn't told anyone.

Taalo deliberately put space between himself and the lodestone. "This is unscientific and unwise," he said to Endigala. "We should ask Famri for translations before handing it over."

Lord Endigala silenced him with a look.

Inica had been told, all his life, that Tyrrans worshipped the stars and the Phrenii, but Taalo didn't behave like a god was using his precious lodestone. Instead, he was frightened. At this point, Inica thought it prudent to ensure the charm Shalah gave him was touching his breastbone. Lady Gedere stood beside him and her slim hand, slightly trembling, tentatively took his. He responded, engulfing hers in his strong grip.

"It is time to give this spell form and release the souls." In Famri's voice, thunder rumbled. The demon glowed internally with firelight, red coals hidden behind melting snow. Its glow outdid the torches and lit the courtyard with red daylight. Waves of intense heat rolled away from it, even to where Inica stood on the other side of the lodestone.

Lord Endigala didn't move. "Before I give you the lodestone, I need assurance of your support. We made an agreement, Famri. Will you swear to abide by it?"

"By the fire that makes me, I will hold by that agreement. I will take Betarr Kain for you." Famri stamped a delicate hoof. The gates behind it burst into flames and the guards nearby scattered.

The demon began chanting strange words above the stone, its voice mingling with thunder. The sound was mesmerizing. Inica didn't know how long he stood motionless, listening to the spell as it was released from the lodestone. The souls bound within the lodestone soared out, glittering in many colors, swirling upward with many voices. Their agony from imprisonment and their joy of release filled his blood with fire. His heart pumped the inferno throughout his body until he could hardly endure it.

The last strange words of the spell hung on the air with an echo. Lightning struck and dawn arrived.

The Whythern Marsh, Kitarra

Draius didn't think Cerith could continue. Thunder sounded as a storm moved above them. Lightning flickered through dark clouds, giving her glimpses of him slumping in his saddle. He slowed and turned into a sloping but clear area within a grove of bushy willows.

She smelled water. A small stream spilled into a rocky basin. Cerith slid off his horse and she dismounted. The horses went to a small pool and started drinking. She helped him to a sitting position against some rocks. In the flickering lightning, his wound seemed worse than she suspected.

"Heal me." The words were harsh, a stark contrast to his usual smooth, silky voice.

She opened his doublet and his light skin appeared luminous against the dark blood running down his shoulder. Was the bullet still inside? She extended her senses to see into his body. His head drooped onto his chest as he started losing consciousness. Thunder boomed overhead. Pulling out the Kaskea shards, she clenched them in her fist.

His hand grabbed her fist. His gloves were torn and covered in his blood. *Meran blood.*

"No!" she cried.

Brilliant rays of green and copper light shot out through the cracks in their hands. Lightning flashed. Cerith screamed and she was sucked into the Blindness.

Dawn arrived over the marsh.

Betarr Kain, Tyrra

Meran-Kolme Kyle woke an hour before dawn and tried to go back to sleep, but a storm rolled in.

"Not disturbing anyone but myself, so I might as well get up," he grumbled. He had to be on shift at the main gate in a couple hours anyway. As lightning flared, he lit a candle and got dressed.

He stood in front of his one window, as he always did during the final step of putting on his guard uniform: attaching his rank. With the candlelight behind him and darkness outside, he could see his reflection on the glass—between lightning flashes, of course.

Glancing down at the desk next to the window, he smiled at the letter from Miina. He'd already read it about a hundred times. Taking Commander Lyn's advice, he had written to the small dark-haired City Guard woman who made his heart pound every time he saw her. It took him so many days, and so many drafts, to create a letter that wasn't messy and sounded friendly. Miina quickly replied in the same manner and in an encouraging tone.

He frowned as amber light washed over the desktop. Out the window, rays of the same light shot up from the center square of Betarr Kain. Inside the rays, copper streams with glittering motes swirled upward toward the storm above. They disappeared as dawn peeked over the eastern walls.

On the Angim Sea

"This can't be normal weather, can it?" Lornis asked Rhobar.

"Don't know, don't care," Rhobar shouted as he lashed down something that Lornis thought was related to steering the ship. "Go tie yourselves to something and pray to the Groygan gods, the Tyrran ancestors, and the Light of Sareen that we survive."

Black clouds had rolled between them and the stars in the blink of an eye. The crew struggled to drop their mainsail while the ship bucked about on the waves. Driving rain forced Lornis and Naton back into the small aftercastle. Jhari stood on top of the aftercastle because the crew didn't like having the creature near them. Lornis wondered if the Phrenii could disperse this storm and whether he could safely climb up and speak with Jhari.

Lightning cracked and the mast exploded. A whirlwind rose up around him, pulling planks off the top of the aftercastle. He raised his arms to shield his face from flying wreckage. The whirling air, water, and debris glittered blue, before rising up to be lost in the storm.

"What in the—" Lornis turned to Naton, to find him collapsed on the deck. Naton's hand was tight about the Kaskea and bright blue light glowed between his clenched fingers.

Dawn faded the storm clouds above to gray.

The Abandoned Hermitage Near Ruhallen, Northern Tyrra

Lyn rubbed her gritty eyes. Only two lanterns were lit because the starlight was bright. They had put in at the neglected little pier and ten King's Guard, plus Gaflis and the king, disembarked. Everyone had a mount except for Gaflis, who rode behind her. He insisted on coming to monitor the king's health and Lyn agreed.

"I can tie up here." The packet captain viewed the pier with distaste. "But I can't trust it to hold, so I can't rest the animals." He gestured to the line of mules that pulled the boat upstream.

"Why don't you keep to your schedule and go on to Ruhallen," Perinon suggested.

Reluctantly, Lyn agreed with the king. Five able-bodied guards would stay on the packet but since no one knew where the king was at this moment, it should be safe to continue without them. She gave the men on the boat orders to search the king's accommodations in Ruhallen carefully, removing any non-essential item that could be a necromantic charm.

After the river boat left, they followed a short winding path through the hills. Because it was so narrow, they traveled in single file. Lyn posted two forward and two rear scouts, with orders to fan out as they approached the hermitage.

"Storm's coming." The guard in front of her pointed to the east.

The abandoned hermitage stood in a glade at the edge of the Vihrea Hilltops. Lightning danced in the clouds over the Tyrran plains but the clearing was quiet as death. They dismounted and Gaflis watched the king; so far, Perinon was holding up well.

"Askar, check with the scouts and set up a perimeter." Lyn worried; the glade was bigger than she expected and her security would be patchy.

Askar nodded, readied his crossbow, and trotted out of the glade on foot. Gaflis stayed with the horses at the clearing's lower end with the other lantern. As heavy clouds started cutting off the starlight, Lyn carried one of the lanterns and sent all but two guards to do perimeter duty.

She, Perinon, and the guards walked up the slope to the structure that might have two rooms at most. As they came closer, her lamp's light created shadows on the front of the old hermitage that looked like a face. She suppressed a shiver.

"This is where Lahna retired toward the end of her life and where she died," Perinon said in a low voice. "The Vilje-Nelja are responsible for cleaning and repairing it."

Lyn didn't care about the historical significance of the cottage, but whether someone hid within it. She made a sign to one of the two guards with her. He drew a long dagger and silently stepped up the porch to the door.

"Wait," Perinon said. The guard paused at her signal. Perinon had his eyes closed and his hand clenched, showing his ring. The shard glowed slightly with golden light. "Someone is here."

"Cover the door and stand ready," she ordered. The guard beside her stepped back and aimed his crossbow. Then she called in a loud voice: "Whoever is inside, come out and be recognized."

The door opened immediately and the figure that stepped out showed no fear. The guard at the door drew back into the shadows of the small porch and the one aiming a crossbow couldn't help but exclaim. From anyone's vantage point, this wasn't a human. Dressed in dark clothes, only the creature's face was visible. Although humanlike, the creature's skin seemed like molten silver. The almond-shaped eyes shone in the lamplight like an animal's eyes.

Lyn drew her sword as Perinon's breath caught.

"No." Perinon put a hand on her sword arm. "*Mehrham sellâmza.*"

Her eyebrows rose at the strange words.

"*Ishrimzâh mehnun oda,*" returned the creature. The words were lilting and the voice sounded like a human male.

There was an awkward silence. In the shadows, Lyn glimpsed her guard's face behind and to the side of the stranger. She kept her own sword ready. The storm had arrived and thunder rumbled.

"I'm sorry, that's the only Minahmeran I remember. My education included study of the language, but no one expected..." Perinon sounded abashed and his voice trailed off.

The stranger bowed and stepped down from the porch of the small cottage. He had a strangely shaped bow attached to the pack on his back, but it was unstrung. He appeared to carry no other weapon but a hunting knife at his hip. Her guard at the door kept his dagger ready and followed behind. The stranger ignored everyone but Perinon.

"It is enough." The stranger's common Tyrran was accented, but understandable. "I return your greeting and introduce myself as Ihmar, out of Cevicik. I am pleased to meet with Perinon, young monarch of Tyrra."

Lyn tightened her grip on her sword. While she hadn't understood the greeting between the stranger and Perinon, she was sure no names had been used. How did he know whom he was speaking to? The stranger was only a stride or two away from the king. She heard the call of a field grouse, coming from the rocks on the west side of the glade. *Field grouse don't live in these hills.*

"Get down!" She dropped the lantern, effectively dousing it.

The stranger leaped toward Perinon. Lyn moved to intercept him. The two of them crashed together and took down Perinon as a result. The thumps of arrows or bolts hitting wood mingled with low thunder. There were screams of pain and she raised her head. Lightning flashed high overhead, showing stilted, but bright, views of the action. Her guard on the porch was down in front of her, a crossbow bolt in his throat. The other turned and circled, looking for the source.

"The rocks to the west," she shouted, and then lowered her voice to ask, "Is the king safe?"

"I'm fine." Perinon's muffled voice came from under hers and the stranger's bodies.

Crossbow bolts might penetrate even plate mail and none of her party wore more than chain. Where were her scouts? She cursed, looking about. "We have to find cover."

She pulled Perinon up and helped him stumble to the east side of the hermitage. She tried to shield his body and saw the stranger trying to do the same, holding Perinon's other arm. Her shoulders were tense, waiting for a bolt to hit her as they scrambled around the corner, then crouched. Sunlight seemed to already be touching the wall.

She took a deep breath when the hermitage was between them and the deadly crossbows. "Are you well, sire?"

"I think so." The king stared at his ringed hand. The embedded Kaskea shard glowed with golden light—she'd mistaken it for sunlight. Perinon's eyes rolled backward and he sagged against the stranger. Dawn touched the rocks across the clearing.

Betarr Serin, Tyrra

Peri yawned and covered his mouth with his hand so neither of the women who walked ahead of him would hear. The predawn air was cold. They walked on the Betarr Serin walls and he shivered while Lady Anja and Lady Aracia talked together in low tones.

Suc-cess-or-can-di-date. He stepped to the rhythm, placing his feet in the middle of the stones, keeping to the pattern of the stonework. He heard those words from everybody yesterday, as he met a lot of matriarchs. Lady Anja treated him more like a grown-up than any of the others. Lady Aracia acted like he was real young and Lady Leika—well, he didn't like her eyes. She could be pretty when she smiled, but her eyes always looked mean, like a bully's.

Lady Anja said they were training him for an emergency, in case he had to stand in for cousin Perinon. *To be prepared, you have to learn the politics,* she said. He should start paying attention *all* the time now, even during this secret meeting with the Meran-Viisi. He didn't like secrecy before he had any breakfast. This talk was boring and his stomach grumbled.

Lightning flashed and thunder rumbled, stopping the matriarchs' conversation as they glanced at the storm coming from the east.

He stood on a bulwark step, looked out over the wall, and saw Mahri and Dahni running swiftly up the road of the plateau. He wondered if someone was sick. The Phrenii were in front of the gate when lightning flashed and cracked. They began to glow and stretch, entwining and reaching toward the sky, until nothing remained but two streams of sparkling gold and green. The streams twisted, whirled, and rose up into the clouds.

"What happened to the Phrenii?" he cried, pointing to where the creatures had been, almost right below him.

"The what?" Both matriarchs turned toward him, looking puzzled.

"The Phrenii. They're gone!"

"Whatever are you talking about, child?" Aracia asked.

The dawn of a new day arrived.

CHAPTER SEVENTEEN

The Fevers Return

Lord Endigala's Estate, Chikirmo, Groyga

Everyone was pushed backward when the lightning struck. Luckily, Inica broke his lordship's fall. As he stood, he rubbed his shaved head to get rid the tingle he felt before the lightning hit the lodestone. He vaguely remembered voices from the stone and a surge of power before the strike.

He helped Lord Endigala to his feet and his lordship's eyes widened. Turning, he peered through the dissipating smoke at Famri and gaped. The demon had transformed into a woman. She was the image of the goddess Falcona, at least as most artists depicted her. Her copper skin complemented an otherworldly body. Standing taller than Inica and Endigala, her orange hair was streaked with red and flickered all on its own. Inica looked away. His eyes watered like he had stared into a fire and he blinked rapidly. In a semi-circle behind Famri lay a few bodies that were apparently too near the lightning.

The force of the strike, or perhaps the spell, blew people over in the courtyard. Other than those behind Famri, no one suffered more than a minor injury. People on balconies and farther away seemed to fare better. As everyone recovered, he heard murmurs of "Falcona? It's Falcona."

"No, I am called Famri." She held her arms up and smiled widely, showing dazzling teeth. Dressed as a handmaiden of Falcona in antique and expensive Groygan armor, she laid a hand on her chest. "I will honor our agreement and lead the *ebi corgo* to Betarr Kain whenever you want."

"Ah. Yes." Lord Endigala rubbed his head. "Once I get confirmation that the mission in the north is completed, I'll move on the Council."

Famri nodded and took a moment to examine her arms and hands. "After this transformation, I feel powerful. Do I seem changed, my lord?"

Endigala paused, then smiled. Inica noted it was purposeful. "I don't think so. Why?"

She suddenly turned on Inica. "What about you, Honored Sword? Do you note any changes?"

He looked into her flickering orange eyes and read cold, hard, and conniving self-service deep within them. *Regardless of her discussion with his lordship, the rest of us are not supposed to remember.* He shook his head.

"Good." She turned about and demanded, "Does anyone know me?" Her voice filled the courtyard. Shalah stood beside Gedere behind the lord. She did what everyone else in the courtyard did, and shook her head in the negative. Of course, there was one person who just couldn't toe the line. Taalo stepped toward Famri, separating himself from the crowd.

"You think you've got enough spirit now to control the *ebi corgo*?" Taalo's gray hair stood straight up.

"You doubt my elemental powers, little man?" Famri drew herself up so she towered over Taalo.

"Perhaps we should see an example. Fire is one thing, but control of water and spirit are—"

Famri's hand shot out with fingers spread and Taalo's clothes exploded into flame. He screamed as he slapped at the flames, dropped and rolled, all to no effect. Famri gestured with her other hand and nothing happened. Puzzlement crossed her face so quickly Inica might not have seen it, if he hadn't been focused on her rather than Taalo. She tossed her head and the flames went out. "I don't perform for your benefit."

"Can you heal him?" Lord Endigala asked while Taalo moaned.

Inica watched Famri's face, figuring that *healing* still wasn't in her repertoire. Lord Endigala was testing her.

Scooping Taalo up into her arms as if he weighed nothing, she walked to the fountain and dumped him in the water. Then she dusted her hands off dramatically. "I've done all the healing he deserves."

Lord Endigala glanced at Inica and Shalah, and then pointed at Taalo. *You two take care of him,* was the message. His lordship offered his arm to Famri, who laid her hand on his sleeve gracefully. "Let's go to the maps and examine our schedule. When Kitarra is contained, we must gain approval for an invasion. Influencing the Council is our most important..." Endigala's voice faded as he and Famri walked toward the hall.

Meanwhile, guards examined the bodies of the dead and organized them for burial. Tradespeople assessed the damage to the gate and portico. Inica, Shalah, and Gedere gathered at the edge of the fountain as Taalo was fished out and put on a stretcher at Inica's orders. The necromancer whimpered through clenched teeth.

"I'll have him taken to the family wing." Gedere went to Taalo's side and pushed singed hair off his forehead. "Whatever made you do such a stupid thing?"

To Inica's surprise, the burned man answered her. "Had—had to—see if Famri got powers—from the others. I think—Kaskea—stopped that." Taalo ended with a short laugh, or perhaps a grunt of pain, which he cut off with clenched teeth. Famri had also mentioned the *Kaskea* and Inica resolved to find out more about this Tyrran artifact once Taalo had healed enough to have a conversation. Gedere gave instructions to the stretcher bearers, but stayed with Inica and Shalah as the necromancer vanished into the family wing.

"What an idiot," Inica said.

"But a brave idiot," Shalah said.

"I'm not sure I'd call him *brave*, but we now know more about the extent of Famri's powers." Gedere frowned. "He told me yesterday the lodestone's spell had two purposes: to usurp the soul of the Phrenii and bestow it upon the spell's releaser, and to make sure the hearts of human-kind would no longer remember them."

"He *told* you?" Inica asked. Taalo had been opening up to Gedere, but this was unprecedented.

"I caught him right after his lordship learned all this—from the demon. By the way, I thank you both for holding my hands. Your charms pro-tected me as well."

"Right." Inica realized he never even questioned why Gedere remem-bered. Shalah had been standing on her other side. Gedere was somehow aware of everything that happened in Taalo's workshop. This plus her incomplete rendering of her dream were puzzles he had to address later. "We should tell his lordship what we know."

Shalah put a hand on his arm. "If Famri learns—"

"His lordship knew this magic would erase our memories and yet he only protected himself." Gedere interrupted. "He must have worried about our discretion and thus, feared for our safety. Famri might have threatened to kill us *all* if we kept our memories."

Shalah agreed. "We should keep silent and ensure the Tyrran idiot stays quiet as well. Let Famri *prove* she can control the *ebi corgo.*"

The Abandoned Hermitage Near Ruhallen, Northern Tyrra

Ihmar felt the necromantic spell wash over him. Luckily, the death magic was designed for humankind and not for him. He continued to huddle behind the corner of the cottage as he heard shouts, more thumps from crossbow bolts, and the glade went quiet.

They waited. Nobody moved.

"We got 'em, Commander," a gruff voice called, near the rocks where the attackers hid.

"Askar. Thank the ancestors," Lyn whispered.

"Don't know if we got 'em all, though." Askar and the scouts laid out five bodies. Lyn went over to assess the damage. Two King's Guard and three assassins lay dead. Lyn and Askar spoke quietly over the bodies in the middle of the glade, not realizing that Ihmar could hear their conversation.

"How did they find us?" Lyn asked.

"Him, of course, the silver man." Askar gestured in Ihmar's direction. "This was a trap."

"I'm not sure. If he wanted to assassinate the king, he would have done better by keeping to the rocks with his friends and having his bow ready. He also shielded the king with his body as we ran for cover."

"He knew he wouldn't be shot by his cohorts."

"Maybe." Lyn rubbed her eyes and looked over the bodies. "One of these men looks familiar. I think he's former King's Guard, which is disturbing. Search the bodies for any connection to their lineage and take everything off them. Remember, anything could be a necromantic charm."

Ihmar frowned as the King's Guard deliberated and Gaflis tried to revive Perinon. He knew the spell targeted the Phrenii, but he wondered why these people had no concern for them. They also didn't trust him, so he kept quiet.

"Make a stretcher," Gaflis ordered. Guards began to ferret about for supple and strong wood.

Ihmar observed the shard on Perinon's ring. Five hundred years ago, Cessina deliberately broke the Kaskea into five shards, but he wondered what purpose the shards could serve now. It pulsed irregularly with golden light, but was fading.

The storm that whipped up so fast, now evaporated to nothing. The sky was clear and the day promised fine weather.

"We must take him to Ruhallen," Lyn said, once Perinon was tied to a makeshift stretcher. "Askar, stay here with two guards until we send a wagon for our bodies and horses. Look for *their* horses, tracks, anything to help us identify these assassins." She walked over to Ihmar. "You're coming with us." Her flat tone brooked no argument.

He inclined his head. "I'm quite concerned about what happened to the—to your monarch."

"Regardless of your concern, I have to search and disarm you."

It was unpleasant to be touched by a human, but he didn't protest. He carried only a bow and hunting knife, which Lyn unsheathed and examined with wonder.

"What sort of metal is this?" She tested the flexibility and strength of the knife.

He shrugged, not familiar with metal smithing. "It's called *kamermar*."

"Why is your bow strung with these extra strings and wheels?"

"The pulleys ensure the draw is steady from start to end," Ihmar said patiently and added, "I use it for hunting."

"So you say." She stripped him of his pack and searched his pockets, muttering something about charms.

He was troubled by that. Lyn had instructed Askar to search for charms on the bodies, as well as doing the same through his things. Humankind must be entangled with necromancy, if even simple soldiers worried about bound death-magic.

They prepared to travel to Ruhallen. They didn't dare drag the king's stretcher behind a horse: the birches grew close in spots and the grade was steep and rough. At the bottom, rocks and thick pines still prevented the use of a horse, so two guards continued to carry it. The Tyrran guards split: half in front of the party and half behind.

Ihmar directly followed the king, leading the stretcher bearers' horses. The Tyrrans were surprised when he said he didn't know how to ride. "We don't have these kind of beasts." Lyn muttered something that sounded like "bloody useless," and shook her head as he introduced himself to them. Putting hands on their foreheads, he found them simple but strong of heart.

Eventually the ground leveled, the pines opened up, and they were looking across a pond to a farmhouse nestled in front of a stand of birches.

"They'll have transportation." Lyn rode off toward the farmhouse.

The rest of the party continued slowly with the stretcher, with Ihmar and the spare horses following. By the time they arrived, the farmer and his family were over the astonishment of finding the King's Guard pounding on the door. The farmer's son hooked up a team and wagon.

Ihmar stood to the side with the horses and tried to remain inconspicuous. A breeze carrying the promise of winter stirred the fading birch leaves... Someone watched him. Turning, he saw the girl in the doorway of the farmhouse, the same girl who kneeled in the glade and touched the sad soul who lived there.

"Berina, get compresses," the farmer shouted as Perinon's stretcher was slid onto the bed of the wagon.

The girl disappeared back into the farmhouse. Lyn poked him and pointed to one of the benches that lined the sides of the wagon bed. He nodded, and climbed in it. Now that he'd shown himself, his best option was to stay as close to Perinon as he could. The Tyrran monarch was in rapport with one of the Phrenii and perhaps he would know what happened to them, once he became conscious.

Berina ran out with compresses and applied them to Perinon's forehead and neck. Gaflis and the farmer's son climbed into the wagon to steady the stretcher, the King's Guard mounted up, and they were ready to go. As the wagon bounced and creaked over the rough roads, Gaflis gave all his attention to the king and Ihmar came under the children's scrutiny.

"Are you a Groygan?" the son asked.

"Don't be rude. Of course he's not Groygan." Berina took on a superior tone with her brother, who might be older because he was taller. Ihmar couldn't estimate their ages.

"What is he, then?"

"He's one of the silver people." Berina spoke with such certainty that he studied her face. She looked down, flushing.

"Like the silver people really exist." Her brother snorted. "Stop living in children's tales. Next you'll be speaking of unicorns."

Berina winced and Ihmar saw anger and perplexity wash over her face. "Are you just being vulgar, or stupid? You know you shouldn't use that word—if the Phrenii exist, why shouldn't the silver people?"

"Vulgar? What word?"

"Why not call them the Phrenii? We have them on the Tyrran flag and the King's Guard wear their likeness." Berina pointed at guards on the left side of the wagon, too far away to notice the children's argument. On their chests were embroidered a stylized side view of a creature with a strong jaw, a thick mane, and a single horn.

"That's a mythic creature that represents nobility and truth."

He caught Berina's glance and shook his head slightly, willing her to be quiet. She looked puzzled, but complied. Now that he had time to think, he thought he understood the powerful spell that washed over everyone. But who had such power in this era? Humankind had rediscovered necromancy and regained the ability to bind the power of death, but he thought them still in a stage of infancy and convinced the elders that no drastic action was necessary. They could wait until he provided them better information. Now he wondered if he was mistaken.

However, the death-magic had interesting holes. His own memory and mind wasn't affected, so the maker hadn't considered any other races but humankind. Then there was Berina, apparently unaffected. Had she been protected due to her innocence or her age?

When they reached Ruhallen, Lyn rode ahead to notify the local matriarch. The farmer drove the wagon into the square where people gathered as news rippled through the village. The crowd parted for a thin woman who had white braids drizzled with grey, but stood straight and strong. Beside the matriarch was a man who carried a satchel; he climbed into the back of the wagon to examine the king and had a muttered conversation with Gaflis. Ihmar figured the man was the local herbalist or chemist. Both Gaflis and the other man felt Perinon's flushed forehead.

"Ague?" The man opened his case to show a bunch of powders.

"Not likely. He's recovering from…" Gaflis seemed to search for appropriate words. "Stress might be the best description."

Meanwhile, the chemist tried to lift Perinon's wrist, but the arm was stiff and uncooperative. "I don't understand why he's so rigid. His pulse is weak. Perhaps he suffers—"

"It's the Fevers!" A villager had pushed up to the wagon and pointed at Perinon's face.

"Impossible." Gaflis's eyes followed the man's gesture. On one cheek were small, telltale blisters, just beginning.

Ihmar drew back. Until now, he thought the young king was experiencing shock from the death-magic and the breaking of the Phrenic circle. But if Perinon had "the Fevers," as humankind named the set of plagues that hit them a generation ago—one of those diseases was deadly to Minahmerans. No amount of herbs, powders, solutions, prayers, or even true magic could save him.

There were mutterings and prayers to ancestors in the crowd that now pressed *backward*, away from the wagon.

"Lady Niisa, why don't you ask him?" Berina's voice rose clearly over the commotion. She pointed to him, still sitting across from her in the wagon. "He's a sorcerer. Perhaps he can help."

The square became quiet as everyone's eyes turned to him.

Lady Niisa ignored Berina's comment and snapped out orders. She sent a messenger back on the river packet boat to Betarr Serin. The king was transported to her house, which was best suited for caring for him. Supplies had to be moved, rooms had to be prepared, food had to be cooked and above all, normal business had to continue. Soon everyone was rushing about, doing something useful.

Niisa's eyes then settled on Ihmar and Berina, still sitting in the back of the wagon. "Both of you come with me."

Below Bryn Celar, Northern Moors, Kitarra

"Where did you find his grace? Was he ambushed?" Suel peppered Tenil with questions as the two men headed into the main tunnel. Bordas lengthened his stride to keep up with them and suppressed a wince; a cut on his thigh needed attending. He wiped the mud from his face. It had dried now that he was out of the mist and no longer sweating. The dirt kept his face from shining while helping Cerith's people with their night-time sorties.

"They were found at one of the northern springs. The duke is wound-ed. Difficult to transport them—but you'll see the problem yourself." Te-nil's voice bounced about the tunnel. Neither he nor Suel gave Bordas more than a glance as he followed them. After the last two nights, he should be accepted by any of these people without question, considering his blade-work.

The evening when Markus made his move and sent his men to seize the estate, Cerith asked Bordas to accompany Suel and four other men, while he stayed behind with Draius. So Bordas helped make half-hearted forays against Markus's perimeter and each time, the duke's group re-treated into the Whythern Marsh. Anyone foolish enough to follow was ambushed once drawn far enough inside the marshland. They did this four times during the night, and he dispatched fifteen of Markus's guards, some of which were Groygans.

Then the short, but terrible lightning storm curtailed all operations. After that, Bordas took a respite at this small fortress in the moors, but Cerith and Draius hadn't yet arrived. While everyone else questioned why his grace stayed behind to help "that Tyrran woman," he berated himself for not staying with Draius.

After a few hours sleep, he again accompanied Suel on a foray through the marshes. Suel searched for Cerith along routes that supported horses. When they got close to the city, they ran into three Groygans on foot who were not wearing the solid black of the council. *Endigala's guards are now protecting the perimeter of Suellestrin?* These appeared to be scouting, perhaps after the same quarry as them. Suel thanked him for taking care of two of the guards and then helping with the third, who had pulled Suel from his horse.

Bordas, though, had an advantage over the average Kitarran guard: he was trained King's Guard and riding a battle-trained Tyrran horse against men on foot. He reminded himself that Draius had much of the same training as he did, as well as a better horse. Cerith, as well, was supposed to be superior with the sword. He convinced himself the two of them would be safe.

But when he walked into the cave and surveyed the strange scene, he wasn't sure. Roumithea, Tenil's wife, was replacing the bandage on Cerith's right shoulder. Gunfire had hit it, but there was no damage to the joint or bones. The duke lay on a cot, with his left arm out, clasping Draius's clenched right hand. She seemed comatose, just like Cerith, but without any wounds.

"Why are they holding hands?" Suel stared at the two figures.

"They're gripping something." Roumithea glanced up at the men. "Tenil tried to separate them, but I was afraid for their fingers."

"Ridiculous! A body goes limp when insensate. They must be awake."

Bordas understood the undertone of hysteria in Suel's voice. Everyone here needed Cerith. Plans and strategies might already be mapped out, but what good was a revolt to take the Crown of Kitarra when the person who should wear it was unconscious?

He walked over to Draius, knelt beside the cot, and covered her free hand with his. He thought there was a tremor, a slight response—Draius still lived; she just couldn't be concerned with her body right now. The hair on the back of his neck rose.

"I tell you, we've used smelling salts and everything else we can think of," Roumithea said while he watched Draius's eyelids. Underneath them, her eyes moved. "I've sent for my mother. Perhaps she can fight this malady."

"There's no cure for this," Bordas said. "We must wait for her to find her own way back to her body."

The Kitarrans looked at Bordas, who had to try to explain the—he had problems remembering— "It's a Tyrran artifact. That's part of the Kaskea they're clutching."

He answered their questions and understood the doubt that grew on the Kitarran faces. In fact, he struggled to make sense of his own answers. His logic had gaping holes, as if he tried to stitch together a fable. He knew the Kaskea allowed those of Meran blood to communicate through something called the "Void" and they went through the "Blindness," supposedly the place where those with Sight dreamed. But he couldn't tell them the original purpose of the Kaskea or why it had been broken. He remembered *how*; it was broken in a battle between the last sorcerers, named Cessina and Nherissa. He recalled the facts: it happened in the summer of Tyrran Year 998, by the new calendar, and occurred at Nherissa's tower, north of Betarr Serin. But if he could remember the dates, location, and combatants, why didn't he know *what* they fought about?

"So she's pulled the duke into this Blindness, as you call it." Suel's voice was grim and he drew his knife. "She can't hold him in that place if she'd dead, can she?"

"No!" Bordas stood and moved to protect Draius. Surprisingly, Roumithea did the same.

"Roumithea." Tenil's voice warned his wife to stay out of this, but she glared back at Suel with challenge, her chin raised.

"I won't allow this." She advanced on Suel, hands on hips, looking up. The top of her head barely came to his shoulder and she quivered with rage. Suel stepped back.

"We'll wait for Enita's word." Suel put his knife away. "But I'll do whatever's necessary, even if comes to cutting off her hand."

"She carries a child. You will not harm her." Roumithea's words stunned the three men, causing a few moments of silence. She still glared up at Suel.

"How could her husband let her go with you, into this danger, when she might be with child?" Suel and Tenil stared at Bordas accusingly. He didn't respond. He'd had enough problems convincing the Kitarrans that he and Draius weren't married, and that Tyrran women were allowed to work and travel with unrelated men. Duke Cerith, after hearing Draius's background, accepted Tyrran culture much more than his people.

"She only recently figured out the days," Roumithea added. "It is still early."

Bordas sighed and looked down at Draius. Worry seized him. "Our women are strong, but—" he stammered. "Is the baby...?"

"I see no sign she miscarried." Roumithea gave him a small smile, but there were lines between her eyes. "But if more days go by and she doesn't eat, it won't be good for the baby. My mother will know what to do."

"So we put all our hope in a wise woman? Trust in her Sight? Bah!" Suel threw up his hands and stomped out.

Roumithea shooed him and her husband out, although the arguments didn't disturb the two patients. Bordas took a last look at the recumbent forms on the cots and whispered a prayer to his ancestors.

Ruhallen, Northern Tyrra

Ihmar ended up in a study within an ancient house where books, manuscripts, and scrolls filled one wall. Lady Niisa settled in a great armchair, with Lyn on one side and Berina on the other. Lyn had an official King's Guard expression on her face: hard, suspicious, and uncompromising.

He stood in front of the matriarch, as though on trial, while he considered his next action. He had set himself on a course that didn't require cooperation from the humankind—but that was before the violent death-magic had washed over him, before Perinon collapsed, and before there'd been any indication of the Fevers.

"Legends come alive and walk among us," Niisa murmured. "He is Minahmeran."

"And he's a sorcerer." Berina's voice was confident.

"He may be in league with those assassins," Lyn said.

Niisa watched Ihmar with curiosity and questions in her eyes, waiting.

He bowed and addressed her as the Tyrrans did. "My name is Ihmar, my lady. I have the gift of sorcery but no instruction in magical healing, particularly for treating humankind. I can't operate like your—" He stopped, unsure how to address the recent loss of the Phrenii.

Berina followed his thought. "Yes, my lady, send for the Phrenii! They can heal the Fevers if they arrive in time."

Lyn stared at the girl like she was insane.

"I suppose if the silver people are appearing, other legends might also. Still, we can't depend upon myth, child," Niisa said gently.

"What's happened to—why are you all—" Berina's voice started to squeak with frustration and he cut her off.

"Yes, something *has* affected you and I can prove it." He borrowed authority from Niisa, a tiny trick he hadn't used in more than a hundred years. "Berina, find a document which discusses the Phrenii."

The girl went to a section of old books and scrolls, ones without labels. She pulled down a bound sheaf of parchment leaves, about as thick as her wrist, and held them with both hands. "This is Sorceress Lahna's last journal."

"How do you know that?" Niisa frowned.

"A puzzle, my lady, but for another time. First we must deal with the Phrenii and the illness of your monarch. Find an entry that discusses the Phrenii specifically," he told Berina.

The girl laid the journal on the small stand in front of Niisa and started turning leaves. Lady Niisa made a startled sound. "I don't remember gaps in her writings. Why would that be done in a time when parchment was so expensive?"

"I see only writing that is faded from time." Berina shrugged. She found a page toward the end of the journal. "Here, although her letters are difficult for me to read, is where Lahna recorded a conversation with the Phrenii. She warns them against seeking individuality. She had dreams—"

"She was crazy," Lyn said. "And I'm wondering about the sanity within this room. There's nothing on that page to be seen; it's clean as a new sheet."

Ihmar saw it crammed with blocked letters. To him, they were plain, but now he knew enough from their varied reactions to guess how he could counter this. He reached for life-light, forming a conduit to the Void, endangering everyone in this room if he lost control. Usually he would take the precaution of meditating and clearing his mind, but there was no time.

"*Başarilar delahrim gedaninar*," he murmured.

The surge through the conduit was sweet, but painful enough that no living being could hold it open for long. The lettering on the journal pages glittered. The three humans, intent upon the page, jerked backward. Lyn covered her eyes and Lady Niisa's mouth opened. The knowledge shined in her eyes: she remembered the Phrenii, the creatures who once protected their king and country.

He closed and tied off the conduit. The adult eyes dulled, but they still stared at the page. Berina appeared unaffected. The results were disappointing: he proved the effects of the death magic were reversible, but he also proved their strength. There weren't enough sorcerers available in the world to reverse this for all humankind.

"What did you do? I remember..." Lyn's voice trailed off and she scratched her head.

"The gaps are gone." Niisa looked over the page. "What I can read, though, are mad ramblings."

Controlling a conduit to the Void tired him and he took a deep breath. "I wanted to permanently change everyone in this house, perhaps even in this village, but the death-magic executed this morning was too strong. I was only able to reverse one document and stir your memories."

"Are the Phrenii gone forever?" Berina sounded anxious.

He shrugged. "I don't have enough information yet to answer that."

"Let's agree that something affected our history and our memories." Lyn's gesture included all the documents in the room. "Shouldn't we be concentrating on the king's health, rather than this?"

Someone cleared his throat. Gaflis stood in the doorway and behind him hovered the chemist. At Niisa's nod, they stepped into the room.

"Officer Lyn is correct, my lady. From the king's symptoms, it looks like the Fevers—two others are showing signs as well." The physician's eyes flicked over to Berina. "One of them is young Erno."

"My brother!" Berina started for the door.

"Stay here." The chemist blocked her way. "We've separated those with the Fevers into the other wing and we can't allow you access. They can spread through touch."

At least humankind remembered some teachings from the Phrenii, even if they didn't have magical healing support from the creatures any more. The Fevers were really two diseases and sequestering the ill was the best course for either.

"Can't you do anything useful here, *sorcerer?*" Lyn clenched her teeth.

"Remember, I have no training in healing and I have as much love for my life as you do. If I succumb to the fever that is exchanged through touch—" His voice was flat and he held Lady Niisa's gaze. "Then I will die. For you, death from this is but a chance; for me, it is certainty."

Ihmar turned to Gaflis and the chemist, and bowed. "I can provide guidance for the treatment of clothes and articles that are touched by the victims. I can improve your powders and tonics. However, if I exhibit symptoms, I must end my life quickly. After my death, you must burn my body in a fire hot enough to melt my bones to prevent leaving latent pockets of the disease; otherwise, they can last for thousands of years."

There was silence in the room.

CHAPTER EIGHTEEN

A Royal Line Ends

Serasa-Kolme Residence, Betarr Serasa, Tyrra

AFTERMATH OF RECENT STORM

The Harbor Master fears several ships that recently left port may be lost, but specifics won't be known for days. Lightning strikes caused fires, the most damaging occurring to the Royal Archives. Children of all ages ran about the streets, traumatized, and claiming a group of unicorns are missing. Physicians recommend seclusion and rest for children suffering this collective delusion. Extreme cases of hysteria may need treatment of dwayberry, but only when attended by a physician.

— The Horn & Herald, *Third Millday, Erin Seven, T.Y.* 1471

Peri tiptoed to the corner of his bedroom and pressed his ear against the wall covering the shaft. This way, he could hear the matriarchs' conversation clearly. He had feigned sleep when Aunt—when *Lady* Anja had looked in on him, but he didn't think he fooled her.

You must pay attention all the time now, Peri. You will work with people who lie or hide the truth. You must learn politics. Da—*his father*, since he wanted to grow beyond childish names—knew all about these politics but never spoke of them. Anja mentioned them once and moved him to this room, perhaps ignoring the fact it sat beside the shaft for the lift used to move supplies between floors. The shaft also happened to pipe voices between floors.

"He's sleeping," Lady Anja said.

"You should ask a physician to dose him for hysteria." That was Lady Leika's voice. "This tumult brought back trauma from his kidnapping last spring."

"Did you give him powders?" Lady Aracia's voice sounded loud. No one ever hushed her, as he often was.

"No, I didn't think it necessary. He's not hysterical," Anja said. "Nor traumatized from his abduction."

"Does he insist he lost some *unicorns?*" Leika sounded amused.

Peri clenched his fists. He hated that word. It was vulgar and not to be used for the Phrenii. He had been reprimanded for using the word once and now adults used it everywhere. Soon he realized the more he protested about the Phrenii, the worse it would be for him. So he shut up.

"Any news on his health? He didn't look well the last time I saw him." Leika was talking now and Peri had missed part of the conversation. He pressed his ear tighter to the wall.

"I received notice the king arrived at the lodge and his trip has been restful and restorative." Aracia's voice sounded light, but her eyes would be cold. Her eyes were often cold, but they were never mean like Leika's.

"The lodge? I thought he traveled to Ruhallen." Leika's voice sounded thoughtful.

"Yes, he made the decision to continue north and visit holdings which rarely get a visit from the king." Aracia's voice sounded as frigid as a winter wind rattling the windowpanes. "I took that as a sign he's feeling better."

"Better? Well, good!" Leika's voice sounded bright, but false. "Perhaps you *do* have time for these negotiations. I suggest the Meran-Viisi and Serasa-Kolme work out their differences regarding *this* successor, so that we may move on to selecting older ones."

Leika called for her cloak, so she was leaving. Anja made sure that her coach was ready. There was a long silence below and Peri thought that Aracia had left also. He was about to go back to his bed when he heard her voice again.

"I need to hold her off longer. We should also move the boy to my residence, for his own protection."

"She wants you to know she tracked the king's location." Anja's voice was colorless.

"I hope that's all she knows. Before I came here, I received a letter straight from the river packet, from the Vilje-Nelja matriarch in Ruhallen. Perinon is gravely ill."

Peri's eyes widened.

Anja's voice remained calm. "Does anyone else know this?"

"Not yet. The worse part is that the Vilje-Nelja suspect the Fevers are returning." Aracia sounded tired. It had a lost tone that a matriarch never used, like she was defeated.

"This time we might discover a defense." The hope in Aunt Anja's words wasn't reflected in her voice.

The Fevers struck Tyrra with ferocity before Peri was born, but every child knew what happened: one in five died, even *with* healing provided by the Phrenii. He clenched his hands into fists, trying to fight the paralyzing fear creeping over him. What would happen now that the Phrenii were gone?

Aracia's voice rose. "I can't select an older successor when I can't trust any of the other five-star matriarchs! Leika pushes Councilman Muusa, who's too old by my standards yet has received a Meran-Viisi education, but the master of arms suspects he's involved in Sevoi's murder. There is also strong reason to suspect the Pettaja-Viisi, the Groygans, *and* the Sareenians are involved in the deaths of the other successors."

"That doesn't seem possible…" For the first time, Aunt Anja became emotional. "You really think Peri may be in danger?"

"I don't know, but he would certainly be safer surrounded by the King's Guard."

"I never thought the day would come when the Crown feared our own people." His aunt sounded sad. "How would Leika benefit from Muusa being selected as a successor?"

"Councilman Muusa is extremely pliable and, apparently, has already fallen under Leika's sway." Aracia sniffed. "I'll never tell him this, but Perinon was right. He never wanted to appoint Muusa as the replacement for Reggis."

"Why would Muusa ever be considered a valid successor, considering his age? Don't you, as Meran-Viisi, have the final authority in selection of successors?"

"First, she's in the position of validating *everyone's* education and background. Second, I have the authority but any successor I choose must have the matriarchy's support," Aracia said grimly. "Remember that no one knew about Peri. I was supposed to be left with no suitable successors, panicked and willing to consider non-traditional substitutes. As I examine this plot, it grows more frightening because it could effectively usurp the Crown if Perinon dies *promptly...*"

As Aracia's voice died away, someone started pacing. When Aunt Anja finally spoke, he could tell she was the pacer. "This explains her insistence on examining Peri's education. She'll say his education is wanting, to force you to rule him out in favor of an older successor. Maybe we should move him to your lineage earlier than we intended."

"I doubt she'll move against Peri before he takes the Meran-Viisi name. Until that happens, she won't take him as a serious successor—that keeps him safer. We have to draw out our *negotiations* while moving him to my residence and getting him a tutor she can't dispute. Pretending to wrangle over contract provisions will also delay evaluating Muusa. If this will be too drastic for the boy, we can..." The matriarchs' voices faded as they went into another room.

Peri tiptoed back to his bed. His whole world had collapsed yesterday morning. Now there were no Phrenii to find, no Dahni or Mahri to ask for help. He wished he could talk to his mother. *She* would remember because she was in rapport with Dahni. Perhaps Lornis would remember because he was Phrenic-healed, but he was gone somewhere, nobody would say where or why. There were only adults like his Da and Aunt Anja and these matriarchs—no one who remembered the Phrenii. Now they would move him to Betarr Serin, change his lessons, and he wouldn't even see his cousins any more.

He burrowed deeper into his bed, trying to shake off the cold that took hold of his body. He felt wounded, like the time he took a bad fall playing defenders-of-the-fortress and tore the skin away from his palms. The Phrenii had been torn away and to pretend they never existed caused more pain. Didn't Dahni say there would be problems ahead? Hadn't they pleaded to children to remember them?

Peri made a resolution: *he* would never forget.

Suellestrin, Kitarra

Renca Be Endigala, previous Honored Sword for Lord Endigala and now aide to Vitna Be Nettona, wrinkled his nose in disgust. The Ungoughts were rotten to their core, if King Markus was their prime example. Renca hadn't met the nephew, Cerith, rumored to be just as unstable as Markus. However, he reserved judgment on Cerith: anyone who evaded the large number of guards hunting him, plus evacuated all his people and supplies from his estate in an efficient manner, might be a worthy adversary.

"Cerith's withdrawn into the marshes, perhaps even to the moors. We'll never find him now." Markus thumped the table. Wine-laced spittle and bits of food spouted from his mouth.

Renca moved his watered wine out of range. He finished his meal long ago. When would Markus finish eating? The man had an insatiable appetite and, as a result, continually replaced his wardrobe.

"There are rumors in the streets that he'll return and unseat me. That talk will stop, even if I must hang all the gossipers myself." Unbelievably, Markus reached for yet another leg of mutton.

"Sire, one might win over the populace better by avoiding executions." Nettona, sitting on the other side of the king, used a wheedling tone.

Renca nodded in agreement. King Markus could learn from that Sareenian, Avo Cabaran, who shocked the mapped world with *To Have and Hold Power*: a work that explained why monarchs should manipulate the hearts of their people. Cabaran publicly mocked the Ungought family, naming Markus as a contrary example, so perhaps it was better that Markus didn't read.

"I can control my own people. I need you and your men to find Cerith for me." The king pointed a greasy finger at Renca.

"I lose patrols to ambushes if I send them too far outside the city. My men are stretched to control your perimeter, keep your people from fleeing, and quell the riots. I have another unit of guards arriving tomorrow. At that point, we can organize a better hunt for your nephew."

"Fleeing the city? Riots? Posh—your problem is finding Cerith and I can't be concerned with your men getting lost in the marshes." Which showed how out of touch and uninformed Markus had become. Nettona had purposely isolated him.

"We're certain the ambushes are directed by your nephew, sire, with Tyrran help. Honor Renca must move more guards into Suellestrin to counter Cerith and ensure your personal safety." Nettona poured more wine for the king. All servants had been dismissed.

"I should have executed him with his father and brother, when he was young. Instead, he repays my clemency with treasonous plots." Markus's ranting began to sound unintelligible to Renca, like an animal's snarling and mewling. He noticed Nettona fingering the charm made by Lord

Endigala's necromancer. Markus wore an invisible one about his neck, paired to Nettona's. The charms had been made with Markus's hair and designed to influence only him, but were untested. Nettona would have to "experiment and find the best means to influence the subject," the necromancer had written.

The right leverage turned out to be the nephew. With their history and the extreme distrust between Markus and Cerith, Nettona merely amplified the paranoia and got Markus to request Groygan troops to quell these "treasonous plots." Cerith's intrigues were imaginary but when Renca considered the careful and successful ambushes on his men, he wasn't so sure any more. Endigala's necromancer had also provided charms designed for Queen Tintia, just as untested. Renca kept those aside, having no need for them yet.

Markus was bright red and his mouth frothed.

Renca reached over the table to grab Nettona's forearm. The pupils of the councilor's eyes had elongated with pleasure. "Stop it. His health may suffer."

Nettona's yellow eyes glared back at him, and then blinked. He released his hold of the charm and shook off Renca's hand. Markus was making heaving sounds; perhaps his dinner was coming up.

Something caught Renca's attention, just at the edge of his eyesight. Turning, he stared at the curtained doorway that led to the family apartments. Had it moved? There was a dark slit between the two fabric panels and he couldn't see if anyone stood behind them.

Markus gasped, his face now a mottled purple. He leaned back, clutching his left shoulder with his other arm.

"I said to stop!" Renca glared at Nettona.

"I did." Nettona watched the king. "We'd better call for his physician."

Markus went still, falling back into his chair.

"No!" Nettona leaned over the king and shook him.

Renca felt for pulses in the wrist and neck. There were none. "Gods, Nettona, now you did it! You just gave Cerith the Kitarran Crown."

"We can't have that—he has Tyrran leanings," Nettona said soberly. "Besides, I have no way to control him."

"It doesn't matter. With news that Markus is dead, the duke can ride back into Suellestrin and even the nobility might welcome him." He jerked his head toward the anteroom, where several Kitarran servants, as well as court members, awaited the king.

"But your guards—you can hold Suellestrin, can't you?"

"Maybe when my additional unit arrives tomorrow," Renca said. "It's tricky controlling a city population, especially *if* there's a rebellion to contend with. We've got artillery units moving into the fishing flats, but using them would be as useful as shooting ourselves in the foot."

"Then it's best that Markus not die *tonight*. We'll wait for your guards to arrive tomorrow. Then we can deal with this." Nettona gestured at the body.

Renca nodded. He went to the anteroom and stuck his head out. Approximately ten Kitarrans rose to their feet in a flurry, eager to have time with the king. Three Groygan guards prevented anyone from entering the king's dining chamber.

"The king doesn't want to be disturbed tonight." He hoped his smile was nonchalant. "But I need my aide."

The sycophants began murmuring, but he shut the door solidly on them. Inside the dining chamber, his aide Maso took in the scene: a half-finished feast for at least five men and a dead king. His facial expression didn't change.

"No one else is allowed to enter this chamber," he told Maso, while he thought about how to handle the body. He didn't know much about Kitarran customs when it came to death. The godless Tyrrans burned their dead, but the Kitarrans didn't have much wood in this gods-forsaken country, so they probably buried them. Would the queen require a viewing of the body?

He suddenly remembered the movement at the curtained doorway to the family apartments. "We must see to the queen and the servants."

Nettona had been thinking also. "Yes, Tintia can act as regent for Markus's son. The Kitarran nobility would accept that."

"Come with me." He stepped through the curtained doorway, followed by Maso, and drew his long knife. The corridor to the family apartments was dark and short, but still managed to make two turns. Renca went through the unlocked door at the end. They entered a well-appointed sitting room lit by two lamps. The lamps smoked, requiring attention, but no one was in the room. The king's rooms were to the right and the queen's were to the left. He gave a signal and pointed to the king's side.

Maso was gone for a few moments. He returned to wipe the blood from his blade on a finely woven tapestry hanging beside the door. Everything had been silent.

"How many servants?" Renca whispered.

"Two."

"Now for the queen's apartments." He burst through the door, expecting surprise from the occupants. However, the two women in the room looked up expectantly.

The young queen sat at an oak table in the middle of the room, holding a silver chalice in her hand. Her attendant was kneeling at the hearth, stirring a steaming liquid in a small pot. The room smelled of herbs and something sweet. Renca sheathed his long knife. Something was wrong here, but he couldn't quite put his finger on the problem. Tintia viewed Renca coldly, waiting for him to speak.

"We need to check on the male heir." He didn't bother with formalities.

"Don't wake my children," Tintia said in a flat tone. The queen's attendant moved to block Maso from the inner bedchambers.

"My lady, we're seeing to his safety." He changed to a respectful tone, realizing this woman would soon be regent. He flicked a signal to Maso, who pushed past the attendant and went into the children's room.

"Two young children, sleeping deeply," Maso reported. "An infant male and a female."

Tintia displayed admirable composure. She stared down at her wine, swirling it. She deliberately raised the silver cup to her lips.

Sleeping deeply. He leaped across the room and with a swing of his hand sent the silver chalice sailing in an arc to land on the hearth. Wine splashed into the small fire, making it sizzle and sputter. Tintia looked up at him with angry blue-gray eyes. For a moment, the only sound was the ringing of the chalice rolling in a semi-circle on the stone.

"Wake the children," he commanded Maso. Tintia's face was blank, the face of a woman who considered herself already dead.

"I was mistaken, Honor. They're not sleeping. The male is dead and this one has but a faint heartbeat." Maso reappeared carrying the girl child. She was roughly three years old and her hair was the same color as Tintia's. Her head lolled back over the aide's arm in an unnatural manner. Even though she was female and couldn't hold the Kitarran Crown, by their law, she was Markus's heir and had value as a hostage. He shook her head, then slapped and pinched her cheek. She wouldn't wake, so he had Maso put her back on her bed. She had obviously been given a poison or a concentrated sleeping elixir, which was slowing her heart.

"Is there any way to counter it?" He demanded of the attendant. The woman's eyes flickered from him and back to the queen. Then she shook her head imperceptibly.

Renca took a moment to control his anger. Why had Giada handed him this fate? Sitting here, in godless Kitarra where it rained most of the time, with no rightful heir to control the population. He stomped back to the table and lowered his broad frame into the chair facing Tintia. How much of the deadly brew had she taken? Her strange round pupils were dilated. The color of her eyes reminded him of the reflection of sky off the Mirror Sea: clear and frigid.

"I must follow my children." Her voice was hollow.

"No. You will live." His answer was irrevocable.

He gave another signal and observed Tintia as Maso backed the attendant into a corner. Tintia's eyes didn't move or flicker as the woman whimpered and tried to fight, but she did flinch at the crunching sound of the woman's neck breaking.

"You're not the only one who can hand out death," he said quietly. "I need to know how many servants attended you this evening. Then we must speak about the future of your people."

He knew she no longer cared whether she lived or died. A small part of him admired her, but if he was to hold Suellestrin for the Council and Lord Endigala, he needed more than apathy from her. The Kitarran nobles, luckily, were sheep. They liked to play political games, but in the end they would support Tintia as regent—they just couldn't find out the infant was dead.

He reached into the sack on his belt for the necromancer's charms.

Ruhallen, Northern Tyrra

Ihmar worked beside the chemist when a member of the King's Guard found him, telling him that Commander Lyn required his presence. Lady Niisa had arranged to keep him away from the sick humankind in the village but he didn't dare offend Lyn, who seemed at the ragged edge of her control. Two days had passed since they'd brought Perinon into Ruhallen and more cases continued to appear. He suspected Perinon suffered from more than disease, but nothing could be done but hope the young monarch survived.

He found Lyn with Askar at the western edge of the village, examining the belongings of the assassins. Neither looked like they had slept.

"That makes nine, including the king," Askar said to Lyn.

"How goes the king?" Ihmar asked.

Askar looked up and shook his head.

"Well, sorcerer, let's see if you can be useful. Examine these items for me." Lyn's voice was flat. She waved her arms over the planked table where the assassins' clothing and gear had been dismantled and catalogued.

"What am I looking for?"

"You say you're not in league with these men." Her eyes narrowed. "If so, these men followed us and found the king by some way other than normal observation. Perhaps they used magic."

He nodded, not bothering to correct Lyn's vague term of "magic." Life-light couldn't be bound into objects, but necromantic power could. Anything he discovered might bolster his own claim of innocence because the King's Guard still viewed him with suspicion. He held his hand out, barely above each item, as he walked around the table and concentrated. When his hand moved over a group of small steel mirrors, he flinched and pulled it back. It felt like a wasp stung his hand; it even throbbed, the death-magic acting like venom.

He murmured a spell, then leaned over the table and looked down into the mirrors. They all stopped reflecting the deep blue autumn sky but only one showed something real. Instead of black, he saw young Erno's face, blistered and still, and he knew a companion mirror had been lifted with the hope that some breath, some life, might come from the boy's lips. He jerked back.

"Cover those!" His voice broke as he turned away, hugging himself. Erno was dead, the first casualty. There would be more.

Askar quickly threw a piece of clothing over them.

"What does it do?" Lyn asked.

"Those are all necromantic charms and one of them is hooked to something your physician carries, perhaps another mirror. I doubt he knows what he carries."

The King's Guard pulled Gaflis and all his equipment away from his charges.

"What's happening?" The physician was tired and angry, disrupted by having his bags and tools searched.

"When did Erno die?" Ihmar asked.

Gaflis looked stunned, as well as saddened. "How did you—? He only just passed on to his journey to the stars. I was going to notify his father and sister."

Meanwhile, Askar and Lyn were putting all the instruments Gaflis used on the table. He found no mirror and ran his hand above every item. He shook his head when Lyn looked at him in question: no necromantic charms.

"What are you carrying?" Lyn asked.

Gaflis protested, but Lyn insisted. Ihmar stood to the side, observing silently. The humankind needed more sleep or they would collapse in the coming days. Eventually, the physician emptied all his pouches and pockets and the mirror was found. Honestly horrified when he learned what it was, he sat down and rubbed his temples with his fingers. "It came from the field kit kept for me at the Betarra hospital. I didn't need it while we were on the river."

"This is how they followed the king's position," Lyn said. "Who would have placed it in your bag?"

"Anybody. My kit is clearly marked. What have we come to, when a physician's tools are used to aid murderers?"

"*Darkness and Fury.*" A woman's voice echoed and everybody looked up. "*Darkness and Fury shall take hold throughout the world. Only by returning elemental true magic shall humankind survive.*"

Thunder boomed in the crystalline sky. Everyone flinched, including Ihmar. Gaflis crouched and covered his ears. No living being had said those prophetic words. The Tyrrans had a fascinated horror in their hollow eyes and every one of them sagged. A sudden and unfamiliar pang of sympathy for them tightened Ihmar's chest.

"You must all keep up your strength and get rest," he said. "Your struggle is just beginning; you can't falter in the long nights to come."

"Whose voice was that?" Lyn asked harshly.

"I think she was a sorceress called Lahna." All the Tyrrans nodded when Ihmar said the name.

Askar scratched his head. "The locals say her prophecies sometimes ring from the ground, but I didn't believe 'em."

Gaflis shook himself, as if waking from a dream. He started repacking his kit. "Well, her words don't help me. If you're finished, commander, I'll take what tools are safe and continue my work."

"Make sure that you and the chemist spell each other and allow for rest periods," Lyn warned the physician. Then she beckoned him with her finger. "Ihmar."

This was the first time Lyn used his name, which was hopeful. He walked around the table.

"I'll leave all these charms in your care. Destroy them, unless they can help you in your work."

"Work?" He frowned.

"You're going to right this wrong, aren't you? Bring back the Phrenii? They're the *elemental true magic* in Lahna's prophecy, aren't they?"

This went far beyond his assignment to "gather information" and he started to say he couldn't help, but stopped. A flash of Ildizar sneering about the dithering elders and constraints went through his mind. The elders would never consider what Lyn suggested to be within the scope of his duties. On the other hand, this was a *meaningful* task, which he hadn't encountered for a long time. *This is a problem I'm trained for; this* should *be my mission.* He had already exposed his presence with minimal repercussions. So far the humans showed little curiosity about Minahmerah or whether it still existed, probably because they were worried about other things—like their very survival. The prophetic words stored in the very bedrock under Ruhallen were not uttered for humankind alone. "I'll need full access to Lahna's journals. I must also learn the location of each piece of the Kaskea."

"Agreed, as long as Lady Niisa allows it. As for the shards, we're not sure where they all are. It's a long story." For the first time, her facade crumbled and she turned away for a moment. "I'm sorry. I lost my husband and my unborn child in the Fevers of the early fifties. I remember talking with someone—inhuman—" She paused and he could tell she was struggling to patch together the memories he'd stirred up. "I think it was one of those Phrenii and it reassured me that Tuomas had found the path to the stars..."

Her voice trailed away as her eyes focused on something behind him. He turned and glanced at the edge of the thick fir forest and the road that went to the river landing.

"Who is that, standing in the shadow of the trees?" She pointed.

There was no movement, so it took him a moment to find the figure. A familiar young man with light braids and eyes that already had laugh lines. "Erno? Yes, that's Berina's brother. "

Lyn gasped when the specter moved. As they both watched, it walked through some tree trunks and disappeared into the forest. He thought Erno gave them a forlorn glance before leaving. "Do your recently departed normally haunt the living?"

"No." Her eyes were wide. "They look for—no, they are *helped to the path by the Phrenii.* Oh, no."

The destruction of the Phrenii had caused more problems than Ihmar realized.

CHAPTER NINETEEN

Alone Among Strangers

Below Bryn Celar, Northern Moors, Kitarra

Draius tried to enter the Void. Again and again. She pounded against a ceiling she couldn't see. *Forever.* There was no time, no place, only this accursed Blindness filled with hunters intent upon ripping her sanity from her. Eventually, blades of light pierced her eyes. She squinted and they faded to mere lanterns. Above her, she saw rough-hewn rock

"Dahni?" No sense of the creature stirred in her mind.

"Bordas was right. You found your own way back from your dreams," a voice said.

With effort, she turned her head sideways. Her leaden limbs wouldn't move. Beside her bed sat Enita, whose face began to crinkle into a smile.

"Not dreams," she said thickly. "The Blindness, with no way to the Void and no Dahni."

"One can communicate with others within their dreams, but you may not have caught Dahni during his sleep." Enita dribbled water into her mouth and she realized she had a desperate thirst. "Slowly," Enita murmured. After she gave Draius more water, but not enough, she went to the door and called for someone.

Roumithea entered the room, all efficiency and bustle. They hauled Draius into a sitting position, washed her face and torso with cool water, changed her nightshirt, and thrust bread and broth upon her. Through the process, she tried to protest that she could dress and wash herself, but she couldn't even speak entire sentences. Both mother and daughter ignored her until she sat upright, food in front of her. She drank some broth, and then became ravenous. Roumithea called for more bread.

Enita put a hand on her wrist. "You should chew everything completely. You have several days to make up for, just like his grace."

Memories of the flight through the marshes and Cerith's wound came back to her. She stopped eating and groped for the Kaskea, feeling only one shard. "Where's the other one?" This lead to tedious questions about the nature of the Kaskea and what it did. She found out why she couldn't establish rapport with Dahni. It seemed as if the Phrenii had never existed. No one remembered them. Enita tried to convince her that she dreamed them up, yet a shard hung around her neck, which Enita couldn't explain.

"How long have I been...?" She paused, trying to find the right word.

"We're not sure. It depends upon when your—your fit started. Three days have passed since the duke stayed behind to evacuate you," Roumithea said.

"What time is it now?"

"About three hours before midnight." Roumithea replenished her bread.

As always, her mind ticked off the days. She had been almost three days without water or food. It was an eight-day, give or take some hours, since she was thrown into a Kitarran jail. It'd been sixteen days since she stole the shard from Taalo and showed him mercy he didn't deserve, but forty-eight days since she was tasked by Perinon to retrieve it. *Forty-eight days* since she spoke with, or touched Peri and Lornis. "I must see Bordas."

The two women glanced at each other before Enita said, "He's unavailable—you should speak with the duke first."

"Fine, then I'll go speak with the duke." She started struggling with the bedclothes.

Roumithea pursed her lips. "You're not strong enough to stand, Missy, much less walk."

"Then I'll crawl to him." She worked up to taking small steps while supported by Roumithea and Enita. The women were shorter than her but surprisingly strong; even old Enita was now much healthier than when they'd first met in the jail. Two bowls of broth sopped up by bread, plus several walks across her room, plus another layer of clothing, allowed her to walk out of her room leaning on Roumithea. With each step, she felt stronger.

She thought they were within natural caves, but the tunnel appeared man-made, supported by thick, dark beams. It was dim, lit by lanterns about every eight or ten strides. People passed by, intent upon their own business. She saw marsh people and Kitarrans carrying food, supplies, armor, and weapons. Many had bound wounds; many looked haggard. They passed several rooms, or room-like caves, hewn from solid rock. All about her, she felt the moisture. Her skin prickled.

"Where are we?" she finally asked.

"You're under Bryn Celar, in the northern moors."

"Bryn Celar is a town?" she ventured.

"No, it is a huge hill protected by standing stones. All these tunnels are under Bryn Celar. Some of this structure was created by our ancestors and the duke has added much more." The marsh woman stopped at a door framed with masonry. "You're on your own, Missy. I haven't a mind to disturb the duke. He woke several hours before you and he's taking reports as fast as he can."

Roumithea stepped down the tunnel and out of sight around a gentle curve. Draius was left alone staring at the heavy planked door while bracing herself against the wall. She knocked. There was a muffled call to enter. Cerith and Suel looked up from the table they bent over. One of

Cerith's arms was immobilized with a sling. He had dark hollows under his eyes and the bones of his face stuck out sharply.

"Draius." Cerith seemed awkward, showing none of his usual grace. Suel had a strange look on his face, perhaps a mix of wariness and concern.

"I need to speak with you about..." Her voice died away as both men stared at her with guilty expressions. Something was wrong.

"Please take a seat, Draius, while I finish with Suel."

She gratefully edged over to a wooden chair beside the door, made for utility and not comfort. She was exhausted by her efforts. Cerith and Suel were looking at a map.

"They've extended their perimeter to here?" Cerith pointed.

Suel nodded. "Scouts report search parties are pushing deeper into the marsh, but because they're unsure of the footing, they always use three established trails. We can choke them off at these points."

"No, I want them going into the marsh; they're more vulnerable to natural accidents and if they keep by established trails, they'll never find Bryn Celar."

"We've attacked them only on these two routes, hoping to hide our location." Suel tapped the map.

"By their patrol patterns, I don't think that fooled them. We must be unpredictable in pressing their perimeter, so they spread themselves thinner. Set up your ambushes closer to the city. Decide which sites to use each day by dice rolls or drawing chits from a hat, then make the attack quick and withdraw straightaway."

Suel frowned. "Use dice to plan tactics?"

"I don't mean for you to pick unsuitable sites. Depend upon the marsh guides, they know plenty of good places for ambushes. Just make our attacks more random so they have to shrink their perimeter." Cerith smiled wanly. "Remember, ambushes alone will not take back Suellestrin."

Suel bowed and turned to go, but paused by Draius. He looked down at her with that strange expression again. He bowed to her before leaving through the door and she smiled tentatively. He'd never shown her any respect before and when she glanced at Cerith's face, she suddenly knew Suel was expressing sympathy. Her smile faded and dread caused her chest to tighten.

"Bordas is dead." Cerith's words were heavy.

"No." Bordas had to get home to be contracted. Who was he marrying? She searched her mind for the details—never forgotten, just sometimes misfiled.

"I'm sorry." Cerith's voice was gentle, causing her eyes to blur. "Bordas supported our operations with all his energy. He was a driven man. For that, we honor and mourn his passing."

She couldn't hear Cerith over the rising roar in her ears: the sky wept and the Mirror Sea expressed its anguish. Those cold waters swirled and went deep, far deeper than the roots of the mountains, to the deepest calm where she longed to be, where something ancient stirred—

"Draius! Stop! Don't you know what you're doing?" Cerith shook her with his good arm and his fingers dug into her shoulder painfully. She blinked away tears. Water seeped out of the hewn rock walls and dripped about her. Outside the door, there were shouts and the sound of people running.

She looked up at him with confusion.

"Yes, you're causing this." Her shard dangled from his hand, pulsing with bright green light. "Put aside your grief before you drown us all. There will be time later to mourn Bordas."

She wiped tears from her face. The shard's pulses slowed and its glow faded. It became a simple piece of slate with etched lines.

"We've been given wondrous powers." Cerith pulled out the other shard from about his neck.

Unfortunately, he was now bound to the Kaskea. She remembered him reaching out with a blood-covered hand to clutch at the Kaskea shards. *I should have been more careful.* "That's a *Tyrran* artifact and I'm responsible for its safekeeping."

"But I'm bound to it now." Cerith's shard flared with copper light and there was a low, barely perceptible, rumble. He held his hand, palm out, toward the hewn stonework of the wall and with a sharp crack, a large chip of rock flew into his hand. He smiled at her and tossed it into the corner. It slid on the floor, bounced back from the wall and spun for a moment, audible in the quiet room.

She lowered her head, disturbed. Before, use of elemental powers had required cooperation of the Phrenii. The creatures had to accept the bearer's intentions and the bearer had to be resistant to the lure of the elements. Remembering his brother's death by drowning, Perinon had warned her about playing with Dahni's element before she had experience. What puzzled her was how Cerith used those elemental powers without the Phrenii. For that matter, she obviously had *all* Dahni's powers and she wasn't sure she *wanted* them.

"That isn't your power to use," she said stiffly.

"Not originally, of course." He regarded her with his bright glance, making her uncomfortable.

"You *do* remember the Phrenii." She took a deep breath of relief; she wasn't the only person in the mapped world who remembered them.

"Yes, but they're gone now." Cerith walked to the wall and laid his hand on the stone, looking at it with wonder. "I never realized how beautiful granite could be."

"Sahvi is—was the element of earth and the aspect of influence," she said.

"She spoke to me, very briefly, during the bonding."

"*She?* They're neither male nor female."

"I beg to differ. For the brief exchange we had, I definitely spoke with a female. She begged me to *remember* her—then I was pulled away into murky chaos and swimming monsters."

"It's called the Blindness." She recalled her last rapport with Dahni. *Remember me. Keep me alive*, the creature told her. "Famri was fire and protection, Jhari was air and prescience, and Mahri was the keystone, representing Spirit. Dahni was water and..." Her voice faded and almost broke. *Dahni, where have you gone?*

"Healing." Cerith finished her sentence. "My shoulder had a serious wound, but it's almost fully healed."

She sat up. "Where's Bordas?" she asked fiercely.

"You can't heal him now."

"Where is he?"

The Abandoned Hermitage Near Ruhallen, Northern Tyrra

Before heading back to the hermitage, Ihmar paid a visit to Lady Niisa and requested access to Lahna's library.

"Commander Lyn told me what she's asked of you. You can borrow anything you need, but the collection is large." Niisa gestured at one side of her library, covered with shelves. "That part was cataloged by the Pettaja-Viisi with whatever they shipped down to the Royal Archives many, many years ago. Then there's the locked room with more to be cataloged, whenever they deign to send somebody here to sort it. They forbade us to use the materials after the thief of the Royal Archives tried to rummage through them—although he didn't receive as warm a welcome *here* as he did in the sister cities."

Ihmar looked at the overflowing shelves and blew his breath out in frustration. Given his talents, he could just take everything and leave Niisa thinking she'd suggested it. However, it would be unethical to meddle with her mind, even though she was only human. He should find another way. "I'll need access to the non-cataloged material. Should I petition these Pettaja-Viisi?"

Niisa snorted. "They haven't sent anyone in response to our standing request for cataloging in my lifetime, and aren't likely to before my death. I've never approved of Leika. She thinks that her five-star-lineage automatically bestows her with authority. She's mistaken. It's the *Vilje-Nelja* who are responsible for preserving Sorceress Lahna's legacy and as their matriarch, *I* can grant you access." She reached into her skirts and pulled out a key and offered it to him.

"Thank you, my lady." He bowed as he took the key.

"Call me Niisa, please. I suspect we're both old enough to use each other's given name." Ihmar nodded, because that was the easiest answer; he was still young, about four times her age. "I'll find you the catalog, which marks the pieces taken to the Royal Archives. Your biggest challenge will be finding what you need in all her writings." Her eyes glinted as she looked up at him. "I assume that next, you'll be wanting Berina's help?"

He nodded. "I think she communicates with the soul who stays near the hermitage and I think that soul is Sorceress Lahna."

"Sorceress Lahna successfully walked the path to the stars. That was confirmed a couple decades after her death by both star watchers and—" She frowned and, courtesy of the spell he tried on her earlier, she was able to work around the holes. "Yes, by the *Phrenii*. It would have been considered heresy, three days ago, to suggest Lahna's soul didn't reside in our ancestral stars. Today, I don't know."

"You can't dispute that Berina has memories and knowledge beyond her own life."

"I don't. Does she have the Sight?" Niisa bluntly asked.

"Possibly. If so, she can help me tremendously in the Blindness. She might even be able to walk the Void, with my help."

"Does she have the abilities to *apprentice* with you?" Lady Niisa's eyes narrowed.

He paused at the unexpected question. Humankind no longer worked elemental magic, what they called "true magic," the source of which was the Void. But was that due to lack of inherent talent or lack of proper teachers? Was the *lack* of talent actually a *scarcity* of talent, with no one able to test for it? The Phrenii sensed such talent, but they were not good teachers—for instance, their knowledge of disease didn't transfer well to physicians.

"Ihmar?" Niisa was still waiting.

"It would require a commitment of many years before we'd know if she had any talent for elemental magic." He didn't know if he could deal with a *human* apprentice, but there would be time to consider that issue later. Lots of time, considering his apprenticeship lasted almost a hundred years.

Niisa nodded grudgingly. "An honest answer. Whatever her talent, Berina must be the one to make the decision to work with you. I'll send her out to the hermitage tomorrow morning. See that you are honest with her, as well."

"I will answer all her questions honestly and to the best of my ability."

She sighed. "You'll find that she quickly changed with the death of her brother. Her enthusiasm and belief in the Phrenii have wavered, replaced with adult resentment and resignation. I was foolish to hope that someone so close to adulthood could hold on to their innocence, especially when faced with the Fevers."

"Unfortunately, resentment and disbelief feed upon each other. By myself, I cannot hold back humankind's urge to disbelieve, to perversely assume a world with no hope and no wonder."

"No, you can't." Lady Niisa's smile held a hint of sadness. "But if you can bring back any bit of hope and wonder to Berina's eyes, I will be forever indebted to you."

When he left Lady Niisa's household, he carried a tied sheaf of papers under one arm and the sack with the necromantic charms with the other. When he got to the hermitage, he put the papers carefully on the small table. He was going to carry the sack outside, but paused. Lyn had suggested they might be of use in "his work" and he had intended to bury or destroy them. He was prohibited from performing death magic, but the evil had already been done and the power bound into the objects. Would the *use* of the mirrors also drain the Void? Two of the polished metal mirrors were linked to each other, but the other two were obviously communication devices to somewhere or someone else. After agonizing consideration, he wrapped the sack into a tight bundle about the charms and put the bundle on top of a high, narrow cupboard.

He ate a small meal of bread and cheese provided by the village and took a nap. He woke in the evening, drank several cups of water, and meditated before attempting the Void. Even with all that preparation and taking the proper precautions, he only managed to reach the Void through an exhaustive attempt.

The Void no longer showed the world below in perfect cold white detail, but ailing with some malady. One small area of Chikirmo was almost blackened. In the Sareenian desert south of Illus, the Void showed mottled gray growing over what used to be pristine sand. The same gray mottling appeared over small areas of the Tyrran sister cities and Ruhallen. It reminded him of mold and it had to be the effects of necromancy.

Show yourselves, Phrenii! He shouted with his mind. Although one could hear the thoughts of others in the Void, one couldn't breathe or use one's voice. There was no answer. *You are the portals; you have responsibilities to humankind!* He sensed a quiver below him, but there was still no answer.

He picked points to punch down through the Blindness to look at the real world. It was obvious the Phrenic elemental powers still existed, but they seemed to be running amuck. The earth shook in the rocky footings on the edge of the Whythern marshes, as if the feet of the northern moors twitched. Drought encroached everywhere due to the lack of rain, with the exception of a small area near the Mirror Sea—which matched with Commander Lyn's estimate of where Commander Draius might be. All across the Angim Sea, the wind was absent, becalming ships which had to use whatever oars they had available. However, small whirlwinds circled Illus. In northern Tyrra, the spirit of the land had been crushed and the Fevers had moved in like a dark miasma—how could they look like a physical manifestation?

Curious, he took time to examine the area around Tyrra as he worked his way back to his body along the shining thread. A pall hung over the country and the Whitewater was shrouded in an unnatural haze. Darkness centered on Ruhallen and extended to a gradual smokiness over the sister cities at the mouth of the Whitewater. He saw no great fires, no source for the darkness over Ruhallen but the Fevers. It was strange that humankind disease, fearsome but natural, would cause such a physical change.

Small cold glints caught his eye and he pulled back to observe. They hovered at the edges of humankind settlements, like they were attracted to, but couldn't partake, in the warmth of human society. Were these the lost and wandering souls abruptly tied to an earthly existence, now that the Phrenii were gone?

Ihmar plunged back into his body with relief. A distinct barrier now existed between the Blindness and the Void. His body was drenched with sweat and his arms shook as pushed himself up and staggered to his bed-roll. Random thoughts flitted through his mind. Perhaps the Kaskea pro-vided humankind with some control of the Phrenic elements. Maybe each shard retained the power of its aspect or the memories of the individual creature. Before sleep took him over, it occurred to him that he'd seen no problems with the element of fire.

The next morning, he rose and washed his face in the cold water in the wash pan. Then he went to the stool and table, barely visible in the early morning sunlight. Today he would start perusing Lahna's journals. Somehow the Kaskea shards held the key, some solution he couldn't see. He couldn't believe the Phrenii had disappeared for good. Beings made of starlight could be forgotten, dispersed, splintered, reflected, or changed, but they couldn't be destroyed, could they?

Someone knocked lightly on the door.

On the porch, instead of the regular delivery of food in a basket set be-side the door, he found Berina. She stood awkwardly, holding the heavy basket on one arm and a bunch of papers and scrolls tied together with twine under the other.

"You'll need these." She thrust the documents at him, and then set the basket down.

"Has Lady Niisa asked you about working with me?"

"Yes." Her voice was listless. "I'm needed in Ruhallen. More people are getting sick and those of us who are still healthy must pick up their jobs."

"You might have the Sight, Berina." At her name, her gaze snapped back to his face. "You feel Lahna's soul, don't you? You dream of places you have never visited and people you have never met."

She nodded and looked down as she shuffled her feet. "But what can I do to help find the Phrenii? In Ruhallen, I can wash sheets and cook food for the sick. Here…" Her voice trailed away as though she was too tired to speak.

"There is greater need for you here. I can help you walk the Void and you can help me through the Blindness. If you're willing to apprentice with me, no one can tell you what to do with your life again." He raised a finger to stop whatever she was about to say. "*No one.* You will be free to make your own decisions—and your own mistakes."

Below Bryn Celar, Northern Moors, Kitarra

Bordas lay in the "cavern of the dead," as the marsh people called it. It was large, cool, and opened to tunnels that went to deeper, smaller caves that contained final resting places for the dead. The newly deceased were laid out in rows, marked by lit candles. Bordas looked like he was sleeping. His sword was lying on top of his body lengthwise, held in place by his crossed arms. A precious beeswax candle burned near his head.

"The arrow punctured below his armpit and went deep to his lungs. He stayed on his horse and arrived back here last night alive, but barely. Nothing could be done but to ease his passing." Cerith bowed his head.

"He shouldn't have put himself in danger," Draius said bitterly.

"He was driven by the guilt of harming that boy. He was also angry with you for ordering him to leave you when his orders were to protect you. After being forced to do something dishonorable, he wanted to leave his mark of honor on the world."

"That boy is fine now—if you had only let me speak to him! And I merely ordered him to return the Kaskea shard to the king." She clamped her jaw shut because she didn't like the defensive sound of her words. *I'm trying to assuage my own guilt.*

"But he couldn't do that *and* continue to protect you; they were mutually exclusive missions." She took a deep breath: when described so logically, she realized she put Bordas in a terrible position. Cerith continued, "By the time he arrived here, no one would smuggle a Tyrran out of Suellestrin by ship, which is the fastest way to get to the sister cities. Nettona controlled Markus and all Tyrrans were arrested on sight. Nobles with strong Tyrran blood, like me, had our loyalties questioned. Bordas said he couldn't just stand by and watch."

She didn't realize Suellestrin was already hostile to Tyrrans when Bordas arrived, but he still carried important news about the *ebi corgo*. "Even if he couldn't carry the shard back, he should have tried to get his information back to the King's Guard."

"He did. His letter for the master of arms was put into one of my diplomatic pouches. At that time, I had several officers I could trust to carry that to the Kitarran ambassador in Betarr Serin." Cerith looked pensive. "Now nothing's sailing for Tyrra, given the attention the Groygans are focusing on the docks."

Bordas, at least, got a letter out. Her heart rose. "When did the pouch arrive?"

"If everything went well, the ship might have docked around the time we evacuated across the marsh. Of course, the pouch would go through our embassy and the ambassador would schedule a meeting with your master of arms."

"Would they read Bordas's letter?"

"I don't know. I wrote an accompanying letter asking them not to open it, saying the master of arms would consider an unopened sealed letter more legitimate."

"Did Bordas let you read it?"

"Of course not." He smiled. "He did tell me the gist: he told them he was staying in Kitarra until you joined him. If an eight-day passed with no sign of you, he would re-enter Groyga. He also passed on news of the *ebi corgo*. They're a nasty bit of business and I'm glad they haven't shipped any up north."

For a moment, she wondered why Bordas had given his loyalty to Cerith so completely. Perhaps when he met Cerith, he saw someone who he could believe in and depend upon. Once again, she wiped tears off her face. *If only I woke sooner, I might have saved him.* She put her hands on Bordas's chest, trying to extend her senses, push out the darkness, heal...

"Draius." Her spoken name brought her back. The candles were low and flickering. She lay across Bordas, exhausted, her back aching. Cerith pulled her upright, his hands on her shoulders.

"When they were here, even the Phrenii couldn't bring someone back from death." Cerith sounded tired. "He's gone."

"His pyre will start his journey." Her heart was heavy. "I must collect his ashes and bones to take home to his reliquary."

Cerith shook his head. "No pyres—we don't have the wood to spare. Besides, it would attract attention to Bryn Celar."

"But he must be sent on!" Her voice cracked.

Cerith put his arm about her shoulders and pulled her, inexorably, toward him. She let herself lean against him and rested her head against his chest. His solidity and the thudding of his heart distracted her from the rushing water in her mind.

"The marsh people believe the candles will light the way for the soul. When the candles go out, his soul has left and he is on his journey." Cerith's voice was soft.

"Do Kitarrans believe in the journey to the ancestral stars? The path?" Her breath slowed as she gazed at the candle near Bordas's head.

"We believe in the same afterlife that Tyrrans do, but we don't need the ceremony of a starlight wielder and a pyre to start our journey to the stars. Let them move Bordas back into the caverns. His body will be pre-served naturally and someday he can go home to his pyre."

She relaxed at his words and his arm tightened about her. He rested his head upon hers. The candle near Bordas's head suddenly flamed bright and guttered out. Smoke rose and it wafted up to drift in front of—of Bordas's face? *He stood looking at her from across his own body.* She yelped, pulling away from Cerith.

"What in the world?" Cerith saw him too, thank the ancestors. He picked up the lantern with his good arm and held it over Bordas's body, directly in front of the specter. The lantern light went right through it. There was no shadow.

"Have you ever seen someone's soul?" She wondered if this was some sort of ancient marsh magic.

"Never." He shook his head. "How can we prove that's really his soul and not some sort of demon?"

"It feels like him." Bordas, or his specter, continued to look at them with an expression that seemed both sad and puzzled. She moved closer. "Bordas? Do you understand me?"

The specter nodded.

Encouraged, she persisted. "The Groygan boy lived. I healed him and he's doing fine. Do you forgive me now?"

She held her breath as Bordas looked like he was searching his memo-ry. That might seem like a long time ago for someone who had just tran-sitioned from life to death. Then he smiled and nodded.

"Ask him what's happening. Why is he *here* and not on the path?" Cerith whispered in her ear.

"Complicated questions for someone who doesn't speak." She tried anyway. "Do you know why you're *here* with us?"

Bordas gave her a puzzled look.

"Are you trying to go to the ancestral stars? Are you lost?" The specter nodded and walked through pallets of dead bodies toward the cavern wall. The further he drifted from the lamplight, the harder he was to see.

Cerith hissed through his teeth. "He's not alone."

She stared and he was right: other ghosts gathered at the dark edges of the cavern. They were mostly motionless. "Oh, no." She put her hand over her mouth, feeling nauseous. "Without the Phrenii, they can't *find* the path to the stars. No, no, no—we must get the Phrenii back."

"How would you suggest we do that?"

"If I had any sense, I would have stayed in Chikirmo and hunted for it. If Taalo was there, then the lodestone of souls had to be there. It's the lodestone that destroyed them and it's my fault. Perhaps I can—I should leave." She stalked toward the cavern entrance.

"Wait!" He got ahead of her at the cavern mouth and blocked her. "What are you planning?"

"To go back to the sister cities. Perinon stopped looking for the lodestone because I lied. I *lied* about where it might be. Maybe he'll know what to do now, maybe there are prophecies—"

"Draius, your safety is my responsibility now. You are a Tyrran woman, alone and with child."

Her eyes widened. "I didn't think you exchanged gossip with Roumithea."

"Roumithea is only concerned for your welfare. Have you considered that you might not be able to return to Tyrra before your child is born?" His voice was cold. "Even if I knew a safe route, I can't afford any guards for your escort."

"Give Chisel back to me. I can travel alone." Her voice became sullen.

"If you go *through* Suellestrin, you'll be arrested. Going around the west side requires a trained marsh guide and they never travel by horse, only by foot. You must realize I can't allow you to leave."

"What about going by ship?"

"You would run into the same problems that Bordas did."

"I mean by small boat, launching from the northern moors and passing by the city on the east." Her skin prickled from the water all about her.

Considering how King Valos died, a boat might not be such a good idea. The Mirror Sea had a mesmerizing call...

Cerith was talking and she had missed a sentence or two. He was finishing with, "I must consider the future of Kitarra and how to take back my city. Together, with our new powers, we would make a formidable alliance."

"What are you suggesting?"

His head cocked. "It'd be beneficial for both of us. I must hold together an alliance between the marsh people and the Kitarrans, despite an age-old antagonism between them. A wife from either side would be unacceptable to the other, but you are Tyrran and from the bloodline of the king. Besides, a marriage to me could alleviate your current difficulty."

"Make me reputable, by Kitarran standards? In Tyrra, we would welcome Lornis's daughter, regardless of whether I'm contracted to him." This wasn't the full truth and her cheeks burned. Certainly, matriarchs in both lineages would be delighted and she'd be surrounded by helpful midwives as well as the Phrenii—her mind swerved away from the past. Regardless, the matriarchy would probably force a contract upon her.

"You know you carry a daughter?" His eyes brightened. "I would raise her as my own. My body knows we belong together, just as yours does."

She bent her head to hide the heat in her face. He felt her emotional turmoil and considered it attraction! "You take advantage of my situation, your grace. You ask me at an inopportune time and I distrust your motives." She waved her arm to gesture at the whole cavern of the dead, cold and dark, lit here and there by twinkling candles.

The smile faded from Cerith's lips. His Tyrran became clipped and he sounded like an upper-city gentleman. "My motives are trustworthy and I make a generous offer, considering your situation. I won't rescind my proposal, but consider carefully before you reject me."

A soft cough caused both of them to spin about. Cerith's face was still carved of stone, but hers became even hotter. Tenil stood near, his face smeared with mud. How long had he been there? He kept his eyes on his feet.

"You have a message?" Cerith's voice was back to his normal silky tone, having that strange combination of businesslike brusqueness and unconcern.

"Many urgent ones, your grace." Tenil glanced at her before rattling off his messages. "News from Suellestrin is that King Markus is dead from a fire in the royal family's wing. There will be no showing because the body is badly burned. Also dead are seven servants, the children's nanny, and Princess Elene. Queen Tintia has been installed as regent for her son Markus, but the infant is under constant care due to smoke in the lungs. Another unit of Groygan guards arrived in the city when Markus's death was announced. News from scouts in northern Groyga is that an artillery unit bearing the colors of House Endigala recently set up at the fishing flats with the stated purpose of 'protecting the Saamarin from unauthorized traffic.' However, the cannons can easily bombard Suellestrin's docks and walls. There's news marked for Serasa-Kolme Draius as well: Lord Chintegrata is called to a sudden Council of Lords meeting, initiated by House Endigala. His intelligence thinks House Endigala will press for an invasion of Tyrra."

Tenil's words pummeled her. She drew her air in with a ragged gasp— she had been holding her breath. Cannons at the mouth of the Mirror Sea? Invasion of Tyrra?

Cerith turned to her. "Groygan artillery units carry spyglasses. You can't leave Kitarra by water."

CHAPTER TWENTY

Treacheries

Serasa-Kolme Residence, Betarr Serasa, Tyrra

Peri sat on his bed and said goodbye to his old life. His things, which had all been scrutinized carefully by the King's Guard, were packed. Since no one could sense a *passive* necromantic charm, he and Lady Anja had been asked exactly when each item was procured or made. If he owned it more than a year, he could move it to his room in Betarr Serin. If he owned it less than a year and couldn't prove it came from someone reputable, then they put it in a bag to be crushed and burned. They were particularly hard on toys or anything entertaining. Unfortunately, all his boring books and study aids came from the Pettaja-Viisi, so they stayed with him.

He wanted to say, "Bet you'd like the Phrenii around *now*, because they can sense necromantic charms." He swallowed that snide comment, because word through the cousins' grapevine was that mentioning the Phrenii or their magic would get you dosed up with laudanum and confined to your room for an eight-day. Adults were getting downright scared about the holes in their memories.

After they packed and loaded his belongings, he asked Lady Anja for a moment alone. He had been in this house less than two years, but it

336

was an improvement over their quarters in Betarr Kain. It changed when Da—*Father*—had to move to the barracks, but he got used to that. His father and mother were *dealing with their differences*, as Lady Anja described it. All in all, even with Berin drugging and kidnapping him, even with the breaking of his parents' marriage contract, these years in the sister cities were *much* better than those at Betarr Kain.

Someone came to the door. Maricie, the maid, called Lady Anja. He heard some low conversation and recognized the voice. *Da!* He ran out of the room and clattered down the top stairs before he caught himself and slowed down. *You must act more grown-up when you're living in Betarr Serin with me*, Lady Aracia had said.

His father, Serasa-Kolme Jan, glanced up from his murmured conversation with his aunt and matriarch, Lady Anja. Jan looked handsome as usual, dressed in his City Guard uniform. According to his mother, Jan made women "swoon." He had asked what that word meant and Draius pantomimed it for him, making him laugh.

He paused on the stairs, his eyes on level with his father's, and wondered what to do. When he was five, he would have jumped into his father's arms. Last year, he would have flung himself at his father and hugged him around the waist with both arms. Now he wasn't sure if that was grown-up enough, so he stepped down the last steps and said, "Hello, Father."

Jan's smile widened and he extended his right hand to Peri, who likewise extended his right hand. Jan clasped his hand and pulled him close while his other arm tightened momentarily around him, and then thumped him on the back in a friendly way with his hand. Peri had seen men greet male relatives and close comrades this way. He followed suit, feeling rather grown up.

"I'm sorry I haven't been by for a while, but we've been busy." His father steered him into the front parlor.

Peri noted he hadn't taken his cloak off, so this would be a short visit. His heart fell, but he tried to nod in a pragmatic way. "I know. The Sareenian charm problem. Master of Arms Kilpi explained everything." He liked the new master of arms, who talked to him like an adult. He didn't soften things, either. Peri shivered, thinking about those toys killing the previous master of arms, plus four Meran-Viisi successors. Essentially, those murders led to all this change in *his* life.

"Yes. This is a real mess for the City Guard." His father looked at him appraisingly.

"Maricie, please bring us some tea." Anja said. The maid bobbed and finished closing the parlor door. Peri hoped his favorite nut cakes came with the tea.

"Your eighth birthday isn't until tomorrow, so I brought you an early present." His father reached under his cloak and brought out a long thin box.

"I figured everybody forgot 'cause we've had so many horrible things going on." As Peri took the present, tears stung his eyes and he took a moment to blink them away.

"Nobody forgot." Anja smiled. "Tomorrow you'll start taking lessons at our house in Betarr Serin, where your cousin Ilke lives."

"Not at the Meran-Viisi house?" Peri felt relieved.

"No, though you'll be living there. We're moving the Serasa-Kolme lessons up there and you'll have a new tutor. I think you'll like him."

All because of him, because he had to move up to Betarr Serin and live in a place crawling with the King's Guard. *For his own safety*, although no one said that to him directly. At least he'd get away from Lady Aracia and have lessons with his cousins every afternoon but Ringday. He untied the twine about the heavy but small box, opened it, and breathed, "This is for me?"

He took out a brass spyglass that appeared well used, but cared for. It was as thick as a large carrot, but about twice as long when extended. The name "Serasa-Kolme" was engraved on the side. He raised it, looked out the front glazing, and said, "Oooooh." That didn't sound very adult, so he put it down in his lap and caressed the engraving. "Where did this come from?"

"Your Serasa-Kolme grandfather, Lady Anja's brother, used it during the long war with Groyga. I had new lenses ground for it. They're clearer and sharper. "

"Used by my much *older* brother." Anja grinned at his father.

There had been so much tension between his father and Anja lately; he was glad to see them relaxing together. Only one thing would make this present better.

"I wish Mother could be here." He regretted saying this when the smiles faded.

"We all do," Anja said.

His father nodded and leaned forward. "Look, Peri, I want to speak with you before you move up to Betarr Serin. Do you know what being a possible successor to the Crown of Tyrra will mean for your future?"

"I think so." He swallowed. "I'll have to learn more than my cousins and I can't talk to them about it. About being a successor, I mean."

"That's true—although if Lady Aracia publicly announces your position, you can talk about it. When you get older, you may not get a choice about your jobs. It may even come to changing lineages."

Peri winced. He overheard an argument between his father and mother, before their marriage contract was broken. Jan worried that Draius would try to move Peri to the Meran-Viisi. *I'll provide for him myself before I let the Meran-Viisi have him,* his father had said, although everyone knew that raising children without matriarchal support was very expensive. "I know you don't want me to be Meran-Viisi."

His father moved to one knee beside his chair and put a hand on his shoulder. "If you heard that, I'm sorry. At the time, I was angry and prideful. The records will always show that you're *my* son. You don't have to carry my lineal name."

"But Mother's lineage?"

"It's the king's lineage. If you must change lineages, it would be the one to take. Am I right?" His hand tightened on Peri's shoulder. "I'm proud of what you're doing for Tyrra. Your mother will be, too, once she's home."

"I hope so." Mostly he just hoped his mother would come home. Once she was here, the Phrenii might come back as well and *everything* would be right again.

"This will require sacrifices. Draius knows this and she'll support you every way she can," Anja said.

"This talk is getting too serious for your birthday. We should celebrate." His father stood. "Nin baked your favorite tea cakes and she's packed a box of them to take with you."

Today was turning out better than he expected. Tea arrived with all Anja's staff: the cook Nin, the Sareenian maid Maricie, and the old grounds and carriage keeper, Cerin. Peri stuck his head out the parlor to invite in the two King's Guard members, but they shook their heads stoically and said they were "on duty."

"The cake has lots of nuts. Are you sure?" Peri asked. The leader of the guard detail shook his head again, but the side of his mouth quirked.

Inside the parlor, the staff wanted to wish Peri well on his birthday and his move up to Betarr Serin. Maricie was last and she burst into tears.

"Whatever is the matter?" Anja asked. "You'll be seeing Peri frequently if I decide to close this house and move to the upper city."

"No, I won't." The maid cried harder.

Peri, who was closer to the staff given his age, motioned Anja away while he drew the maid across the room. He was surprised when everyone moved back at his gesture. "This isn't about me leaving, is it?"

Maricie gulped and shook her head.

"Tell me. Please." He used the expression he reserved for special situations, like when he was caught stealing sweets in the kitchen.

"I must go back to Sareen, Master Peri. For my own safety, they say." She tried to wipe her eyes with her apron and he automatically offered her his kerchief.

"Who says?"

"I received a letter from my distant cousin in Illus. Rumors are flying about and our relatives are writing to us, begging us to leave Tyrra." Maricie pulled a letter out of her apron.

"May I read it?" She handed it to him. Everyone was being nicely obliging today and he wondered why.

Sareenians, with the exception of some reclusive desert tribes, spoke and wrote Tyrran. Peri could understand most of the careful script, but it was filled with unfamiliar names and words. "Pater So-and-so said... and So-and-so wrote... Lord and Lady So-and-so are readying ships... so you can evacuate..." These were probably important people in Illus, the place where Lornis might have gone. Captain Kilpi would be interested in this, but since Peri didn't have his mother's perfect memory, he'd never be able to repeat this.

"She wants our entire family to leave. We're not safe in Tyrra, *if we ever were*." Maricie had a point. Her uncle had been murdered, in an especially nasty way, by the same necromantic conspiracy that kidnapped him. She pointed at Jan, or rather, his City Guard uniform. "They're already arresting Sareenian merchants."

"They're trying to find murderers—like what Mother used to do. She found the people who killed your uncle, right?"

Maricie nodded, appeased by the mention of his mother. In her mind, Draius's honor outshone even the Crown of Tyrra. She had squeaked with delight when he told her the Kitarran embassy had word from Bordas that he was safe and waiting for Draius to join him.

"Can I show this letter to the master of arms?"

"I can't cause trouble for my cousin in Sareen." Maricie was hesitant, worried more for her family than herself.

"I will only show it to the master of arms, I promise. Maybe he can find the truth behind these rumors." He tried the innocent pleading look again. "I'll bring it back in a day or two. *Please*, Maricie."

"Will you protect my cousin's name?" She kneaded her hands in her apron.

"Yes, I promise. And whatever I learn, I'll tell you."

"All right, then." Maricie hugged him and whispered in his ear, "May the Light protect you, Master Peri." When she backed away, she still had tears in her eyes.

Everyone bid him goodbye. Lady Anja said she'd be seeing him tomorrow when the new tutor was introduced to him and his cousins. As he went out to the coach with the Meran-Viisi crest, he told the guard detail leader that he had to see the master of arms before going to the Meran-Viisi residence.

"Yes, ser," was the answer.

As he settled into the coach and waved goodbye to Cerin and Maricie, he realized how young and insignificant he felt. When would he be capable of handling anything that came his way? *Perhaps never*, was his thought. His coach stopped at the Palace of Stars and he wanted to run up the stairs, but walking was more grown up. The guards matched his pace up the stairs perfectly. Luckily, Master of Arms Kilpi was willing to see him at a moment's notice.

"What can I do for you, Peri?"

"I've got strange news out of Sareen." He flourished Maricie's letter.

"So does *The Recorder*, although the news is bad, not strange." Kilpi waved the boring journal that nobody but matriarchs read—and the master of arms, apparently. All it contained were records of births, deaths, contracts, and other dreary stuff. He handed it to Peri. "At the top of the page, to the right."

The Harbor Master reports a Sareenian ship has verified the total loss of the Horn of Victory and all souls on board. It was owned by Frisson Rhobar, partially financed by the Meran-Viisi and underwritten by the Vakuutis-Nelja. Bodies cannot be recovered for pyres and what follows are the known lineal losses:

Purje-Kolme: Ardri 72, Vaelta 54, Kiv 22, Nim 19

Purje-Nelja: Erika 36, Lakso 54, Hamm 47

Kulte-Kolme: Lornis 29

Sareenians (ages unknown): Frisson Rhobar, Naton Deldanta, ...

— The Recorder, *Kingday 3, Erin Ten, T.Y. 1471*

Peri's hand shook as he returned the paper. He wiped some tears away with the back of his hand.

"That report was two days ago. I'm sorry, but we must assume Lornis is dead. He was a good man; I never understood why the council wanted his arrest, just because of that—that—artifact. What was its name?" Kilpi struggled with holes in his memory that disconnected the *why* from the *what happened.*

"It was called the Kaskea," Peri said hollowly. "I guess it's at the bottom of the Angim Sea now."

Chikirmo, Groyga

As Inica marched behind Lord Endigala into the hall where the Council of Lords met, murmurings rose. Every Lord was allowed one Honored Sword as a bodyguard, but without weapons. Inica wore full battle armor and a flowing scarf of blood red silk tied to his upper right arm. With his left arm, he carried a bundle in a sack. The scarf caused murmurs: House Endigala was declaring war.

Inica followed Lord Endigala to the head of the long table, watching the face of each Lord as they walked by. A few minor Lords blanched and looked away; they feared House Endigala looked for smaller houses to swallow, but those were petty, small goals—too small for Endigala. He was surprised to see Lord Chintegrata in his regular seat near the head of the table. Supposedly, Taalo took care of him with a specialized charm. But here he sat, though age lined his face and he shaved his head to avoid gray hair. To be fair, Inica shaved his own head, as did many guards. Regardless, Chintegrata had been targeted because he was the most powerful and significant impediment to House Endigala's plans. He still refused to accept any *ebi corgo* as workers and raged about them being soulless, all the while using Falcona for support.

As they approached, Chintegrata's amber eyes held stoic resignation. Inica made a mental note to review house security: too much knowledge glinted in the lord's eyes. Chintegrata had a wide network of agents and plenty of intelligencers at his beck and call.

Lord Endigala sat down in the seat nearest the head of the table, saying nothing. The hall became silent. House Endigala called for this meeting, so everyone waited. The lords—which included a few ladies—were ranged down one side of the long table with their Honored Swords standing behind them and facing the gallery of the sacrosanct. Currently, eighteen houses sat at the table. Three of these houses were in the throes of reorganization, thrown into chaos by the mysterious and untimely deaths of their lords. These experienced and prominent lords, with rich houses, happened to stand in House Endigala's way. Endigala wielded Taalo like a fine scalpel, resulting in three fresh faces at the table, inexperienced and pliable. House Chintegrata was supposed to go that way as well, but the lord was present and, unfortunately, fairly healthy.

"The time has come for Groyga to carry our gods forward and subjugate the godless." Endigala's familiar words caused shadows of skepticism on more than a few faces. This was the rallying cry for the disastrous Fifteen Year War with Tyrra, which ended in stalemate. Years of internal struggle followed as the Temples contended with the Lords' Council for control of Groyga. The final solution was the gallery of the sacrosanct, which held those who carried the title of head priest for their temple and represented their god. Inica looked over the gallery. All gods were represented today. The lords now faced this gallery, a change from the past decade that showed the rising, but subtle, power of the temples. No longer did any lord or lady present their back to the representatives of the gods.

"Some of you still doubt me, but today all your concerns will be settled." As Lord Endigala's voice rose, Inica looked at the patched and re-patched mosaic on the wall behind the gallery, where bits of onyx, slate, marble, and barog-eye struggled to show the "Triumph of Condotga."

In 783, Tyrra's King Voima extended Tyrran influence while Groyga fragmented into clans, split by intractable leaders. It took Condotga to cement the original Council of Lords and establish the Great Houses. Through his hard work, these lords now held their seats on the council. Lord Condotga had forced cooperation, making his point by throwing the head of his most obstinate challenger on the council table. These days, the council provided a united front to the outside. Internal battles were hidden, waged through subtle politics behind closed doors or in the shadows with poisons, bribery, and agents. It was fitting that Condotga's "gesture," which many found barbaric today, was frozen in time on the council's wall. Inica's lip curled as he waited for his cue.

"Many have urged caution due to the fear of supporting more than one battle front." Endigala referred to Lord Chintegrata's most viable argument, supported by the Temple of Falcona. "Sareenians are easily bought, but not Kitarrans. Kitarra, even though it is estranged from Tyrra, might not forget the country that birthed her. We worry they might run to the aid of mother Tyrra. We need worry no more about Kitarra. Everyone may have heard that King Markus Ungought was lost in a fire three days ago, but that isn't the entire truth."

Lord Endigala paused and silence reigned: no murmuring, fidgeting, or whispering. "The truth is that *we* now control Kitarra, for the glory of Groyga and her gods." Endigala's words rang through the hall.

After that sentence, Inica dumped the contents of his sack on the table, in between the Lords Endigala and Chintegrata. Contrary to popular opinion, a human head doesn't always roll well. Inica tried to give it enough momentum to roll down the table but instead, the grisly trophy slid an arms length and tottered over on its ear. The royal circlet was still on the brow and the placid features of Markus, recognized by a few lords, faced the other end.

Several lords jumped to their feet while others stared in amazement, their eyes moving between the head and the mosaic. Chaos erupted in the gallery of the sacrosanct as priests consulted their gods. Some stood, their necks craning to get a better view of the table.

Inica observed Lord Chintegrata. No surprise showed on that lord's face as he lifted a fine piece of silk to block his aquiline nose. Inica was now convinced that Chintegrata had either placed his own operatives in Kitarra or had penetrated House Endigala's security. Before he left for Tyrra, he would order Shalah to scour the guard ranks and servants, looking for traitors.

"Now is the time to subdue our ancient enemy! We have rebuilt the ferries so they can hold troops and weapons of war. We will start with Betarr Kain..." Lord Endigala was shouting, but his words couldn't rise over the babble. Then he pounded on the table for order. Lord Chintegrata also pounded for order and in a few moments, the two most influential Lords in Groyga had the floor again. Chintegrata sat and motioned for Endigala to continue.

Whispers in the gallery had to be addressed first. Turning to the sacrosanct, Endigala asked, "Do I have the support of the gods?"

Giada, Master of Fate, had always supported House Endigala. The temples of the minor gods had been bought off and Endigala nodded as each minor god signaled approval through their temple, from Erina, the Mistress of Time, to Fortgis, the Master of Music.

Finally there was Falcona, Mistress of Spirit, and the counter-balance to Giada. The head priestess of Falcona's Temple, the mouth of Falcona, stood. "Falcona welcomes souls from wars against the godless. She wishes to let the Groygan spirit run fierce and free." There was clapping, but she held up her hand for quiet. "But, Falcona objects to the *waste* of spirit. She questions wasting our spirit and people in a winter campaign."

Inica pressed his lips together. Lord Endigala anticipated the objection against starting a campaign so late in the year, but expected the objection to be voiced by Lord Chintegrata. For Falcona herself to present this concern was disquieting. Warfare was expensive during late autumn and winter because of the weather and because manpower was difficult to obtain as soon as harvest season started. In the mapped world areas about the Angim Sea, campaign season started in Erin One during what the Groygans called spring and the Tyrrans called false-spring, and went until the middle of Erin Nine. Today was Honorday *Three* of Erin *Ten*, so the campaign season was officially over, at least for contracted Sareenian galley squadrons. Autumn ended in Erin Eleven.

Endigala hesitated. His lordship intended to operate throughout winter, but he didn't want to divulge detailed plans at this time or to this audience. "Our autumn is mild and winter may be as well, if the recent dearth of wind for sea-going vessels continues. Even so, the Tyrrans would never expect an attack during this season and our strategy hinges upon surprise."

The priestess persisted. "The gods turn a blind eye to warfare in the winter season, because it's their time to test us with the elemental demons."

"*Demons?*" Endigala tensed, as did Inica. No one in this hall should remember the Tyrran demons. In theory, the Phrenii were even erased from the sacred texts.

"I refer to the winter demons mentioned in the *Texts to Falcona*, chapter five, section twelve, verses seven through twenty-five."

"Ah, yes. Forgive me, priestess, for my failing memory." Endigala smiled. Inica also relaxed: this was proof that Taalo's charm had worked and Lord Endigala possessed all his memories, contrary to his apology. "I understand your concerns and the first stage of this invasion will not risk many Groygan lives. "I intend to take the Kainen peninsula using forces of *ebi corgo*, which many of you have heard about. I will pit the soulless against the godless."

Voices surged after Endigala's words. Although this might negate Falcona's argument, the use of *ebi corgo* raised doubts about the campaign's success. How could such creatures be controlled? Of course, directing the council's and the gallery's attention toward stage one was intentional, because once they approved this step, the next step's approval would be easier, and so on—his lordship had explained this manipulation of the psyche to Inica in detail.

"We have someone who can command them." Lord Endigala motioned to Inica, who walked toward the side door. Once the council was in session the main doors were barred, but they accepted the need for a waiting area that allowed witnesses before the council. He let in Famri.

When she stepped into the light from the high windows, another murmur rose. Many in the hall whispered Falcona's name. The armor she wore was a traditional design used by handmaidens more than a hundred years ago. The worked metal parts had no pits or scratches from battle.

"She is *not* Falcona; she's only an echo of the true goddess's beauty and might." The mouth of Falcona watched her with narrowed eyes. Famri walked to Lord Endigala and bowed her head to him, which caused another murmur.

"This is Famri. She will lead the *ebi corgo* in taking Betarr Kain for the glory of Groyga." Endigala proceeded carefully because many of the head priests had talented truth-readers with them. "She's taken a vow of silence but, luckily, she can control the *ebi corgo* with her thoughts." All incomplete truths: Famri could only control the beasts by herding them with fire, which she did do through thought, and she took a vow of silence for this council meeting *because she couldn't lie.* She could manage incomplete truths, but not with skill necessary for this audience. Of course, the Phrenii were known to be incapable of lying,

Endigala pushed on before the mouth of Falcona could question Famri. "She has agreed to retake this vow today, in front of the council, the temples, and the Groygan flags." He gestured upward to the flags of the houses on the wall, below the Groygan flag of the barog cat on a yellow field. Famri put a hand over her heart and, there being no sword hilt available since no one was allowed to carry a sword, she laid her other hand on the table.

"Do you vow, before the gods and people of Groyga, to take Betarr Kain for the glory of Groyga, by any means possible?" Endigala gave the terms of the vow. She nodded and took her knee. It was all theatre, of course, but it worked. When she rose to her feet, there were some quick applause and exclamations. Lord Chintegrata thumped on the table for quiet.

"I also vow, before the gods and people of Groyga, that I will control the Kainen peninsula within the next erin. I offer my entire house to Falcona as weight behind that vow." Lord Endigala's words quieted the entire hall and Inica's blood ran cold. This oath put the entire House of Endigala at risk. There was a keen light in Chintegrata's amber eyes.

"The goddess is satisfied." With those words, the mouth of Falcona finally sat down. She would leave the implementation up to the council while her temple ensured Falcona's support. Her voice, though, didn't sound sincere to Inica. Everybody else accepted her pronouncement: up and down the gallery, there was the thunderous sound of stamping feet.

When the hall quieted, Endigala spoke again. "Once the Kainen peninsula is ours, however, House Endigala expects support for the second stage. We'll strike directly at the heart of Tyrra, their sister cities. For this, the council must prepare a fleet that can prevail over the Tyrran Navy and every house must commit galleys to bolster it. Our navy, as provisioned by this council, is still short of Tyrra's numbers."

There was muttering from all the houses; a winter sea campaign was even riskier. Endigala had to apply more persuasion of half-truths. "The King's Guard will be drawn away from the sister cities because Tyrra would have to retake Betarr Kain, which will be held by my people. Considering their *personnel problems* of the past eight-day, this will require a major effort from inexperienced leaders. While they're involved on that eastern front, we will take the sister cities." He obliquely referred to the results of their secret operation called Desert Wind, which was only partially successful. Nonetheless, Tyrra's Crown and King's Guard leadership were weakened. Unfortunately, the goddess Falcona had traditionally frowned upon trickery in warfare, considering it less than honorable—but to have any chance of conquering Tyrra, they had already aligned with treacherous types and performed deceitful deeds.

More than half of the council cocked their heads with sudden understanding on their faces. Those houses received enough intelligence from the sister cities to realize Endigala was taking some credit in sidelining the Tyrran king and eliminating their master of arms.

Lord Chintegrata was experienced enough to *not* let his face betray his knowledge, although Inica suspected he already knew about Desert Wind. "How many extra galleys will be needed?" Chintegrata asked.

Endigala suggested that if the Council of Lords provided fifty new war galleys from tax revenues and each of the houses commissioned four, they could add 122 new ships to their aging fleet. This caused pained expressions, especially on faces of the less well-to-do lords.

"*When* would they be needed?" Chintegrata asked.

"Before the end of Erin Eleven, preferably by the middle," Endigala said.

Some of the lords gasped. Chintegrata shook his head. "You think our shipbuilders can create that many galleys within a couple of eight-days?"

"We can pay the Sareenians to build some."

"Why don't we just skip the shipbuilding and *contract* a couple of Sareenian squadrons?" Chintegrata threw up his hands. "The down side is the amount of money it'll take to get someone to commit during winter. And once the Tyrran Navy took out Rhobar—"

"Fortunately, we weren't the ones hiring him," Endigala said. "As long as we aren't offending the Church of the Way, there are plenty of Sareenian venture captains available. They're more afraid of the Church than the Tyrran Navy."

"But are they any *good*? What will they cost during winter?"

"I don't know the answer to either question. Rhobar was one of a kind, but there should be comparable contractors." Lord Endigala frowned. "My problem is contractors won't be so willing to do the invasion ground work and secure the city. We should depend upon our *own* guards at that point."

After Lord Glotta agreed to handle the contracting of venture captains, the council hammered out an agreement. They would create a fleet of 120 warships. Half of the required ships would be Sareenian contractors, presuming that Glotta was successful. The other half was divided up with each house providing two galleys with oarsmen and full complement of guards, and the council providing the remaining, either with existing ships or ones newly built from tax revenues.

A final provision was suggested by Falcona and endorsed by Lords Chintegrata and Glotta. These ships, including the contracted ones, could only be used if *House Endigala held the Kainen peninsula through Erin Eleven.* Inica felt a little chill at seeing the mouth of Falcona add additional stakes to House Endigala's gambit.

"Then, and only then, will those galleys sail." Lord Chintegrata nodded, his face impassive.

Two obvious points were left unsaid: the first was that storms on the Angim were usually prevalent in the winter erins, and the second was the current treaties with Tyrra. What Tyrrans didn't understand was that agreements made with the godless didn't have to be honored.

Endigala mentioned the third obvious point. "The Council of Lords must shut down the Tyrran embassy. Whether you expel or kill the ambassador and his staff is your choice, but you must do it *tonight.*"

After the council ended, Inica followed a jubilant and confident Lord Endigala out into the square. The normally brilliant azure sky was muted to pastel blue by the haze that lay throughout and over the city. The weather of the past four days had becalmed all ships and created a worldwide pall. Inica knew the cause: there hadn't been so much as a breeze since Famri released the lodestone's spell and destroyed the Tyrran demons that controlled air, water, earth, and spirit. He glanced at the tall demon, cloaked in the body of a beautiful warrior, standing on the other side of Lord Endigala. Fire, of course, had not deserted them, but he had to suppress the urge to cover his nose and mouth with his sleeve. The shroud overhead trapped the smoke of every cooking fire and nighttime brazier. Even the beggars held rags over their nose and mouth as they breathed in, while clumps of phlegm from coughing fits were spit aside.

"Famri, you'll start across the Saamarin after darkness falls. Inica, ensure that bombardment support is in position by dawn. Now that we've got approval of the gods and the council, we must strike like a cobra." Endigala dropped a coin into a beggar's cup, and then rubbed his hands together.

"Yes, my lord." Inica's gaze settled on the great red columns of the temple of Falcona. He shivered. House Endigala did not have the *full* support of the gods.

Betarr Kain, Tyrra

With Commander Lyn gone, Kyle had been switched to lead the guard shift that ran from midnight through dawn. As he walked down to the gate he swung his lamp about, looking at how unfamiliar the buildings looked in the nighttime mist that had descended on the city. Normally he would have used the starlight to find his way; usually the nights were dry and clear in Betarr Kain. He sniffed as he approached the two shifts of guards. The air didn't smell of water so much as—was that smoke?

"Sama's Inn is burning!" A boy ran down the road toward him and the guards. "We need help with the buckets."

"Two of you go to the inn. Everyone else stay here, including the last shift." Kyle pointed to guards who would have been dismissed at the end of their shift. He couldn't relieve the prior shift yet; something was wrong tonight—he felt it in his gut. He grabbed the boy's arm as he started to run back. "Wait, Auri! How did the fire start?"

Auri's face was frightened and tears smeared the soot on his face. "No one knows. Like a bolt from the stars. Why?"

"Why, indeed?" murmured Kyle, releasing Auri's arm. A guard on his shift, a woman named Jouka, came over to look down at Auri.

"Perhaps a curse from the ancestors?" Jouka was the only one brave enough to say that.

Auri stared at Jouka's face for a moment, unwilling to answer her. Kyle looked up and saw not a single star; either the mist or the smoke had made the starlight impenetrable. They all flinched as the wooden thatched farrier's shed suddenly exploded in flames, ten paces away from them. Without any wind, the fire settled down and persistently ate away at the dry wood while it made the thatch smolder.

"Darkness and Fury," Kyle swore, as Auri raced away for more help. Up the street, a wooden stall in front of the potter's place burst into flame. The potter's structure was stone, but the ceiling was thatch and it would soon catch. His stomach clenched. This couldn't be the work of the ancestors.

"Lower the portcullis and close the gates." He gestured at the iron portcullis and the heavy ironclad gates.

"But we can use seawater," Jouka said. Yes, the sensible action would be to open everything and allow a water bucket brigade down the cliff.

"This is sorcery," he shouted. *"Lower it!"*

Jouka's eyes widened. She jumped as another roof erupted with flame and ran toward the geared wheel that allowed one person to lower the portcullis. It would, however, take more than one person to raise it. They might be trapping everyone inside Betarr Kain to burn alive.

Kyle ran up steps to the top of the walls and pulled out his spyglass. From a higher position, he took stock of the many parts of the town exploding and burning. Luckily, Tyrrans loved to build with stone and the Kainen peninsula had one of the biggest Tyrran quarries, just west of the fortress by a league or two. But stone structures used interior wooden beams and here, close to the Tyrran plains, they had thatched roofs. It seemed like anything that could burn in Betarr Kain was going up in smoke.

Tearing himself away from the disaster, he stepped on the ledge that would raise him above the wall and looked north. Low rocky hills sat between the fortress and the Saamarin. He should be able to observe much of the road to the ferry and the ferry itself, but more smoke obscured his view. Through the haze glowed a huge coal, all which remained of the ferry master's shelter. Grass and low bushes smoldered along the road almost all the way to—he gasped at the seething, dark mass of bodies between barriers of dark flame on each side of the road. The only time he saw them was when a body bumped against them, momentarily causing a flare in the smoky miasma. These forces streamed through the rocky hills right to their gates!

The bell to signal attack was right beside him. He moved as if in a dream, much too slowly, to grab the rope and pull it, back and forth, back and forth. The clanging of the bell mingled with the fire-fighting chaos but underneath all the noise, he felt the thump of siege ladders against the thick wall. How could this happen so fast, without any warning?

He heard a cry from Jouka below. The gate smoked, even though it was clad on both sides with iron. Somehow the interior wood was burning and heating the iron. Jouka stood surrounded by smoke, using something that looked like her steaming jerkin to close it. Another guard, Vainamon, slashed and stabbed at the portcullis, which buckled from the sudden mass of bodies pressed against it. Claws on malformed arms reached toward Vainamon through the grate. They managed to close the gates, but the iron brackets sagged from the heat and they couldn't use the timbers made for those brackets. They were bracing the gates as he called for more archers.

"Bows to the wall!" His words repeated, post after post, along the wall. As an afterthought, he drew his sword.

Cannons thundered from the two northern corner bastions, almost simultaneously. Kyle peeked through the nearest arrow slit, but nothing could be seen. As well, nothing had come over the walls, not a rock or a bolt. He took a chance and stepped up again to look over the wall. He wasn't sure the cannons hit anything. When he stepped down, Sihd was beside him, propping a hakabut for use through the arrow slit.

"Groygans? How'd they surprise us?" Sihd wore his sleeping shirt under his jerkin, stuffed into hastily tied breeches.

"Not Groygans. Humans need lights, torches. These are creatures of the night. They have no weapons that I can see, other than their claws and teeth."

"Well, they should be easy to dispatch with our long bows and guns." Sihd set up his pre-measured powder papers with bravado.

"Except I just counted twenty siege ladders on this side alone—" Kyle abruptly turned to call down to guards arriving below. "Siege ladders!" he bellowed. "Bring up oil and torches! Every blade and bow to the walls!"

While his orders repeated down the walls in two directions, Kyle had a young guard carry a message to the bastions. "Tell the gun crews to load grapeshot and concentrate on the ground forces coming at the gate." Those jutting structures had been put on the corners of Betarr Kain to hold off bombardment from sea or land, but these creatures were already climbing the fortress. At least the spikes on the bastion flanks and elsewhere might hamper the siege ladders.

They poured oil from the walls, soaking bodies below, and threw lit torches on it. The torches, sadly, helped them see how vastly outnumbered they were before strangely sputtering out. If one counted every man, woman, and child within the fortress of Betarr Kain, the number might come to three thousand. The torches illuminated three times that number of attackers, and more still flowed over the rise of the road to the Saamarin.

"I don't know if the gate will hold," Jouka said, wiping the sweat from her face. Her jerkin was burned black in a strange pattern, but it still held together. She helped him tilt a vat of oil into the gutter designed for just this purpose, and then threw down a torch. They both swore as the torch sputtered out. Down the wall a couple paces, a man leaning over the wall

to hack at attackers instantly ignited. He screamed and rolled until someone could douse him with water.

"Everything and everyone inside the fortress burns like tinder, while
oil won't even flame on the outside!" Kyle crouched against the wall, frustrated. He yelled, "Water to the wall," but didn't see any free guards or
even adults. Instead, Auri and other children of similar ages formed a
bucket brigade themselves for the defenders on the wall. He wished he
could tell them to stand down, but he was beginning to think they were
all trapped in a sudden fight to the death.

"At least the oil made the ladders slippery." Jouka stepped down and
leaned against the wall, panting. "They're almost here."

On his other side, Sihd fired the hakabut and then drew his sword.
A few paces down the wall came screams and shouts, sounds of weapons thudding against bodies. There were snaps, clicks, and shrill keening.
Jouka looked at him and flinched when a cannon boomed again. Unfortunately, their guns could only fire three to four times an hour and this
attack was barely half an hour old, by his estimation.

"Get ready." He gripped his dagger in his left hand and his saber in his
right. These creatures weren't armed, so if he kept away from their claws
and teeth, he'd survive. *Keep far enough away to slash, use the dagger to protect from secondary...*

Of course, his training assumed human antagonists who wanted to
stay alive. He slashed at the first small hunched figure that reached the top
of the wall. It fell, and he cut down another and another. He tried to use
his height to his advantage and jigged about, keeping in mind the bolts of
fire that came out of the air. Eventually a creature dodged his blow and
caught his arm. He yelped from the shooting pain. His powerless hand
had dropped his sword but worse, he was being dragged over the wall.

Halfway over the wall, someone grabbed his leg and Jouka shouted.
He kept trying to stab the creature, while grappling with his wounded
arm. The creature scrabbled to hold the slippery ladder. It made a keening sound as his dagger went into its side, losing its grip on the ladder. He

and the creature were locked together as they hung, struggling, from the wall. Someone held him below his knee, but the grip slid and loosened. He fell—bounced against something—twisted—blacked out.

CHAPTER TWENTY-ONE

The Devastation of Betarr Kain

Betarr Kain, Tyrra

Kyle wouldn't be in this much pain if he were on the path to the stars, so he must still be alive. He clenched his teeth over his groan as he tried to move. Heavy bodies lay across him, under him, but everything was still. He heard no other groans or voices, felt no vibrations.

He couldn't open his eyes. He freed one arm and touched his face, which was covered with something crusty and sticky. After scratching away the crust, he opened his eyes.

At first, he thought dawn approached. As he squinted, he realized he looked up at the Betarr Kain walls and battlements, sitting in a cloud of dark smoke. The smoke was thick; it filtered the sun down to a hazy spot in the sky. No breeze stirred the air.

A yellow and red flag hung limp on the wall above. Lying on top and all about him were creatures he never saw clearly until the light of day— well, smoky twilight. With long fangs and claws, their grotesque positions in death made them more inhuman. He lay in a pile of bodies at the foot of the Betarr Kain walls and Groyga controlled the fortress.

How long had he lain here? Weighed down by bodies, but given space to breathe by the grace of his ancestors, he tried to assess his condition by moving slightly. He whimpered during the process, choking back screams. His right forearm was probably broken. His left knee and ankle were painful, but nothing seemed broken in his legs. After several hours—the spot of the sun had traveled across the hazy sky—he pulled himself free. He paid attention to any other movement about him, any sign that someone, or something, was alive nearby.

He rolled so his body faced away from the walls and looked out on a sight that drove all hope from him. The rocky hills to the North used to be sparsely covered with stout pines, sturdy brush, and grasses that gave the hills green, orange, and red spots during the fall season. They would appear to be covered with fuzzy hair in a riot of colors. Now the smoky haze showed a stark landscape in grey and black. Skeletal sticks stood on those hills, twisted into the tortuous shapes of death. In places, large pieces of wood still glowed and smoke rose lazily, hardly distinct from the haze. Behind those hills, the northern forests still stood green, running all the way up to Kitarra. They called to him, offered him cover, if he could only get there.

Close to the fortress, the brush and grasses along the roads were burned to a black crisp. The ground was the color of glassy tar. Nothing was left to burn. Darker smoke had settled in the low places of the road and a figure stepped out of that smoke. He blinked his eyes in an effort to clear them. The figure stood out because of its red, hooded cloak. It waved its arm and, in that flowing movement, he realized it was a woman. Flames billowed from the edge of the forest, almost a league away, and settled down as more smoke added to the haze. The sky above the northern forests glowed, so abruptly that it was obviously unnatural. Several creatures—similar to the dead ones about him—scampered out from the smoke and cavorted about the woman, looking like puppies dancing about a master with food. His heart pounded as the figure strolled leisurely along the road. Now he knew Betarr Kain had fallen to Darkness, if such a sorceress now existed in the mapped world. Who, or what, could withstand her?

Silence slowed the passing of time while he watched the sorceress, her cloak drifting about in the windless air, walk toward the gates of Betarr Kain. It was absolute quiet: no footsteps from the road, no groans of wounded, no chitters from the creatures about the sorceress, no challenges from sentries, no sounds of gates opening or closing, and of course, no roar of cannons as this usurper entered Tyrra's eastern-most fortress. Was anyone left alive inside? He was lying near the northwest corner of Betarr Kain, in the shadow of the jutting bastion—which didn't make sense because he surely fell from the wall closer to the gate.

He slid along on his back, working his way over a mound of bodies. They defended the fortress against so many of these creatures. When he touched ground, he knew from the pain shooting from his left ankle that he couldn't walk. He should crawl anyway, even on the painful knee, until he was out of sight of the fortress. Holding his right arm tight with his left, he tried to roll his torso around. He ended up sliding off the mound and his head finally rested on the ground, face to face with familiar, but clouded eyes.

"Jouka," he whispered, his eyes blurring with tears.

Her helm was off and the leather gorget that should have protected her neck was gone. Claws had gone for her throat and taken most of her jaw as well. Her blond braids were soaked in blood and her right hand still clutched her sword. He couldn't tell if she had lived after the fall from the wall. If only they'd been wearing mail! Their security had become lax under the treaties and there'd been no indication Groyga would make a treacherous attack, much less with these creatures. In fact, if it were not for the Groygan flag hanging above, he'd have a hard time believing they were behind this—this *evil*. At one time, he barely regarded Groygans as human with their strangely colored hair and eyes, but he would give anything to see a Groygan body among the dead, rather than these things bred from Darkness and Fury.

Looking about, he realized that many of the bodies lying at the base of the walls appeared to have suffered through an inferno. How had he managed to survive the fall from the wall and the heat? Other bodies must have protected him. He counted about five dead creatures for every Tyrran body he saw—but each was somebody he had worked and lived with in this outpost far from the center of Tyrran civilization.

He lost all control when he recognized Auri's body on the far side of Jouka. The boy was completely burned and curled, frozen in agony. Deep, heaving sobs wrenched his body, causing pain. With effort, he stifled them. There could be sentries on the walls and inside Betarr Kain. A three-clawed appendage of one of those creatures peeked out from under Auri's body. The claws twitched. He pulled Jouka's spare dagger out of her boot with his good arm. He surged to his knees while he reached for the creature. The pain from rising to his knees almost made him faint. The creature wore no armor, only what might be called a long shirt made of leather. The edges of his vision went gray, but when it cleared he cut the creature's unprotected throat.

He had to get away from Betarr Kain. West of the Kainen peninsula lay thinly spread farmsteads. Would someone have seen the smoke, or did it merge into the heavy pall over all the country? He thought about farmers coming to investigate or to deliver their produce. They would be slaughtered.

He wondered if the sorceress was burning the forests as a way to hide what happened here at the lower part of the peninsula. Most of eastern Tyrra might think that wildfires started in the hills beside the Saamarin, which happened every once in a while due to lightning. No one in eastern Tyrra would expect this smoke to be anything but a massive wildfire; no one would expect that Betarr Kain could fall in just one night. This was still hard for him to believe.

He cleaned the dagger and put it in his belt. He still had one good arm and leg. He moved slowly, crawling painfully and trying to stay in the light shadows of the fortress. He hoped his slow progress made him harder to see from the walls. By the time he got around the northwest bastion, he was shaking with exertion and pain.

That's when he saw them, grouped together in the shadows. *Ghosts*. They seemed sad and lost. Why weren't they on the path to the stars? Most didn't move, making them harder to see, but Jouka and Auri stepped forward. Jouka's arm rose and her specter pointed in a northwesterly direction toward Plains End.

He nodded. *I'm going there, Jouka, as fast as I'm able. We'll take back Betarr Kain. Then you'll be avenged and you can start your journey to our ancestral stars.* When he stopped shaking he continued crawling, always moving in a northwesterly direction.

Betarr Kain, Occupied Territory of Groyga

Inica was aghast at the *waste*.

"Hostages would benefit us. Is there no one to question?" He tried to contain his rage as he held a rag over his mouth and nose as protection from the heavy smoke and smells of death. Such careful planning, and yet this had all gone wrong because of Famri.

His part of the mission went well. He knew the Angim was becalmed and bereft of currents, meaning they would depend upon oars. He commanded four of Lord Endigala's heavily armed galleys and left Chikirmo's harbor as early as possible to use the shoreline by daylight. To the relief of the navigator, the night skies cleared once they moved a league away from shore. It was then a matter of anchoring close to land, as to avoid traffic coming out of the Saamarin.

When dawn came, he expected to provide Famri with cannon support. They moved away from shore and tried to fix their target, but couldn't. They faced a long bank of fog or smoke that covered the coast of Tyrra. They couldn't see the Betarr Kain battlements, let alone any flags or signalers. The galleys moved north under the silent guns of Betarr Kain—silence that filled them with hope—into the mouth of the Saamarin, before Inica set them ashore at the Tyrran side of the ferry.

A cheer went up when the Endigala ferries came into view, abandoned after many uses. The galleys let Inica and a company of guards off at the ferry pier and then anchored themselves further out. It seemed safe enough, given the silent cannons.

Inica and his company set off, walking into the smoky haze. They marched by the destroyed ferry house—the cheers faltered here, perhaps because the agonizing death of the ferry operator and his family was disturbing, even to the hardened guards. As they went further, silence weighed on everyone as they walked through colorless desolation, a silence broken only by coughs. Inica covered his nose and mouth, and most of his guards followed suit. The silence was no longer hopeful and the blackened landscape sucked all the spirit from them as they trudged along the road. Their boots made shrill crunching noises that violated the silence, no matter how lightly they stepped.

When they came over the last hill, everyone stopped, stunned at the sight of so many bodies. The Groygan flag flew over the carnage and drew no cheers.

"Gods, how many *ebi corgo* can be left after this?" muttered Inica as he crossed the bridge to the gates, climbing over bodies while looking *up* at piles of more bodies in the twenty-foot-deep ditch. He had to admire the tenacity and fortitude of the Tyrrans who killed six *ebi corgo* for every guard in Betarr Kain.

He was astonished that Famri took the fortress without the use of cannon. It still stood, its walls undamaged. But, once they'd made it through the gates, the sorceress obviously allowed the surviving *ebi corgo* to run rampant. He stalked about looking for Famri, noting piles of civilian bodies, body parts, and incinerated *ebi corgo*—heaps of those creatures as he worked his way to the center of the town. All the buildings were burned out shells with nothing of value remaining inside.

In the center square with the clock tower, he finally found Famri staring down at carefully ordered small bodies. When he stomped up, protecting his nose and mouth, he noted these Tyrran children had died from claw and teeth wounds. She seemed pensive, but what really irritated him was that she was doing nothing to make the fortress defensible again. When he was within speaking distance, he complained about the lack of hostages.

"No one escaped." The sorceress stood motionless. "There is no one suitable to question."

"You let them kill everybody, destroy everything?"

She turned and he glimpsed devastation in her eyes. "They killed the children."

"You mean you lost control of them. What else did you expect?"

"I had to punish them." Her gaze flicked over to an alley off the square.

He drew his breath; stacked there was a huge pile of *ebi corgo*. It looked like they were herded into the dead end, piling over each other, and then incinerated with the buildings. "How many of your creatures are left?"

"They are not *my* creatures!" Her red eyes flared. "Your house created and bred them."

He made a placating gesture with his hand and touched his forehead. "My apologies, but I must know how many are left for defense."

She sniffed. "About three hundred."

"That's all, out of *seventy-five hundred?*"

"They wouldn't be good at defending this place." She shrugged. "Think of it as a winnowing process; those that are left are the smarter ones."

"I remind you that we must now hold this fortress *ourselves*! Think how easier it would be if we also possessed their resources and provisions." His hands clenched into fists and he struggled to relax them. No hostages for bargaining meant that once the Tyrrans realized this, they would raze Betarr Kain to the ground. To make matters worse, he had no trinkets to reward his guards, no food, and nothing to drink except water from a well now clogged with ash. He added, "You destroyed our means to survive. How are we going to feed our people, or the *ebi corgo*? Where are we going to billet everyone? Most of the buildings are so gutted by fire that they're useless—everything but stone is melted into worthless slag."

"The *ebi corgo* have already made their nest in a burned-out stable. I saved these two buildings for us. One of them was an officer barracks." She waved behind her at a small hall of records or administration beside a larger building with three floors and many windows. These buildings also had the only slate roofs on the square, discounting the clock tower.

While the barracks appeared untouched, the hall of records had many broken windows. Burned window coverings hung behind them. "Did you burn items inside the records building?"

"Of course. I had to destroy…" Famri paused. "Dangerous records had to be eliminated."

Meaning any records of Famri in her old demon form? "Those could have helped me establish the number of—"

"I know the number of guards garrisoned here during peacetime." She smirked. "I know how many horses and weapons they had, but not their food stores."

"Well, start with the number of guards and able crossbows, long bows, and swords." He wouldn't worry about cavalry, considering he would soon be under siege.

"During peacetime, such as yesterday, they generally had twelve hundred guard members here: one thousand assigned to the Betarr Kain Guard with two hundred rotating King's Guard. Of those, four hundred could be issued crossbows and another four hundred long bows." Famri tried not to look proud. "Of course, they had training on any weapons issued. The rest of the approximately three thousand souls were family members and support personnel."

Inica knew that, in her other form, Famri had been responsible for ensuring this eastern border was protected. "And during wartime?"

"This fortress easily held up to three times that number."

"And do you have any idea how we're going to hold it with three hundred *ebi corgo* and a single company of guards? The whole point of taking Betarr Kain was to present the King's Guard with a resource-consuming siege to take it back." He ground his teeth.

"I thought the *whole point* was to convince your Council of Lords that House Endigala could be effective without using Groygans. That has been done." Dimples in her cheek formed as her smile widened. "Surely you can request more guards."

"I *can*, but that doesn't mean I'll get them." He clamped his jaw shut. House Endigala did not have an unending supply of people, but he didn't want to bring that up with Famri. His lordship could recall troops from Kitarra, provided everything was under control up there. Inica now had to write a letter with all the hard truths. About to excuse himself to do just that, he noticed Famri wasn't paying attention to their conversation anymore.

She stared across the square where the shadows grew long. Her eyebrows knitted into a worried frown. He glanced over his shoulder and thought he caught movement in the hazy shadows, but it was nothing.

"I must rest in the hall of records. You and your people stay in the barracks." Famri appeared distracted.

"Before you do that, call off the *ebi corgo* so my people can search this town." Inica glanced at the body of a young Tyrran girl and a suspicion was growing, a suspicion that even he wanted to flinch away from. He realized Famri had avoided saying whether *everybody* had died.

"As you wish. I can frighten them into their nest for the night." She waved a hand and something flashed in the air and created a sudden boom. *Ebi corgo* scampered to the burned-out hulk of the stables, down the hill to the southeast.

After Famri turned and walked into the hall of records, Inica called two of his sergeants over. "First order of business is to get the guns serviced and ready. We'll be blocking Tyrran ships from the river mouth."

One saluted and headed toward the walls. The other waited.

"The Tyrrans will learn about this soon and we must clean up the bodies before they march on us," Inica said. "Unfortunately, the *ebi corgo* only understand simple commands. Tomorrow set them to work digging large pits; their advantage is that they don't need tools to do that. Use any cart you can find—I'm requesting more—to move the bodies out of the fortress and into the pits. Then burn whatever you can."

"Where are we getting the wood, Honor?"

Good question. Everything on the peninsula had been burned to a crisp already. However, smoke still rose over the northern forests, which were green wood that Famri somehow managed to burn. "Get Famri's help. I think she can make anything burn."

The man flinched, but nodded.

"*Tonight*, though, I want you to set a detail on digging and cleaning out that well. We're going to need it when the Tyrrans lay siege to this place. The rest of the company must search this place from top to bottom."

"What are we looking for, Honor?"

"Firstly, any unburned resources we can use: tools, food, blankets, anything. Secondly..." He sighed. "Look for children."

"Ex—excuse me, Honor?" The aide looked about at the destroyed town. "How could they have survived this?"

"I'm not a sorcerer, but I'm pretty sure that even destructive magic can be selective. They might be hiding or covered with bodies. Also, I'll need a messenger in about two hours."

The man recovered, snapping back to attention. "Yes, Honor."

Inica waved him away absently, realizing that he needed to confront Famri on some unpleasant details. He squared his shoulders and turned toward the hall of records. When he stepped inside, he saw a light in the room in the back, which looked like a library with scrolls, books, and maps. He glanced about at the burned contents, regretfully considering how many useful maps might have once been there. Famri was sitting on a cleared spot on the carpet, which had only been singed in places.

"Come in, Honor." In her hand was an open bottle of amber liquid.

"Where did you get that?" Inica stepped closer. He could smell the liqueur now and, unbidden, his mouth watered. Usually, he liked his drink strong, not sweet, but this stuff was tempting.

"Many of the cellars still exist. This was in a burned building across the square. There are more bottles, but it'll take some digging. So sweet, and yet it burns." She took another swig and sighed. "This makes it all worth it."

She was starting to appreciate food and drink; as a demon, she'd never tasted anything. They were going to have to talk about the issues of "becoming human" and he was furiously thinking about how to come out of that conversation alive. He said, "I'll have my men start digging out the cellars."

"Yes, I'd like more of this." She took a long swig at the bottle. He wondered how well the sorceress could hold her spirits.

"Lord Endigala's orders were to hold this fortress for him when the Tyrrans came to reclaim it, and to block the Saamarin as Tyrra once did against Groyga. Did you understand that?" he asked.

"Of course. Have I not taken this facility swiftly, as requested? Will this not satisfy his lordship?" She took another long drink.

"Quickly, yes. To his lordship's satisfaction? The answer is no. There are rules to warfare. The taking of a city is done for both strategic purposes and for the usefulness of the city. You made this fortress less useful by taking away its labor, its shelters, and most of its resources."

"I'm sure we can manage." She shrugged.

He persevered. "One of the most important rules of warfare: when the population gives up or the combatants surrender, one stops the slaughter. I could see many civilians clutching white kerchiefs, hoping to be spared. When there's no need for retribution, the survivors can be put to good use. Now when the Tyrrans send their forces, their thirst for revenge will be fierce and sustaining." Despite his attempt at control, his voice had risen in volume. Famri didn't respond, which didn't bode well for the coming discussion. He started walking the perimeter of the room, looking at the shelves. Perhaps something useful survived the conflagration.

"You know nothing, Inica. You think I have no need for retribution? These people caged me with their expectations. I have exacted revenge for years, for eras, of protecting them and yet having them shun me. They would never have allowed me this soul." She drained the bottle. Her voice was becoming morose and starting to slur.

He paused at a surprisingly functional and latched door that had no sign of charring. She was starting to refer to her life as a demon, which he didn't want to point out to her yet. He asked her a general question, which could be about her past or about the destruction of the *ebi corgo*. "What about the children?"

"I love children, I do, but their fear is so much sweeter than their affection. I only just discovered this..." She rocked back and forth, her back to him.

Inica listened at the door and heard movement inside. Famri started to murmur in some strange language. He opened the door. Inside was a small ransacked storeroom and two children huddled in the corner. One was about six years of age, either male or female. The other was a pre-pubescent female, perhaps ten; it was always hard to estimate the age of Tyrrans, considering they didn't grow as fast and were longer-lived. They looked up at him with dirty faces and light-colored eyes. They had bruises and scrapes on their legs, bare because they were clad in their undershirts. They clutched each other, trying to share body warmth.

"Close that door, Honor." Famri's voice had an edge and she no longer sounded tipsy.

He turned around slowly and nearly stumbled forward a step as two small bodies hit him from behind. The smaller child attached itself behind his right leg, wrapping arms around his thigh with a surprising grip. The larger child pressed against his buttocks, holding on to his belt and digging her knuckles against his chain shirt, which had to be painful for her hands.

"Help us. She's not Famri anymore." He heard the girl's whisper and the hair on the back of his neck rose. The children *remembered and recognized* her.

"You said there were no survivors to question."

"No *suitable* survivors, meaning adults. Why concern yourself with these two?"

"A child is useful as a hostage and can even perform some labor. As commander, I reserve the right to put survivors to use as I see fit." He observed her. Did she sway a little? This was now about asserting his authority; if he couldn't face down a drunk Famri, how would he ever command a sober one?

"Take the girl; she's almost sullied anyway. Put her to work cleaning and feeding your men, if you wish, but the boy is young and sweet, like the liqueur. He's mine." She came close and caressed the boy's face and shoulder, in a sexual way. The boy wrapped his arms even tighter about his thigh. This felt unreal: he was disconcerted these children would consider a Groygan Honored Sword their savior.

"I'll take both children. Remember, Lord Endigala put me in command of holding this fortress. You only hold authority over the *ebi corgo*."

"I couldn't save all the them. Just let me keep this one." Her face crumbled.

He had to chance honesty. "Famri, some of us remember your past life." At the edge of his vision, the young girl nodded. "In your past life, children didn't put expectations on you, did they? They never shunned you, either. Didn't you seek out their company?"

Famri's eyes flared with inner fire, but she didn't move.

"In your past life, you were innocent yourself." He was truthful: he believed she was a demon, but one created to be an innocent servant of the Tyrrans. "But you're different now—your feelings are mixed up. You feel a deep need, but you cannot love children like adults, nor use them for your pleasure. The gods and all humankind consider that a perversion. You must fulfill your needs elsewhere."

The sorceress seemed to withdraw, almost shrink away from them. He started walking out, trying to remain dignified with the small boy clutching his leg. The girl kept holding his belt, but circled to keep his body between her and Famri, who made no move to stop them. Once outside the building, the children collapsed. He picked up the boy and carried him with his shield arm while pulling the girl along, unresisting. When he looked down at their faces, tears streamed down their cheeks.

Bryn Celar, Northern Moors, Kitarra

Draius didn't take the possible Groygan invasion of Tyrra well, not in her weakened condition. When she learned there was only one-way pigeon flight from their embassy in Betarr Serin to Kitarra, she lost all control.

"You *have* to let me go! I have to warn them," she screamed at Cerith.

The duke was unmoved. He had to be just as tired, having woken only a bit before her, but the man had an iron will. "The Lords' Council may not approve Endigala's scheme, whatever it is. Let's wait for news from Chintegrata. If the worse comes to pass, I'll try to spare a sympathizer I have in Suellestrin. Perhaps he can get across the Whythern under cover of darkness in a marsh boat. But you can't make that trip."

"You don't understand! I have a *son* in the sister cities and—and—the father of my unborn child." She tried to lower her voice. Her fists clenched and she stepped toward him, only to be grabbed by guards who Tenil must have called. She flailed at them and her body collapsed. They ignominiously carried her back to her quarters.

After that, she spent several days in agonizing tedium and worry, being escorted to the dining hall and then back to being locked in her rooms. She couldn't help obsessing about how Endigala would invade and whether her family and comrades were in danger. He would start by making a grab for the Kainen peninsula. Would he use the *ebi corgo*? Had the Kitarran ambassador passed along Bordas's letter? She thought of Lyn and Kyle, stationed at Betarr Kain. Jan had been posted there; it was where Peri was born. Every time she thought of her son, she wanted to curl up and cry with worry and loneliness, the ache of not being able to hold him.

When she started this mission, she tried to only think of Peri before she went to sleep. In that half-drowsy state, Dahni sent visual flashes and she knew he was safe. When the Phrenii disappeared, she lost those assurances about her son. She and Cerith still held Phrenic abilities from Dahni and Sahvi. Healing and influence. She could still take out the Kaskea and watch it pulse with green light, but what help was that? It couldn't tell her if Peri and Lornis were safe, and she still couldn't walk the Void.

From the whispers in the tunnels and dining hall, she realized few Kitarrans trusted her. No difference in opinion existed between the marsh people or the Tyrran-descended ones: they all thought she put Cerith into unnecessary danger. Moreover, she didn't have any excuses. She made a bad decision and, worse, shamefully violated her promise to not use the Kaskea. Through her waking hours, either Roumithea or Enita accompanied her. The marsh people respected Enita, but that respect didn't rub off on her. While Tenil sometimes joined them when eating, most Kitarrans avoided her.

She didn't encounter Cerith after she lost control in the cavern. Occasionally she caught a glimpse of his back, striding along while getting briefed by someone. He kept busy, while she went insane from inactivity.

"There must be something useful I can do around here," she complained after hearing a third morning of preparation. Before dawn, there came the sound of feet pounding through the tunnels, squeaking leather armor, and clinking metal.

"Perhaps you can help with this mending." Roumithea sat working on a pile of clothing while she paced the room.

"I've never been taught to mend or tailor."

"Too simple for you?" The edge in Roumithea's voice made her flush.

"I admire all honest work, but I swear by the Healing Horn, you don't want me touching that mending or you'll end up with worse. I can't even thread a needle."

"What did they teach you as a child, then, if not the basics of living or keeping house?" Roumithea knotted her thread with a twisting motion that bewildered Draius.

"Our education isn't divided. Until the age of fifteen, girls and boys are taught the same lessons, which are specific to the lineage. Meran-Viisi training meant learning past battle strategies and tactics, Tyrran history, memorizing treaties, and understanding our government and the King's Law. It all bored me terribly, especially history and law. One day, when the weather seemed better for swimming in the canals, I announced to our tutor that there could be no value in going over the dry events of the past."

"Ah, the arrogance of the young." Roumithea's words distorted as she bit off a thread.

She chuckled and Roumithea smiled back, hopefully warming up. "Our tutor put a quick stop to my rebellion." She changed her voice to mimic him. "Draius, while you can memorize everything I set in front of you, let me ascertain whether you have learned the lessons our ancestors taught us." She paused and sighed. "He ruthlessly proved that rote memorization was not the same as true analysis. After that humiliating afternoon, I applied myself better in history and law. I already loved the mathematics and geometries of the star watchers, which we studied because one of us might take the title of Starlight Wielder for the Meran-Viisi. All those lessons helped me fulfill my true calling: to hunt down and apprehend criminals."

"Not much call for hunting criminals here." Roumithea's voice softened. "Not for your mathematics either, but I can check if Suel has any problems he can give you to analyze."

Or that he will trust me to analyze. She mentally translated Roumithea's words. "I can use Phrenic healing to help your wounded."

"Thankfully, the missions have been successful recently. Nothing but minor wounds since..." Roumithea's voice faded away and she picked up another piece for mending.

Since Bordas died. Draius crossed her arms tightly across her chest, hugging herself, and continued pacing. Perhaps she could walk away her guilt. She hoped Bordas wouldn't show up—the specters had a tendency to drift out of walls when one talked or thought about them, hence Roumithea's reticence to mention his name. By now, everyone in Bryn Celar and the neighboring village were aware of the lost souls who sadly watched them from the shadows.

The duke's guards ran out of luck later that morning. Tenil knocked, fresh from a mission with his camouflaging mud still on his face. He and his men were noticed within longbow range of the Suellestrin walls and one man was critically wounded. Draius hurried after him.

The man's wound was painfully similar to Bordas's, but this time she hoped to do something about it. She sat on a stool and put her hand out over his body, trying to sense where the arrow penetrated. It entered his side and went between the ribs to puncture his lung. Under normal circumstances, he would soon die and the physician had given him some precious herbs to numb the pain. They didn't help much and the wounded man breathed shallowly.

"Withdraw the arrow according to my directions," she said to the physician.

"That'll kill him." The physician looked up at Tenil.

"If she does nothing, he'll die anyway." Tenil was right.

She nodded. "It'll be painful and he'll have to be held down so I can follow the arrowhead."

An assistant was called to help hold down the wounded man. She closed her eyes to concentrate better and shouted directions over the man's grunts and clenched-jaw screams. The arrow had to be pulled slowly away from the lung, then angled and twisted to get it through the ribs. As the arrowhead came out, she tried to knit together his lung, staunch any bleeding, and push the Darkness out of his body.

She was close to fainting when she felt a hand on her shoulder. Tenil still stood behind her, wonder on his face. The Kaskea shard around her neck lit the room with green light. She looked at the man as the light faded and was disappointed. "I'm sorry. I'm not as good as Dahni—if the Phrenii healed him, he might have walked away."

"But he's breathing well and no longer bleeding!" The physician sounded delirious. "He'll heal, my lady. Just give him a couple of days to rest and he'll soon be walking."

She tried to stand and nearly tilted off the stool. Tenil offered his arm and she took it, leaning on him as she stood. She glimpsed the swirl of a dark blue cloak on the edge of her vision and turned to catch Cerith's back as he left through the doorway. So the duke had observed as she worked on the wounded man. She had no sense of him or the element of earth as she worked, so he must be getting better at controlling his Phrenic powers.

"I should look at the other wounded," she said.

"No one else requires your attention and you need rest." Tenil sounded so much like his wife, Roumithea, that she smiled. She was hustled back to her quarters and fell sound asleep. She missed the mid-day meal, but Roumithea brought food for her and something else: a pile of printed publications from Tyrra.

"Did Cerith send these?" A surge of excitement mixed with homesickness swept over her as she looked through the pile. The issues of the Horn & Herald and The Recorder were well-read and none more recent than four days ago. They went back to the time when she and Bordas first entered Groyga. "How do they manage to get these?"

"I don't ask. Suel brought them. He's concerned about the political situation in Tyrra and asked for your analysis. Whether those orders came from the duke...?" Roumithea shrugged.

"Oh." She was disappointed, and then berated herself. It didn't matter if the orders came from Cerith; she had something to read and keep her mind busy.

She ate and then started on the daily *H&H* pile. While it was often pure sensationalism, it was also much more interesting to read than *The*

376 | LAURA E. REEVE

Recorder. She tried to read them in order, thinking about the news rather than skimming the pages. Since she was able to recall every page she read like a painting, she could sometimes be lazy and avoid processing the information, instead waiting for a trigger to call the page to mind. After an hour, she understood why Suel mentioned the "political situation" in Tyrra.

After the *H&H* had reported her transfer to Betarr Kain, a rift formed between Perinon and the King's Council. As she read the reported quotes, she realized the council learned she was trapped on the wrong side of the Saamarin. That made sense: her situation was a security issue the King's Guard would brief to king and council, while keeping it from the public. The political posturing regarding "custody of the Kaskea shards" took on new meaning because the council had to be aware that one shard, at least, was out of the country. Andreas, both the writer and editor of the *H&H*, missed those implications.

Councilman Muusa appeared to be spearheading the council's attempt to gain control of the remaining shards. Muusa was temporarily appointed to the King's Council and would keep his seat only if he won in the elections at the beginning of next year. Draius knew enough about politics to realize he probably had powerful backing or he wouldn't attempt this. She searched for clues in Andreas's sly commentary and decided Muusa either had influential friends on the council or clever backing from the matriarchy. Either way, he managed to stir up a hornets' nest regarding an artifact most Tyrrans weren't interested in: the Kaskea.

Then she read about the murders in the early hours of second Honorday, only ten days ago. Sevoi's murder saddened her: she didn't know the master of arms very well, but she had respected him. The other deaths that same night of her Meran-Viisi cousins alarmed her and made her suspect necromancy. Andreas didn't catch that, although he noted both King's Guard and City Guard were searching the trash near the murder sites. She nodded when she read Lornis had been assigned to the investigation. He would do well.

She put down the *H&H* as she wondered about the commonality between the victims. Even though she was Meran-Viisi, none of these cousins had been in her lesson group with the exception of Laakso, her replacement as OIC of Investigation. Laakso had the same education as Perinon and Valos—she paused. There were rumors that the Meran-Viisi matriarch kept a list of successors to the Crown ready, although the public didn't know who was on the list. Even the Meran-Viisi children only knew about the heir presumptive and only after there was an announcement. In her time, they all suspected it was Valos, Perinon's older brother. However, if their father hadn't died early due to the Fevers and Valos grew too old, he'd be replaced by another heir presumptive. At that time, being children, she and her cousins figured the age for replacement on the successor list was nineteen, since that seemed very old to them. Now that she better understood the average Tyrran lifespan, around 120 years, she figured they didn't drop off the successor list until later. How much later, she didn't know, because the matriarchy liked their kings young and malleable, which was why their education started so early. Having not kept up with the "cousin's grapevine," she never heard any gossip about the next heir presumptive. Since Perinon had no children, had it been Laakso?

The next two issues of the *H&H* were full of the murder investigations and she sympathized with Captain Rhaffus, who had been doggedly followed by Andreas. They also showed more rancor coming from Councilman Muusa toward the Meran-Viisi—even though that was his own lineage—complaining they were being secretive about the king's "failing health." What was happening with Perinon? Muusa also thought the king should be considering more candidates to bear the Kaskea. She shivered, remembering Siuru, and wondered if Muusa hoped to be a viable candidate. *What an idiot.* She also noted that several Sareenian merchants had been arrested by the City Guard and their "inventory of toys" confiscated. It was about time, because those necromantic charms in the market made her ill.

The major headline on the next issue was KING TRAVELS TO SUMMER LODGE. Perhaps he really was ill? She turned it over and scanned the back page, catching a small column at the bottom and drawing in her breath. This was the list of recent arrests, as well as warrants for arrest. Underneath the warrants was listed one "Kulte-Kolme Lornis, wanted for treason." *Treason?* That was impossible.

There was a knock at the door and Roumithea opened it to reveal Suel, dressed in muddy field gear.

"The duke wanted you to know about this." His hand fiddled with the hilt of his sword. "The Tyrran forests across the Whythern are burning red, too hot for man or beast to travel through."

"How did it start? Lightning?" she asked.

Suel shook his head. "Our observers say the whole forest suddenly burst into flame but then, with no wind, it smoldered like a brazier of coals."

"The *whole* forest?"

"From the Saamarin to as far west as the eye can see." Suel swung his arms wide.

"Could someone travel along the edge of the Whythern?"

"No, it's too hot. Wildlife that can't fly away is jumping into the river, with the small animals trying to stay in the shallows and not drown. I assume that if they could stand the heat, they'd stay on land. A contact in Suellestrin says they're worried the heat may cause fires *across* the bay of the Whythern. One good thing is the lack of wind. Huge, glowing cinders rise, but merely float down again."

"Thank you for telling me," she said dully, thinking of her homeland's beautiful forests and their wildlife.

After Suel left, Roumithea put a hand on her arm. "Are you all right?" Her tone held concern.

"No." She was numb. "That's not a natural wildfire."

"I'm sure it isn't. Maybe you should go to bed again. You're still recovering and you've got a baby to consider."

She nodded.

Roumithea undressed her like a child and tucked her into her glorified cot. She slept fitfully, having nightmares of deer and rabbits bursting into flame. For a while, she swam in a cool, dark river and called them to safety. When she stopped and treaded water to look up at the night sky, she saw her ancestral stars. *Why can I see them? There should be too much smoke.*

A voice called her. "Draius, can you hear me? Can you see me?"

She looked around and saw a girl, perhaps fifteen years old, sitting in a flat-bottomed marsh boat that floated on the other side of the river. "Yes."

"Draius, you have to help us make things right."

She swam toward the boat and as she reached the center of the river, sensed something circling her. Something hungry, hunting her like prey. She spiraled down into darkness.

CHAPTER TWENTY-TWO

The Politics of War

Bryn Celar, Northern Moors, Kitarra

When she woke the next morning, Draius stared at the ceiling as everything came back to her: the probable invasion of the Kitarran peninsula, Tyrra's northeastern forests destroyed, King Perinon retreating to the royal summer lodge, and the rancorous politics between the Crown and King's Council. She clenched her fists. *All I can do is watch helplessly as everything and everybody I love is threatened? There* must *be some way I can help them.*

She forced herself to get up for breakfast. After choking down some food in the dining hall—only her ancestors knew what it was—she went to check on the wounded. The man she recently healed was mending, but not yet awake. The physician was happy to talk, although no one needed her healing.

Back in her room, she viewed the finished stack of *H&Hs* and picked up a different publication, taking a deep breath. Today Enita shadowed her and sat in the corner of her room peeling bark from a pile of branches. The old woman claimed she created a pain medicine by crushing the bark and boiling it in water. The process appeared to be tedious.

She held the earliest issue of *The Recorder*. Most Tyrrans avoided it, published once an eight-day and containing a dry rendering of births, deaths, marriage contracts, import and export shipments, production figures, and currency rates. Matriarchs read it from cover to cover; she suspected it played an important part in their communications. It also helped them keep their finger on the economic pulse of Tyrra.

By their appearance, someone else had read them carefully. She took a deep breath and tried to think like a matriarch. She started reading. By the second issue, she understood some of the patterns. It all concerned resources: exchanges of funds, goods, labor, and the marriage contracts, of course, represented the exchange of people.

Last erin, Netta's Vakuutis-Nelja marriage contract ended and she was "traded" back to the Tahti-Nelja. Netta's affair with Jan had been the breaking point for Draius because it was public and humiliating, and because she suspected Jan really cared for Netta. She remembered Lady Anja dismissing the possibility Jan and Netta could ever marry, because the matriarchy believed she was sterile. She felt a pang of sympathy. Netta, like all Tyrran woman, would never be able to control who she married.

She reached for the latest *Recorder*. She noted a regular transfer of funds starting from the Meran-Viisi to the Serasa-Kolme. She knew some of this money paid for her son Peri's education because Aracia was considering him for the successor list. Putting down the paper, she thought for a moment. This started just before the *Horn & Herald* noted that King Perinon left for his respite earlier than scheduled.

Perhaps Peri's status went to full candidate? This had been thrust upon Peri at a time when she could not be there to support him. Her eyes watered. She blotted them and sat up straight, trying to get through the rest of the blasted publication.

She turned the page, ran her eye down the entries, and read the name KULTE-KOLME LORNIS. Her breath stopped and her heartbeat pounded in her ears as she read above his name: "Bodies cannot be recovered for pyres and what follows are the known lineal losses." Lost at sea? That didn't make sense. She gasped as she tried to breathe. A roaring sound filled her ears.

"Is something wrong?" Enita asked.

She stood. Thinking she might vomit, she kept her hand tightly on her mouth to hold everything inside—including her emotions. She paced the room or the *cage*, as it had become. *This is just another prison.*

"I'm getting out of here." She ran for the door.

"Draius!"

She stumbled down the tunnels leading to the stables, which she had been allowed to visit once. Her breath heaved in sobs. Drops of water hit her face and fell about her. She bumped into people. Voices called after her but she didn't stop for anyone. She found Chisel and rested her head against the horse's neck. She let the warmth of his coat soak into her.

"Chisel." She breathed the horse's name and he whickered back. He didn't appear restive, so someone must be exercising him. She went over to tack storage and grabbed a saddle. Leading Chisel out of his stall and tying him, she brushed him and positioned the saddle.

"Are you going somewhere?" The clipped question came from behind her.

She whirled guiltily and hoped no tears showed on her face. Cerith was dressed for riding and wearing his dark blue cloak and livery. His garb was pristine, as always, although his boots were muddy. He held a wrapped roll, probably a document, and tapped it against his thigh as he waited for her answer.

"I see Enita wasted no time in calling my jailer." She went back to buckling the saddle girth under Chisel's belly.

Cerith ignored her sarcasm. "She's concerned for you. What if you take a fall riding and lose the baby?"

"Fall?" She stared at Cerith blankly. She didn't recall ever falling accidentally from a horse, having been set on her first horse at the age of four. "I'm more likely to stumble in those dark tunnels." Her voice was tart as she tested the girth. She proceeded to bridle her horse.

Cerith made no move to stop her. He stood still as a rock formation, so solid she could sense and gauge his exact position with her back turned. "Accidents can happen, my dear Draius. Should I believe Groygan myths of savage Tyrran women riding late into pregnancy and lying down in pastures to give birth?" There was an edge under the silkiness. "Or are you intending to reject my protection by trying to travel home?"

Like she rejected his proposal? She couldn't face him and she couldn't lie. Pressing her forehead against the saddle flap, she smelled the leather and its protective oils. The Mirror Sea lay eastward, deep and dark and attractive, pulling at her. When she first entered the stables, she planned to ride for those dark still waters and throw herself into them—anything to get away from the grief. Now rationality took over, preventing her that relief.

"I'm a practical woman, your grace," she said bitterly, speaking against the saddle flap. "I have no provisions for such a journey. Besides, the path into Tyrra is blocked by fire, the route down the Saamarin is blocked by cannon, all ships are becalmed, and apparently any horseback rider unfamiliar with the Whythern marshes is as good as lost. Please—I need the *Light*—just like the lost souls that surround us."

She was exhausted. Bordas was gone, but couldn't find the path to the stars because the Phrenii were destroyed. Peri needed her, but she couldn't be there to protect him. Now Lornis was gone and he would be forever anchored to the earth as well. She lived in a stronghold buried at the feet of these cold moors and here she must stay, if she wanted to protect her unborn baby. *Lornis's baby.* She fought to keep tears from squeezing out of her closed eyes. Several moments of silence passed and she waited, leaning against Chisel.

"Enita says you suffered a great loss." His voice was soft and made her eyes tear.

She didn't answer, trying to keep her composure. She couldn't break down in front of him again.

"Very well," he said finally. "If you're willing to take a sedate ride with a companion, then perhaps you should visit something important to us. A place sacred to the marsh people."

She thought he'd call for this companion, but he meant *he* would ride with her. He put the document into a breast pocket, went into the tack room, and returned with a cloak.

"You'll need this." He threw it at her and then whistled. Two of the largest dogs she'd ever seen came running down the row of stalls leading to the outside village. They greeted him with eager whimpers and snuffles. He returned their adoration with head and ear scratching, easy to do since their heads came to his hip. "Wolfhounds," he said, noting her stare. "With winter coming, the wolves will hunt further south and you should always take protection when you ride."

A boy came around the corner, leading Delfi. She winced. Not only did Delfi remind her of Bordas, but also the gelding was saddled and ready. Cerith thought she was making a run for Tyrra, against his orders, his advice, and all common sense. He had been prepared to pursue her with a horse that Chisel would recognize. Her cheeks burned first with anger, rejecting this misplaced sense of responsibility he had for her. Or was it possessiveness? Then embarrassment replaced the anger: he had no reason to believe she would follow his orders, once she broke her word to him.

"Thank you, Bevyn." Cerith smiled at the boy. The roof was high and he mounted fluidly.

Bevyn ducked his head shyly, but not before she saw the admiration and devotion that shined in his eyes. He looked about twelve years old and had a similar symbol to Enita's tattooed on his forehead, although his design was simpler. Her ire rose at the thought of Cerith manipulating and using the loyalty of these marsh people, all for his own gains.

"How fortuitous that your grace has a dead man's horse of such capability." Her tone was spiteful and she regretted her words immediately.

She seemed powerless to stop the Darkness growing within her, fed by her grief.

Any trace of the smile that Cerith had for Bevyn was wiped away. He gathered his reins deliberately before answering and while there was no irritation in his expression, she sensed anger in the bedrock below her, as if the earth threatened to tremble.

"I don't think Bordas would mind, considering he made me pledge, on my honor, to protect you. It was his duty to safeguard you and he passed that duty to me when we evacuated the estate. Besides, I had to pick a horse that could keep up with yours, didn't I?" His tone was light and he cocked his head with a smile, using the same beautiful and impenetrable facade he had used at his ball. A barricade slammed down between them, like a door closed against the light. Nothing emanated from the bedrock any more, not even anger.

"That was uncalled for. I'm sorry," she mumbled. She avoided looking at him and mounted.

"Get the doors, Bevyn. Remember to barricade them after us." Cerith's orders were clipped.

They went out the stable doors at a sedate trot and she noted how Bevyn watched her. No wonder the Kitarrans thought she was ungrateful and self-centered. This conversation between her and the Duke would be circulated throughout the fortress by the time they returned.

Once outside, Cerith headed northeast. He paused on a rise to give her time to look around. The dogs took up guard positions to the north and east. Winter was definitely coming to the moors. The air was heavy with fine mist but she breathed the chill deep into her lungs, tasting the water that rolled toward the marshes from the Mirror Sea. She also tasted the sharpness of wood smoke.

"The marsh people have hidden this fortress for hundreds of years." Cerith nodded back toward the stables.

The term "fortress" was not entirely accurate for Bryn Celar because no fortifications could be seen. At the top of the huge hill was a crown of stones, irregularly placed, and several had fallen. She had difficulty picking out the slate roof of the stables from the natural formations of the tall, wide hill. The stonework of the stable walls was hidden by cunning use of earth and rock, piled against the walls some time ago so that the hardy short grass and brush of the moors had grown up the walls and on to the roof. Almost everything else was under the hill, although there was what seemed like a small village with a smithy, pasture, and several sheep runs to the west.

She gazed out toward Suellestrin and tears welled at the glow in the southern skies. The horizon was one long and continuous coal that melted into dark smoke. It intermingled with the low cloud cover that hung over the land. The day had been forced into twilight and the clouds overhead had a strange taint from the fire and smoke. If the Whythern Marshes were flat, she could have seen Suellestrin, but the marshes were crowded with hillocks covered in scrubby trees and thorny bushes. They also had treacherous bogs and sucking holes masquerading as innocuous pools. This was why the annoying rebels stayed one step ahead of the Groygans.

"Strange that these people support you," she murmured. Through her haze of grief, curiosity stirred.

"Perhaps you'll understand after I show you this place."

She tore her gaze away from her homeland and eastward, where she saw part of the Mirror Sea spreading away like burnished silver. It perfectly mimicked the gray color of the northern skies. Her breath caught and without thinking, she turned Chisel toward it.

Cerith's hand whipped out and caught her rein. "No. You must control your element, not have it control you."

"Easy enough for you," she returned. "No one eats rock or earth. You don't drink it, wash with it..." Her voice trailed off at the thought of a large luxurious bath, not available in Bryn Celar. Even the memory of a bath overwhelmed her senses. She could slide down under the surface of the warm water and forever be finished with this pain.

"Didn't your cousin Perinon teach you to master your element?"

Cerith's voice brought her back. He was still holding her rein. She didn't remember talking to him about Perinon's warnings or about Perinon's older brother, King Valos, who had succumbed to the call of water. But he was right. She nodded slowly, slipping back into numbness.

"Follow me." He released the rein once it was obvious she wouldn't run for the sea.

She paid little attention to the rocky moors and let Chisel pick his own way. If she had made different decisions, would Lornis still be alive? Why had she resisted his urging for a marriage contract? She pictured his brown eyes, sparkling with humor, and his long shining hair. She could have been happy with him. If she had been newly married, she would have reason to resist when Perinon posted her to Betarr Kain. Yes, she could have changed her cousin's mind, she was sure. Then she would be making a new life with Lornis in the sister cities and he would never have contemplated a trip. Why was he on that ship anyway? Unfortunately, her rationalizations were marred by the niggling counters made in the back of her mind. Maybe she *wouldn't* have been happy with Lornis and *no*, she couldn't have changed Perinon's mind about this disastrous mission.

"Look, Draius." Cerith's voice sounded deep, hollow, and full of power.

Her skin prickled and she drew her cloak closer. The mist had become fog and they were going down into what might be a basin. She recoiled when the first standing stone loomed massive out of the fog, right in front of her. "It's huge! Is that all one stone?"

"Yes, and they were set without any engineering devices." He gestured roundly with his arm. Meanwhile, his dogs circled at the edge of the basin.

She looked about, trying to see the shape of the ring of standing stones, much larger than those on Bryn Celar. They enclosed half of the basin and faced eastward to a gap that would show the Mirror Sea, if she could see through the fog. In the focus of the semi-circle was a hill that held a jumbled structure of stone. The large stones of the semi-circle had all supported lintel stones, but some of those had fallen. Even in disrepair, this basin was a place of power. She sensed the deepness of the stones, their influence rippling through her. "Who raised these? The rock giants?"

"I suppose Tyrrans call them by that name." He dismounted and walked to the closest standing stone, putting his hand on it. "Enita's people believe that these stones touch the root of the world, where the power of earth and rock resides. These stones are ancient." His hand caressed the stone like it was living flesh. She thought a shiver went through the bedrock below them.

"Who needs to master his element now?" she demanded.

His laughter washed over her like a warm wave, his power of influence radiating through her and making her skin tingle. She shook herself to get rid of the feeling and decided to dismount. Leaving Chisel outside the standing stones, she walked a path about the inside of the semi-circle. He followed and she sensed the solidity behind her, like he was the most stable stone in the formation, standing always at her back. She paused at the last standing stone, at the most northeastern point. Its rough and worn surface had carvings around its girth, at a point above her head. She put her fingers on the stone and felt the slickness of the water from the fog. Leaning forward, she placed her cheek against the stone and absorbed the cold, deep power of water and earth.

"This is the safest place for you in Kitarra." His voice was soft, close by her ear. "Here you can grieve."

"What do you know of my grief?" Her vision blurred and when she lifted her free hand to her face, she found it wet with tears.

"Your sorrow doesn't carry the anguish of a mother's loss, so it must be—"

"*Lornis.*" She moaned his name and the sky above erupted with rain. She clung to the side of the huge standing stone, sobbing, and the rain responded by pounding the earth. He moved closer, protecting both of them with his cloak. Pain took her over and she dove into Darkness. She didn't know how long she was gone, but she eventually heard her name. Cerith's voice called her. She opened her eyes, thinking she still leaned into the standing stone, but saw his eyes a handspan away. Drops of water clung to his thick lashes and his eyes searched her face.

She pushed herself away, but her feet stuck and she almost fell backwards. He caught her shoulders and she glanced down. They stood in water up to their ankles and her feet had sunk into the earth. The grasses and sedges on these harsh moors subsisted in thin layers of dirt and gravel; her feet stood on firm bedrock under the mud.

Disconcerted, she stepped away from him, her feet making sucking sounds as she lifted them. She had told herself not to break down in front of him, yet that was exactly what happened. She willed him to say something, anything that might be taken as condescending so she could vent her anger and embarrassment upon him.

Instead, he motioned toward the gap. "The water is draining from the basin."

She searched for ridicule in his face, but it was blank and as still as the standing stones about them. His eyes were unreadable. She looked about the basin, blinking hard to clear her eyes. The rain had dispersed the fog. The jumble of rocks in the raised center used to be a platform, set in front of another structure.

"While this circle reflects the power of those who built it, the most interesting part is yet to come." He started toward the hill in the center, his boots making sloshing sounds. She didn't want to poke around in ruins, but the water level was falling so she followed. She thought she was already handling her impulses better: she sensed water all about, felt the tug of the sea to the east, but ignored its pull.

He led her around to the eastern side of the central hillock. Just like Bryn Celar, there was a structure built into the earthen mound but it was very small. The jumbled blocks on the other side had been the upper parts of walls and perhaps the supports for beams. The remains of a doorway faced the Mirror Sea.

Something bothered her. As Cerith bent his head to enter the opening, she asked, "Was this built later than the circle?"

He paused; smug satisfaction mingled with some other emotion on his face. "No."

"It must be. This is human-sized and was built by later settlers."

"The marsh people know who built this circle and when. They were built at the same time. See, the carvings here are the same as those on the stones." He raised his hand and caressed the symbols on the lintel piece of rock across the opening. The symbols matched what was carved about the girths of the standing stones; moreover, they looked similar to the circular symbols tattooed on Enita and Bevyn's foreheads.

"But the rock giants..." Her voice trailed away.

When taking their history lessons, the exploits of King Voima were the favorites of Tyrran children. His defeat of the northern rock giants when establishing Kitarra for Tyrran settlers was legendary. She remembered the pictures that went through her mind as their tutor described the battles: giants twice the height of any normal man swung huge weapons that caused mayhem. The legends said they had eyes in the middle of their foreheads, although the tutor cautioned that this might be an exaggeration. She gasped. "Voima and his sorcerers didn't fight monsters."

"No, they defeated humans, the ancestors of the marsh people. Voima pushed them north until they were no longer a problem." Cerith's voice was light as he continued to trace the carvings with his long graceful fingers.

"Perhaps they were called giants because they moved and placed these standing stones?" She was almost horrified, thinking back on her childlike satisfaction at the defeat of monsters.

"Just like other humans, they once had magic to do great deeds. Make no mistake, Enita says they were a savage and aggressive people." He turned about and his voice became brusque. "But you can see why the marsh people believe they should control these lands. Likewise, the Kitarran nobility, as descendants of the original Tyrran settlers, think they should control Kitarra."

"How will you hold them together, your grace?" For once, she wasn't sarcastic or facetious. He faced an enormous problem.

"I have gathered support from both sides. Enita has been the key for the marsh people. I also made promises. If you noticed, we're one of the few countries in the mapped world that doesn't have representational governance. Even Groyga, with its Council of Lords, is better than our singular monarchy. Many will pledge fealty for the promise of representation." She caught momentary uncertainty in his eyes.

"I should help you." The words jumped out of her without any forethought. Once she said them, she knew they were right.

He shook his head. "Your fealty is only to Tyrra. You've made that clear."

She wondered if he obliquely referred to his proposal of marriage. They never spoke of that, even though he said he wouldn't rescind his offer. "If I help you push the Groygans out of Kitarra, it's one step toward helping Tyrra. These are Endigala's forces—I can help you understand their strategies and organization. In addition, I still have the favor of Lord Chintegrata." At least, she hoped she did; Chintegrata also had to support the Council of Lords.

"What if your loyalties are tested? What if you must decide between Tyrra and Kitarra?"

"What decision will you make when my cousin Perinon demands the Kaskea? It was made by Tyrran sorcery and by our right it's a Tyrran artifact. Will you give it up?" She looked up into his face, that chiseled and facile face surrounded by blond hair that curled from the dampness, and wondered how much she trusted him. Likewise, his eyes searched hers, perhaps with the same question.

"I believe this binding with the Kaskea is for life." He smiled. "While my people don't recall the Phrenii, I remember the creatures wouldn't support Voima, or any Tyrran King, in deliberate warfare. If the Phrenii still existed, they wouldn't see me as Kitarran, would they? Even they wouldn't be able to free me from the Kaskea."

She tore her gaze away, remembering Dahni's attitude toward the sanctity of life. Her chest tightened with another pang of loneliness and she realized, with surprise, that she missed the creature in a tangible, emotional way. "If the Phrenii wouldn't ask you to divide your loyalties, why ask me to divide mine?"

"Clever sparring, but we ask each other unanswerable questions, never revealing our hearts." He chuckled and the sound slid along her skin like a caress. She shivered and pulled her cloak tight.

The smile faded from his face. "I make you no promises, Draius. My goal is to retake Suellestrin and regain control of Kitarra. I have no plans to assist Tyrra. That's too far in the future."

"But I just can't stand by. I've never been so helpless," she whispered.

"Maybe if you practiced control of your element, perhaps called enough rain to put out those fires." He waved toward the glow in the southern side. As she turned and fumbled for the Kaskea, he stopped her. "Long distance control takes a lot of concentration and strength, which you don't have today. Better get some rest before wrestling with your element. This is not to diminish your healing powers; my people and I thank you for your help."

"But what can I do *now?*" Glancing up, she saw him regarding her with a strange expression. She looked away, suddenly uncomfortable.

"Come, I must have you back to Bryn Celar before twilight or Enita will have my balls. We'll talk on the way." He grabbed her elbow and marched her back toward their horses.

What kind of influence did Enita have over a man whose bloodline put him in direct contention for the Kitarran throne? She wasn't able to ask that question of the duke because he filled the ride back to Bryn Celar, deluging her with Kitarran politics. She had to ask about strange pronunciations and the spelling of names, connecting them with the reports of Kitarra she had read. Periodically he would ask a focused question, perhaps to ensure she absorbed all the information. By the time they arrived at the stables of Bryn Celar, her head was whirling. He seemed determined to disgorge every piece of intrigue and intelligence possible. She would remember all his words, but that didn't mean she could instantly weave the facts into a fabric of sense.

There were sidelong glances at her as she followed the duke through the tunnels. As expected, the story of their argument had circulated and it hadn't helped her reputation. The exception was Enita, who greeted them with smugness and a small smile at the corners of her mouth.

"Cerith, the comhla commander and Suel are waiting for you." Enita pointed down a tunnel.

He nodded. "Come with me, Draius."

Pulled along in his wake, she barely had time to wonder why Enita addressed Duke Cerith Ungought of Whythern as an equal, flouting Kitarran protocol. Two patrol commanders gave rapid reports to the duke while he strode down the tunnels. As they walked, they picked up a few more people wearing the King's Comhla livery. When they entered a room that was a planning center, as indicated by the maps that hung from the walls, she noted many more in comhla colors. Suel was an exception, still wearing the Duke's livery. Tenil told her that the King's Comhla was officially disbanded, but it had been revived in the northern moors. There were even a few marsh people in comhla livery.

"What's she doing here?" Suel demanded.

"She knows Groygan tactics and strategies better than any of us," Cerith answered.

"Your grace, we can't expose our identities to someone we don't know," said the man who appeared to be the comhla commander. "We would be trusting a stranger with our lives."

Cerith nodded. "What if she took the oath of the King's Comhla?"

There was silence while everyone considered this. Cerith cocked his head at her. She knew he was asking her to trust him, to trust that she could live within the terms of this oath.

"I can make this oath," she said. "As long as I do not, through this oath, forsake my loyalty to my king."

"Your grace, she hesitates! Not only that, she makes provisions." Suel scowled at her.

She glared back. "Because anything sworn upon my honor is *permanent*. I have already sworn fealty to Tyrra's king and his laws."

Suel dropped his gaze first. She took a deep breath and looked at the men and women wearing the livery of the comhla, one by one. They all nodded. She tried to still her nerves. By taking this oath, she could help protect her son and country, but she might be taking an irrevocable step away from both of them.

Betarr Serin, Tyrra

WAR!

News of the Groygan invasion of the Kainen peninsula arrived in the sister cities yesterday evening. The King's Council unanimously declared war on Groyga and is expelling all Groygan embassy staff today. Meanwhile, our King's Guard prepares to take back Betarr Kain. As well, the full extent of the northeastern wildfires and whether the invading forces started them is unknown. The Horn and Herald *is dedicated to providing all relevant news of the invasion to our readers...*

— The Horn & Herald, *First Hireday, Erin Eleven, T.Y. 1471*

Peri shifted uncomfortably on the wooden bench, trying to keep his buttocks and thighs from going numb. For once, he hoped to see an exciting council meeting. Last night they declared war on Groyga and even that meeting managed to feel routine and boring. Before they voted upon the declaration of war, Lady Aracia was appointed regent for King Perinon because he was absent from the cities. Apparently, the Meran-Viisi matriarch traditionally stood in as regent.

Yesterday, though, Lady Aracia did cause a minor disturbance when she revealed the assassination attempts on King Perinon near Ruhallen. Several of the treasonous culprits had been killed. Because of this and the Fevers and other problems—Peri couldn't remember everything she said—the king had decided not to leave Ruhallen, worried that a "hasty departure might start a panic." She wove this story for the council yesterday evening and, knowing she lied by omission, Peri had wondered how long she could hide the king's illness.

Councilman Muusa had diverted today's meeting again and, unfortunately, he could make anything boring. Peri wished he could watch the impromptu parade down in Betarr Serasa, where the King's Guard was kicking out the filthy Groygans. It'd be more exciting and *instructive*—a word he kept hearing from Lady Aracia—than watching council meetings. His cousin Ilke would be on the wharves; she'd probably claim she hit the ambassador with a rotten apricot.

He glanced up at Lady Aracia, wondering if she might excuse him from the rest of this meeting, but her icy glance stilled his hope. Today was going to be about money and the matriarchy was attending in force. He sat wedged between Lady Anja and Lady Aracia. Aracia had become rather drawn and even sterner in the past eight-day. She also seemed older today. He glanced at Anja, who had started displaying little frown lines between her eyes.

Master of Arms Kilpi briefed the council on the Tyrran guard responses. He said five companies of cavalry and ten companies of infantry headed toward Plains End, which would be the staging area. He claimed this left the security of the sister cities thin, although several members appeared skeptical. Peri did the math in his head: a siege train of 120 cavaliers and 240 foot guards, plus "logistical support" wagons and experimental cannons light enough to travel on wheels, moved across the Tyrran plains. Plains End already had a few permanent companies of King's Guard, which would also march on Betarr Kain. When asked about the guards at Betarr Kain, Kilpi said they were "neutralized." Peri assumed this meant the Groygans had taken them prisoner—talks with Kilpi were always *instructive*.

Today Kilpi asked for more money and more horses and more guards—then he proposed conscripting Tyrrans between the age of nineteen and thirty. This caused quite a stir and Lady Aracia murmured in Peri's ear, "Conscription means that young people will be required to serve in the King's Guard. We haven't done that in more than one hundred years."

"I fear we won't be able to take back Betarr Kain with our current force of King's Guard," Kilpi added.

Then the captain of the Naval Guard stood and stated they hadn't decided whether to use bombardment from sea against Betarr Kain. They didn't have enough information yet and nobody wanted to destroy their own fortifications. Then he stated there weren't enough galleys and naval personnel to protect the Betarr Serasa harbor from a full-scale seaborne invasion from Groyga.

"Why hasn't the Naval Guard ensured they have enough resources to protect the harbor?" Councilman Muusa asked.

Kilpi cocked his eyebrow at the captain of the Naval Guard, who sighed. "Because, Councilman, ships don't last forever and they are decommissioned and dismantled on a regular basis when they can't be made seaworthy. The king continually requests funds to replace these ships, but in the past few years he's been denied them. I believe the denial of his request this year, Councilman, was specifically spearheaded by *you*."

Muusa sputtered. "Invasion by sea isn't an immediate threat. We all know that autumn shuts down warfare."

"Yet Groyga marched over our border—" Kilpi began.

"It's too blasted expensive. No sensible leader would attempt it," Councilman Muusa interrupted.

Discussion degraded to a boring squabble about past decisions and funds, a subject that Muusa could drone about for hours. Peri started daydreaming, thinking about how they'd celebrate when his mother came back. Lornis was gone but maybe his father, who had been exceedingly pleasant since he moved to the upper city, might step in. His father and mother might get back together—

He jerked his head up when both matriarchs nudged him in the sides. Something important was finally happening.

"We'll start with the Meran-Viisi pledge. The council recognizes Lady Meran-Viisi Aracia." The King's Council now called upon each lineage for support in the war effort and the crowded hall became quiet as Aracia stood.

"The Meran-Viisi make up the backbone of the King's Guard and I guarantee that every able-bodied member of our lineage is working toward the defense of Tyrra." Aracia's voice rang through the hall. "In addition, we have liquidated assets and pledge ten thousand gold tyr toward Tyrra's offensive and defensive forces."

Peri gasped, as many others did, at the sum. Cheers and clapping came from the benches behind him, where matriarchs crowded in with their staffs and common observers.

"We suggest these funds go toward galleys already available from Sareen, rather than investing the time to build our own." Aracia's clear, icy voice rose above the hubbub and quieted it.

At the front table facing the benches, fourteen of the fifteen Councilmen nodded. The exception was Muusa, who looked to Peri's left, where Leika sat. The next lineage to pledge would be the Pettaja-Viisi, but Leika's pledge would be paltry when compared to Aracia's.

"Lady Aracia, one more question, please." Muusa's voice was pleasant. "Yesterday, you were vague about when we can expect King Perinon back in the sister cities. Surely the people would benefit from his moral support."

The hall became deathly quiet, as if everyone held their breath. He heard the rustle of Aracia's skirt as she took a step toward the Council. Anja reached for Peri's hand. Her grip was tight and he felt her stiffen. He now knew why he had to be here today.

"This morning the Meran-Viisi received disheartening news. King Perinon has taken ill and will remain in northern Tyrra until he is well enough to travel. As a safety measure we have established Meran-Viisi

Perinon, formerly Serasa-Kolme, as the heir apparent." Pandemonium broke out and Aracia had to shout out her last words: "This is merely precautionary. We expect his majesty will make a full recovery."

Hardly anyone heeded her last words. Shouted questions rose above the uproar, most of them variations of, "Does the king have the Fevers?"

Aracia motioned for Peri to stand. That was the problem with going by a nickname; he almost didn't realize she spoke about *him*. He stood and faced the crowded benches, his mouth dry. The noise in the hall seemed to triple and hurt his ears. Cheers for him mixed with heated discussions and shouts, generally about whether cousin Perinon had the Fevers and whether the Fevers threatened the sister cities. In the back of the room, a short, pudgy man who Peri recognized as Andreas, editor of the *H&H*, ran for the doors. This revelation, or confirmation as some saw it, of the king's illness was more exciting than how the war would be funded.

The council mediator started tapping a bell for order. This didn't calm the crowd and Councilman Aivo called for guards to start clearing the hall of non-essential personnel. As the more disruptive spectators were escorted out, Captain Rhaffus and Peri's father Jan entered the hall. They walked up the side to stand to the right of the benches. Peri stood taller, wanting to make Jan proud during his presentation.

"I present Perinon, from Meran-Viisi succession, as heir apparent to the Crown." Aracia laid her hand on Peri's shoulder, but she now spoke to a quieter hall with a third of the people it previously held.

It was done. Several matriarchs nodded at Peri as he went back to his bench, but most kept still. Of course, a different heir apparent might be announced next eight-day. He glanced at his father, but Jan's face was as unreadable as any matriarch's.

"We'll continue with the pledges," the moderator said, after Peri sat down. "The Council recognizes Lady Pettaja-Viisi Leika."

Boredom again threatened as he listened to each matriarch pledge, in order of lineal precedence. He tried to track amounts, but not everything was pledged in money. Some matriarchs pledged people with expertise or supplies or labor. He didn't need to track the figures on a slate to grasp that Leika made a very *stingy* contribution, considering the wealth of the Pettaja-Viisi. He liked that word; he learned it from Lady Anja, who once said that Leika ran a "stingy lineage."

"The Council recognizes Captain Rhaffus of the City Guard."

Peri sat up, interested again. Captain Rhaffus and Jan walked into the empty space before the Council, so that he could only see their backs. Slightly taller than Rhaffus, Jan made a fine figure of an officer. Peri hoped that one day he would look the same, perhaps even wear the same uniform. Then he realized he might never wear the livery of the King's Guard or City Guard, if cousin Perinon died before his time.

Captain Rhaffus was speaking and he'd missed the beginning words. "It's important to continue the investigation, now that we're at war. The murder of the master of arms and four Meran-Viisi in sensitive positions was a treasonous act that weakened our defense and could be a boon to Groyga."

"I thought we concluded that misguided Kulte-Kolme wanted to protect the Kaskea from Sevoi. After all, he did steal two of the shards before he fled the country." Muusa sounded indignant.

This was about Lornis. They wanted to blame him for murder! Peri started to stand, but felt Anja's hand on his shoulder. She shook her head.

"That was your conclusion, *not* the City Guard's. We have proof Kulte-Kolme Lornis couldn't murder Sevoi; he was in Betarr Serasa at the time and witnesses have sworn he was nowhere near the other three victims in the lower city. We also know Lornis took the shards of the Kaskea at the king's command." Jan's voice was cool and collected. Peri knew his father didn't like Lornis, so it seemed odd that Jan was defending Lornis's honor. His mother Draius would say this was a political move to support an agenda within the City Guard.

"Then, as I always maintained, the king was misguided. Why can't we close this case and get on with more important issues, like driving the Groygans off our land? At this point, Sevoi's murderer will never be found, so what does this matter?" Muusa threw up his hands.

"This matters, ser, because you're the only person who visited Sevoi that night and you're the one who ordered us to drop the investigation," Rhaffus said.

"What about the other murders? Are you demanding the City Guard leave them unsolved as well?" Jan asked.

"Is the City Guard insinuating that I had something to do with these murders?" Muusa's voice was loud and tight. The benches behind Peri started humming with whispers and low conversations. The moderator tapped his bell for order and the hall quieted.

Master of Arms Kilpi stood and was given leave to speak. "I agree with the City Guard and I submit that this could be a matter of national security. The City Guard must continue their investigation."

"Not if they obstruct and divert this council with false accusations." Muusa's face was white and strained.

Peri glimpsed movement in the corner of his eye. Leika stood, waiting for attention.

"The Council recognizes Lady Pettaja-Viisi Leika." Most of the King's Council looked surprised. Matriarchs seldom participated in public politics, nor were they interested in matters of the King's Law.

Leika walked up beside Captain Rhaffus and as they turned to face each other, Peri gasped loudly. He looked down as Leika's gaze jerked toward him. She had a black eye! Well, not a bad one like he got from an elbow in a rough game, but the edge of a bruise circled her eye and ran down on her cheekbone. The bruise was healing, casting yellow and green along the side of her face.

"This appears to be going nowhere. If it will help the City Guard move forward in their investigation, I can make a statement to clear Councilman Muusa." Leika's voice was crisp.

Rhaffus regarded Leika curiously, his jaw working, but he made a quick bow and gestured for her to continue. Wasn't anybody going to ask

Leika how she hurt her face? He glanced up at Lady Anja and she shook her head. Why not? If he had a shiner, every adult he met would be asking him what he did to get that bruise. He slumped in his seat, disgruntled at the unfairness in the world. Lady Anja's hand crept over his, again giving him the signal that something was important, somehow, to his safety.

"I saw the Councilman after his meeting with Master of Arms Sevoi," Leika said.

"At what time? For how long?" Rhaffus asked.

"He arrived after the evening meal and stayed the night. I can vouch for his frame of mind. He could not have been murdering Sevoi; his mood was mild and considerate." Leika raised her chin, challenging the captain.

Rhaffus seemed skeptical and Jan's eyebrows rose. Peri rarely saw his father express surprise in public. All three of them turned to look at Muusa, who became pink and flustered. Rhaffus turned back to Leika and his eyes deliberately lingered on her bruises. "I wouldn't have considered the Councilman to be the type to interest you, my lady. He must be more adventurous than I thought."

At those words, Muusa turned red and started coughing.

"You should never judge a man by his appearance, captain." Leika's voice was cold.

"I don't, which is why your statement about his *mood* cannot take the councilman off our list of suspects."

"But Councilman Muusa visited the master of arms at my request," Leika said. "The Pettaja-Viisi wanted to see the Kaskea safely back where it should be: under our care and on display for all the people of Tyrra."

"Yet those shards were easily stolen from your care. That's why the king took them into his possession for safe-keeping, by his own words." Jan's voice was bland.

Leika's eyes narrowed as she stepped back. She cocked her head as she looked Jan over, her gaze going from his feet to his head. She licked her lips with the tip of her tongue and a strange, dark, possessive look came into her eyes. Jan's face never changed. Peri didn't need Anja's signal to know that Leika "owned" Muusa and she wanted to "own" Jan, also.

"Did you send a gift with Muusa that night? A gift for Sevoi?" Rhaffus's questions chilled Leika's expression.

"Of course not. I only asked him to present our appeal. The Pettaja-Viisi have always protected our knowledge and our artifacts, for our future and for our children." Leika jerked her head toward Peri. "The Kaskea is part of our heritage and the king always carries one of its shards."

As Leika primly marched back to her seat, Peri tried not to sigh. Adults had forgotten about the Phrenii and the true purpose of the Kaskea. They thought the king carried a shard because that's what Tyrran monarchs had always done. They considered the Kaskea valuable, but only for its own sake.

"I move that the City Guard reopen and continue their inquiry into Sevoi's murder, as well as the others that occurred that night." This was the first time Councilman Aivo had spoken. Aivo was quiet, but the most respected councilman ever elected. Muusa pursed his mouth in displeasure, but he couldn't gainsay Aivo and he cast his vote in favor, making it unanimous. Captain Rhaffus and Jan bowed. They strode out of the hall and Peri wished he could follow.

He had realized the point of Lady Anja's signals: the Pettaja-Viisi and Councilman Muusa were *his* enemies now. They were closer to him than the Groygans swarming over the Kainen peninsula and perhaps more deadly.

Betarr Serasa, Tyrra

Kilpi hated telling Peri that he couldn't come down to the docks with him, but he was late. He could ride fast and alone, while Peri had to take guards. "I'm sorry, but I can't bring you along." Out of the corner of his eye, he saw Lady Aracia nodding in agreement. "I'll be sure to brief you about everything, though."

That mollified Peri. "You'll do that tomorrow, first thing after breakfast?"

"Certainly, ser." Kilpi smiled. Now that Lady Aracia was the regent for the crown, he would brief her every morning. Having the possible future king of Tyrra listen to the updates would be good training. He liked talking with Peri, who seemed surprisingly adult for his age. He was also quick-witted, bringing those rumors circulating about the Sareenian community to Kilpi's attention. *I guess Peri's had to grow up pretty fast in the last two erins, what with his mother missing and the murders making him heir apparent.*

The Betarr Serasa docks were crowded and Kilpi carefully pushed through the throngs that came to see the Groygan Embassy staff for the last time. If he had a tenth for every time he heard "good riddance, I say," from an onlooker, he'd be rich. He skirted the ranks of men and women in shining silver and green uniforms and dismounted, throwing his reins to a guard on the end. These three companies of King's Guard had escorted the Groygans through streets filled with shouting towns-people.

Velenare Be Glotta, Ambassador no longer, stood by the ship's gangplank and faced Ruel, newly promoted to captain of the King's Guard. She waved Kilpi over. "Ser, I'm waiting on a report."

"I'm glad you made the time to say goodbye, master of arms." Velenare sniffed and gestured at the crowds. "Many thanks to your guards, who have kept the commoners from harming us." In his last hour on their soil, his Tyrran was unexpectedly impeccable, even sporting a slight upper-city inflection.

"I would have thought you'd be gone by now," Kilpi returned. "Then I could put the King's Guard to much better use."

Ruel pulled him aside. "We're trying to ensure that we've found his entire staff."

He looked over the twenty Groygans accompanying Velenare. "Where are Lottagre and Garra?"

"That's what I asked. He says he shipped them home four days ago. I sent a runner to the Harbor Master to check the manifest of the ship."

So everyone waited in the chilly air. No sunshine came through the clouds to warm them. Behind the lines of King's Guard the Tyrrans seethed, brave enough to throw rotten fruit over the heads of the guards. They often missed the Groygans, but once in a while Velenare dodged a well-aimed missile. Kilpi chuckled and Velenare motioned him closer.

"You will pay for this humiliation," Velenare said.

"And *you'll* pay for every resident of Betarr Kain who has been harmed." Kilpi's voice was gritty and he let his sheer, naked hatred show in his eyes. As opposed to those throwing the rotten fruit, he knew how many Tyrrans might have survived the attack on Betarr Kain. Meran-Kolme Kyle's *very* short report—carried by two dedicated messengers, each galloping straight through a day and a night, each changing horses five times—had been bleak. Velenare nervously stepped back, eyeing him.

The runner came back with the ship's manifest from the harbor master's office. It verified that two Groygans named Lottagre and Garra boarded and left for Groyga that day.

"Why did you send them home?" Ruel asked.

Kilpi sensed Velenare tense up. The Groygan was preparing an important lie, one that they must believe. "Although this is none of your business, I sent Garra away because he was disruptive."

This didn't need to be verified: Garra notoriously picked fights with Tyrrans who walked past the embassy gates.

"And Lottagre? Your Honored Sword?" Ruel asked.

"He picked up too many Tyrran mannerisms for my taste," Velenare said, more easily this time. "Besides, there are pressing matters in House Glotta that require his attention. When I sent him back, I had no idea we were going to be at war within a few days."

Ruel looked skeptical, but when her guards came off the ship and reported it clean, she went ahead and let the Groygans board. "We won't meet again, Glotta," she said over her shoulder.

"Don't wager on that, Captain Ruel," Velenare snapped as he followed the last of his men up the gangplank.

She and Kilpi waited until the plank was pulled up, the ship unmoored, and they were pulled away from the dock by dinghy. Eventually, they headed toward the harbor mouth under the power of their oars. Their one sail hung slack like all the others in the harbor.

"I have a question for you." Kilpi motioned over one of the hands who released the Groygan ship moorings. "I'm no expert on ships, but the one carrying the Groygan ambassador looks very Sareenian to me."

"That it does, ser. It seems the Groygans are buying ships from the Sareenian city-states, probably to avoid the time and labor of building their own."

Just like we'll be doing. Kilpi exchanged a look with Ruel, who used to be Deputy for Resources.

"The Sareenians have no compunction about selling ships to both sides in a war," she said.

The Sareenians were also trying to frighten their people here in the sister cities into leaving, which would cause labor shortages and possibly cascade into shortages of food and other important items. He had to look into this building undercurrent of subversion he sensed—after all, the necromantic charms they were trying to purge from the sister cities came from Sareen, by way of Sareenian merchants. Ruel, though, shouldn't be bothered with this. She would be leaving immediately with the last company of cavalry to head to Plains End. She would lead the grim mission of retaking Betarr Kain.

Kilpi bid her goodbye. "May our ancestors bless and protect you."

She saluted him. "For Betarr Kain."

Captain Ruel had ridden off with her companies, cheered by towns-people lining the sides of the streets, when someone tapped Kilpi's shoulder. A Kitarran guard bowed, dressed in dark blue livery with unfamiliar symbol of a silver tree under five stars.

"Master of Arms Kilpi, I carry something addressed to you, which arrived at our embassy an eight-day ago." He offered him a letter.

It was from Bordas, dated fourteen days ago, and it had been opened. Kilpi turned it over, noting it was actually addressed to Sevoi's home. "Your ambassador already told me the substance: our man Bordas is waiting in Suellestrin for Serasa-Kolme Draius."

The guard shifted his weight and raked his fingers through auburn hair. "Well, he sent much more news. Being a duke's man, I pushed for giving you the entire letter, as the duke requested in his packet. However, Sevoi had just been murdered and it has intelligence regarding Groyga. King Markus explicitly ordered our embassy to *not* release intelligence on Groyga to Tyrra, so the ambassador only released the information about Bordas and Draius. He sent a message home by pigeon to ask whether this policy should be continued, using the pretext of having a new Tyrran master of arms."

"What was their answer?" Kilpi shoved down his ire with effort. How long had this Kitarran no-sharing-intel-on-Groyga policy been in effect?

"We didn't get one." The Kitarran shrugged. "We learned King Markus died in an accidental fire. There have been no messages since. When we realized, with the rest of Tyrra, that Betarr Kain had been attacked, the ambassador directed me to give this to you after the Groygan embassy staff left."

"Why after?"

"He couldn't have Velenare see this hand-off. I'm not sure your intelligence grasped just how much Markus favored Groyga." The Kitarran pressed his lips together. "It's better in your hands, now that we're just waiting for policy changes from the regent. I hope it proves helpful, ser."

"Thank you." He bid the Kitarran guard goodbye before opening the letter.

While he walked, he skimmed over the opening information about Draius. Suddenly he stopped in the middle of the busy entrance to the docks, letting the crowds bump and brush by him as he read the entire letter. He started running for the guard stables near the Betarr Serasa main square.

He had to send a messenger after Captain Ruel—she needed to know about these *ebi corgo*.

CHAPTER TWENTY-THREE

The Broken Kaskea

The Abandoned Hermitage Near Ruhallen, Northern Tyrra

Ihmar apprenticed with a sorceress who espoused safety first when dealing with elemental magic and, in particular, walking the Void. She taught him to shield his mind before entering and to keep it shielded throughout his visit, even when going through the Blindness. Through the years this became habit to him. This time, these habits saved his life.

Berina left to do errands in the village while he walked the Void. The Blindness was more tumultuous than ever—the sleeping minds were plagued with nightmares and the lost souls now participated in the chaos. The hunters reveled in more than enough prey. He felt guilty subjecting Berina to this night after night with the directed dreaming.

The barrier between the Void and the Blindness had weakened since the last time he had attempted this, but he couldn't guess why. He rose into the Void and, keeping his mind shielded as usual, started to assess the shape of the world. Thus, when the seething and disordered mind joined him, he built another layer of calm walls and merely waited.

"Show yourselves!" The mind raged with a distinctly female voice.

He drifted closer and *saw* her rising from the Kainen Peninsula.

"Who is dousing my fires?" The woman was Groygan and dressed in armor.

He wondered whether this sorceress was the one who had invoked the lodestone's spell. After reading Lahna's writings regarding the lodestone of souls, he was convinced it could destroy the Phrenii and bestow their collective soul upon the invoker. It seemed the only answer to the mystery of their disappearances.

"Dahni, I know it's you." She put her fists on her hips and faced north toward the Mirror Sea. "You and Sahvi always impeded me. If you're hiding behind the Kaskea, I'll find you. Or maybe I'll hunt down the bearers and destroy their shard. Either way, I win."

He discarded his earlier hypothesis that she was a human who knew enough sorcery to correctly pronounce the lodestone's spells. If so, he should sense two souls, not one. Besides, she was visible to him. Only the Phrenii could be actually seen because they were beings of the Void. He wasn't, so he couldn't be seen but he could be sensed. He strengthened the walls around his mind to shield himself. The Phrenii had been extremely good at sensing and identifying others inside the Void.

Another theory grew—an uncomfortable one. She couldn't be the embodiment of all the Phrenii or she wouldn't be hunting Dahni and Sahvi. The most damning evidence was the one element that still endured in the world below, while the others withered. Well, he had an obvious but dangerous way to test this. He loosened the shields about his mind.

She looked about, sensing him. "Who's there?"

Not being made of the Void, he only communicated through thought. He tried to put volume behind his one word. *Famri!*

Her head jerked around. "A Minahmeran sorcerer?" Whether she perceived him or his mental shadow, it didn't matter. She located him. Her eyes narrowed and glowed. "I figured you were all dead."

I know what you did to the others.

A ball of white fire narrowly missed him as he dove for the Blindness below. The ability to call up fire in the Void had identified her as well.

Knowing she might follow him, he sped through the Blindness so swiftly he doubted any hunter noticed him. He jumped for his body and pushed through the shock, like being dumped in ice water, and opened his eyes.

He sat comfortably on a mat in the back room of the ancient hermitage, while Berina puttered around in the front. It sounded like she'd brought food from the village and was storing it away. He cast his senses about for elemental magic, any leaked spell residue or conduit not tied off neatly. Yes, he had been taught well—he felt a moment of sadness for his teacher, who had succumbed to fever before her time. Lastly, he reestablished the shields about his mind.

"How long will he be doing this Void walk? Is he meditating?" That was Lyn's voice; the commander must have come back to the hermitage with Berina.

"No, but he prepares for it by meditating." Berina glanced up as he came to the doorway. "Oh, you're back."

He surveyed the bucolic scene: Berina was making lunch and Lyn lounged at the table, nibbling an apple. The weather had finally chilled, just as they entered winter. The small wood stove in the corner kept the structure cozy. He realized this place seemed more like *home* than any other he'd lived in before. He was also becoming fond of these humans; he wanted them to live out their short lives in peace, but that didn't look likely after identifying himself to Famri.

"What's the matter? I'd say you looked like you'd seen a ghost, but..." Her smile slipping sadly off her face, Berina tilted her head toward the rocks at the edge of the glade where departed souls gathered in the shadows.

"I discovered who invoked the lodestone." He pulled out a rickety chair to sit opposite Lyn. "It was Famri. She nearly just killed me in the Void. She's now the equivalent of a powerful human sorceress and we'll have to be very careful—she'll be hunting for us—for me, most likely."

Berina's jaw dropped. "She? Human?"

"So they were betrayed by one of their own? Famri's the unicorn—er—the element of fire?" Lyn looked to Berina for confirmation. She was trying to learn everything about the Phrenii again, which was difficult for someone who had no memories of ever seeing them.

"Why would Famri do this?" Berina whispered.

"My guess is that it—she—wanted individuality." Ihmar waved at the sorted piles of documents that lined one wall, kept far away from the stove. "Lahna harped about that, saying it would be the downfall of the Phrenii. It appears she was right."

"She also predicted the Kaskea would save them."

He drummed his fingers on the table, wondering if he should feed the hope in Berina's eyes. "It's possible." He used a cautious tone. "Apparently, Famri hasn't come through the lodestone's spell with all the Phrenic elements. She was in the Void trying to figure out who was 'dousing her fires' and called out Dahni by name. There was no response, of course, and she said that if they were *hiding behind the Kaskea*, she would find them." He decided not to worry Berina with Famri's threat against the Kaskea shards and their bearers; that threat was hollow because Famri had to move like a human now and the shards were spread across the mapped world.

"Perhaps they're *in* the Kaskea and hiding *behind* the bearer!" Berina leaned forward eagerly. "They might still exist but without enough power to have their own bodies. Maybe their elemental power transferred to the Kaskea bearer—if so, then *Draius* is the one who's dousing Famri's fires."

"That woman has the most stubborn will I have ever seen." Lyn nodded. "She would fight back any way she could. This also means that Famri started the wildfires in northeast Tyrra and Draius made it to Kitarra."

Ihmar eyed both of them. Without having more than a bare introduction to the concept of elemental magic, Berina had just made an intuitive leap to the same conclusion he had, with his hundreds of years of study. Lyn and Berina, between them, had figured out the names of four of the Kaskea bearers, even the mysterious male in Kitarra. The fifth shard had been unresponsive to his probing and Lyn told him it was at the bottom of the sea. That, though, could have been overcome. The real reason was now obvious: Famri was permanently severed from the Kaskea.

"So what's your plan?" Lyn slapped the table with her palm.

Then he remembered why the commander was here. He and Berina intended to present their plan, which he saw in an entirely different light now that he had encountered Famri in the Void. Originally, they hoped to call the Kaskea bearers back to Tyrra. *Now* the bearers could do something much more important: they might be able to provide an earthly anchor for the Phrenii and help him reinstate them as portals to the Void. This was a lot to ask of anyone, but to communicate this request through dreams?

He laid out the adjusted plan for Lyn.

She was not impressed. "Berina will be doing all this by *directing her dreams* to people many leagues away? Well, that sounds unreliable, at best. Why can't you help out with your sorcery?" Lyn waved her free hand and fluttered her fingers. "Can't you hobble Famri with your hocus-pocus?"

"No, because her ho-cus-po-cus can easily overwhelm mine. She's still one of the Phrenii, so she's a natural at sorcery and knows its language and pronunciation. She's an elemental made of life-light from the Void, so she essentially *is* magic—which means she has a ready and unlimited source of elemental power, while I have to establish a conduit to the Void. What's worse is that when I do establish my conduit, she can track me down from the Void."

"What about your previous spells?" Berina sounded anxious.

"No. I don't leave residual magic around and I tie off my conduits completely. She didn't know I existed until this afternoon. I bet she starts paying attention and watching for me in the Void."

"What does this mean for Berina and her Sight? Will Famri hunt her?"

"Not if she looks like any one of the other humankind sleeping in the Blindness. I can teach her shielding techniques and go with her, but I can't use magic without attracting Famri's attention."

"What would she do to us?" Berina asked.

"Best not to give her the chance." He shrugged and exchanged a glance with Lyn. She probably realized, as he did, that Famri was behind the fall of Betarr Kain.

Lyn went back to punching holes in his plan. "But why concentrate only on Commander Draius? Wouldn't you get better results trying to communicate with all four bearers?"

Berina answered her. "Because I've read about her, I know her name, and she's Tyrran. That commonality helps me find her in the Blindness when I sleep. Besides, she's the only one who's reacted to me and been receptive. The king's mind is still feverish and the other two are foreigners about whom I know very little."

"It doesn't sound like you'll ever coordinate the four bearers." Lyn's forehead furrowed.

"They don't have to be coordinated. I will have to invoke a complicated spell to see if the Phrenii are indeed residing within their respective shards of the Kaskea and make them ready. After that, it'll be up to the bearers to commit themselves."

"I thought you said that magic would attract Famri."

"It will." He looked up at the sack that still sat on the top of the cupboard. "But I might find a way to distract her. I'll need more mirrors—ones that aren't necromantic, please."

"I'll get you whatever you need, as long as you can make this world right again. Are you sure that bringing back the Phrenii will help those lost souls find their way to our ancestors?"

He hesitated. "I hope that restoring even one aspect of the Phrenii will help them. No one's ever attempted this before, but we'll give this our best effort." Beside him, Berina nodded.

"Fair enough." Lyn finished her apple.

Northern Moors, Kitarra

Draius dreamed about the girl again. This time she was in the glade before the ancient hermitage, which she remembered visiting as a child. It was warm and she smelled late summer flowers.

"There are four minds," the girl said slowly. She held a bouquet in her hand. "But only two of you are sane enough to make the decision."

Draius started gathering her favorite blossoms. The girl's words were familiar.

"Dahni is still with you. We are clearing the way for their return but you must make a hard decision, one that will affect your entire life. You must provide an anchor, a soul, for your aspect." The girl sounded tired, like she had memorized and said this many times.

"I used Dahni's power to bring rain to the wildfires." She was getting better controlling her element, because… Because she had something to do for Cerith. The hermitage began to shimmer and she caught sight of the Mirror Sea behind it.

"Draius! You must make things right!" The hermitage came back and the sea faded. "Dahni must share your soul for your entire life. We will be making the preparations tomorrow. If you offer your soul as an earthly anchor, Dahni can come back and help the dead find peace."

"Here in the moors?" The vague shapes of standing stones start to appear.

The girl shook her head. "They cannot violate both time and place. Dahni can only be remade in the same place, once time is changed."

"I want Dahni to watch over Peri in the sister cities." Then everything jumbled and she was with Peri in the Betarr Serasa marketplace, then she opened her eyes in the dark of Bryn Celar.

Enita had laid a quiet hand on her shoulder. "It's time." She lit a lamp and hurried out of the room.

In the past nights, she had plenty of dreams with the girl in them, but she couldn't give them much attention. Even with her perfect memory, what happened during sleep was difficult to remember when awake, unless it was triggered. Besides, since she became a member of the King's Comhla, her days had been filled with practice controlling her element as well as preparing for this night. It was midnight and they would be mounting an attack upon Suellestrin before dawn. She heard people passing each other in the tunnel, exchanging tense updates or boosting morale. All Bryn Celar was getting ready.

She smiled as she got into her comhla livery. Cerith turned out to be smarter than she expected. The oath of the King's Comhla required loyalty to the *rightful* Ungought heir to the throne, which was why Markus had finally disbanded the comhla. As long as she trusted Cerith, she could live within the oath. In the past few days she was not only starting to trust him, but to respect him.

She wouldn't be part of the armed attack; the comhla had come up with a special use for her elemental powers—*not mine, but Dahni's*, she reminded herself. As she dressed, she noted these recently fitted breeches were not as snug as her old ones. In an erin or so, she'd be limited to wearing kirtles.

"Are you sure you can do this?" Enita was back, handing her a bowl of gruel even though breakfast was hours away. She became concerned that Draius wasn't gaining enough weight, even though she protested her pregnancy was proceeding much as it had when she carried Peri. Perhaps Tyrran women were different from northern marsh women.

"You'll be with me, if I need care." She was bemused by Enita's attention to her pregnancy; it seemed like she and her child had a surrogate matriarch.

"Humph. This is the last time I'll allow you to ride."

Draius shoveled down her gruel while watching Enita pack enormous amounts of extra clothing. "Don't bother with those, Enita. The forward post is three hours ride and if we fail tonight, we'll be abandoning it and making a run back to the moors."

"I also made sure Cerith is well outfitted. There's always need for dry clothes," Enita said.

"Particularly those sized for a tall Tyrran woman?" she asked dryly.

"Are you ready?" Enita snapped. "I can't carry these packs by myself." The tattooed symbol on Enita's forehead rippled and her whole face showed tension. The old woman was usually composed, providing a calming strength and wisdom that others relied upon. Enita needed that strength tonight, for her people, for Cerith.

"Whatever happens tonight, the duke will survive," Draius said softly.

"I hope so." Enita nodded and the bun of graying hair at her neck bobbed up and down. Draius had braided her silver-blond hair for war, the braids close to her head and resting on the back of her neck out of her way.

"Besides, he'll be using his Phrenic powers, so he'll be safe." She mouthed hopeful words, because Cerith had to maintain a high profile and always be visible; the comhla planned well-timed riots in the city, but unless the populace believed the duke was returning, they would sputter out.

Enita's dark eyes looked searchingly at Draius. "You have no idea how important he is, do you? Or what part you and your child must play?"

"I've been having strange dreams lately, but nothing about my child." She deflected any questions regarding Cerith by asking, "How do *you* know a dream contains true Sight or a meaningless prank played by your mind?"

"I don't. The Sight shows possible consequences, nothing more. When one of my dreams suddenly makes sense of reality—that's the Sight guiding me. But right now, the Sight hasn't told me who's going to carry this old woman's pack."

"I will." Draius laughed as she hoisted the pack over her shoulder. Another difference between her and all the northern women was her superior strength, which became obvious in the last eight-day.

Outside Bryn Celar, they joined the last group leaving for the forward post. The clouds above blocked the starlight and made the velvet night close in about their lanterns. She tasted the water in the air, as available to her as the sea that sat about a furlong to the east.

A man wearing the dark blue of the duke's livery was holding Chisel's bridle. He bowed when she approached. "My—my lady," he stuttered. His nerves made Chisel dance about. She automatically patted the horse's neck while she searched her memory. This was the man with the deadly lung wound.

"I'm glad to see you're well enough to get about," she said as she mounted.

"My eternal thanks to you, my lady." He bowed again and she noted determination on his face. "I'm well enough to guard your safety, if you'll have me. My left side isn't strong enough to draw a bow, but my right arm can use a weapon."

With one word from her, this man could stay behind in safety. He *should* remain at Bryn Celar and continue to heal, but she knew what it cost, *in spirit*, to feel helpless. He anxiously waited for her decision. She nodded. "Your name?"

"Pearth, my Lady." A smile transformed the man's face and he scrambled, somehow, up on his pony—or that was probably a horse. Chisel towered over the Kitarran mounts. These people had to start breeding more height in their horses. At least Delfi was carrying Cerith as he pushed through the city. Delfi was trained to protect his rider from close threats on foot. She muttered a low prayer to her ancestors as they wound their way to the forward post.

A few hours later, she was in the forward post looking at a map of the city. They were on a stable hillock near the Mirror Sea, in the ruins of what might be an old shrine. Interestingly, one couldn't find it from the south or the west. The path by land wound in from the north and then crossed a narrow gravel causeway to the shrine. From this shrine, one had to travel by water around a marshy point to find the road, which was a half hour's ride from the edge of Suellestrin.

"Is it time?" Enita asked.

"Not yet." Draius glanced about the sparsely occupied post. Pearth hovered behind her, intent upon fulfilling his role as personal guard. Tenil and a marsh man stood near the map. Outside waited a few runners. A force of mixed marsh and Kitarran guards waited beyond the southern marsh point, to be used under various scenarios planned by Cerith and Suel.

Unfortunately, the forward post couldn't receive or send news quickly because of its location. Runners took time. Horses actually took longer because they couldn't take the paths the runners could. The instantaneous mode of communication would be—she sensed the ripple of Cerith's tension flood the bedrock below the ruins.

"The duke just collapsed the walls about the northeastern gates." Her voice was loud and crisp. Everyone looked up and Tenil came to look at the map.

"You're sure?" He sounded doubtful and she realized none of them felt anything.

"I'm certain. My turn, now." She walked out of the shrine followed by Enita, Tenil, and Pearth.

The cloud cover above the Mirror Sea thinned and clusters of stars shone through. Draius looked up and saw the Meran-Viisi constellation through a hole, with the sorcerer Cessina shining brightest. *How fitting.* She stood on the gravel and boulders that stuck out into the water. She felt the ancient power stirring below the shining surface of the water and fought her urge to dive into that stillness, that peace. Her hands trembled and she clenched them. Her baby moved and she exclaimed.

"Are you all right?" Enita asked.

"I'm fine, I'm fine," she murmured, concentrating on the rock below her feet. She was mistaken; it was far too soon for the baby to be moving or kicking.

Enita huffed, but didn't say anything.

She put a hand on her belly, gathered her strength, and *pushed* with her mind. Tenil shouted and Pearth muttered something like "Starlight above." Enita tried to hold her up as her knees sagged. She opened her eyes to see a huge wave of water traveling away from them. That wave should swamp the fishing flats and, more importantly, erode the foundation under the Groygan cannons. Since the fishing flats were merely sand mixed with a little mud, the cannons would sink, tilt, or even move from the force of that wave. Hopefully, it would take days to dig them out. The docks and ships at Suellestrin would be damaged, but it couldn't be helped. These days, all the foreign ships were Groygan anyway.

She had to lean on Tenil when she walked back to the forward post. The effort of moving so much water left her limbs like noodles. Once in the post and under the tarps, Pearth brought her a cup of cool water, which she drank eagerly.

"Is this going to happen to the duke?" Worry creased Tenil's forehead.

She shook her head. "I don't think so. I had to do something powerful, something I couldn't practice. Cerith has been able to practice more and has taken to his element better than I have to mine. Collapsing the walls will take a toll, but he's got more strength and control than..."

Her voice trailed off as she met Enita's eyes. *You have no idea how important he is, do you?* She realized how appropriate the element of earth was here, in Kitarra, the birthplace of Enita's people. Here they had erected the standing stones and some still worshipped the Mother Goddess of the Earth. Nothing could have been more fortuitous for the marsh people than to have Cerith bind to the Kaskea and master the element of earth—and he mastered that element as if he'd been born for it. He *was* born for it. She sat up.

"We'll draw away forces to the docks." Tenil was pointing to the map and speaking to his men.

"No," she said. "They won't care about the docks."

"That's the plan," Tenil protested. "By whatever means possible, we pull men away to defend the eastern side."

"Their leader is smarter than that. I can't believe I haven't seen this before!" She hit her forehead with her palm. "They never extended their perimeter far beyond the walls because they don't *need* to waste their resources. They have been taunting us, not the other way around."

"So? If there are less troops than we thought, our plans will go all the better," Tenil said.

"This isn't about territory for them, but about control. This is about *Cerith*." She looked at Enita, whose eyes glittered back at her in the lamplight.

"The duke is well protected," Tenil protested.

"Not protected enough, if this is one big ambush. Whoever's running things in Suellestrin has been waiting for Cerith to enter the city—although having the northern walls collapse had to be an unpleasant surprise. They'll have their troops fold in behind ours because they *don't care* about protecting the city or its inhabitants. All they have to do is land the right arrow and everything is finished. There can be no Kitarran control of Suellestrin *without* the duke."

Cerith and most of the comhla were wearing armor. It wouldn't help against cannon fire, of course, which was why they attacked the northeastern gates where the cannons could only be aimed at ships out on the Mirror Sea. Powder weapons were scarce in Suellestrin, although one had already wounded Cerith. Armor couldn't withstand well-placed longbow arrows, either, but the comhla expected normal siege warfare, not hoards of assassins lying in wait for the duke.

Tenil's eyes hardened. "This calls for different tactics. I should be taking my men in behind the duke's force."

"Let's check his route." They went to the map and Tenil noted Cerith would be traveling streets that went between tall buildings. There would be many archers and only one target they cared about.

"We'll be late, even if we ride hard." Tenil pointed where they estimated Cerith to be, near the northeastern gates.

"Is there any way you can warn Cerith?" Enita asked Draius.

"Not directly, but I could dump water and hail on the town. He might realize something's wrong. But that much water would reduce visibility and damage bowstrings..." She cocked her head, thinking.

"Powder weapons don't work well in hard rain, either." Tenil caught the same thought. "Everyone would have to go hand-to-hand, which would be much safer for the duke." He exchanged glances with his assistant before turning back to her. "We'll ride hard for the gate. I'm hoping we can provide security behind the duke, but it'll be almost half an hour before we reach the walls. Do whatever you can, my lady."

She was taken aback by the faith she heard in his voice. They left, having to use a raft and pole around the marshy point before they joined their horses and guards.

Enita wrapped a blanket around her as she sat in front of the map, staring at the city streets. She pictured where the duke's men were, versus where the riots were planned and where Tenil's men would be. Then she invited the clouds to come, willed the water and hail to fall, and pulled at the grief in her soul. She wallowed in her pain, thinking about Lornis and Bordas and especially Peri, who was trying to get by without her in the sister cities. Tears fell unnoticed. Occasionally Enita wiped her face and Pearth gave her drinks of water.

Surely dawn had come and gone. Enita had massaged the cramps out of her neck and shoulders twice before a tremor ran through the shrine, this time strong enough to make the cups on the table rattle.

"He's safe. He wants me to stop," she mumbled. Pearth caught her as she fell out of her chair. He gently laid her on some blankets. Before her eyelids slammed shut, she saw through the opening of the shrine. Dawn had just begun.

Betarr Kain, Occupied Territory of Groyga

Initially, the ghosts wandering about Betarr Kain didn't bother Inica because they were just Tyrrans and *ebi corgo*. Famri insisted he shouldn't see ghosts of the *ebi corgo* because they had no souls and, as for the Tyrrans, what did he care about their afterlives? But now he was seeing a specter of *one of his own men*. A Groygan.

"Oh, no." Shalah stopped going over the next requisition order and followed his gaze down to the shadows behind the burned-out smithy. "Is that Algo?"

"I think so." Inica sighed.

"Maybe Surmagla sent him back?"

"I'm pretty sure when Surmagla lets someone return to the realm of the living, they get put back in their body. Besides, I can't imagine a god being impressed by someone dying of sepsis because they wouldn't clean a bite from an *ebi corgo*." His first mentor would say Algo "had more bone than brain in his head." Famri offered to execute the offending biter, even though it was one of her smarter creatures. Inica refused the offer, because he couldn't help feeling that Algo had it coming. The guard bullied and kicked the creature until it snapped and bit him, then paraded the bite around, ignoring recommendations to clean it.

"This doesn't bode well for our own afterlives, does it?" Shalah's voice was low.

"No, it doesn't." Algo's specter proved the lodestone had disrupted the Groygan afterlife as well as the Tyrran one. Groygan souls didn't need to find a path, so why did Algo look so lost? Inica got an uncomfortable notion his afterlife wasn't going to be much different from that of the godless. That begged the ultimate question of why they were invading and subjugating Tyrra. He remembered Lord Endigala's speech before the Council of Lords: *The time has come for Groyga to carry our gods forward and subjugate the godless; I will pit the soulless against the godless.* From where he stood, it seemed the *ebi corgo* did have souls and their own gods weren't taking care of business any better than the missing Phrenii. Staying away from that blasphemy, he asked, "In the twelve days since Famri changed, did you hear anything about ghosts?"

Recently arrived from Chikirmo, Shalah was a welcome reward from Lord Endigala. "Come to think of it, I caught one rumor, but paid no attention." She shrugged apologetically.

The easternmost cannon boomed, warning a Tyrran merchant away from the mouth of the Saamarin. The ship had turned up-river behind a Groygan ship. Since there was no longer the favorable wind for going up-river, both ships were under oars and going against the current. The shot went over the Tyrran ship's prow. Inica's artillery sergeant was well trained in ballistic angles.

Shalah watched as the Tyrran crew gave up and turned back. She had eagerly taken the offer to leave Taalo's workshop and come out to Betarr Kain, although her exuberance cooled once she saw the shape the city was in. Her comment was, "At least the walls and bastions are untouched."

"Report on yesterday's cleanup details." Inica started walking the ramparts, keeping his view toward the sea.

Shalah shuffled her notes. "They've finished searching the remains of all the buildings."

"Any more survivors?" As he expected, they found some infants and small children untouched by Famri's fire.

"We found another baby too late—it had been without water and its cries couldn't be heard." Shalah kept her eyes down. "That should be the last one, hopefully."

He hoped that as well. Digging children out of burned out ruins destroyed the morale of his guards. It also brought out the commonality between them and the enemy—not something you want to point out to warriors preparing for battle. "How many does that make?"

"We have fifteen children aged six and below, of which seven are infants. Then we have only four above the age of six. Famri wants them all to go."

"Of course she does. Too much temptation," he said softly.

"Honor?"

"Don't let her be around any of the children without supervision."

"Yes, honor."

He told Shalah to think of Famri as a spoiled child—one with frightening powers—suddenly thrust into an adult body. Add the fact she had been a unicorn, attracted to innocence, and Shalah got the idea immediately. "Send the young ones back to the estate and let the household raise them. They're still valuable for hostage exchange. We need to have some children inside the fortress to display occasionally, to keep the Tyrrans negotiating. Keep the four older ones here, but move them to different quarters and don't tell Famri."

She nodded.

He leaned over the parapet to contemplate the swirling mass of Tyrran and *ebi corgo* specters below. The bodies had been cleared and burned, but they remained. It was strange that Famri didn't see them, while everyone else could. Perhaps she was able to create blinders for her eyes and mind. Otherwise she'd become deranged, considering what she just did to people she had sworn to protect.

They climbed down from the walls and started toward the center of the town. Famri muttered as she passed them, walking faster. He and Shalah stepped to the side to let her go past. He never knew how to exchange pleasantries with the sorceress—*what a nice day, isn't it, and doesn't the smoke from those corpses look good in the morning light?* This time he didn't have to worry because she passed them by without a glance.

"I know you're working through Draius. Hiding behind her, hoping she'll quench my fires? Now the Minahmerans are involved. Did you call them? I'll watch what she's doing. Show yourself or suffer..." Her voice faded as she went up the hill.

"Did she say the name *Draius?*" Shalah asked.

"Yes, she did."

"Isn't that the spy that Taalo—"

"Yes." Inica rolled his eyes. "I hoped never to encounter that name again, but Famri's gotten into a tizzy about some sorcerer using the Kaskea bearers against her."

"The *what?*" When he waved away her question, she added, "Then this Draius is alive, perhaps still in Groyga?"

"Only according to Famri, who I suspect is going mad. I figure Draius is dead and even if she's not, she's none of my affair any more." Inica's tone was final.

Near the Village of Ruhallen, Northern Tyrra

Today Ihmar would be risking exposure to Famri, but the sooner he prepared what was left of the Phrenii, the better. Berina told him that morning that she'd done all she could with Draius. Their frequently targeted Kaskea bearer had been told multiple times about their plans, although the woman still seemed unsure about sharing her soul with Dahni.

"Ser, if you plow under two more rows to the east, we'll have enough bare soil," Ihmar said to Berina's father Arvo.

"No need to use 'ser' with me," the taciturn farmer said. "Especially when you're seeing so much of my daughter."

Uh-oh. Ihmar looked at the edge of the tilled soil where Berina helped Lyn and Askar unload mirrors from a wagon. "Arvo, I'm more than a hundred years older than her. We work well together, but there isn't anything—uh—romantic between us."

"What a shame," Arvo replied. He raised the plow's blades and shook the draft horse's traces, directing it toward the eastern side of the field.

All the mirrors were laid out according to Ihmar's direction. They formed two facing semi-circles, like clam shells. Then Ihmar went to the circle center and pushed two shortened shepherd hooks into the soft ground, set less than a pace apart. From those he hung the two necromantic mirrors, uncovered, each facing out toward a semi-circle. Using scrap wood blocks and squared logs from Arvo's woodshed, he carefully

set each large mirror upright and angled toward their respective necromantic mirror.

"What's he doing?" Arvo used a low voice, but Ihmar heard him.

"It's all about the geometry," Berina answered.

"I can see the mirrors all angle light toward the center, although they're
so much bigger than those middle ones, I don't understand the point."
Arvo sounded impatient.

"Well, elemental magic is called life-light because it behaves like regular light. It reflects off mirrors—ordinary ones, that is. Those center mirrors are actually necromantic. They absorb most of the light that hits
them so someone with the paired mirrors will see what's going on, but
they do reflect a bit of their death magic back."

"And the point of doing this is...?"

"First, we hope a reflected conduit will be more difficult for Famri to
sense. If she tries looking—it's technically called *scrying*—from the Void,
she'll get necromantic echoes which may confuse or even impair her.
She's still one of the Phrenii and they always avoided death magic. I know
this doesn't make sense to you now, Father, but it might later."

"If you say so." Arvo sounded both impressed and befuddled by his
daughter's knowledge.

Ihmar grinned. Lately, Berina had been absorbing information like
hard tack absorbed broth—he realized that they hadn't eaten a mid-day
meal. He double-checked the angles by looking straight down upon each
mirror. The benefit of this setup was that some life-light would hit the
necromantic mirrors, which might do something interesting to the mirror on the other end. Looking around, he verified positions for the last
time.

"Everyone but Berina should get to the edge of the plowed dirt," he
ordered.

"Perhaps you should stay with me." Arvo tried to catch Berina's arm,
but she evaded him.

"I'm his apprentice, Father," she said firmly. "I must assist him—don't worry, we've made this as safe as possible."

Ihmar decided to do this through four individual spells, hopefully making his draw upon the Void small and imperceptible. Berina had been correct when talking to her father. When Ihmar apprenticed, he was tasked with drawing reflected life-light for years to make him completely comfortable with it. He still did exercises to keep it feeling natural.

Mahri would be first, since Perinon's shard of the Kaskea was physically close to him and he'd met the bearer. This would take little power, but was tricky because Mahri's element was *spirit*—the focus would be more abstract than holding a rock, for instance. This required Berina to step into the center, between the necromantic mirrors, and hold his hand. She still believed in the Phrenii and more importantly, she believed in her king and his ability to invoke spirit in his people. Arvo yelped as she took Ihmar's hand, but he ignored it as he picked a polished steel mirror and opened a conduit. He located the Kaskea shard, which held much of its element, and called all spirit from the Void. Golden, almost white light surrounded them while he reminded the element that it was named *Mahri* and commanded it to hide within the shard until it had a soul to anchor itself. The light faded. He tied off the modest conduit and shielded his mind.

Berina brought a bucket of water into the circle and left to stand outside it. They were careful to have no more than one elemental focus within the circle whenever Ihmar opened a conduit. He plunged his hand into the water. Dahni was easier to call, perhaps because most of the element already hid within Draius's Kaskea shard.

When the green light faded, Berina took the bucket and dried his hand. Then she placed a rock in his hand, one he was familiar with, having practiced with it. Cerith Ungought, the Duke of Whythern, was easy to find because he had been using the element earth rather significantly since midnight, but the element had quieted several hours ago. As copper light surrounded Ihmar, he found the element almost exclusively residing within the Kaskea shard. He merely prepared Sahvi for an anchor, hoping it would come from Cerith.

"Now it is going to get difficult." He took a deep breath as he tossed the rock outside the circle. Berina locked gazes with him and nodded. While she could now feel conduits to the Void, she couldn't yet create one and help him. Unfortunately, he couldn't create wind as a focus from the air about him, because that would divert Jhari from hiding in Naton's shard. He had to call wind—air—Jhari from the Void and use the called element as a focus at the same time. Bracing himself, he opened two conduits at once by extending his hands toward mirrors on either side—lining them up nicely with the necromantic mirrors. He knew Naton's location from Lyn and thus, where the shard should be. Naton's mind was incoherent; luckily, he needn't deal with the man, only the unreasoning element—the element that was the most difficult to control.

When he called air from the Void, it came willingly and whirled around him, whipping up dust and dirt. Concentrating in the midst of the blue light and whirlwind was difficult and he was grateful for all those "meaningless" control and meditation exercises his mentor made him practice. While his eyes were closed against the dust, with specks of dirt hitting his face and his clothes flapping about him, he was able to enunciate the sorcerous language of the spell and concentrate upon it. He reminded Jhari of its name and commanded the element to hide in the Kaskea.

Suddenly the conduit was cut and *not by him*. Since it wasn't tied off correctly, residuals of elemental magic sparked off the dust still flying about him. "Run!" he yelled.

Berina turned and started toward the wagons where all the observers waited. He felt a slight shock as he broke through the spell circle. Quickly catching up to Berina, he scooped her easily up and ran with her in his arms. His people were stronger than the humankind and she didn't weigh much. As he ran, he concentrated on shielding their minds.

He was close to the wagons when he was knocked to his knees. Berina rolled out of his arms and started crawling under the wagon. He followed.

Looking back, they saw a pillar of fire raining down flames through the haze that kept out sunlight. Counting off the seconds, he figured the pillar kept roaring for almost half a minute. Famri was displaying her stamina and the depth of her power.

When the fire stopped, he saw all the mirrors were melted, even the expensive glass ones. Having Arvo plow up a field of wheat stubble had been an important precaution. Ihmar rubbed his head and realized the hair on the back of his head had melted. He shucked his smoking cloak.

Lyn bent down from the protected side of the wagon and looked them over. "You both all right?" After they nodded, she asked, "Were you able to finish your spells?"

"I was interrupted toward the end, so Jhari might still be a problem. Mahri can't do anything until Perinon wakes. Dahni and Sahvi are ready, so now it is up to Draius and Cerith."

"Let's pray this works and that only two of the Phrenii can help those poor souls." Lyn motioned toward the forest growing at the edge of Arvo's pastures. In the shadows of those trees, the dead had undoubtedly watched Ihmar as well.

CHAPTER TWENTY-FOUR

Remade From Starlight

Northern Moors, Kitarra

The shard's light woke Draius. It had come loose from her clothing and lay on the blanket under her chin. She squinted as the green pulse lit the overhead tarp and tumbled walls. It faded and daylight seeped in. Last night she thought a structure protected her, but now she realized she was just bivouacking. Through an opening, which was just a hole in a crumbled wall, she heard Enita and Pearth quietly talking.

"What time is it?" she called.

"Just past mid-day, we think. There's no sun or shadows." Enita came under the tarp.

Pearth handed her a cup of water and a hard roll. As she softened the bread with water and gnawed on it, more than her stomach felt empty. All the grief that poured out of her in those dark hours before dawn had left her hollow. She attained a sort of peace, but it was fragile and could crack.

"We just had a messenger from Suel. They secured Ungought Hall and most of the city. They think they captured the Groygan leadership. The duke calls for us and he requests dry clothes." Enita's voice held a note of satisfaction.

Draius smiled. "Did the Sight tell you to bring along so many of his belongings?"

"No, practical forethought." They chuckled, relieved by the message, not the dry clothes.

As the last people to leave the forward post, they had the duty to pack up and ensure the ancient shrine was left pristine. Draius and Pearth rolled up the heavy oilskin tarps and hauled them across the causeway to their horses and pack animals.

"You sure they'll be able to pack everything out?" She doubtfully viewed the three donkeys, seeming rather diminutive next to Chisel.

"They brought everything here. Divide the weight evenly among the three." Enita huffed as she lugged over the kit bag of codebooks, building plans, maps, compasses, spyglasses, and other tools necessary for tracking one's infiltrators.

As she strapped it down, Draius surveyed the two hills to the north. One sat to each side of their path. "Did anyone report back on the wave I pushed into the fishing flats last night?"

"Oh, yes. The messenger said it was effective." Enita nodded energetically.

"How effective?" She glanced at Pearth, who nodded as well.

"Very effective, my lady," he parroted.

Suddenly suspicious, she untied the flap and fished around in the pack of tools. Pulling out a thick spyglass with a good lens, she walked toward the hill nearest the Mirror Sea. "Maybe I should see for myself."

"That's not necessary," Enita called after her and Pearth bleated, "No need, my lady."

No ground fog existed this afternoon, only overcast skies. When she got to the top of the hill, she extended the spyglass and peered at the fishing flats. She suspected they were brushing aside her fruitless effort—what she saw took her breath away. What first appeared to be smashed piles of kindling were the remains of fishing boats, docks, and huts. They washed inland and stopped against the rocky cliffs rising up around the

Saamarin. Most of the cannons suffered nearly the same fate, but hadn't been pushed as far. They sat deep in mud and stuck out at odd angles, their bores plugged with muddy debris. Their carriages were splintered or buried; the force of the water and mud had twisted off most of the wheels. She focused in on movement; people dug out bodies and laid them out in a higher area to the east. There were rows and rows of them. *Very effective, indeed.*

By the time Pearth reached her—to be fair, his lung was healing from a puncture—she was sitting on the ground with her elbows braced on her knees and her face covered by her hands. The spyglass lay beside her. Pearth picked it up gently.

"Please tell me the local fishermen had fair warning." Her hands muffled her voice.

"I cannot, my lady. If they fled the flats, the Groygans would know we moved on the city. They—even you, my lady—couldn't have anticipated what your magic would do."

She lifted her head. "When you say 'they,' you mean the duke and Suel and..." She hadn't been introduced to the comhla commander by name. Her breath trailed away into a sob.

"I assume so." He sat down beside her. "You dealt an irrevocable blow to Endigala's artillery. Otherwise, those cannon would now be firing on the city and its docks. We would have to use Suellestrin's fixed cannon in return. There would have been great loss of life, regardless."

They sat for a while until she realized this didn't help anything but the moisture seeping through the seat of her britches. "We'd better get to Suellestrin." She got up and Pearth followed, more slowly.

They couldn't ride side by side because the trail was narrow. It first wound north and the branch they needed to take to Suellestrin was impossible for her to spot. Enita, however, knew where to scoot between two bogs edged with switch-brush.

Behind each horse trailed a donkey on a lead. The animals had to push through the thin, woody blades of the switch-brush and Draius stopped, once on the road to Suellestrin, to check them. The donkeys had bleeding gashes on their bellies and legs, while the horses only suffered cuts on their legs. She took the time to heal them, because they never hesitated to do their duty.

Once Enita could ride beside her, the old woman started telling stories that usually featured some feckless Kitarran noble doing something foolish. Draius eventually started laughing and challenging Enita to *prove* each story was real. However, their good humor dampened when the walls of Suellestrin came into view.

"What a mess," Pearth muttered.

Draius nodded, feeling guilty again. Cerith had done damage by collapsing the entire northern wall of the city, but her pounding rain and hail had been widespread. Many slate roofs in the town had disintegrated, creating piles of broken shingles in the streets. They let the horses pick their way through piles of refuse that had lodged in the strangest places. Surprisingly, townspeople worked on repairs and everyone appeared in decent humor, or as good as they could be when recovering from a flood and a battle in their streets. As opposed to the first time she went through Suellestrin, tied up in a wagon, the skies were clear and the city was washed clean of its brooding and sullen manner.

The horses took their time to test the depth of puddles and find ways around debris, so it was late in the day before they came to Ungought Hall, where King Markus had resided. The king's residence was built into the wall that went around a huge block of gardens, buildings, and support facilities. Suel waited on the steps, his arm bandaged and in a sling. He looked like he went swimming in his clothes and let them dry on his back.

"Do I need to look at your arm?" Draius asked as she dismounted.

"I'm fine," Suel said.

"Cerith?" Enita asked sharply.

"The duke has hardly a scratch." Suel's eyes dropped. "We took heavy losses until the rain came. Then their bows became useless and we could spread out and do our work." He nodded at Draius.

"Did Tenil make it?" She worried about Roumithea, waiting back at Bryn Celar.

"He took a slight wound to his leg, but he got through and told us why you changed plans." Suel's voice was gruff. "You were right—we didn't expect to use everyone as shields for the duke. I don't think he expected it either, to take such losses merely for his protection."

"Better take me to the wounded, then." Her heart was heavy.

"No, the duke needs you inside. It's too late for anyone who suffered deadly wounds last night and our physicians are handling the rest." Suel motioned for Pearth to take the horses. He started walking up the stairs; she and Enita followed.

"We're now dealing with the Kitarran nobility," Suel said in an undertone as she moved to walk beside him into an atrium. "Some have supported the duke, but aren't yet willing to be public with their support. Then there are Tintia and her *missing* children."

"What?"

There was not time for discussion. They stood at large double doors and Suel threw one open with his free arm. She followed him through the door, with Enita behind her. At first glance, the babble and smells and crowd were chaotic but after drawing a breath, she could make sense of everything. The room smelled like wet wool, wet leather, and other scents best left unnamed. Tracks of mud crisscrossed all over the polished stone floor. To one side, with their arms bound behind them, kneeled Groygan prisoners. She recognized the guards watching them, all in the livery of the King's Comhla. Knots of people carried on intense conversations. They appeared to be Tyrran-descended Kitarrans and by the quality of their clothes, nobility or wealthy merchants.

"Attention!" Suel bellowed, cutting through the chatter. "Announcing Serasa-Kolme Draius, cousin to the King of Tyrra, Commander in the Tyrran King's Guard, and holding honorary rank of Lieutenant Colonel in the Kitarran King's Comhla."

She didn't even know Suel knew her full name, let alone how to pronounce it. Her mouth dropped as the room hushed and everyone turned to look at her. Enita gave her a push from behind. She took a tentative step and Suel nodded. The Kitarrans parted for her so she headed straight forward, where Cerith's head was visible above the crowd.

When the tableau at the dais emerged, she paused. On the slab of raised stone was a chair, ornate enough to be a throne. Tintia sat in it, but it was not the same Tintia she had seen at Cerith's ball. This woman looked old and haggard, but more than that, she had no life or soul in her face. Her light blue eyes were empty of reason, chilling Draius. Her red hair was artfully arranged, obviously done by the lady's maid who stood respectfully behind the throne. However, Tintia was blind and deaf to everyone in the room.

Cerith and Medrew Ungought faced each other. Draius remembered Medrew from Cerith's ball, as well as from his briefings on Kitarran politics. Medrew was now the only other living male over the age of twenty who carried the Ungought name, albeit he was a distant cousin and didn't have a title—probably why Markus let him live. Medrew had supported Cerith surreptitiously when it came to ousting Groygan influence, but Cerith suspected Medrew had aspirations of his own. By the angry expressions Draius saw when they both turned toward her, Medrew was already making trouble.

Medrew was of medium height and build, but by his stance and movement he had some of the same physical grace as Cerith. There the resemblance ended. He had the ruddy complexion of a Kitarran, with none of the Meran coloring or delicate bone structure Cerith displayed. Medrew was handsome, in his own way, with a slightly crooked nose. Perhaps he broke it in his childhood.

"Since when has the comhla recruited Tyrran beauties?" Medrew exclaimed. His clothes were crumpled and splashed with mud, but he ignored this as he smiled and extended a hand toward her.

Cerith, however, coming from battle and still wearing some of his chest and thigh armor, looked impeccable. His armor and boots were clean of mud and his dark blue cloak draped smoothly down his back. He didn't seem sodden or crumpled or even tired, although he couldn't have slept for at least a day. He also extended a hand toward her.

"Since I reinstated the *King's* Comhla," he answered.

Without hesitation, she stepped forward and took Cerith's hand. She sensed everything with a jolt as their ungloved hands touched: Cerith's facade was strong as stone, but he was operating under bone-crushing fatigue and grief. The weight of the armor and injuries, the weight of seeing so many of his supporters and comrades die—she wouldn't have been able to bear it. She went down on one knee and bent her head to hide the shocked sympathy on her face.

As the universal symbol of fealty, this rated high with the Kitarran nobility. There were gasps behind her. After all, the Kitarrans thought she was "royalty," since she was Perinon's cousin. Cerith's grip tightened, perhaps thanking her for the gesture. Then he pulled her back to her feet with surprising strength. He guided her to stand beside him and then offered his hand toward Enita. Soft muttering started.

"Welcome to Ungought Hall, Mistress Enita," Cerith said. "With my return, I've rescinded the ban upon certain marsh people. Anyone with markings may freely enter the city."

"Thank you, your grace." Enita held her head high and took the Cerith's hand, then curtsied. Draius realized no other marsh people were present. This might have been the first time in years, perhaps ever, that a wise woman of the marsh had been received in Ungought Hall. Cerith was breaking precedent and many Kitarrans, including Medrew, were scowling. The mutterings rose to full voice and people began to cluster again into private conversations.

"If you think support from local savages and foreigners is going to help you, you're mistaken," Medrew said to Cerith.

"The Crown might rightly pass to Markus's son," said Gwerth, a Kitarran who held the title of count.

"If so, where are the children?" Cerith asked.

Medrew shook his head. "No one's seen them since Markus's death."

"And she's oblivious to our questions." Gwerth motioned to Tintia.

"Who's been serving her? Why didn't they notice this malaise?" Cerith was angry. She glanced around, noting the supports were stone pillars. Cerith could easily kill them if he lost control.

"Nettona and his men kept us away from her and the children." Medrew pointed toward the prisoners. Several other nobles mumbled agreement.

"The regular servants weren't allowed to attend her. We're not sure who was serving her." A noblewoman had joined their cluster and finally answered Cerith's question. "I had to summon my own lady's maid for this afternoon, your grace."

Enita put a hand on his arm. "Draius might heal her."

Cerith cocked his head at her and she shrugged. She didn't know if Phrenic magic could heal mental problems. Stepping up on the dais, she bowed and when she got no response, approached the young queen. Tintia's light blue eyes didn't turn toward her or even flicker. Putting out her hand to touch Tintia's hand, she recoiled with familiar nausea. *Necromancy*, but it seemed tied to something else... She stepped back, noting Cerith moved farther away as well. Everyone became quiet as they noticed the activity on the dais. There was nothing about Tintia's neck but the gown and her necklace, which appeared to be made of gold. Of course, the charm could be hidden like Lord Chintegrata's. The tie she sensed to something else in the room disturbed her. She remembered seeing Nettona reach inside his doublet at the ball and King Markus spewing anger and spittle at Cerith.

Thinking she'd better find the controlling charm first, she asked, "Who's been running this place?"

Cerith's mouth twitched in amusement and he turned to Medrew, his eyebrows raised.

"Uh, well, the Groygans." Medrew's face colored. "Vitna Be Nettona started out as the king's counselor, then more Groygans arrived, and then Markus died in that fire—well, it all just happened, didn't it, like a runaway carriage! We couldn't do anything about it."

"I suppose not. Just like you allowed my uncle and his Groygans to persecute me like a common criminal?" Cerith's tone was acerbic.

Medrew flushed even more. "Come now, Cerith, it all washed out right in the end."

"At the cost of many men who were worth *your* weight in gold, cousin. I'll never forgive, or forget, that." Cerith's voice was low and vicious like a whip. Medrew went white and Draius sensed a tremor of anger in the stones beneath her feet.

"I don't think Nettona commands the Groygans, your grace." She diverted Cerith. "Nettona is a political appointee and we've been up against a military mind."

"You can ask Nettona yourself." Cerith nodded toward the bound Groygans.

She walked down the line of prisoners, keeping her distance because a few spat at her. Some muttered "Tyrran bitch" as she went by. Cerith walked behind her, as she looked each of them in the face. Most wore the black and crimson of House Endigala. Behind the row of kneeling Groygans, Suel kept abreast of her and indicated Nettona, in the solid black of the Council of Lords.

"They're incensed by you, my dear Draius." Cerith seemed amused by their antagonism, but she wondered how long he could keep up his facade under the exhaustion.

"This is not the commander of Lord Endigala's men." She let disdain drip from her voice as she paused in front of Vitna. His yellow eyes glared at her. Sweat ran down his face and he stank of fear, but not necromancy.

Two prisoners past Vitna, she paused again. This hardened soldier stared back at her without emotion. He also was dressed in solid black and sported a gash and bruises on the side of his face.

"Be careful." Cerith spoke into her left ear. "I'm ashamed to say Suel and I took this one down by surprising him from behind. He's the one who wounded Suel."

"Hmm." She made a dismissive gesture and watched the man's eyes narrow a little. She paced to the end of the row, just to be sure the aura of necromancy emanated from him. Then she came back to stand in front of him. Cerith patiently stood behind her, while Suel stood ready behind the prisoner.

She turned to murmur under her breath to Cerith. "Can you *sense* the necromancy? On him, it's much fainter—I think he's got the controlling charm."

"Does necromancy feel like nausea?"

She nodded, hoping Cerith was learning to sniff out the charms as well. Turning back to Suel, she asked, "His name?"

"The nobles say his given name is Renca."

"Honor Renca," she said abruptly and was rewarded by a slight jerk of the man's head. "What's your rank? Lord Endigala wouldn't trust this city to just anyone. You must be a First or Second Honored Sword."

Renca gazed back at her calmly and she was right: this was the most dangerous Groygan in the room. He was the one who had controlled Suellestrin. He might have kept the city if he'd managed to kill Cerith.

"This is their military mind?" Cerith's voice was tight.

Suel grabbed the back of Renca's shirt to pull him up on his knees. When Suel did that, Renca's mail shirt and leather under shirt pulled away from his neck, exposing a silk cord. His charm didn't need to be obscured like Tintia's. She ignored Cerith's question, pulling her knife out and stepped toward Renca. Cerith made no move to stop her and Suel held Renca in place.

"Well, what do we have here?" she asked softly. This time, she wasn't going to let her hands be burned. Her knife slid down Renca's throat to slip under the cord. She could feel the vile thing through the knife. She lifted her blade and a little sack came out from under his shirt. Even the stitching was familiar.

She worked to still her nausea. "I see that *nunetton* Taalo now has world-wide distribution." She flicked her knife and cut the cord. The sack landed in front of Cerith, who backed away from it. Tintia screamed. She came pushing through the crowd toward the prisoners. Gwerth, Medrew, and the chamberlain followed her. Still screaming, she flew at Renca, but Medrew and the chamberlain caught hold of her. She fought them, twisting and screaming fragments of sentences, trying to get at the Groygan.

"They're gone—you didn't let me—you made me—bury them!" Tintia collapsed into Medrew's arms, sobbing hysterically, while he seemed bewildered. Draius, though, suddenly understood whom Tintia meant: *her children*. The nausea came back, but for different reasons. Holding her blade for slashing, she turned back to Renca while the hall exploded in babble.

Renca eyed her blade and pushed backward against Suel. "She poisoned them herself. I only stopped her from following them to Surmagla." His eyes met hers and she knew he spoke the truth. He used a normal tone and, with all that chaos, only she and Suel could have heard him. She nodded at Suel, who shoved Renca back down in a sitting position.

Turning, she saw Gwerth reaching for Renca's charm and she shouted, "Make sure your skin doesn't touch it. After we find the one on her, they have to be burned."

The charm about Tintia's neck had become visible, perhaps because it was no longer being controlled. Draius carefully cut it off, but it brought no relief to the poor woman. Now that her grief could be released, she had to be carried away with the help of the lady's maid, chamberlain, and several sympathetic nobles. Gwerth trotted away, holding the charms gingerly by their cords with gloved hands. Renca started laughing. Enita tugged on Draius's arm. She was in a madhouse.

"He needs you." Enita pointed toward the end of the hall past the dais. Cerith was leaving. Even at that distance, she sensed his control cracking.

"What can I do for him?"

The old woman gazed back at her solemnly, her dark eyes glittering. "You have to *make things right.*"

Suellestrin, Kitarra

Draius stood motionless for a while—she didn't know how long. She was exhausted, but she recognized the look in Enita's eyes. Her Sight spoke, not her. The babel in the hall faded as dream after dream flitted through her mind. *Make things right.* She suddenly remembered what the girl repeated over and over. She had a decision, a personal one, to make about Dahni.

She slowly walked away from the chaos and took the stairs that Cerith had climbed. If anyone called to her, she didn't hear them. Soon she was lost. Whoever designed the stairways and corridors of Ungought Hall must have been a maniac. When given the choice, she turned away from the burned wing that had housed the royal family; she doubted Cerith would have gone there. Near the end of what seemed like a third-floor passageway, she peeked around the corner. An offshoot corridor accessed several rooms and she saw Tenil speaking to two guards in comhla livery. She approached quietly.

"He's going to be fine and, yes, he *does* want to be alone," Tenil said as he leaned on one crutch. "You go get some rest and I'll attend him." He noted her presence and added, "My lady Draius! Do you need anything?" The guards gave her a curious look as they passed, but Tenil's greeting and her comhla uniform gave her permission to be here.

"I thought you had a minor wound. Why are you using a crutch?" She extended her hand and waved it over his thigh, her fingers blurring with green light.

"It's just a little support—" Tenil gasped and put more weight on the leg. Then he stood normally and observed the crutch thoughtfully as he twirled it. "You shouldn't waste your healing on me, when there are other wounded who need it more."

"Blasted things!" Cerith's voice came through the closed door behind them.

"I'm on a mission from Enita. She's seen something..." She gazed meaningfully at Tenil. "I need to speak with him."

"He *really* doesn't want anyone in there, so your choice of funeral." Tenil motioned at the door. She took a deep breath and opened it to an opulent bedchamber. Cerith whirled about, his cloak on the floor and his fingers caught in the buckled straps holding on his breastplate. His facade had dissolved; anger, pain, and anguish mixed on his face.

"Relax, it's only me." She closed the door behind her. "You can't take your armor off by yourself." She didn't suggest calling for a valet or whatever they called them here. He didn't want anyone seeing him in this state. Helping him remove the breastplate, she noted Suel's assessment of "hardly a scratch" was an understatement. Cerith's torso had been bleeding from a blow pushing the armor and muslin undershirt into his side. She cautiously tugged at the dried bloody fabric and he winced.

"What were those—those things you called charms?" He kept his eyes averted.

Down in the hall he had played along, but he couldn't know the history that Tyrra hid for so long. As quickly as possible, she explained necromancy. It was an evil art invented by the sorcerer Nherissa more than 500 years ago. He used pain and torture and death to bind power into inanimate objects called charms. Tyrra tried to suppress all knowledge of this art for eras, but it was rediscovered. That was how she ended up bound to the Phrenii.

While she wove her story, her fingers flitted over his side, pushing away the pain and separating the shirt from the flesh. "Necromancy is anathema to elemental magic—what we also call *life-light*—which is why you and I react so badly. The Phrenii told me it could drain the Void of life-light. They feared the lodestone specifically because its spell would unmake them." The shirt came loose from the skin, which now looked pink and healed. She brushed off the flakes of dried blood.

"Where is this lodestone now?" He didn't seem to notice, diverted by her story. He sat on a settee and started pulling off his boots.

"It *was* on a ship scuttled by pirates. We found the pirate responsible and he assured us that it was at the bottom of the Angim."

"You don't believe that any more. In the cavern of the dead, you mentioned this lodestone and said something was your fault."

She grimaced, wishing he hadn't remembered that. "That *nunetton* necromancer, named Taalo, must have dredged it up again. You know, I was the one who let him escape. Not just once, but *twice*." Her tone was bitter. "I suspected he had seen the same thing I did in the Blindness—a distinctive shoreline where the ship washed up. My mistake was withholding that information from my king, hoping to protect everyone, but it has all come to ruin. The lodestone destroyed the Phrenii, and now I'm supposed to *make things right?*"

His eyebrows furrowed. "You just raised more questions than you answered. Can we postpone all this talk of lodestones, blindnesses, and ruination for later?"

This can't be put off by either of us, unfortunately. She ignored him and walked over to double doors with small panes of glass and opened them. If she could change any of the bad decisions she made… But she couldn't. *Make things right,* Enita said. The girl in the dreams said the same thing, but how could sharing her soul with Dahni actually work? When examining her memories, she noted the girl gave her no assurances.

Walking out into the surprisingly mild night air, she viewed the lights of Suellestrin from a third-floor balcony. Looking up, she was startled by the stars in the night sky.

"It's unusual to see the stars so clearly here." Cerith's voice was quiet. He padded across the balcony in his bare feet like a barog cat. Standing beside her, he started to caress the stone balustrade.

"Strange weather, when winter's coming," she said awkwardly, wondering how to ask about his dreams. Had he also seen the girl in them? He was in control again, almost his old self, but something was different.

"You can't take blame for the woes of the entire mapped world, just because one criminal escaped you." His hand traced patterns upon the stone, as if he touched flesh.

"And you can't blame yourself for all the lives spent to get you here. They were given willingly."

"That's cold comfort." His hand stopped. He flattened it on the balustrade and sighed. "Suellestrin is finally mine, but I didn't want it by the deaths of Tintia's son nor at the cost of so many of my friends. They shielded me with their horses and their bodies."

The agony in his voice pulled her to him. Even gone, the Phrenii still made her averse to bloodshed. He must have suffered tremendously when fighting in the streets. Without realizing it, she was holding him. At first he clung to her, but after a few moments he collected himself.

"This is compromising, my dear Draius," he whispered, sounding much like the Cerith she first met.

She pushed herself away. His face was in shadow and the starlight glinted off his hair. There was still something different about him, as if there was no barriers left between them.

"Why did you ask me to marry you, when you knew I carried another man's child?" She went on the offensive.

He turned his face toward the lamp-lit room. "It was the gentlemanly thing to do."

"That's not the entire truth."

"Blasted Kaskea." His tone was mild, but he backed away. "I told you I had limited options because I was balancing support for the nobles, the honest working people of this city, and the marsh people. You didn't come with problematic alliances and you were unique. But now I'm considering a lifetime with a creature that lets me see into the hearts of others. That changes things."

"You've had the same dreams." She closed the distance between them.

"Yes, the Tyrran girl told me everything, although I didn't respond. I can feel Sahvi waiting for my commitment. She's very patient. But I'm still trying to deal with the ramifications: I will live a longer but more lonely life, with no human confidante or companion beside me."

"Being bound to the Phrenii doesn't mean that you or I can't have a loving companion—"

"Are you sure? You didn't commit to Lornis before you left Tyrra. Why not?"

That hurt, the more so because she had to answer with the truth. *Blasted Kaskea.* "We were intensely attracted to each other and I trusted him with my life, but something felt wrong. Maybe it was a bit of Phrenic prescience or I was worried about marrying again. I doubt I'll ever know why I hesitated. I admit that I've only had two..." She looked down at her hands as she intertwined her fingers.

"Marriages?"

"No, two men."

"Oh." He tried to hide his surprise, but the Kaskea shard and fatigue bared his emotions.

"One of them was picked for me, so I don't have much experience in recognizing lifelong mates." She reached up and fingered a lock of his hair. "If I told you I *wanted* to accept your proposal, what would you say?"

"You shouldn't push me when I'm exhausted. I might spout nonsense." His eyes were uncertain, something she didn't expect. There was also something darker in them: primitive and elemental.

Her body tensed. "Nonsense like *I need you,* or *I love*—"

He kissed her. At first his lips were on hers lightly, tasting her. She reached up and spread her fingers into his hair. She pulled his head down tighter and he opened his mouth for her, letting her explore and taste him. He made an inarticulate sound in his throat. Pulling her tight, he turned and pushed her back against the wall. She kept forgetting how strong he was—yet she responded in kind, almost ferociously, her need spreading from her chest and downward. The need was painful, aching, all over her body.

Then he shoved her away. It felt like someone ripped away a part of her body and she groaned. Her heart pounded and her body flushed with heat. She unbuckled the top of her comhla uniform, which exposed the Kaskea shard. It blinded her with pulsing green light.

"Now you're bribing me with a marriage of convenience and curse me with Darkness, I'm considering it." Cerith leaned on the balustrade, his bruised and scraped hands clenching, digging at the stone. When he turned toward her, an answering copper light pulsed under his shirt and splashed up on his face when he moved. "In Kitarra, marriage is for life, the same commitment being asked of us by the Phrenii. We can already read each other's emotions—do you really think we can stand a lifetime together, when you don't even love me?"

"But I do. I learned that last night as I sat helpless, praying you would survive." She wanted to say so much more, but he would know if she spoke the truth and whether it came from her heart. She stepped close. "I had to trust you before I could love you. Trust and love go hand in hand."

"Ah, but I loved you the moment I first met you. That was *long* before I ever trusted you." His fingers stroked down the side of her face, jaw, and neck. "It seems we took different paths but we arrived at the same point."

She caught his hand and looked at the intertwining trails of green and copper fire that wound about the two of them. "Sahvi is waiting." Her voice didn't sound totally her own; another female voice echoed hers. "Will you bind to us for life?"

"I will." There were echoes of Dahni in his voice. "Will you do the same?"

"Yes." She added the most serious oath she could. "On my honor."

Copper and green light flared all around them. Then it was gone, leaving only the pulsing glow of their Kaskea shards. She began to be aware of noise below as people streamed outside and stood on the street, pointing and calling. They stopped kissing. All around the city and surrounding countryside, globes of light floated upward. The higher they rose, the more transparent they became. Eventually, they disappeared against the blanket of stars above. They often drifted up in clumps.

"Bryn Celar." Cerith pointed to a group of tiny lights rising on the horizon.

"Bordas and the others. They've found the path."

"Freed, thanks to Dahni and Sahvi."

"Some credit should go to us and the girl who kept invading our dreams." She turned back to him.

He was looking her over head to toe, thickening waist and all. "You're so beautiful."

"If you like long and lanky, then I'm your girl."

"Yes, you are mine." He trailed his lips down her neck while he undid the rest of the buckles on her doublet. She wanted to stroke his chest and, frustrated, ripped his shirt open rather than taking it off over his head. No longer covered, each of their Kaskea shards washed the other with color.

"We're lit up for all the city to see." He pulled her tight against him, bare skin touching, quenching some of the light. His eyes filled with copper flecks. Whether they were his eyes, or Sahvi's, she didn't care. She wanted to seep into his stillness and surround the deepness, making his strength hers. *Water and earth seek each other* came the thought, but she wasn't sure from whom.

"Does it matter who sees us?" Draius/Dahni asked.

"We really should go inside," Cerith/Sahvi said.

She put her arms about his neck and he swept up her legs to carry her through the doors.

Betarr Kain, Occupied Territory of Groyga

Inica was woken by an alarm. "Honor, the Saamarin flooded!"

The midnight watch commander decided to roust everyone. As Inica jogged to the ferry landing with the sergeant, he learned more. "The landing's covered with bodies and debris. We're trying to see if the pier is damaged. It'll take days to clean up."

At approximately three hours past midnight, a wave of water pushed out of the mouth of the Saamarin. It carried wood, bodies, household items, and the flotsam of what might have been fisherman vessels. The debris had slammed into the cliffs that lined the river as it increased speed, so its components were barely recognizable when it floated out into the bay. The guards at the ferry said the water rose above the pier before it settled down to its normal height. That left mud, bodies, and random detritus on the landing. Some of the pier supports leaned, possibly weakened.

Inica scratched his head. He had heard of violent flash floods, but they usually happened in mountainous areas where there was a steep incline. Granted, the Saamarin had cliffs on each side, which could add to any flood condition.

"Honor, these are our people." Shalah called him over to examine a tattered crimson and black uniform that managed to stay with its battered owner. She pointed to an embroidered symbol. "They're artillery."

Inica stared at what looked like an axle from the carriage under a cannon. This all came from Kitarra. He sucked his teeth contemplatively, and then called over the sergeant. "Separate the bodies into House Endigala, other houses, and non-Groygan piles. Pile the trash separately and we can use it for fuel when it dries. I'll send two details from the fortress to help. Get the landing useable by tomorrow."

"Yes, honor."

He would send a message to Lord Endigala after the sun rose and he could make a better assessment. Back at the fortress, a scout from eastern Tyrra arrived. After he gave his report, Inica told Shalah to assemble the group sergeants and Famri for a meeting in the hall of records.

"Our scout says possibly five companies of cavalry and ten companies of infantry are arriving in Plains End, based upon preparations," Inica said.

At the table with him sat Famri, Shalah, and four group sergeants. The Groygans appeared dismayed while Famri stayed motionless. Recently, she seemed preoccupied—at least, whenever she deigned to meet with them. Otherwise, he wasn't sure where she was and what she was doing.

"Their cavalry is a problem," Shalah said.

Inica glanced at Famri. She shrugged. "The *ebi corgo* have an innate fear of horses, buried deep in their instincts. They are only worthy opponents for soldiers on the ground."

"More *ebi corgo* and reinforcements will be coming across the river, whenever the ferry starts running," Shalah said. His sergeants looked glum. Groyga couldn't provide the sorts of horses and horsemen needed to deal with the Tyrran cavalry.

"They can't take back this fortress with cavalry," Inica said sharply, wondering if he should knock some sense into their heads. "We just need to *hold* Betarr Kain and keep the King's Guard busy through this erin, which is why I haven't requested more than two companies of our own cavalry for sorties. There are some logistical issues now because of the flood at the landing, but that can't be helped."

He stopped at the sound of feet running past their room and shouts outside. Through the window, it still appeared to be an hour or two before dawn. The sky was clear and the starlight strong. A flash of copper light washed the burned-out buildings across the street. Something cracked and echoed, but not a cannon—the sudden deep sound penetrated his chest. Everyone stood and they all grabbed for the table as the building's foundations shook.

"No!" Famri screamed. She left the room. He followed, saw her open the main door to the building and jump back, dodging a falling stone and snarling inarticulate curses.

Everything went still. He exchanged puzzled glances with Shalah.

"In the plaza," came the shouts.

He and his guards ran for the central plaza where the marketplace of Betarr Kain had been held. Standing on the steps to the town hall stood a unicorn. It appeared to glow, being the pure white of starlight but casting a copper light back on the stone walls of the hall.

"That's Sahvi." Shalah stood beside him and used a low murmur that only he could hear. "Earth and influence. More than strong enough to counter fire."

"Get the children." When her eyebrows rose, he added, "They're the only beings in this city that Sahvi values and we may need to bargain for our lives."

She ran for the rooms where the four Tyrran children were kept.

"Should we shoot it, Honor?" asked one of his sergeants.

Inica gave the man a wilting glance. "If Famri hasn't dealt with it, why do you think we can?"

"Honor, a report." A company sergeant came running up. "My man aimed an arrow at the creature, but he missed. He's in a fit, on the ground and foaming at the mouth. Suggest a blanket order to avoid confronting the creature."

Inica recalled that using weapons against the Phrenii caused insanity or death. "Agreed. Get that order dispersed."

The creature was about the size of a deer. Famri stood in the center of the square, facing the mythic creature. Many of the *ebi corgo* gathered in the far corner opposite Inica and his guards. He moved deliberately to stand a few paces away from, and slightly behind, Famri. He noticed no one followed him.

"How could you be here?" Famri was asking as he came close.

"Look around you. We are back." Sahvi's voice was female and captivating; he didn't expect that. Her voice could be clearly heard all about the square, yet she didn't need to shout.

Catching movement in the corner of his eye, he glimpsed glowing orbs rising around the gate and walls—so many that they made the battlements glow. Others now rose within Betarr Kain. They came in two sizes: ones the size of melons and smaller ones the size of apples. Unlike fruit, they were uniform and becoming transparent the higher they rose.

"I'm asking how could you be here without a soul? I took ours." Compared to Sahvi, Famri's voice sounded harsh. She stamped her foot.

"And sullied it by destroying the path for the souls. We remade it from starlight." He noted the unicorn didn't answer Famri's question. Sahvi gestured with her horn toward the *ebi corgo* and continued in her silky voice. "Look carefully at them, Groygans, and then at the souls leaving this earthly plane. You called them *soulless* and Famri didn't enlighten you."

Strangely, the *ebi corgo* appeared entranced by both the orbs and, especially, the unicorn. They kept trying to edge closer to Sahvi, while Famri ordered them back with gestures. They moved backward at her signal, but more and more were gathering and starting to push at the ones in front. Her control of the *ebi corgo* was fraying and she finally sent them running with a blast of harmless fire.

"Yes, run to your nests!" Famri yelled at their backs and crossed her arms. A sneer formed on her lips. "Why should I care about the afterlives of mortals?"

"Because you *are* mortal now, my dear Famri. Even if you expect to live as long as Cessina did, which is unlikely in this age of science, it is but a drop in the bucket compared to the time you have had." Sahvi sounded amused. "Didn't you consider that particular outcome when you carried out the lodestone's spell?"

Famri didn't say anything, but a crackling sound grew.

Sahvi's regard turned to him. "Honor Be Recorga. What would your gods want of you, once you know the *ebi corgo* have souls but the minds of children?"

"That would be between me and my gods, demon, and of no consequence to you." He wouldn't meet the creature's eyes and his voice was gruff to hide his fear. If Sahvi was right and the *ebi corgo* did have souls, the gods would consider their forced labor and use in warfare a black mark against House Endigala and everyone associated with breeding the *ebi corgo*.

"Remember that her power is influence. Don't let her sway you," Famri muttered.

"I should level this fortress and your gods would approve." Sahvi raised a hoof and he knew her threat was real and imminent.

"Wait!" He saw Shalah appear with the four children. "Would you consider taking these children in exchange for—" He was interrupted by the children squealing and running for the unicorn, calling her name. Shalah tried to follow and hold them, but he waved her off. Once Sahvi knew they existed, this was inevitable.

"No! They should be mine." Famri raised her arm. "They're not for you."

"Don't *invite* retribution, you fool." Inica leapt forward and tried to force Famri's arm down. He grunted in pain and had to pull away. His hands and forearms were burned. From her hand, a wave of flame traveled across the square and hit a wall of stone that suddenly appeared in front of the reuniting unicorn and children. With a deep groan, it went back into the earth leaving piles of displaced cobblestones.

Sahvi reared and landed with two front hooves together on the cobblestones. The ground and cobblestones rippled away from her as if they were leaves floating on the surface of a pond. Famri was taken by surprise and fell, while Inica ran back toward his guards. The ripple reached him quickly and gained strength as it went through the city. Cobblestones flew through the air and might have knocked him unconscious if he hadn't wrapped his arms over his head. After it passed, he found himself up to his knees in loose gravel and rocks.

He looked back at the square. Famri was awkwardly digging herself out of a perfect grave-sized hole and Sahvi was trotting toward the gate with the children following. The guards at the gate shrank back, but kept at their posts. With a leap, Sahvi sailed to alight on top of the barbican, the stone structure about the gates that included two small towers on each side. Inica twisted about while he concentrated on freeing one of his legs.

"I give you warning." Sahvi sounded like she spoke right next to him. "You have trespassed upon Tyrran lands and taken the lives of those I have sworn to protect. There will be consequences." It stamped one hoof, making a sound like a gong that went on and on. Inica covered his ears as he struggled to free his other leg.

The barbican started to waver and a ripple of destruction ran along the walls of the fortress. Guards jumped or escaped however they could. Betarr Kain's defenses crumbled: gates twisted, guns slid, bastions crashed, and battlements toppled. During this, Sahvi daintily stepped through an unbelievably stable and protected hole in the ruined walls. The children followed.

"By all the gods!" Inica stared about at his previously secure fortifications. The rubble still seethed and rumbled. A haze of dust created halos around torches and drifted slowly upwards to follow the orbs.

Betarr Serin, Tyrra

It was an uncommonly warm evening, considering that winter was almost upon them, and Master of Arms Kilpi decided to walk the watch posts on the walls of Betarr Serin. He used to do this as Captain of the King's Guard to check on the security of the city. Since Captain Ruel had left for Plains End, it wouldn't hurt to keep the post guards ready and on their toes. The night sky was clear for the first time in—he didn't know when, but it'd been a long time. He took a moment to recognize his ancestors before making his rounds. He started from the north. As he hoped, the northern and northeastern posts he visited were ready. No one dozed during their duty.

However, the posts on the eastern-facing main gate were a different story. He heard the riot long before he arrived. When he came in sight of the posts on the walls, no one challenged him because they were empty. When he stepped down the stairs to street level, he saw why. His guards at the front gate faced a rabble of more than two hundred children violating the new curfew.

"Open the gate! Open, open!" They chanted, pushing at the bewildered guards who kept them away from the interior portcullis. Only that and the outer gates were closed.

Two guards ran over to Kilpi, shaking their heads.

"Don't ask me, ser, why they're here. We can't get them to go home." One was the shift commander for fortress security, a lieutenant who appeared frazzled.

Kilpi chewed his lip. He had six guards here at the gates. That number couldn't cover the wall or escort the children back to their homes. "Go to headquarters for more guards."

"Yes, ser!" The lieutenant sent the other guard running up the street toward the Palace of Stars.

Their interchange attracted the attention of someone at the edge of the small mob. As the boy walked toward them, he pushed back the hood of his cloak and Kilpi realized it was Peri, the new heir apparent.

"Ser?" Kilpi bowed. The boy appeared flushed, but not as excited as some of the younger children.

"Good evening, master of arms." Peri inclined his head; he was getting much better at his etiquette.

"Are all these—is everyone here at your request?"

"Of course not." Peri cocked his head. "But your guards should open the gate soon."

"That violates our security procedures. You know that."

"Would you rather have the gates blown to bits when the Phrenii arrive?"

Kilpi cocked his head. He wanted to disregard this all as ridiculous, yet there was something in young Peri's demeanor that made him pause. Something stirred in his mind, like a memory awakening.

"Open the gates," he ordered the lieutenant.

"Ser?"

"By my authority—is that good enough?"

"Yes, ser!" The lieutenant gave the signal and with a screeching sound, the King's Guard started cranking up the inner portcullis. The children stopped their chanting immediately. Many started clapping and laughing, but Kilpi noticed most of them backed away from the gate area, even though they wouldn't be in the way of the opening gates.

"They should hurry," Peri said urgently.

The men had taken down the bracing beams and were opening the heavy gates clad in iron. It took two men per each gate, four in all. A drizzle started. Kilpi looked up, trying to figure out how a cloudless night could produce any rain, when Peri shouted, "Look out!"

He felt like a wet, warm blanket hit him, just as a brilliant green light expanded. He staggered back as the gates flew open, each sending two men airborne. He glanced at the lieutenant standing next to him. Water ran down the man's braids and face and dripped off his nose. His own clothes were soaking wet.

Out of the green globe of light stepped a unicorn about the size of a brawny deer. The globe of light disappeared with a sharp crack. The children surged forward and surrounded it, caressing its coat and attempting to hug it. The creature appeared to exchange greetings with them. Some squealed, hugged its legs, or swung from its tail. However, not one attempted to get on its back.

"Ser, do you see—"

"Yes, I see it too." He shook his dripping sleeves. "We better check on your guards, lieutenant."

Both exterior and interior portcullises were undamaged, but one of the outer gates had twisted off its hinges. None of the King's Guard had been injured; they just had some bruises from tumbling.

"What's that?" The lieutenant pointed above the wall. A transparent globe—or maybe a very large bubble—of light was rising into the starry sky. He glanced down the main thoroughfare of Betarr Serin and noted a few other globes rising here and there. The guards returning to the posts on top of the walls gestured downward and identified more, probably rising from the lower city.

"More guards are coming to help secure the gate, lieutenant. You'll have to make do with the inner gates and the portcullises tonight. We'll get things repaired tomorrow." Kilpi watched the impromptu parade of children with their creature of legend start traveling up the street. What most disturbed him tonight wasn't the strange globes of light or the appearance of the creature. Somehow, deep in his heart, that seemed *correct*. What niggled him was how Peri got all the way to the gates, during curfew, without an escort. When Peri had moved into the Meran-Viisi residence, he'd reorganized the King's Guard shifts himself. After Sevoi's murder, he didn't want to take any chances with the new heir apparent.

"I'm following them." He suspected this parade was going all the way to Meran-Viisi residence.

CHAPTER TWENTY-FIVE

Lull Before the Storm

The King's Residence, Betarr Serin, Tyrra

Kilpi stopped Peri before the he jerked on the bell. "Is it necessary for you to wake the *entire* household?" He put a hand on the rope. Being Meran-Viisi, he'd prefer not to get on Lady Aracia's bad side. "It's several hours past midnight."

"This is important. The Phrenii are back and they can help us."

"Why isn't everyone already awake and looking for you? Perhaps you should tell me where your personal guard is."

Peri ducked his head and glanced sideways at Kilpi. Wisely, the boy said nothing.

"I may have caused this, Meran-Viisi Kilpi." Dahni intervened. By this time, Kilpi knew that the creature talked and the children considered it to be male. "Those who believe were made aware that I would return. Likewise, many who actively disbelieve, slept sounder than usual."

"Hmm. You're saying that Peri's personal guards, all five of them, fell asleep? Not believable when many adults, such as myself, are awake..." His voice trailed off. Dahni cocked his head he could view Kilpi better with his faceted green eyes. Kilpi was vividly reminded of all the times he sneaked out of his bed when he shouldn't: to go wading in fountains at night, to play tricks on stodgy tutors, to meet girls in the alley behind—

"Fine, if this is what you want." He backed away from the bell. "I just don't think we should bring everybody inside, since Dahni is the important visitor. Correct?"

Dahni and Peri both nodded and, like wisps of fog being blown away, the other children dispersed. Then Peri yanked and yanked and yanked on the bell, grinning all the while.

"Hold yer horse," yelled someone in the courtyard. A King's Guard came to the wrought iron gate. The poor fellow went into shock. Not only was Peri not in his bed, but he was accompanied by the master of arms, who wanted to know how the heir apparent left the residence unaccompanied.

Peri, with the single-minded confidence of a young man on a mission, rousted the Meran-Viisi residence. Kilpi entered the parlor first, meeting a harried Lady Aracia who was securing her dressing gown.

"Kilpi, what's going on?" she demanded, forgetting his title as she struggled to compose herself, fussing with the ties of her housecoat.

He averted his eyes to avoid the "I'm your matriarch and I can make you pay for this" look. Lady Anja hurried in and now he stared. Her silver-blond hair, when unbraided, cascaded down her back to below her waist. Her dark blue eyes, sleepy and unfocused and without the hardened matriarch gaze, captivated him. She sometimes stayed in the Meran-Viisi residence to be near Peri. She might, if she wished, stay in her lineal estate maintained by her niece, but she preferred her modest Betarr Serasa house. He knew all this, because he was told about each of her visits during regular King's Guard reports, yet he had never met her.

Dahni and Peri and his retinue of King's Guard, now sheepishly attached to their charge, entered the parlor. The room became crowded. No one cared about Kilpi any more and he could observe Lady Anja unnoticed. Other household members crowded in and about the parlor door, all straining to glimpse the magical creature. Cellas pushed into the parlor late, having taken the time to dress properly, and ensconced herself in a corner.

Regardless of all the protocol he was learning, Peri was still an excited eight-year-old boy. He blurted out his long and involved story while the matriarchs ordered their tea. Why not? The kitchen staff had been rousted with everyone else.

"Then my mother helped bring Dahni back using the Kaskea, with the man she calls Cerith. They're gonna get married and they brought Sahvi back too. That means we have water and earth on our side and that can help with the war, can't it? Also, the Phrenii are changed from before. Dahni only knows what's happening with my mother, not with Sahvi, which is strange because they used to be one mind. Dahni is a he and Sahvi is a she and they're individuals. They still have elemental powers and Dahni can still heal. They used to be able to tell when people lie, but Dahni says—"

"Whoa, Peri," Kilpi said. "They can tell when someone is lying?"

Peri looked at Dahni and the creature answered. "My abilities have been weakened but I suspect that when Draius is present, our capabilities will be the same as before."

"Commander Draius has to be present?" His dream of the perfect interrogation tool evaporated.

This was the first time the matriarchs had seen Dahni speak. Anja leaned forward and Aracia set down her teacup with a clink, causing tea to slosh out.

"Sorry," Aracia muttered. She stared at Dahni. Somewhere in the back of her mind, memories were probably stirring. This was happening to everyone; he heard murmurings at the door and they rippled out into the hall.

"Peri," Lady Anja interjected herself smoothly. "Are you sure your mother is safe and healthy?"

Kilpi cocked an eyebrow. He had the habit of thinking of matriarchs as cattle breeders, who had no concern for the individual bulls and cows.

But here was a matriarch who first asked about the health and welfare of Draius, before asking after the intriguing marriage that Peri mentioned.

"She loves me and misses me and she's well. She's having a baby."

Dahni added, "Draius and I only exchanged thoughts and scenes through rapport. More complicated communication must occur in the Void, which I would prefer to put off for a few days. She needs a respite after helping oust the Groygans from Suellestrin."

Kilpi made a mental note to ask the creature for more information about Suellestrin. The Kitarran Ambassador, who lost some of Kilpi's trust by holding back Bordas's letter, had been stranded for more than an eight-day without news from his homeland. Now they might make a trade: in exchange for instant status reports regarding the happenings in Suellestrin, the Kitarrans could teach them how to breed homing pigeons, perhaps provide them with breeding stock. The time it took for horse-back messengers was hampering his communication with Captain Ruel in Plains End.

"If she's getting married, we can always hope that children will follow." Aracia sounded doubtful. "Who's this fellow you say she's marrying?"

Peri gestured helplessly at Dahni, who complied.

"Duke Cerith Ungought is ninth in the Ungought line that holds the throne of Kitarra. Tomorrow will be his coronation as king of Kitarra. He and Draius plan to marry soon, but the child she carries is a daughter by Kulte-Kolme Lornis."

The authority of the creature's information seemed unquestionable. Both matriarchs sat back and their eyes glazed. They blinked and looked at each other.

"Daughter?" Aracia was stunned, forgetting her matriarchal hauteur. "I'm going to enjoy entering this into the ledgers."

"Which of us should notify the Kulte-Kolme?" Anja asked eagerly.

Kilpi hid a small smile. It was almost comforting to watch them discuss the well-being of Peri's mother, who had been effectively lost to them for several erins. Even though Tyrra sat on the brink of a major war, one that promised to be bloody, everyone could be diverted by an impending birth. *Life carries on, regardless.*

Betarr Serin, Tyrra

NEWS ABOUT THE SISTER CITIES

Yesterday the fire brigade was called to the Pettaja-Viisi estate because "flames spewed out of mirrors" in their library. They managed to save over half the contents of the vast Pettaja-Viisi library but as to the fire's cause, Lady Pettaja-Viisi Leika only stated, "It was an unfortunate accident and we will recover." The unnamed household member who called upon the brigade is now missing. Since Sareenians are leaving the sister cities in droves, this past eight-day the markets offered hardly any foreign goods at all: no tools or cotton from Sareen, no silk or spices from Groyga, and no wool from Kitarra. Food stores for the winter are looking glum because of the drought. The recent root vegetable harvests are smaller than normal. The lack of rain also affects the start of the winter wheat; farmers say the harvest next year will be meager. On a good note, the specters of our recently departed who have been hiding in the shadows are gone. Last night, many witnessed them turning into light and floating up toward our ancestral stars, so they finally found the path.

— The Horn & Herald, *First Fairday, Erin Eleven, T.Y. 1471*

Orze Be Lottagre knew Lady Leika intended to kill him by her sudden insistence upon savoring everything she could, all within one night. Once he realized she made this decision, his tension and excitement were heightened—which was helpful for his performance.

"Please. Now."

He looked up, across her flat stomach and between her breasts, to her raised face, flushed and unfocused. Her body jerked with pleasure, but she wanted more. She wanted final fulfillment and, most of all, she wanted him spent. He turned her over so he'd have more control and she couldn't read the knowledge in his eyes. Besides, looking down at the quirt marks across her buttocks sobered him. While he understood and met her needs, they weren't his needs. Seeing those red welts helped him focus on his mission. She never noticed that he didn't even participate in the final throes.

He couldn't afford a bit of languor. She wouldn't do the deed herself, but he didn't rule out being attacked by her servitors while he lay in her bed, which was a favorite and effective Groygan technique. Moving slowly as if relaxed, Lottagre got into his clothes. Inside, he was on edge. He turned away when she broached the topic.

"I think you'll be safer in one of my houses in Betarr Serasa."

Still turned away, he asked sullenly, "You're sending me away?" His mouth twitched as he played the part. This was fortuitous because he needed to be in the lower city anyway, connecting with the others.

"Don't be cross. I'm going to miss you." There was the ring of truth in her voice. "The fire was a close call—you or the charms might have been discovered. Besides, there's the curfew and the additional King's Guard running around Betarr Serin. This will be better, really."

It'll certainly be safer for a traitor hiding an enemy of the Crown. Lottagre was surprised by the sudden and rigid security the new master of arms introduced as soon as the Tyrrans had news of Betarr Kain. He had thought all the Tyrran Guard services were complacent, but he wouldn't make that mistake again. He studied her face as she lay on the bed, her long legs twisted with the linens. He still couldn't tell whether she'd been affected by the invasion of the Kainen peninsula or the necromantic murders their pillow talk made possible. If so, she hid her emotions well. Her finesse in getting rid of a liability—whether a household member who blabbed too much or a Groygan spy who knew too much—was admirable.

"There are men outside to escort you. They'll take you in the closed coach down to the lower city. It has a hidden compartment."

Was he supposed to be alive or dead during the transit? He hoped they would take the practical route and try to kill him down there; after all, Betarr Serin was small and clean and sounds echoed in the walled streets. If they took him down to the old canals of Betarr Serasa where warehouses and wharves dominated, they could be as messy and noisy as they needed.

Taking her hand, he bowed. "Until next time, my lady."

"Goodbye, Orze." She rarely used his first name.

He had been truthful. He would see her again. Lottagre sauntered out of the house and assessed the two burly Pettaja-Viisi waiting for him by the coach, both armed with long knives.

Suellestrin, Kitarra

Draius woke to gray light and a cold room. Of course, no one lit a fire for this room. The household staff, as well as the rest of the city's inhabitants, was unbalanced by Cerith's takeover. She looked around at the opulent guest suite, then closed her eyes and dropped into rapport with Dahni. She reveled in the flashes of home she saw and even admitted to missing him—yes, the creature was now male for some reason. Regardless, Peri was safe and she had Dahni back, meaning she could communicate with both of them.

Outside the windows, heavy dark clouds hung over the city. Snow was coming. She rolled over to look at Cerith and drew in a sharp breath. No doubt, he was the most beautiful male she had ever seen. His body looked like carved alabaster, much lighter than hers. What startled her were the purple, blue, and black bruises over all his body. She knew he'd taken a beating when he entered the gates, yet she never suspected this. Even the right side of his ribcage, where she'd healed him last night, sported a multitude of colors.

She passed her hand over his entire chest. He had a cracked rib! How had he cleared Ungought Hall of Groygans, dealt with those political snivelers of the nobility, and made love to her—all with a cracked rib? Last night, she hadn't sensed the pain that *should* have come from this hidden injury. She went to work quietly, healing as much damage as she could. Her fingers lightly touched bruises and scrapes, leaving a green glow.

Cerith stayed in a dead sleep of exhaustion, although his eyelids flickered with a dream.

Pleased with her work, she leaned back on her heels. Cerith sighed, breathing deeply now that the rib was healed. She noted his erection and wondered if it would be selfish of her to wake him—

Someone tapped quietly on the door.

Still naked, she looked over their ripped and tossed clothes, finally finding a long shirt to cover her. She tiptoed over the cold stone to the door and cracked it. When she recognized Enita, alone, she opened it wider.

"The color might suit you, but the blood doesn't," Enita said with a smile. She carried a basket on her hip.

She glanced down and realized she wore Cerith's bloody and ripped shirt. Remembering why she tore it, she flushed. "You needn't look so smug. After all, this wasn't really your plan. You just nudged it along."

"I was shown a way." Enita corrected her. "One that led toward Light, rather than Darkness. I only hope he won't change too much."

She looked over her shoulder. Cerith was still sleeping soundly. "I'm sure Sahvi will only enhance his abilities." *As if he needs more strength or agility.*

Enita seemed to follow her thought. "He was always physically superior—I watched him grow up. But I'm not referring to the Phrenii or the Kaskea; I'm talking about his heart. He's been though much pain." Her eyes turned somber.

"I swear to you *on my honor,* I have no intention of hurting him or betraying him. He has my loyalty, respect, and love."

"I believe you." Enita's eyes became warmer and a smile started in the corner of her mouth. "And last night, all of Suellestrin could view the passion between you two."

Her face flamed with embarrassment but she held her head high. "Cerith proposed marriage a while ago. He said I had no *problematic alliances.*"

"How romantic of him. Just like a man to use justifications in his proposal." Enita laughed, then continued in a more serious tone. "You know he'll resist sending assistance to Tyrra while Groyga sits at his back door."

"Yes, well, I'll work on that. After all, Kitarra is cut off if Groyga controls the mouth of the Saamarin."

"Don't *assume* his support, Draius. The Sight only showed me that you and Cerith were integral in taking the mapped world toward Light. There are many challenges ahead. You both will live a long life—but that doesn't mean it won't be fraught with heartbreak."

Her good mood broken, she stared back at the old woman. A shiver suddenly ran down her body. "Will we be happy?"

"That depends entirely upon you and him, as it should. The Sight isn't concerned with anyone's happiness." Enita's voice became brusque. "I'm here on an errand. Suel requests your presence. If you've had enough sleep, he needs healing for both men and horses."

"Yes, of course, but—" She shifted from foot to foot on the cold stone floor. Given all the ripping of clothes that occurred last night, she had nothing to wear.

"Your backup uniform." Enita thrust the basket at her. "And clothes for him, as well."

"I'll never again joke about your fondness for preparation and packing."

"And I'll be holding you to *all* your promises, Draius." The old woman's eyes narrowed.

Cerith was awake when she carried in the basket. "You're still marrying me, right?" He folded his arms behind his head.

"Yes, but you should probably start doing whatever one does before one's coronation. Isn't it tomorrow? Enita brought round some clothes. I have to get to healing people and horses." She dumped the basket on the bed.

"I don't want to take a chance on losing you." His mouth quirked with annoyance. He sat up, letting the covers fall from his chest, which looked healthier than it had only a few moments ago. "I think, under the circumstances, we should marry *before* the coronation. Only the ancestors know what sort of arcane laws the nobility might trot out to prevent the Kitarran sovereign from marrying a foreigner. Before the coronation, they have no control over me." He held out his hand. "Would you be content with a small ceremony *today*, attended only by our loyal friends? Sahvi will be coming."

She laughed and took his hand. "That will be perfect."

Forenllas, Sareen

Avo Cabaran's cell couldn't be called a dungeon. He was too well known, read across the entire mapped world, for Pater Urbano Dimoni to execute or mistreat him. But Urbano, unlike his predecessor Lorenz Dimoni, didn't want Avo's writings to be disseminated. So Urbano shut Avo up in a tower on the edge of Forenllas, in one of three high rooms his jailers called the "luxury suites."

At least he had writing materials and could correspond with his family. He had regular meals, but of questionable quality. Because of the moderate temperatures on the Sareenian island, he was rarely cold unless a sea storm came through. When a tempest blew in from the north, he had to close the shutters to his north-facing window and huddle in his blankets, but at least he had protection.

Avo was writing, of course, on the First Fairday of Erin Eleven in Tyrran Year 1471. This was the last erin of autumn and when winter started, his incarceration would add up to two years. He sighed as he blotted the last paragraph of his diatribe against the Church of the Way. No one would read this. He couldn't smuggle it out as a letter, because his jailers checked them and they were terrified of Urbano because he was a well-educated despot who paid attention to detail.

The sound of a ruckus filtered through his door. Someone was being hauled up to one of the luxury suites and fighting the jailers all the way.

He put down his pen. While he desired companionship, he hated this game Urbano played. Prisoners would be locked in the two cells on either side of him and he would become attached—then they'd be executed and Urbano would require him to be present. Avo sighed. He needed to retain his humanity and that required interacting with others, no matter how painful it might be.

They brought two prisoners. The one deposited in the west cell sounded like a sack of potatoes when hitting the floor. The man going in the east room took several thumps with cudgels—Avo winced—before he was securely locked up. The jailers left and the prisoner threw himself against the door to shout through the grill.

"You whores of Falcona, you tell Dimoni that he's spawned from the bowels of Darkness," roared the eastern prisoner. If that language wasn't bad enough, there followed such a streak of mixed Groygan, Sareenian, and Tyrran curses that Avo's ears rang.

The prisoner exhausted himself. Avo left his desk and addressed the eastern grate high in the wall. "Excuse me, ser, but are you a sailor?" he called politely.

"Who's there? Wait."

There came the sound of a stool being moved and Avo sighed. "You shouldn't try to look through—" The prisoner smacked his head on the ceiling. He waited for the cursing to stop before he continued. "The walls are thick and the opening is small and high, which make it impossible for us to see each other. We can, however, converse."

"Bad luck to be traded to Dimoni," the man muttered.

"May I ask your name, ser?"

"Frisson Rhobar," answered the eastern grate.

"My word, I meet the most interesting people in these cells." Rhobar supposedly had received amnesty in Tyrra and given up the seafaring life. "I'm Avo Cabaran."

"Cabaran? I read your *Discourse on Forenllas.* You've got balls, going up against both the city fathers and the Church." Gruff admiration came from the grate.

"Some take criticism better than others."

"Well, we'll find out how long Urbano Dimoni holds a grudge. I may be looking at an execution here."

Having good manners, Avo didn't agree aloud. Any city-state would execute the venture captain, who some called privateer and others called pirate, but not for the reasons Rhobar thought. "Your mistake, ser, was going up against the Church. I made that error and once made, I found out who's really in charge of all the Sareenian city-states."

A groan came from the western grate, filled with pain and bewilderment.

"Who's that?" Avo asked.

"It's a long story. Let's just say something's rotten in Illus. That's where we were taken prisoner, and then we were traded. By the way, he's stronger than he looks—it took four men to subdue him."

Avo was impressed. "What's his name?"

"Kulte-Kolme Lornis. He's Tyrran City Guard."

"Never heard of him."

FROM THE AUTHOR

Thank you! I hope you enjoyed *Souls for the Phrenii* and the world of the Broken Kaskea.

If you have a moment, please help others enjoy this book, too. Lend it or recommend it to friends, readers' groups, and discussion boards.

The next novel in the Broken Kaskea series will be *Names for the Forgotten.* Want to know when it will be released? Visit my web site at AncestralStars.com and sign up for my release announcement email list.

Want to know more about the mapped world of the Broken Kaskea? Here are links with more information:

Characters (ancestralstars.com/lr_kaskea_characters.html)
Cultures (ancestralstars.com/lr_kaskea_cultures.html)
Places (ancestralstars.com/lr_kaskea_places.html)

If you're interested in military-flavored science fiction, please take a look at one of my other series, the Major Ariane Kedros Novels:

Peacekeeper (ancestralstars.com/lr_peacekeeper.html)
Vigilante (ancestralstars.com/lr_vigilante.html)
Pathfinder (ancestralstars.com/lr_pathfinder.html)

ABOUT THE AUTHOR

Laura E. Reeve began writing science fiction and fantasy in the fifth grade, leading to a lifelong obsession for building worlds. Along the way, she spent nine years as a US Air Force officer, holding operational command positions and having the opportunity to escort Intermediate-Range Nuclear Forces Treaty inspectors. Her civilian jobs have ranged from Research Chemist to Software Development Lead. She currently lives in Monument, CO with her husband and a Shiba Inu who runs the household.

Visit Laura's author web site at **ancestralstars.com** or her art stock web store at **ccm.ancestralstars.com**.